Literary Lives

Founding Editor: **Richard Dutton**, Professor of English, Lancaster University

This series offers stimulating accounts of the literary careers of the most admired and influential English-language authors. Volumes follow the outline of the writers' working lives, not in the spirit of traditional biography, but aiming to trace the professional, publishing and social contexts which shaped their writing.

Published titles include:

Literary Lives
Series Standing Order ISBN 0–333–71486–5 hardcover
Series Standing Order ISBN 0–333–80334–5 paperback
(*outside North America only*)

You can receive future titles in this series as they are published by placing a standing order. Please contact your bookseller or, in case of difficulty, write to us at the address below with your name and address, the title of the series and one of the ISBNs quoted above.

Customer Services Department, Macmillan Distribution Ltd, Houndmills, Basingstoke, Hampshire RG21 6XS, England

Angela Carter

A Literary Life

Sarah Gamble

palgrave
macmillan

First published 2006 by
PALGRAVE MACMILLAN
Houndmills, Basingstoke, Hampshire RG21 6XS and
175 Fifth Avenue, New York, N.Y. 10010
Companies and representatives throughout the world

PALGRAVE MACMILLAN is the global academic imprint of the Palgrave
Macmillan division of St. Martin's Press, LLC and of Palgrave Macmillan Ltd.
Macmillan® is a registered trademark in the United States, United Kingdom
and other countries. Palgrave is a registered trademark in the European
Union and other countries.

ISBN-13: 978–0–333–99293–7 hardback
ISBN-10: 0–333–99293–8 hardback

This book is printed on paper suitable for recycling and made from fully
managed and sustained forest sources.

A catalogue record for this book is available from the British Library.

Library of Congress Cataloging-in-Publication Data
Gamble, Sarah, 1962–
    Angela Carter : a literary life / Sarah Gamble.
       p.   cm. — (Literary lives)
    Includes bibliographical references and index.
    ISBN 0–333–99293–8 (cloth)
    1. Carter, Angela, 1940– 2. Authors, English—20th century—
Biography. I. Title. II. Literary lives (Palgrave Macmillan (Firm))
PR6053.A73Z63 2005
823'.914—dc22   2005049196
    [B]

10   9   8   7   6   5   4   3   2   1
15   14   13   12   11   10   09   08   07   06

Printed and bound in Great Britain by
Antony Rowe Ltd, Chippenham and Eastbourne

For Tabitha

Contents

Acknowledgements

Thanks are due to many, but particularly to Susannah Clapp, John Haffenden and Richard Ellis for their recollections, David Walker for reading the whole manuscript through and Helen Craine and Richard Dutton for waiting so patiently.

Introduction: Is She Fact, or Is She Fiction?

It is very difficult to imagine a successful contemporary author ever preserving their anonymity in an age where writers are celebrities whose lifestyles are as extensively reviewed and discussed as their published work. In many ways, Angela Carter was no exception. Particularly in the last decade or so of her life, after the translation of her short story 'The Company of Wolves' to the screen and the long-listing of *Nights at the Circus* for the Booker Prize in 1984, she was hailed as 'the fairy godmother of magic realism',[1] and consequently became a public figure, a status confirmed on her after her death in 1992. A host of obituaries from friends and admirers were published in newspapers in Britain and America. *Omnibus* on BBC1 screened a final interview, *Angela Carter's Curious Room*, BBC2's *The Late Show* paid tribute, and the Ritzy Cinema in Brixton hosted a celebration of her life, at which was played the music she had selected for BBC Radio 4's *Desert Island Discs* programme (luxury item: a zebra).[2] Although Carter had been too ill to record the programme itself, which had been scheduled for what turned out to be the final week of her life, the fact that she had been asked at all demonstrated that she had achieved recognition beyond a select cult following.

In actuality, most of the facts of Carter's life that have entered the public domain were put there by Carter herself. During her career, she wrote a number of autobiographical essays that were commissioned by anthologies and journals – *New Society*, to which she was a regular contributor between 1967 and 1986, published a number of them. 'The Mother Lode' (1976) relates the story of her early childhood during the Second World War, when she and her family lodged with her grandmother in South Yorkshire. 'My Father's House' (1976) and 'Sugar Daddy' (1983), as their titles indicate, focus on her father, laying particular stress on his Scottish origins. 'Notes from the Front Line', and 'Notes from a Maternity Ward' (both published in 1983) use her personal experiences as launching points for wider social analysis. Indeed, even the most cursory flick through *Shaking A Leg*, Carter's collected non-fiction writing, demonstrates her tendency to write pieces of social commentary in a chatty style which not infrequently alluded to incidents in her own life in order to make her point. For example, an essay for *New Society* in 1977 on women wearing trousers in the workplace begins: 'When I started work in the late 1950s...'.[3] Similarly, a piece about vegetarianism opens with the words: 'My neighbourhood wholefood shop...'.[4] As Joan Smith observes in her introduction to Carter's collected non-fiction, she 'had a rare ability to use her own experience as a spring-board for ideas'.[5]

From this, it could be concluded that Angela Carter was not only perfectly happy to reveal the circumstances of her life, but actively drew on it for inspiration in the course of her writing career. Such a train of thought might conclude that Carter is making a characteristically postmodern move here, dissecting the boundaries between life and art, the personal and the professional self. Self-disclosure makes the writer's life itself another text; an 'open book' for readers to peruse at their leisure. To a certain extent, this study supports such an interpretation, since Carter's autobiographical writings are clearly as textually self-conscious as her fiction. Moreover, as shall be demonstrated in subsequent chapters, there are many elements in Carter's personal pieces that evoke echoes of her novels and short stories.

However, it would be naïve in the extreme to interpret these writings as pieces that reveal the authentic circumstances of their author's life, and quite preposterous to regard them as capable of functioning as the 'proof' that Carter used her fiction as a forum for personal confession. On the contrary, it would be closer to the mark to reverse that supposi-tion – rather than the autobiographical details throwing light upon the fiction, the fiction should make us suspicious of the authenticity of the autobiography.

Such an approach is validated by Carter's 'hybrid' writings: not quite autobiography and not quite fiction. 'Flesh and the Mirror', which resembles many of her autobiographical essays written during her stay in Japan between 1969 and 1972, was published in Carter's first collection of short stories, *Fireworks* (1974), and 'The Quilt Maker' first appeared in a short story collection entitled *Sex and Sensibility: Stories by Contemporary Women Writers from Nine Countries* (1981). The status of both as pieces of fiction rather than statements of fact was confirmed by their inclusion in the anthologised collection of Carter's short stories published by Chatto & Windus in 1995, *Burning Your Boats*, yet 'The Quilt Maker', in particular, would not have looked at all out of place in amongst more ostentatiously non-fictional pieces such as 'The Mother Lode' and 'Sugar Daddy'.

'The Quilt Maker' is an extended, typically Carteresque, conceit, which invites reading as personal memoir, but which also deliberately confounds that attempt. It is written in the first person, in a conversational style which places the reader in the position of confidante: 'In patchwork, a neglected household art – neglected, obviously, because my sex excelled in it – well, there you are; that's the way it's been, isn't it?.'[6] Carter includes just enough details drawn from her direct experience to maintain the sense that she's telling a true, and very personal, story, mentioning in the course of her tale her upbringing 'during the Age of Austerity' (123), her extended stay in Japan and her divorce from her first husband. The narrative voice itself is situated in 'the tall, narrow terraces' (124) of South London, where Carter did indeed live at the time, and the anxiety expressed by the narrator about turning forty ('my skin fits less well than it did, my gums recede apace, I crumple like chiffon in the thigh' [124]) can also be aligned with the author herself, who must have written this around 1980, her fortieth year.

Intermingled with the impression of casual intimacy conveyed by Carter's informal, chatty, style, however, is an ever-increasing sense of artfulness. Indeed, it is there from the narrative's opening paragraph, although at this stage it's easy to miss:

> One theory is, we make our destinies like blind men chucking paint at a wall; we never understand nor even see the marks we leave behind us. But not too much of the grandly accidental abstract expressionist about my life, I trust; oh, no. I always try to live on the best possible terms with my unconscious and let my right hand know what my left is doing and, fresh every morning, scrutinize my dreams. Abandon, therefore, or, rather deconstruct the blind-action painter metaphor; take it apart, formalize it, put it together again, strive for something a touch more hard-edged, intentional, altogether less arty, for I do believe that we all have the right to choose. (121)

This is a classic Carter tactic. The linguistic exuberance of this passage, full of asides and elaborations, works to obscure what the narrator is really saying, since the style implies a spontaneity which she actually eschews in her explicit rejection of all that is 'grandly accidental abstract expressionist' in favour of 'something...hard-edged intentional'. The story itself contains a similar conundrum, appearing on the surface to be a spontaneously generated narrative that is apt to veer off the point whenever the narrator's attention is diverted, while in fact very tightly constructed and consciously manipulative.

Because of all its diversions and anecdotal asides, 'The Quilt Maker' is a difficult tale to summarise. The core of the story is a reminiscence concerning the narrator's next-door neighbour, an elderly woman called Letty, whose calls for help in the middle of the night are heard by the narrator. She alerts the police, who break into the flat to find Letty on the floor in a tangle of blankets, having fallen out of bed and unable to get back in. The incident, though trivial, brings Letty to the attention of the apparatus of the welfare state: 'Then the social worker came; and the doctor; and the district nurse; and, out of nowhere, a great-niece, probably summoned by the social worker' (133). The decision is taken to remove Letty to hospital for 'a few days' (133), but the narrator implies that her departure has become permanent. For example, when she tells us that 'Letty lives in the basement with her cat', she immediately amends that statement: 'Correction. Used to live' (127). Given that this is a narrative permeated with allusions to death and transience, whereby Letty becomes the focus of the narrator's own anxieties about aging, it's easy to jump to the conclusion that Letty is dead. At the end of the story, however, Letty returns home, leaving the narrator to indulge in histrionic expressions of regret at the foiling of her artistic intentions:

> I'd set it up so carefully, an enigmatic structure about evanescence and aging and the mists of time, shadows lengthening, cherry blossom, forgetting, neglect, regret...the sadness, the sadness of it all...
> But. Letty. Letty came home. (139)

This tendency of life to refuse to conform to the contrived patternings of art is emphasised to an absurd extent through the allusions to Letty's cat, '[o]ne of those ill-kempt balls of fluff old ladies keep' (132). Abandoned when Letty is removed to hospital, the cat is witnessed by the narrator apparently on his last legs, 'doddering' through the garden with '[h]is sides caved-in under the stiff, voluminous fur' (137). When he disappears, she assumes that he has died – but when Letty returns, he miraculously rematerializes, 'lolling voluptuously among the creeping buttercups, fat as butter himself' (140).

As a piece of writing, this story is characteristically double-edged. The writer is 'a middle-aged woman sewing patchwork' (140), a self-conscious (and self-consciously well-worn) metaphor for the attempt to translate the formlessness of 'real life' into the shapes, textures and patterns of fiction. In other words, it is pointing to the limitations of art, which, because it always has to reach some kind of resolution, is always going to be outrun by life, a never-ending sequence of events with random and unpredictable outcomes. Yet 'The Quilt Maker' also celebrates its own failure, since the return of Letty from hospital and the unlikely resurrection of her cat is a far happier ending than the storyteller herself predicted; and she rejoices in it, even if it does derail the progress of her narrative. The narrator identifies closely with Letty throughout, since she is the means through which the narrator is enabled to contemplate her own, inevitable, descent into old age: 'The significance, the real significance, of the age of forty is that you are, along the allotted span, nearer to death than to birth. Along the lifeline I am now past the halfway mark' (124). In this context, Letty's escape from 'the clean white grave of the geriatric ward' may be 'ridiculous' (139), but it also reminds the narrator herself that, while aging and death are inevitable, the will to live persists to the very end:

We know when we were born but –
The time of our reprieves are equally random. (140)

But this confrontation between art and life is also itself a conceit, a point underscored by the uncertainty regarding the provenance of this story. For the fact is, of course, that Carter's inclusion of autobiographical material does nothing to anchor her narrative in any kind of exterior reality: indeed, it does precisely the opposite. If we cannot establish what is real and what's contrived, then we cannot accept Letty's story as part of a world outside the narrative; therefore, we cannot ultimately accept the conclusion laid out for us by the narrator that she has been frustrated in her assumption that the world outside the text will ever conform to attempts at fictional representation. Instead, Letty's return is a deliberate sleight of hand by a narrator who only *appears* to lose control of her story. In the end, all we are left with is a portrait of the narrator in her South London garden: 'the woman of forty, with dyed hair and most of her own teeth, who is *ma semblable, ma soeur*' (140). Appearances to the contrary, this is not a resolution, but a final turn of the screw. Throughout the text there's a deliberate slippage between the real author, Carter herself, and the implied author, whose autobiographical voice merges with Carter's own. Here, yet another layer is added to the confusion, as the implied author not only objectifies herself by shifting from the first to the third person, but also stresses the implications of that splitting-off by explicitly distancing the observer from the observed. She is 'ma semblable, ma soeur' – 'my likeness, my sister' – but not 'my self'. This allusion to one of Carter's favourite poets, the French symbolist Charles Baudelaire, is the final indicator that, for all its sense of self-disclosure and personal emotion, 'The Quilt Maker' is not actually going to tell you anything that's verifiably true about the actual author, who, for all of her lavish use of the intimate first person, is concealed beneath a mannered and many-layered persona.

However, one of the other things 'The Quilt Maker' does is contemplate the activity of autobiography itself. One of the most teasing elements in this story is its allusions to an affair Carter had while she was in Japan – an episode which is the central theme of 'Flesh and the Mirror' – but, as in 'Flesh and the Mirror', it is represented in terms which tell her audience absolutely nothing about it. The narrator's lover, distanced from her by time and culture, is apostrophised as a mask – a mask, moreover, which may be inhabited by no-one: 'I cast the image into the past, like a fishing line, and up it comes with a gold mask on the hook, a mask with real tears at the ends of its eyes, but tears which are no longer anybody's tears' (126). Tellingly, though, while Letty may be nearer the narrator geographically, temporally and culturally, she is as much a mystery to the narrator as her Japanese lover ever was:

> What Letty once saw and heard before the fallible senses betrayed her into a world of halftones and muted sounds is unknown to me. What she touched, what moved her, are mysteries to me. She is Atlantis to me. How she earned her living, why she and her brother came here first, all the real bricks and mortar of her life have collapsed into a rubble of forgotten past.
>
> I cannot guess what were or are her desires. (131)

The question which is implicit in this story throughout, therefore, is this: in the face of this impossibility of knowing anybody, even one's self – which in this story keeps receding steadily into the distance – what is the point of autobiography, a genre whose central tenet has been defined as 'the ideology of subjectivity-as-truth'?[7] In the final analysis, 'The Quilt Maker' justifies what it also enacts – the endless evasion of disclosure through the substitution of a succession of masks and shifting narrative personae. And if there is no essential self in the humanist or Cartesian sense, then the endeavour to write an autobiography becomes just as 'The Quilt Maker' implies – an endeavour which is all style and linguistic games, with no tangible end to be attained other than the pleasure of the exercise. No wonder Carter said to John Haffenden in 1984 that 'all attempts at autobiography are fraught with self-defeat and narcissism'.[8]

The mask is an apt motif to evoke in a consideration of Carter's life, since she was so extremely adept at constructing them. When one reads the interviews that Carter gave in her lifetime, their repetitiousness is striking, and the extreme control Carter exercised over the areas of her life she chose to make available for public consideration is evident. The autobiographical essays delineate the territory – her childhood and adolescence are most frequently alluded to, her time in Japan is mentioned, although never in personal terms, and the topic of mother-hood is skirted around. Her relationships, both past and current, were hardly ever mentioned. Although she retained her married name throughout her career – it was the name under which she was first published, and hence by which she was professionally recognised – she was actually divorced in 1972.[9] Throughout her life, she retained a dignified silence on the topic, saying only that 'it wasn't so much my husband or myself that was at fault: it was the institution of marriage that was making us behave in ways we didn't seem able to prevent'.[10] Paul Barker, the editor of *New Society* between 1968 and 1986, wrote a posthumous profile on Carter in *The Independent on Sunday* that was full of affectionate reminiscence, but even he professed little knowledge of the relationship (or relationships) so coyly hinted at in the essays she sent him for publication from Japan:

> Her life in Japan was bizarre. She joined a lover there. I think he was Korean, and Koreans are as despised in Japan as (say) Poles are in Chicago . . . She worked briefly for a broadcasting company, but then did anything and everything. She was a bar hostess on the Ginza, where, she told me, "I could hardly call my breasts my own." In one short story collection, there is what seems like direct reportage of being picked up in the street and taken back to a be-mirrored cheap hotel for an instant seduction. I was never sure how close she got to prostitution in Tokyo.[11]

Interviewers, though, appear to have followed the script Carter laid down with compliancy; and she had a tendency, in her later interviews in particular, to repeat her own autobiographical articles more or less word for word. For example, she told Olga Kenyon in an interview published in 1992 that: '[m]y mother learned she was carrying me when the Second World War was declared. Our family had a talent for magic realism – she told me she had been to the doctor's on the very day'.[12] In fact, this is a direct echo of a passage from 'The Mother Lode': 'My mother learned she was carrying me at about the time the Second World War was declared; with the family talent for magic realism, she once told me she had been to the doctor's on the very day.'[13] A little further on in the same interview, Carter simply refers Kenyon to already-published versions of her autobiography: 'If you want to know more about my early life, read my essay called *Family Romances* about all the anecdotal figures who influenced me.'[14] In her study of Carter, Lorna Sage cites a letter that Carter wrote to her in 1977 after Sage had interviewed her for *New Review*, in which Carter wryly commented on this tendency to quote herself:

> The *New Review* piece is smashing. Thanks. The only snag, as far as I'm concerned, is that I only have the one script, alas, so that a number of the details of my autobiography are repeated in the 'Family Life' piece – repeated word for word, what's more. Which is a great tribute to my internal consistency, I suppose; only, my childhood, boyhood and youth is a kind of cabaret turn performed, nowadays, with such a practised style it comes out engine-turned on demand. What a creep I am.[15]

Although Carter's death in 1992 marked the beginning of a process of literary canonisation, with academic analyses of her work proliferating throughout the 1990s, no new biographical material has appeared to throw light on the areas of her life she chose to keep private, nor has her autobiographical 'cabaret turn' been substantially tested or challenged. In spite of the fact that Carter has been repeatedly defined as one of the most important British authors of the second half of the twentieth century, there are no collections of letters, diaries or memoirs in the public domain, and no detailed biographies have as yet been published.

The writer of a study such as this, which seeks to follow the passage of an author's life in order to place their work within a social and cultural context, is therefore faced with a paucity of sources, since Carter differs from the majority of other subjects of the *Literary Lives* series in the respect that her life has not – or at least not yet – become the subject of substantial analysis. Moreover, as has already begun to be demonstrated, and will continue to be so throughout the course of this book, the process of contemplating Carter's life is complicated by the fact that she deliberately plays about with the notion of the autobiographical writing self. Her perennial fascination with masks, masquerade, theatricals and dressing-up, tropes that appear throughout her fiction, in this respect point to the endlessly shifting identity of the author herself. As Lorna Sage puts it:

> Taking into account the writer's life doesn't mean that you have to reinvent your subject as a 'real' person. Angela Carter's life – the background of social mobility, the teenage anorexia, the education and self-education into the deliquescent riches of the ruins of various great traditions, the early marriage and divorce, the role-playing and shape-shifting, the travels, the choice of a man much younger, the baby in her forties – is the story of someone walking a tightrope. It is all happening 'on the edge', in no-man's land, among the debris left by past convictions. By the end, her life fitted her more or less like a glove, but that was because she had put it together by trial and error, *bricolage*, all in the (conventionally) wrong order.[16]

As a woman who began writing in the sixties (her first novel was published in 1966), Carter appears somewhat out of step with her contemporaries; something to which Lisa Appignanesi drew attention when she interviewed Carter in 1987:

> I find it very interesting that most of the women writers who have come out of this last wave of feminism actually write in a very auto-biographical and confessional mode, and you can actually chart their lives from their fiction – you can tell when they have their sexual awakening, their first love, first lesbian experience, the lot. Whereas reading you, of course, is rather more opaque.[17]

As many critics of women's writing have pointed out, the confessional novel became a popular form amongst feminists writing in the seventies, in which the personal experiences of the author become representative of a more general female quest for self-determination. Discussing Kate Millet's *Flying* (1974) – a text which is frequently cited as an example of this trend – Rita Felski argues that however experimental it might appear, its ultimate goal is the recovery of the subject as a perceptible, recognisable, and above all, stable self:

> [E]ven the more experimental forms of feminist confession continu-ally refer back to the perceptions of the female subject as their source and authority; there is a conspicuous lack of interest in irony,

indeterminacy, and linguistic play. Thus Millett, for example, implies that the purpose of her text is to aid the discovery of an underlying buried self, moving her closer to 'recovering my being'.[18]

This is not a statement that could ever be applied to Carter. Indeed, she functions as its absolute antithesis, writing novels which are all about 'irony, indeterminacy and linguistic play', and which stringently interrogate the notion that there is such a thing as a self that is capable of being unproblematically 'recovered'. As she asserted in her final interview for the BBC just before she died:

> I never believe that I'm writing about the search for self. I've never felt that the self is like a mythical beast which has to be trapped and returned so that you can be whole again. I'm talking about the negotiations that we have to make to discover any kind of reality.[19]

It could be argued, indeed, that this stance enables Carter to avoid the double-bind which Rita Felski identifies as intrinsic to the feminist confessional mode, which finds that 'the more emphatically it defines its function as the communication of the real, the more clearly the unbridgeable gap between word and referent is exposed'.[20] Carter's texts, however, explicitly embrace the uncertainties of a vacillating and uncertain subjectivity, which is brought into being through, as she says in the comment quoted above, the never-ending 'negotiations' involved in trying to bridge the gap between what Felski terms 'word and referent'.

In presenting the subject in this way, though, Angela Carter was not unique – typically, she was just in advance of the trend. Laura Marcus notes that autobiographies written by women in the eighties became much freer in their 'use of fiction within the autobiographical text', with the result that:

> [t]he 'fictional' can become the space for more general identifications, or for the trying-out of potentialities and possibilities – what might have been, what could have been, what might yet be – or it can be a way of suggesting how much fiction is involved in all self-representations.[21]

This is far closer to the mark as far as Carter is concerned, and it enables her portrayal of subjectivity to be aligned with postmodernist conceptions of gender identity – in particular, the work of theorists such as

Judith Butler. In *Gender Trouble*, Butler echoes Carter in rejecting the feminist quest for a stable speaking and writing subject, arguing that:

> the identity categories often presumed to be foundational to feminist politics, that is, deemed necessary in order to mobilize feminism as an identity politics, simultaneously work to limit and constrain in advance the very cultural possibilities that feminism is supposed to open up.[22]

The analysis of such cultural practices as drag and cross-dressing enables Butler to assert that *all* gender identity is 'performed', enacted on and through the body in order to bring it into line with the hegemonic norms that govern sexuality. Therefore, 'genders can be neither true nor false, but are only produced as the truth effects of a discourse of primary and stable identity'.[23]

Still, to say that Carter's work portrays the self as provisional and contingent in this way doesn't mean that it isn't possible to make connections between the life and the art. In her examination of modern modes of feminist autobiographical writing, Laura Marcus argues that various anthologies of writing published in the eighties exemplify how '[t]he structures of fiction, fantasy, autobiography and experience are often played across and against each other'.[24] One of the texts specifically cited by Marcus in support of this assertion is *Fathers: Reflections by Daughters*, published in 1983 – a collection to which Carter contributed her essay 'Sugar Daddy'. Although Marcus is not referring explicitly to Carter here, her description is extremely apposite in the context of a study of Carter's artistic approach, which grows out of the tension generated by the collision of opposing modes, genres and conceptions of self.

Carter might not have been into self-disclosure, she might not have used her art to reflect on personal dilemmas, but that doesn't mean that she eliminated herself from her work entirely, or indeed at all. As an intellectual, Carter expressed herself through ideas, believing that 'a narrative is an argument stated in fictional terms'.[25] Appropriately for someone who specialised in medieval fiction at university, Carter was perfectly happy to describe her work as allegorical: 'I put everything in a novel to be read – read the way allegory was intended to be read, the way you are supposed to read *Sir Gawayne and the Grene Knight* – on as many levels as you can comfortably cope with at a time.'[26] She was adamant in her commitment to both socialism and feminism, and firmly believed that her writing was, however fantastical it might appear, firmly rooted in the conditions of the material world. In her widely cited literary manifesto, 'Notes From the Front Line', she emphatically asserted her:

> absolute and *committed materialism* – i.e., that this world is all that there is, and in order to question the nature of reality one must move from a strongly grounded base in what constitutes material reality. Therefore I become mildly irritated (I'm sorry!) when people, as they sometimes do, ask me about the 'mythic quality' of work I've written lately. Because I believe that all myths are products of the human mind and reflect only aspects of material human practice. I'm in the demythologising business.[27]

Such a commitment to materialism made Carter an extremely astute observer of the cultural milieu within which she lived and worked. In both her fiction and her substantial body of non-fiction, she chronicled her times with a thoroughness which has sometimes been underplayed in studies of her work which concentrate on her as a fabulist, neo-Gothic or postmodernist writer. Certainly, her choice of mode has often been regarded as standing at odds with her political commitment. As Joseph Bristow and Trev Lynn Broughton comment:

> Carter's early decision to become a 'mannerist' sometimes appeared eccentric in a writer whose radical political interests were both femi-nist and socialist. Undeniably, her 'mannerist' method stood in serious opposition to the austerity of social realism, the traditional genre for representing the grinding oppression of women, workers and minorities.[28]

Carter stressed her political commitment in many of her essays and frequently in interviews. Her response to Lisa Appignanesi in their 1987 interview, for example, demonstrates that she saw absolutely no contra-diction between being a fantasist and a politically engaged social observer. Indeed, she represents it in terms which makes one almost automatically follow on from the other:

LA: You have said that you are a socialist, yet...
AC: Oh, absolutely! What do you mean?
LA: I mean, the kind of writing that you do has very little to do with that kind of gritty realism that one associates normally with socialist writing.

AC: You mean . . . that sort of Soviet social realism?

LA: Yes, that one.

AC: Well, that's true . . . [but] I think certain kinds of exuberance and restructuring of the way that we perceive reality is an essential part of being. . . . I sound romantic about this, but I believe that it's an essential part about being a socialist, or why bother? I mean, you're not a socialist because you think that it's a good idea for the world to be endlessly recapitulated just as it is this very minute.[29]

Such comments reveal Angela Carter to be fundamentally concerned with issues of class, feminism and national identity, even though, as subsequent chapters will show, she used her autobiographical material to construct herself as a subject living on the periphery of all of these categories. As she wrote in a typical throw-away line in 'The Mother Lode', 'alienated is the only way to be, after all'.[30]

1
Alienated Is the Only Way to Be

Angela Olive Stalker was born in 1940. According to her account of the event in 'The Mother Lode', 'Dunkirk fell as I was shouldering my way into the world'.[1] This meant that the circumstances of her early years were entirely dictated by the war:

> My mother learned she was carrying me at about the same time the Second World War was declared; with the family talent for magical realism, she once told me she had been to the doctor's on the very day. It must have been a distressing and agitated pregnancy.[2]

Her father, Hugh, worked as a journalist, and remained at the family home in London for the duration of the war – a veteran of the First World War, he was, fortunately, too old to be called up for military service. Meanwhile, Carter's mother, Olive, her maternal grandmother, and eleven-year-old brother Hugh, plus her own 'embryonic self',[3] evacuated themselves to Eastbourne, where Angela was born. 'Not a place I'd have chosen', she comments in 'The Mother Lode', 'although my mother said that if Debussy had composed *La Mer* whilst sitting on Beachy Head, I should not turn my nose up at the place'.[4] However, as Carter was to note rather wryly in later life, the defeat of the British Expeditionary Force at Dunkirk meant that, rather than gaining any measure of safety, the family actually ended up living on the front line, since the South Coast would have been the landing site for any German invasion. As a consequence, the family moved again, this time to her grandmother's home village of Wath-upon-Dearne near Rotherham in South Yorkshire. Carter's earliest memories, therefore, were 'of a living fossil, a two-up, two-down, red-brick, slate-tiled, terraced miners' cottage architecturally antique by the nineteenth-century standards of

14

the rest of the village',[5] set in the middle of the South Yorkshire coal-fields. Here, Carter was reared by her grandmother as 'the child she had been, in a sense, for the first five years of my life...a tough, arrogant and pragmatic Yorkshire child':[6] and indeed it is her grandmother rather than her mother who emerges in 'The Mother Lode' as the formative figure of her earliest childhood.

Lorna Sage has described the grandmother's intervention in 'The Mother Lode' as a 'kidnapping...into the past', a shift which enables the piece (in characteristic Carter fashion) to make a narrative transition from the realm of historic actuality – dominated by the Second World War – into the sphere of magical realism, where the everyday is shot through with fantastic referents:

> Skipping a generation took Angela back to 'Votes for Women', working class radicalism, outside lavatories, and coal-dust coughs. Granny ought, perhaps to have surfaced in the fiction as the spirit of social realism – though actually it makes sense that she is in the magical mode, since her brand of eccentric toughness was already thoroughly archaic from the point of view of the post-war and the south.[7]

In one sense, Carter's grandmother is indeed a figure in 'the magical mode'. '[A]n old woman, squat, fierce and black-clad like the granny in the Giles cartoons in the *Sunday Express*',[8] viewed from her grand-daughter's perspective she keeps the entire Luftwaffe at bay through an act of sheer determination:

> [M]y grandmother said there was *one* place in the world the Germans would not dare to bomb.... And although the Germans bombed hell out of the South Coast and also bombed the heart out of Sheffield, twenty odd miles away from where we had removed, not one bomb fell on us, just as she had predicted.[9]

But although the grandmother's fierce protective power verges on the supernatural, Sage overestimates the extent to which she functions in the 'magical mode'. In fact, she embodies a characteristic tension that runs throughout Carter's work, between the excessive, the ornate and the fabulous, and the pragmatic issues of the real world, such as class and political allegiance; issues with which she is closely allied throughout Carter's recollections.

When Carter's grandmother takes her granddaughter back to South Yorkshire, and the scene of her own growing-up, she comes to serve as the means through which Carter can contemplate her origins. Recollected as 'always and ineradicably *there*'[10] by her granddaughter, the grandmother functions as the stable point in a world of shifting class-consciousness, for she is the one figure in Carter's family scenario who remains relatively fixed within a hierarchical class system. Born in the mining village of Wath-upon-Dearne, she worked as a chambermaid before moving to London following her marriage to Carter's East Anglian grandfather. He was a soldier who (Carter supposed, for she did not know for sure) must have come up to South Yorkshire in the later years of the nineteenth century in order to suppress miners' strikes in the area.

'The Mother Lode', as the title suggests, is very much about maternal origins, centred as it is around recollections of the grandmother and the mother. However, Carter's grandfather is a significant – or, rather, significantly absent – figure in the narrative. Dead before Carter's birth, he becomes an object of nostalgia to his granddaughter. 'Of all the dead in my family, this unknown grandfather is the one I would most like to have talked to. He had the widest experience and perhaps the greatest capacity for interpreting it.'[11] Where Granny represents solidity and an unshakable adherence to her working-class origins, Carter's grandfather is the instigator of class-mobility; a characteristic which comes to define her childhood and subsequently her art. Posted to India for seven years before his marriage, he made ample use of the educational opportunities offered by the army:

> When we were clearing out my grandmother's effects, we found a little stack of certificates for exams my grandfather had passed in the army. In Bluchistan, in the Punjab, in Simla, he had become astoundingly literate and numerate. He must also have learned to argue like hell. Furthermore, he became radicalised, unless the seeds had already been sewn in the seething radicalism of the coalfields...coming to consciousness through the contradictions inherent in the Raj.[12]

On his return to England, he married Carter's grandmother and moved to Southwark in South London. '[U]s[ing] his literacy to be shot of manual labour', he worked as 'a clerk in the War Department...then worked in one of the first clerical trade unions'.[13] A member of the Independent Labour Party, his most treasured memory was of once shaking Lenin's hand. His children took after their father, becoming 'indefatigable self-educators, examination passers and prize-winners';[14]

and Carter's mother won a scholarship to a ladies' grammar school – an achievement which distanced her from her defiantly working-class mother, who 'talked broad Yorkshire till the day she died', and embarrassed her daughter on school prize-days by turning up 'with a huge Votes for Women pinned to her lapel'.[15] Carter's mother, on the other hand, spoke 'standard South London English',[16] was fond of fashionable clothes, and was bereft of any real sense of radicalism: for example, Carter recalled that her mother 'used to sing "The Internationale" to me, but only because she liked the tune'.[17]

Focused on maternal origins though 'The Mother Lode' undoubtedly is, it refuses to represent matriarchy as a kind of homogenous sisterhood. Instead, it's riven with generational tensions, since Carter portrays the relationship between her grandmother and her mother as an uneasy one: 'My grandmother could have known of no qualities in herself she could usefully transmit to this girl who must have seemed a stranger to her. So, instead, she nagged her daughter's apparent weaknesses.'[18] Her mother's response to this was not, as one might expect, to capitalise on her education. Instead, she left school at fifteen in order to work as a cashier in Selfridges department store, then at eighteen she married into the middle classes, settling with her journalist husband in the South London suburb of Balham.

However, irony is an inescapable element in Carter's family saga, where the consequence of an event hardly ever turns out as might be expected. Balham may have been 'a solid, middle-class suburb'[19] in the 1920s, but by the time the family returned from Yorkshire after the end of the Second World War, the area – which had suffered extensive bomb damage – was in decline. Although Carter's mother longed to move to a more respectable neighbourhood, Carter's father insisted on staying put, which meant that their daughter was brought up within '[a] self-contained family unit with a curious, self-crafted lifestyle, almost but not quite an arty one, a very unself-conscious one, that flourished on its own terms but was increasingly at variance with the changes going on around it'.[20] So although the shift from manual working class to professional middle class was technically complete, the notion of class as something in a state of permanent flux remains. The Carter family's middle-class identity is 'anachronistic' and 'deviant'[21] in the context of post-war Balham, leading her to recall a life spent out of step with the outside world: 'a twilight zone', or a 'dream-time' in a house 'in which you could never trust the clocks'.[22]

In 'The Mother Lode', therefore, the historical and social context of Carter's childhood is everywhere evoked, yet simultaneously subtly displaced, since the narrative displays a constant tendency to veer off into the kind of magical realist mode so typical of her fiction. Her family's transplantation to Wath-upon-Dearne because of the war introduces Carter to an environment which is at once 'witchy, unpremeditated',[23] and the ineradicable product of political and class conflict, where miners struggled to earn a living wage, and 'scarcely a family had not its fatality, its mutilated, its grey-faced old man coughing his lungs out in the chair by the range'.[24] In the same way, it's perfectly clear why the presence of the middle-class Stalker family in post-war Balham should be incongruous, but it is that very incongruity which enables Carter to portray her home as topsy-turvy or other-worldly, a place in which time moved more slowly than outside, or even in reverse – in the midst of the Cold War, for example, she says that her parents 'recreate[d] a snug, privileged 1930s childhood', complete with 'shoes with silver buckles, organdie dresses and so on'.[25] So if one takes Carter's autobiographical narrative in 'The Mother Lode' at face value, it demonstrates that the origins of her literary techniques lay in the earliest years of her life, in which she was introduced to the idea that time is mutable, that history isn't a strict chronological progression, and that appearances can be deceptive. It was, she said to Lorna Sage in 1977, a 'peculiar rootless, upward, downward, sideways socially mobile family, living in twilight zones'.[26]

No wonder, then, that the oppositional categories of 'fact' and 'fantasy' continually collide in 'The Mother Lode'. This is particularly foregrounded in the way in which a very precisely defined historical moment – the Second World War – elides with the more narratological elements of the piece. On the one hand, Carter defines herself as a war baby, conceived almost at the moment war was declared, and born during one of its most memorable turning points. Nonetheless, one should always bear in mind Carter's own acknowledgement that she comes from a family that possesses 'a talent for magical realism',[27] and she's exercising this proclivity when she speaks of her birth coinciding with the fall of Dunkirk. She was actually born on the 7 of May 1940, over two weeks *before* the beaches at Dunkirk were evacuated: which begs the question, what would she gain by so explicitly – albeit slightly erroneously – aligning her birth with such an event?

There is more than one possible answer to this, the first of which is to do with her perennial fascination with storytelling, myths and tales. Dunkirk is an event which, although historical fact, has also assumed the status of myth; and hence it is both real and imaginary. As such, this anecdote becomes representative of Carter's own favoured literary approach, which consistently destabilises the opposing categories of 'fantasy' and 'fact'. As Carter herself tells it, then, her nativity coincides with the generation of one of Britain's most important national stories; one which was crucial in establishing a lasting myth of the British Isles 'as a righteous nation under God's special protection',[28] and the last bulwark against the evil of universal Nazism.

As the German army advanced on Paris in the spring of 1940, the Allied forces retreated to the beaches of Dunkirk, from which an armada of Navy destroyers, aided by a motley civilian fleet of fishing boats, ferries and recreational vessels, evacuated nearly 400,000 men between 27 May and 3 June. Dunkirk was described by the historian A.J.P. Taylor as 'a great deliverance and a great disaster',[29] for although, miraculously, most of the British Expeditionary Force was saved, by the time the rescue was complete the last of Britain's European allies had capitulated, leaving Britain isolated and vulnerable. Yet out of this moment of crisis arose a new sense of 'Britishness': a collective determination to succeed against overwhelming odds that become known in popular parlance as 'the Dunkirk spirit'. A particularly useful account of the importance of Dunkirk in the formulation and maintenance of a British wartime identity can be found in Richard Weight's book *Patriots: National Identity in Britain 1940–2000*:

> Churchill always portrayed the British as an island people: outward-looking, in need of Imperial and American aid, but ultimately self-reliant. The most memorable phrase of the speech he delivered – the promise to 'fight them on the beaches' – resonated for precisely that reason. So too did Vera Lynn's song 'The White Cliffs of Dover'. So too did the Dunkirk evacuation. 'BLOODY MARVELLOUS', the Daily Mirror said of Dunkirk.... The manner of the BEF's 'deliverance', as much as the deliverance itself, was seen as quintessentially British. Most troops were rescued by large ships from the Royal and merchant navies, but the legend of Dunkirk was constructed around the hundreds of small boats that chugged over to France to lend a hand, in particular the pleasure boats of south coast resorts.[30]

This statement anticipates the second way in which Dunkirk is relevant to Carter's own story and to her storytelling method, since it also throws into high relief a concern with issues of national identity that informs much of both her fiction and nonfiction writing. In the seventies, for example, she wrote a series of essays for *New Society* on different areas of England, from Bradford to Bath. Her autobiography reifies this interest in nationalism; in what it meant to be, not just British, but *English* – a concern that she never lost, even whilst travelling, or living, abroad. Yet this fascination does not stem from a sense of secure national identity, but of its precariousness; hence implicitly debunking the efficacy of the Dunkirk myth to sustain a universal, incontrovertible, concept of 'Englishness' founded on a sense of special destiny. Interviewed by Lisa Appignanesi in 1987, Carter said that although she was 'quite proud' of being 'second-generation South London – second-generation South London middle-class, yet, which is certainly something unusual', she didn't 'feel . . . particularly English' because 'my father was a Scot'.[31] She contemplates her father's Scottish origins in her essay 'My Father's House', which is about her father's decision to return to his home town of Macduff in north Aberdeenshire following her mother's death. This event is portrayed as something of a shock to his daughter, in the sense that it disrupts her identity by bringing her face to face with an aspect of her ancestry which is foreign to her – and yet, because it is her father's, and hence also hers, it is also curiously intimate.

In some ways the two different sides of Carter's family balance each other out. Her Scottish connections are as upwardly mobile as her English ones, from her ancestor Davy, who 'used to live in an earth-floored cottage'[32] to her 'degreeless'[33] uncles and grandparents, to her respectable middle-class journalist father. Another thing which binds the English and the Scottish branches of her family tree together is a certain tendency to strain the limits of credulity:

> My maternal grandmother would light a fire on the Sabbath and piled Sunday's washing up in a bucket, to be dealt with on Monday morning, because the Sabbath was a day of rest – a practice that made my paternal grandfather, the village atheist, as mad as fire. Nevertheless, he willed five quid to the minister, just to be on the safe side.
> What fictional eccentricities are these? But all true, all perfectly well-documented.[34]

Like her mother's family, her father's, too, displays a talent for 'magic realism', although from the other side of mirror, as it were. While Carter's mother embroiders the truth, her father engages in 'true' behaviour that is so extreme as to seem 'fictional'.

Nevertheless, the whole essay is written from an uneasy authorial perspective, which persistently vacillates between the positions of 'insider' and 'outsider' in order to recreate the sense of someone 'easily confused by my own roots'.[35]

Everybody says I look just like my paternal grandmother, furthermore. I can't go out to buy morning rolls, those delicious regional
specialities, without somebody who remembers the old lady grap-
pling with me on the pavement and stressing the resemblance.

They're still a bit bewildered by my accent. My Aunt Katie used to
explain, almost apologetically: 'Hugh marrit an English girl, ye ken.'
And I'd stand there, smiling, feeling terribly, terribly foreign in that
clean white town, under that clean, white unEnglish light which is
nevertheless, in some dislocated way, home – which is where my ain
folk are from.[36]

This passage falls into two quite contradictory, and unevenly distributed,
parts, separated by the dash which appears towards the end of the final
sentence. *Before* the dash, Carter occupies a position of alienation and
estrangement: a product of the soot-stained Edwardian terrace houses,
net curtains and privet hedges of London suburbia, she doesn't feel in
any way part of 'that clean white town, under that clean, white
unEnglish light'. This sense of disassociation is further foregrounded
through Carter's stress on linguistic difference – her Aunt Katie's Scots
dialect is separated from the author's own standard English ('English'
being the operative word here) by quotation marks. Indeed, the passage
as a whole adopts a somewhat exaggerated version of prim middle-class
idiolect – Carter's relatives, she claims, are 'still a *bit* bewildered by my
accent', while she feels '*terribly, terribly* foreign' (my italics). *After* the
dash, however, there's a declaration of belonging which attempts to
blend in by adopting the appropriate form of speech: while this town
may be 'foreign', it is, says Carter, 'where my *ain folk* are from' (my
italics). However, it's difficult to read this as anything but parodic. Not
only is it a flat contradiction of everything Carter has just said, it constitutes only a momentary departure from the very 'English' tone of the
narrative voice. In spite of the lack of the earlier quotation marks, it is
still a conscious attempt at 'dialect' that cannot be sustained precisely
because it is unnatural to the speaker. These 'folk' are not Carter's 'ain'
at all, since if they were, her language wouldn't have to strain to accommodate them. There's a similar sense of strain, indeed, in her attempts
to interest her father 'in the history of his people, now he's gone back
to them at last'. But although she sends him books 'about Culloden and
the Highland clearances', her father 'casts them aside after a prelim-
inary reading. He says they're too bloody depressing'.[37] The point is
clear – Carter's concern with Scottish history only underscores her
distance from it. Like her adoption of a Scottish accent, the attempt is

self-conscious and unconvincing, since 'real' Scots don't have to think consciously about either their history or their accent.

'My Father's House', therefore, elaborately displays the paradoxical location of the speaking subject. Because there was 'bad feeling over my wedding...I hadn't set foot in the place for fifteen years, nor felt the lack of it', claims Carter – yet, 'I felt entirely at home...the first time I got off the bus beside the harbour again.'[38] Two entirely contradictory positions are layered over the same site – Macduff is both familiar and alien, home and not-home. Indeed, Carter speculates that any claim she might make on Macduff as home might in fact only confirm its status as 'not-home': 'the last result of rootlessness and alienation, when you can say – and mean it – "Anywhere I hang my hat is home"'.[39]

The narrating voice thus emerges as marginal subject located in the '[n]ot much of a difference' between Scotland and England – 'not even enough difference to make me a mongrel'.[40] It is a subjectivity that does not exist in an *a priori* relationship to its environment, but is the product of it, as Carter's closing words indicate: 'You don't choose your own landscapes. They choose you.'[41] The landscapes that 'choose' her, and that shape her sensibilities as a writer, may lie on opposing sides of the English/Scottish border, but what they have in common is liminality – middle class in working-class Balham, half-English in Scotland, half-Scottish in England.

In *Angela Carter*, Lorna Sage lays heavy stress on Carter's matriarchal origins, arguing that 'the whole *self-conscious* quality of her 1960s début derives from this sense of a (lost, deliberately distanced) reality: working class, northern, matriarchal...[n]one of...[which] she could *be*, or speak directly for'.[42] This statement, however, does not take into account the other aspect of Carter's identity which comes to the fore in 'My Father's House', and for which she is equally – and equally ironically – nostalgic. Englishness is the inheritance of the mother, while Scottishness is the inheritance of the father, and Angela Carter is the sum of both, yet not quite either. As 'My Father's House' makes clear, it is this that confers upon her an ability to be comfortable with vacillation, paradox and contradiction.

Another element that emerges in both 'My Father's House' and the later 'Sugar Daddy', is Carter's clear affection for her father. Carter was a late addition to the family – Hugh was already in his mid-forties, and her brother twelve years old, when she was born. In her father's case, she never saw this as problematic; indeed, in 'Sugar Daddy' she claims gleefully that he 'was putty in my hands throughout my childhood, and still claims to be so'.[43] Lacking the attribute of introspection, he does not see, much less contemplate, the questions that so consume his daughter. He emerges from the pages of 'Sugar Daddy' as temperamentally conservative; he is a man who 'still grieves over my mother's "leftish" views',[44] and who, according to a letter written by Carter to Lorna Sage after his death in 1988, was discovered by his daughter to have been a card-carrying member of the Scottish Conservative Party.[45] But although he is 'a law-and-order man', Carter's account lays stress on another facet of her father's personality that aligns him with the grotesques that populate her fiction. Behind his Scottish Calvinist 'law-and-order' persona 'lurks a strangely free anarchic spirit. Doorknobs fall from doors the minute he puts his hand on them. Things fall apart. There is a sense that anything might happen.'[46] He talks to cats, jerry-rigs burglar traps out of tripwires and bags of flour, and can 'kick his own backside, a feat he continued to perform until well into his eighties'.[47] Moreover, '[h]is everyday discourse...is enlivened with a number of stock phrases of a slightly eccentric, period quality'.[48] While her grandmother's 'scatological pun[s]' may have introduced Carter 'to the wonderful world of verbal transformations',[49] it is her father who continues her education:

> At random: 'Thank God for the Navy, who guard our shores.' On entering a room: 'Enter the fairy, singing and dancing.' Sometimes, in a particularly cheerful mood, he'll add to this formula: 'Enter the fairy, singing and dancing and waving her wooden leg.'[50]

As Carter admits, this indulgent, slightly dotty, father did nothing 'to prepare me for patriarchy',[51] since 'very little of all this has to do with the stern, fearful face of the Father...there was no fear'.[52] Instead, 'the very words, "my father" always make me smile'.[53]

Nevertheless, for all the affection that is so clearly expressed here, there's also a sense in which the father remains something of an unknown quantity.

> For I know so little about him, although I know so much. Much of his life was conducted in my absence, on terms of which I am necessarily ignorant, for he was older than I am now when I was born, although his life has shaped my life. This is the curious abyss that divides the closest kin, that the tender curiosity appropriate to lovers is inappropriate, here, where the bond is involuntary, so that the most important things stay undiscovered.[54]

This passage gives expression to a theme that runs throughout Carter's writing, and one which became more and more strongly voiced as her career progressed: the nature of the familial bond. Indeed, as she says here, the individuals that are closest to us are also the most mysterious, with the result that what she describes in 'The Mother Lode' as 'the arbitrary affection that grows among these chance juxtapositions of intimate strangers',[55] originates more out of ignorance than intimacy. In Carter's own case, this sense of distance is emphasised by the fact that, as she says in 'The Mother Lode', '[m]y mother and father were well on in their marriage when I was born, so there is a great deal about them I do not know and I do not remember them when they were young'.[56] In both 'The Mother Lode' and in 'Sugar Daddy', Carter portrays her parents as forming a self-sufficient unit from which the children were excluded. Her father worked unusual hours – 'from three o'clock to midnight most days' – and thus her parents 'spent more time alone with one another than do those parents who use children as an excuse for not talking to one another'.[57] In 'The Mother Lode' she recalls her father bringing her mother tea and biscuits in bed on his return home from work in the middle of the night: 'they would chatter away for hours in the early morning. If I was awake, I could hear them through the wall.'[58] An episode in 'Sugar Daddy' reiterates this impression that:

> their children, far from being the *raison d'être* of their marriage, of their ongoing argument, of that endless, quietly murmuring conversation I used to hear, at night, softly, dreamily, the other side of the bedroom wall, were, in some sense, a sideshow. Source of pleasure, source of grief; not the glue that held them together.[59]

As Olive's health began to decline, Hugh cared for her devotedly, 'cooking, washing up, washing her smalls, hoovering',[60] and on her death, he 'buggered off' to his family home in Scotland, 'leaving his children behind to carve niches in alien soil...once my mother was gone, he saw no reason to remain among the English'.[61] In so doing, he not only geographically distanced himself from his son and daughter, but also redrew the lines of an already slightly skewed relationship. Older than normal for a father – as Carter said, 'he was born a Victorian'[62] – he then:

> resigned the post to go and live with his own brother and father, moving smartly out of our family back into his own, reverting, in his

seventh decade, to the youthful role of sib. At an age when most parents become their children's children, he redefined himself as the equal of his son and daughter.[63]

From these narratives, Carter's father emerges as a central contradiction. He is anarchic and conventional; he is a stranger in a strange land, whose stay in England constitutes nothing more than 'an enormous parenthesis';[64] and he is a loving father whose attachment to his wife overrides any other bond.

In 'Sugar Daddy', Carter examines the symbiotic relationship that her parents shared, remarking that it is '[i]mpossible for me to summon one out of the past without the other'.[65] Yet, while she paints a detailed vignette of her father both in this essay and in 'My Father's House', her mother remains an indistinct, half-realised figure. Nevertheless, she is a mother figure that is impossible to escape – 'See how she has crept into the narrative, again', she acerbically remarks in 'Sugar Daddy'.[66] Indeed, when one considers Carter's autobiographical essays, none are primarily about her mother. 'Sugar Daddy' and 'My Father's House' are, as their titles indicate, focused on her father, while Carter's grandmother claims centre stage in 'The Mother Lode'. Nevertheless, Carter's mother 'creeps' into all of them, as Joan Smith observes in her introduction to *Shaking A Leg*:

> Some of her relatives, her father and her maternal grandmother for instance, emerge vividly and immediately from her prose. Her mother, a shadowy figure compared to these domestic colossi, is revealed more slowly as a figure in her own right – and this gradual unveiling suggests, more powerfully than if it had been addressed directly, the uneasy relationship between the women of Angela Carter's generation and the one immediately before it.[67]

In the interview she gave for the BBC2 programme *Angela Carter's Curious Room* shortly before she died, Carter described her mother as 'in some respects a deeply displaced person'.[68] However, she didn't go on to explain exactly in what sense her mother could be considered 'displaced'. In the essays she emerges as a woman who was perhaps slightly constrained by the circumstances of her life. A well-educated girl, she got married young, and by the time Carter was fifteen, she was declining into invalidism.

> She once warned me: 'Children wreck marriages.' I had not realised how essentially satisfied they had been with one another until then,

not that I think she meant my brother and I had wrecked her marriage. If anything, we were too much loved, I don't think she resented us. I do not think she was registering a specific complaint, but making a grand generalisation based on observation, insight yet also, perhaps, she felt a dissatisfaction that was also generalised, had nothing to do with any of us, did not even exist as an 'if only', but as if, perhaps unconsciously, she felt she might have mislaid something important, in the eccentric, noisy trance of that rambling, collapsing house.[69]

The relationship between mother and daughter was clearly problematic – in *Angela Carter's Curious Room*, Carter said that she and her mother 'didn't get on, in the way that adolescent girls and their mothers so often don't'.[70] In the essays, her mother appears an ineffectual figure, attempting to control her rebellious daughter by threatening her with a paternal retribution which was never realised, and apt to resort to emotional blackmail in times of stress – Carter describes her as breaking down in tears during rows, with the result that 'my father, in an ecstasy of remorse . . . would go out and buy her chocolates'.[71] When Carter began to write stories – which she said she began to do from the age of six – her mother, 'not a sentimental woman',[72] would throw them away. There was nothing malicious in this action, however; it was just that 'the fact that I had been scribbling away and writing stories since almost as soon as I could write my mother regarded as a perfectly normal activity for a child'.[73] Both children were artistic – while Carter herself was an inveterate writer, her brother Hugh was musical – and their mother allowed their talents to flourish by finding them absolutely unremarkable. When talking to Lorna Sage in 1977, Carter related an anecdote that, she said:

> always seems to me to explain my family. When my brother, who trained as a musician, was being interviewed for I think the Guildhall School of Music, when he was about fifteen, the bloke in charge of admissions asked my mother when he had started playing the piano, and my mother said, 'Oh, when he could toddle, he started playing tunes'. 'You mean with one finger?' 'Oh, no, with both hands, and he'd hum the tunes . . .' And the man said, 'Didn't you think that was rather unusual?' And mother said, 'Oh, not in my family!' And very, very much later, when I'd had some novels published, and my mother had been prowling around I think Harrods book department, and she'd noticed that my books were on the same display as Iris

Murdoch's, she said to me, 'I suppose you think that makes you an intellectual?'[74]

While Carter's father thought she should become a journalist, apprenticing her to a paper when she was eighteen, her mother is associated with creativity, however off-handedly she may have nurtured it in her children. In her final interview, for example, Carter recalled receiving her introduction to Shakespeare from her mother, who as a young woman would 'take the bus to the Old Vic to watch the Lilian Bayliss popular productions of Shakespeare'.[75]

While Carter may have been, to quote Lorna Sage, 'wry, oblique, protective'[76] concerning the topic of her mother, there is one moment at the end of 'The Mother Lode' in which she confronts this troubled, troubling, relationship, recalling her 'tenth or eleventh birthday' when her mother gave her 'a miniature rose tree in a pot'. It is a gift her ten- or eleven-year-old self finds disappointing, but, says the narrator, now older and wiser, 'I misunderstood my mother's subtleties. I did not realise this rose tree was not a present for my tenth birthday, but for my grown self, a present not for now, but to remember.'[77] From this perspective, the rose tree carries an unspoken message that counteracts the other memories of 'later discords' and 'acrimonious squabblings'.[78] What that message might be is never explored – indeed, Carter speculates that her mother 'may not have been at all aware of' the symbolism behind the gift, 'a present like part of herself she did not know about that she could still give away to me'.[79] But although its implications are never fully understood by either giver or recipient, the rose tree nevertheless endures as an, albeit tentative, image of communication, mother to daughter.

The image of the rose tree with which 'The Mother Lode' concludes indicates the existence of much left unsaid; not only between mother and daughter, but also between author and reader. Indeed, there are guarded hints in Carter's writing that there may have been another complicating element in the relationship between Olive and Angela. In one book review, Carter said that her mother's early death was due to 'a heart condition aggravated by a protracted labour',[80] which adds a tragic double meaning to her memory of her mother's pronouncement that 'children wreck marriages'. Whether or not it was Carter's birth that so fatally weakened her mother is unclear: certainly, the Stalkers had no more children – or no more *living* children, perhaps – after 1940. The notion that it may have been Carter's entry into the world that hastened her mother's early departure from it is an intriguing one, however, and adds a new dimension to the common observation that, in Carter's fiction, the mother is more often than not noticeable only by her absence.

So whatever Carter's autobiographical pieces do or do not tell us about her early life, they certainly provide us with a perspective from which to view her fiction. They reveal her fascination with the generation of stories, and with the way in which a sense of history – social, political or personal – is retained through the exercise of storytelling. They allow us to construct a rationale for Carter's portrayal of gender in her novels: her critique of the mother-figure (which was to be one of the things that would later draw her to the work of the Marquis de Sade), and her ability to critique patriarchy while maintaining a clear affection for men. The essays also show Carter's concern with place and time; an on-going interest in cultural moments, and the part they play in the formation of individual subject identity.

The novel in which Carter most clearly traverses the territory explored in the autobiographical essays is *The Magic Toyshop*, published in 1967. It was not her first novel – that was *Shadow Dance*, which appeared the previous year, 1966. However, it is appropriate to begin with *The Magic Toyshop* precisely because of its anticipation of the later autobiographical material. The novel concentrates on the experiences of Melanie, the eldest of three children who are orphaned when their parents are killed in a plane crash. Although they are prosperous – Melanie's father is a successful writer – they are careless with money. On their death, it is discovered that no financial provision has been made for the children, who are forced to move to South London to live with their mother's brother, a toy-maker, and his mute wife. As Lorna Sage has noted, this relocation comprises more than just a geographical or familial transition, since the children 'exchange prosperity for poverty, country for city, and indulgent present for the authoritarian past, and – most important – a world of common-sense realism for one which works according to the laws of dreams, fairytales, folktales, myth and magic'.[81] Sage's comment typifies the way in which many analyses of this novel concentrate on the metaphorical implications of Melanie's journey, as one that takes her away from the realm of historical actuality into a primarily symbolic and very self-consciously literary space. In their discussion of the novel, Sara Mills, Lynne Pearce, Sue Spaull and Elaine Millard argue that Melanie's 'first sighting of the house and shop places it firmly in a nightmare world of myth and folklore',[82] while Lucie Armitt observes that '[t]hough the toyshop is a far cry from the aristocratic gothic mansion ... the interior is gothic in its most conventional sense.... Once across the threshold all will change for Melanie.'[83] Certainly, the novel invites such readings. Carter herself described it as 'a kind of fairy tale',[84] and it does indeed function as an early example of her highly allegorical, intertextual technique.

Nevertheless, comments Carter later made in connection with *The Magic Toyshop* demonstrate that these 'fairy tale' elements are being played off against a very precisely delineated historical moment – the period in which she herself was a teenage girl. When the novel was made into a film in 1986, she said that the act of rereading it brought this aspect of the text to the fore:

> When the book came out in 1967 ... it was reviewed as a kind of fairy story. But when I read it again I was very struck with the intense sense of adolescent longing in it, an extraordinary sexual yearning. What it reminded me of was endless afternoons alone in a room smelling of sun-warmed carpet, stuck in the Sargasso Sea of adolescence when it seems that you are never going to grow up.[85]

Although Carter's use of the generalised third-person pronoun 'you' here means that she does not directly align this statement with her own experience, the article subsequently becomes much more specific:

> The action of 'The Magic Toyshop' takes place in the Fifties 'around the time when I was 13 or 14,' said Angela Carter, 'pre-youth explosion at any rate. When I wrote the book, I was moved near to tears for a London which had almost completely vanished. Now shops of that type no longer exist. That whole London I grew up in has gone' ...
>
> Angela Carter grew up in Balham ... She was born in 1940, 'in Eastbourne because of the bombs', but the family came back to Balham when the war was over. 'My home was much more like Aunt Margaret's London one than Melanie's country place,' she said. 'My memories are of mild but persistent discomfort. My parents were middle class, but somehow they couldn't get it together. Like most people with a taste for glamour, they had an aptitude for squalor. Balham was really seedy then.' ...
>
> 'When I re-read the book, I was filled with a quite aching sense of nostalgia for seedy upper-working, lower-middle-class London at the fag-end of the Stafford Cripps era.'[86]

This, of course, is another, though slightly truncated, replay of the same old 'cabaret turn' Carter performed in front of most interviewers, but it does contextualise *The Magic Toyshop* itself very precisely as a conscious revisiting, not of exact situations, but of the general place and cultural atmosphere of her personal past.

If we are meant to see Melanie as Carter's contemporary, this means that the action of the novel takes place in around 1953 or '54, and her mention of Stafford Cripps reinforces this sense of period. Cripps was a member of the Cabinet in Clement Atlee's post-war Labour government, which came to power in 1945. In 1947, he was appointed Chancellor of the Exchequer. David Marquand identifies this year as an 'Annus Horrendus' for Labour, which had achieved a landslide victory only two years before, but was seemingly failing to deliver on its election promise to 'Face the Future'.

> In 1945 Britain had emerged from the war as one of the 'Big Three', bankrupt but unbowed, and she had elected a Government pledged to carry through a social revolution. By 1947 it was becoming clear that Britain's status as a Great Power was no more than a polite fiction, that her loss of strength had created a power vacuum which others would fill, and that the country faced a desperate struggle for solvency, in which either the Government's social aims, or its inhibitions against pursuing them wholeheartedly, might have to be sacrificed. It was in 1947 that British troops left Greece, that India became independent, and that the Marshall Plan was launched.[87]

As part of the effort to reverse Britain's sliding fortunes, Stafford Cripps launched a programme of 'austerity', which was founded on the policy of short-term privation for long-term gain. The novelist Susan Cooper has observed that although the population were willing enough to endure privation immediately after the war, '[a]ll the same, hope was burgeoning. It was, after all, the hope of release from the long grinding privations of wartime life which had done much to put the Labour Government so resoundingly in power.'[88] Cripps confounded this cautious optimism, and if anything, day-to-day life became even harder under his strategy for economic recovery:

> Recovery did not mean a flow of goods to the individual consumer; it meant backs to the wall (once more) to 'get Britain going again', with a 'massive export drive', particularly after President Truman had summarily cut Lend Lease, the US aid that had essentially enabled Britain to win the war, in the immediate aftermath of VJ Day. The economist J.M. Keynes was dispatched to Washington to

beg or borrow for Britain's economic survival. The terms of the loan he managed to negotiate meant that a fiscal squeeze had to be clamped on domestic consumption, in order that production would be channelled for export – and, given the dollar-rich US hegemony of world markets, this was to be a long and uphill struggle.[89]

Angela Carter grew up in the environment of austerity authored by Cripps. However, like most children of that time, she did not experience austerity *as* austerity. Instead, she was the member of a generation of war babies who not only lacked any standards by which to judge the privations of the post-war world, but also benefited from stringent governmental regulations regarding their dietary health. Susan Cooper's observation that '[t]he children ... had the best of it all round. ... They were a large and healthy generation, guarded by regulation orange juice, halibut liver oil and milk'[90] is closely echoed by Carter's own description of the period in 'Truly, It Felt Like Year One' that '[a]ll that free milk and orange juice and codliver oil made us big and strong and glossy-eyed'.[91]

By the time Carter was a teenager in the early years of the fifties, Britain was beginning the long, weary climb back to affluence. *The Magic Toyshop* is situated in this period, one in which rationing has ended, but the brave new post-war world has not yet become fully realised. This atmosphere of transition, however, is evoked by Carter through an *inversion* of the historical process, for while society at large may be in the process of moving from austerity to affluence, Melanie travels in precisely the opposite direction – from affluence to austerity. The result is to throw her ensuing experience of depravation into high relief since it ejects her out of the state of unknowing that characterised the children of Carter's generation who had no memory of life before the war. Unlike them, she exists in a state of constant nostalgia for better times. On her first morning in her uncle's house, for example, she visits the bathroom, only to find 'no hot water system' or 'proper toilet soap',[92] and 'a number of sheets of the *Daily Mirror* roughly ripped into squares' (56) serving as toilet paper: a scene which sparks off idealised recollections of her former bathroom, in which '[p]orcelain gleamed pink and the soft fluffy towels and the toilet paper were pink to match. Steaming water gushed plentifully from the dolphin shaped taps and jars of bath essence and toilet water and after-shave glowed like jewellery' (57).

The world in which Melanie lives before her transition to South London is the epitome of bourgeois comfort: a 'red-brick [house], with

Edwardian gables, standing by itself in an acre or two of its own grounds; it smelled of lavender furniture polish and money' (7). Despite the traditional surroundings, Melanie's lifestyle is self-consciously up-to-the-minute, a fact which Carter stresses through the use of detailed description of the interior décor. Melanie's bed has 'a Dunlopillo mattress and a white-quilted headboard', she owns 'a transistor radio of her own', and smart clothes 'made by her mother's dressmaker' (7). Melanie's parents' bedroom contains a 'low, wide bed...generous and luxurious as a film star's', adorned with a 'white crochet cover', and with a 'wicker heart...form[ing] the bedstock' (9) – a taste, Carter makes quite clear, dictated by 'glossy magazine[s]' and 'Sunday colour supplement[s]' (10).[93]

This is as far from austere as it is possible to be, and although Carter does not mention the event in *The Magic Toyshop* except through implication, Melanie is clearly benefiting from a lifestyle which represents the kind of ideal of postwar recovery epitomised in the Festival of Britain, which took place in 1951. As an event which was intended to demarcate the point at which austerity ended and prosperity began, the Festival functions as the concealed pivot around which the social aspect of the book revolves; moreover, as I will go on to argue, the world of Uncle Philip's toyshop, as well as the role of Uncle Philip himself, can be defined through reference to the ideologies the Festival strove to promote.

According to the official guidebook, the Festival of Britain was intended as 'one united act of national reassessment, and one corporate reaffirmation of faith in the nation's future'. By celebrating 'British contribution to world civilisation in times of peace',[94] it showcased British manufacturing, design and culture in a series of exhibitions, or 'pavilions', arranged in a series of thematic 'circuits', each centred around a specific theme – 'The Land', 'The People' and 'The Dome of Discovery'. The display overall was conceptualised, explained the guidebook, as 'a series of sequences of things to look at, arranged in a particular order so as to tell one interwoven story...[which] has a beginning, a middle and an end – even if that end consists of nothing more final than fingerposts into the future'.[95] This 'act of national autobiography'[96] was intended to tell the story of recovery of a national identity centred upon economic, political and cultural achievement, and to reinstate Britain as a power in a post-colonial, post-war world. The guidebook, stuffed with full-page colour adverts for glossy consumer goods such as Hoover electric washing machines, Creda cookers and Sanderson wallpapers and fabrics, underlines the fact that the Festival was also celebration of renewed consumerism – by the middle classes, at least.

The Festival of Britain was situated on the South Bank of the Thames, near Hungerford Bridge, and had offshoots a few miles downstream in Battersea Park, which perhaps makes it tempting to think that this was an event which belied Carter's enduring belief that 'London is a city divided into two by the Thames'.[97] Certainly, as Roy Strong says, the festival was officially 'non-political'. 'All references past or present to divisions of rich and poor, of class, of state as against private education, of state as opposed to private medicine were, of course, glossed over...British "supremacy"...rested no longer on power but on "common ideas and ideals".'[98] However, the guidebook makes clear that the dominant perspective on the Festival was firmly based on the North Bank of the north/south divide; an unconscious bias exemplified by an advertisement promotion for Shell-Mex and BP. It consists of a picture of a grimy industrial scene, followed by the proclamation: 'Shell-Mex House across the river looked onto this view of the South Bank until last year – a view of Britain at work. Now in token of the achievements of British Industry "shining prospects rise"; in Festival Year our windows frame a new horizon – a signal of Britain's recovery.'[99] Such a point of view was further emphasised in the body of the guidebook itself, which commented that the Festival project 'has quite transformed the familiar patchwork of rubble and half-derelict buildings which had for so long monopolised the prospect from the North Bank'.[100] Such statements suggest that the benefits of the regeneration project lay wholly in the aesthetic improvement in outlook for the prosperous folks based on the opposite side of the Thames. Michael Frayn has famously underlined the fact that, for all its claims to universality, 'it was scarcely the British of the working-class that was being fêted...there was almost no one of working-class background concerned in planning the Festival, and nothing about the result to suggest that the working-classes were anything more than the lovably human but essentially inert objects of benevolent administration'. Instead, 'Festival Britain was the Britain of the radical middle-classes; the do-gooders; the readers of the *News Chronicle*, the *Guardian* and the *Observer*.'[101]

Melanie's parents, literate, artistic and fashionable, are thus the very sector of the population who would have endorsed the egalitarian and libertarian ethos of the Festival, and who were the primary beneficiaries of a post-austerity society. Their association with consumerism is foregrounded by a process of metonymic substitution – they never appear in the text directly, but through reference to a series of objects and arte-facts (photographs, furnishings, clothes) that stand in for their absent selves. This raises the implication that they may have been nothing more than the total of their rather extravagant possessions: for example, Melanie finds it impossible to imagine her mother, always 'an emphatically clothed woman', naked, and fantasises that she 'must have been born dressed, perhaps in an elegant, well-fitting caul selected from a feature in a glossy magazine, "What the well-dressed embryo is wearing this year"' (10). In her wedding photograph, too, the flesh-and-blood mother takes second place to her wedding dress, which is 'a pyrotechnic display of satin and lace' (11). Her father, mean-while, a man 'compounded' of 'nothing but tweed and tobacco and type-writer ribbon' (10), is 'quite obscured' by her mother's 'flying hems' (11). Touchingly, though, their facial expressions are the same: 'his shy grin' mirrored in her 'smile...soppy and ecstatic and young and touching' (11). It is this observation that endows Melanie's parents, otherwise so shadowy and distant, with humanity, but it also hints at complicity between them that recalls Carter's memories of growing up in a household in which Hugh and Olive formed 'a peculiarly complex unit' (22) from which their children felt excluded. Melanie, however, attempts to breach that alliance when she tries on her mother's wedding dress; an act which symbolically tries to enter into the frame of a photograph which depicts a scene from which she is separated in time, space and understanding. In fact, the ensuing debacle only emphasises this sense of separation. Melanie struggles into the dress, which swamps her adolescent frame, and, on a bold romantic impulse, goes out into the garden in the middle of the night.

    Although Melanie's subsequent experience in the midnight garden constitutes an attempt to insert herself into the parental bond, what it actually achieves is an emphasis on her distance from her mother and father. She hopes to enter 'her parents' time' (10): a time which is closely associated with a renewed interest in consumerism and aesthetics characteristic of a post-austerity, post-Festival Britain. Instead, Melanie finds herself in quite a different realm, which is ahis-torical, mythic, symbolic. The door of the house swings shut behind her, stranding her outside, in a garden '[w]hich was too big for her, as the dress had been' (18), an event which underlines her exclusion from the parental dyad. There may have been 'few mothers in her books', Lorna Sage records Carter as saying in a late interview, but 'all along the houses stood in for mother'.[102] If this is the case, then the slamming of the door indicates the mother's rejection of her daughter, shutting her out of their world and their time – although it's a rejection which is involuntary rather than deliberate. Melanie's parents are never portrayed as anything less than fundamentally well-meaning, but they cannot prevent the accident that causes their premature deaths, which leave their children alone and vulnerable. Melanie's experience of being locked out thus presages the sequence of events that will force her to leave their home for good.

The garden is clearly linked to Uncle Philip's toyshop in that both are realms of unremitting symbolism, in which everything means something else. When she cuts her bare feet on the gravel path, Melanie recalls the heroine of Hans Christian Anderson's tale, 'The Red Shoes', an orphaned girl who is compelled to dance to her death just as Melanie will soon be compelled to dance to Uncle Philip's tune. When she climbs the apple tree in order to get into the house through her bedroom window, Melanie takes on the role of Eve, who rebels against God's prohibition against the eating of the fruit of the Tree of Knowledge, thus anticipating, to use Carter's own words, the 'Fortunate Fall'[103] with which the book ends.

As many critics have already noted, Melanie's journey to the toyshop itself takes on a symbolic force. Following an interminable train journey to London, Melanie and her siblings are met at the terminus by Aunt Margaret's brothers, Francie and Finn Jowle, and are surprised to find that they have not yet reached their destination:

'Is it very far, still? Melanie asked in a congested, small voice.
'Still farther,' said Finn abstractedly. His profile was wild and eccentric, a beaky nose, eyes still hooded beneath heavy lids.
'Still farther,' he repeated.
'It is beginning to get dark,' she said, for light drained from the streets and Jonathon's face wavered and dissolved in the pool of dark inside the taxi.
'And will get darker,' responded Finn. His voice suddenly warmed. There was a certain ritual quality in this exchange, as though Melanie had stumbled on the secret sequence of words that would lead her safe over the sword-edge bridge into the Castle of Corbenic. (36–37)

The mention of the Castle of Corbenic demonstrates Carter drawing on her background in medievalism, since according to tradition it is the place in which the Holy Grail of Arthurian legend is kept. This, plus the antiphonal, ritualised, conversation between Melanie and Finn, encourage the reader to think of this journey as a pilgrimage or quest with some kind of transcendental 'truth' or revelation as its ultimate object. However, just as in the autobiographical essays, the text interweaves such allegorical or mythic references with firm sense of historical and social context. The taxi is traveling from the prosperous North to '[m]elancholy, down-on-its-luck South London' (38), which indeed constitutes a journey from one realm of social experience to another. No wonder that Melanie, whose recollections of London are centred around the prosperous borough of Chelsea, ends up feeling as if '[w]e might as well not be in London at all' (88).

While Melanie perceives this translocation as an experience of great depravation, for her author it becomes an exercise in nostalgia 'for a London which had almost completely vanished'[104] by the mid-sixties. If this, as Carter claimed, was the London in which she grew up, then Uncle Philip's toyshop is situated in Balham, in the very down-at-heel environment in which she herself was raised; the social 'twilight zone' (11) of a middle-class girl who 'went to primary school with apprentice used-car dealers' (14). While her fictional contemporary is thoroughly bourgeois, Carter herself lovingly evokes a seedy, down-at-heel neighbourhood from which any vestige of stuffy Victorian respectability has long since fled:

> It was a high and windy suburb. The square, its shabby focus, topped a steep hill and these streets ran sharply down once stately and solid streets, fat with money and leisure, full of homes for a secure middle-class with parlours in which its bustled daughters could play 'The Last Rose Of Summer' and 'Believe me if all those Endearing Young Charms' politely on rosewood pianos antlered with candle-sticks; and roast-beef coloured dining-rooms where the gentlemen mellowed over rich, after-dinner port and mahogany reflected ox-roasting coal fires tended by black flocks of housemaids. And now, crumbling in decay, over-laden with a desolate burden of humanity, the houses had the look of queuing for a great knacker's yard, of eagerly embracing the extinction of their former grandeur, of offering themselves to ruin with an abandonment almost luxurious. (98–99)

It is in passages such as this where the gulf between Carter and her heroine becomes most apparent. While Melanie is appalled, Carter is fondly wistful, and clearly does not mourn the passing of the elaborate comforts of the nineteenth-century bourgeoisie. In fact, she has enormous fun at Melanie's expense, recording her appalled reaction to her radically changed environment. Not only is Melanie confronted with a level of physical depravation that she has never before experienced, but her sense of aesthetics, formed by her mother's colour supplements, is also being continually challenged. While her parent's home conforms to dominant definitions of 'taste', Uncle Philip's conforms to its wider environment in remaining untouched by any hint of modernity. Utilitarianism, rather than fashion, predominates, and nearly everything is old or recycled, such as the 'chest-of-drawers painted pale blue with flowers cut from seed-packets glued to it for decoration' (44) and 'the leather-covered armchair of great age' (41) which dominates the back parlour. The few pictures on the walls are either cheap reproductions or Finn's own highly idiosyncratic work – for example, a painting of the family dog that hangs above the 'ugly mantelpiece of beige tiles' (59) in the kitchen. Garish and kitsch, it depicts the white bull terrier sitting 'squatly full-face on a spiky tuft of grass' with 'a wicker, flower-girl basket of pinks and daisies in its mouth. Drops of dew trembled on the flowers. The dog's eyes glittered unnaturally because they were made of pieces of coloured glass stuck onto the canvas' (59–60). Alongside it hangs 'a carved cuckoo clock with green ivy and purple grapes growing around the front door' (60), and the real stuffed cuckoo inside it the counterpart of the 'large gilt cage containing a number of stuffed birds with glossy black plumage, yellow beaks and sharp little eyes' (41) which is the principal decoration in the parlour.

The residential quarters of the toyshop therefore do not conform to any dominant aesthetic or 'look'; instead, they contain an eclectic, hugger-mugger assemblage of objects ranging from the tacky to the tatty. This, however, is in marked contrast to the business of the toyshop itself. Uncle Philip is a master craftsman, 'a genius in his own way' (64), and his creations have become fashionable commodities in a social environment that can now afford to accommodate frivolity. The toyshop's best customers 'come by car from north of the river' (95) in search of same kind of 'little and gay' (95) *objets d'art* Melanie's own mother used to select from the Sunday colour supplements. In fact, Finn tells Melanie that Uncle Philip has been approached by a man from such a colour supplement who 'wanted to do a photo-feature. Toys for grown-ups. He said we – your uncle and me – were a unique fusion of folk-art and pop-art' (95). Uncle Philip loathes such people (a point he makes forcibly when he throws the journalist's camera equipment down the stairs); but he has, however unwillingly, found a niche in a post-Festival economy that has made the craftsman a fashionable icon.

The Festival of Britain, by and large, concentrated on the benefits of mass-production, in accordance with its belief that 'industry is now our lifeline'.[105] However, it did find a place for the individual work of art. The Festival site as a whole abounded in one-off pieces of art and sculpture, but it was the bizarre and quirky Lion and Unicorn Pavilion that showcased 'visible reminders of the British People's native genius' (67). The pavilion's centre-piece consisted of two gigantic corn dolly figures of the Lion and the Unicorn themselves, and one area contained 'a collection of examples of British craftsmanship of all kinds and materials'.[106] Uncle Philip's clockwork monkeys and handcarved Noah's arks become fashionable commodities in a market which has been encouraged, through the Festival, to think of craft as art.

Uncle Philip, therefore, inhabits a contradictory space in this novel's cultural landscape. The situation of his shop in the hinterlands of South London, plus his defiant refusal to court commercial success, is suggestive of a willed marginality; but this is contradicted by the symbolism with which Carter surrounds him, which hints at dominance from the centre rather than resistance from the edge. While the Sunday supplements court Uncle Philip as a profitable eccentric, and market his products on the same level as the Mexican pottery and Spanish ceramics which once adorned Melanie's parents' house, Uncle Philip himself refutes the benevolent attentions of the middle classes. In the basement of the toyshop, he has built a puppet-theatre, in which he dramatises his lust for control on the most literal of levels. This assumption of imperial dominance is enacted through Uncle Philip's control over his puppets, which he has created to serve as instruments for his mastery – a mastery which Finn's corresponding ineptitude only emphasises. It is significant, too, that when it comes to puppetry, Uncle Philip has a preference for the female. He is first seen enacting 'Morte d'une Sylph, or, Death of a Wood Nymph' (127), featuring a ballet-dancer expiring 'gracefully in a waterfall of white tulle' (127), and this is followed by a love scene between Mary, Queen of Scots and Bothwell, with Uncle Philip, significantly, pulling the Queen's strings.

As Melanie's subsequent experience demonstrates, Uncle Philip's tendency to create and control female puppets does not constitute any kind of challenge to the boundaries of gender; he isn't engaging in any form of theatrical cross-dressing here. Instead, his sentimental tableaux are unsubtle enactments of masculine dominance, their force redoubled by the fact that his audience consists of the household over which he reigns so despotically. When Melanie is forced to take the role of the puppet in his performance of 'Leda and the Swan', she might as well be one of his mannequins, tied to him by strings of fear and economic dependence. As Finn reminds her, 'he'll turn you out if you can't work for him. And what would you do then?' (148). The women in the Flower household are thus 'crafted' by Uncle Philip to fit the ideal of womanliness exemplified in his puppets; an ideal predicated on a state of lack which only he can satisfy. He resents evidence of Melanie's growing maturity, brusquely rebuking her for having thrived on 'all that free milk and orange juice' provided by the newly instituted Welfare State – she is too 'well built' and her 'tits are too big' (143) to conform to his prepubescent ideal. His wife is conditioned to starve herself so that her husband's appetite – in both the gustatory and the sexual sense – can be satisfied. Melanie sees her as 'an icon of Our Lady of Famine, pictured as a spare young girl' (113); and as Emma Parker notes in her essay 'The Consumption of Angela Carter: Women, Food and Power', 'Aunt Margaret's fragile form highlights how she has been diminished through a literal process of reduction.'[107]

However, it should not be forgotten that not all of Uncle Philip's literally captive audience are female, since the objects of his tyranny also include Melanie's brother Jonathan and Aunt Margaret's brothers, Finn and Francie. His patriarchal authority is thus potentially limitless, as indicated by the poster he displays in his puppet-theatre depicting 'a great figure recognisably Uncle Philip . . . holding the ball of the world in his hand' (126). Uncle Philip, therefore, symbolises universal patriarchal dominance, and as Aidan Day observes, 'the imperiousness of his patriarchy is emblematised in the power relations between himself, as Englishman, and the Jowles, who are Irish Catholics'.[108] National distinctions thus become as important as gender distinctions in mapping out the extent of Uncle Philip's ambitions, for he can be regarded as the embodiment of a distinctly English imperialism that is founded on the subordination of the 'other' and on the conscious dramatisation of authority.

Such an observation brings us back to the relationship between *The Magic Toyshop* and its social context. Uncle Philip is depicted in the text as a patriarch out of the nineteenth century – for example, he sports 'an impressive gold watch chain, of the style favoured by Victorian pit-owners' (73), and dresses in a manner that reminds Melanie of 'veterans of the American Civil War' or 'Mississippi gamblers . . . in Western films' (12) – although he is not nearly as out of place in a twentieth-century setting as he might at first appear. Certainly, the imperial politics of the nineteenth century are clearly invoked in the narrative; most overtly in the episode in which Finn takes Melanie into the park which contains all that is left, he tells her, of

> 'the National Exposition of 1852 . . . They held it here, in a pleasant village outside London, and run up to a hundred excursion trains a day out to it. They built this vast Gothic castle, a sort of Highland fortress, only gargantuan, and filled it with everything they could think of, to show off. Goods and chattels and art and inventions . . . It was made of papier mâché specially treated to withstand the weather. It was ever so ingenious, the castle.'
>
> 'What happened to it, then?'
>
> 'Someone dropped a match in 1914. It was apt enough. It went up in flames as the lights went out all over Europe. Victoria's final death pyre.' (99)

Finn, as he is wont to do, is spinning something of a yarn here, but it contains enough connection with the truth to be recognisable as a satirical fantasy based on the Great Exhibition of 1851, housed in the Crystal Palace constructed in Hyde Park. This monumental glass structure was indeed crammed with 'goods and chattels and art and inventions', exhibiting the artistic and inventive ingenuity of Great Britain and its Empire. Its glittering spectacle, however, concealed an ideological project to, in the words of John R. Davis, 'act as a vehicle for the establishment of a new order founded by a newly configured élite and characterised by its commitment to the principles of ownership and property, as well as production'.[109] As Davis points out, the Great Exhibition took place at a time when the spectre of civil revolt still hovered in the background of British politics, fueled by the Chartist movement at home and revolutions abroad, and the Exhibition was therefore an attempt to create social stability:

> it could unite the disparate forces of the bourgeoisie . . . raise the levels of the country's production, and thus help the labouring classes; it might strengthen the industrial centre and make it a bulwark against the reactionary landed classes that had been so grievously alienated by the abolition of the Corn Laws in 1846; and thus it could generally help guard against revolution and reaction.[110]

On its closure, the Crystal Palace was relocated across the river to South London, where it was reconstructed in Sydenham, only to be destroyed by fire in 1936. Angela Carter herself was clear that the setting for this scene in *The Magic Toyshop* is indeed the derelict remains of the Crystal Palace, although it is a typically mutated version of the real thing. The grounds of the Crystal Palace becomes another symbolic space within the text; another allegorical garden in which Melanie is inducted into a further stage of development. When Finn kisses her beside a broken and vandalised statue of Queen Victoria, she is introduced to the possibility of a real sexual relationship as opposed to the idealised romances that have dominated her adolescent fantasies. She does not find it a pleasurable experience, becoming 'convulsed with horror at this sensual and intimate connection, this rude encroachment on her physical privacy, this humiliation' (106). Finn lets her go; but his act is nevertheless symbolically aligned with the spectacle of female degradation provided by the statue.

Queen Victoria was, of course, the dominant symbol of her age, and thus the muddy, vandalised remains of her statue can be read as representing the downfall of the imperialistic spirit of which the Great Exhibition was a spectacular embodiment. In the context of *The Magic Toyshop* as a whole, however, she also participates in the parade of degraded females who are forced to bow to Uncle Philip's masculine authority. He recreates Mary, Queen of Scots as a puppet, and presides over the dinner table 'like Henry VIII' (160) – a monarch who regularly despatched his queens. Similarly, Queen Victoria is supplanted by a phallocentric order founded on the brutal assertion of masculinity. The stone plinth from which she has long since been toppled is inscribed with the obscene rubric 'Gordon Cox (Cocks) has a fucking great penis' (104), and Finn comedically emphasises the scatological force of the message when he takes his bubblegum out of his mouth before kissing Melanie and 'deliberately' sticks it on 'Queen Victoria's swelling stone backside' (105).

Carter's reference to the Great Exhibition functions, therefore, as a multi-faceted symbol, particularly in the way in which the demeaned image of the Queen is at once an object of ridicule and sympathy. On the one hand, she is the embodiment of the woman broken by patriarchy; but on the other, she indicates the collapse of Victorian imperialistic certainty. Like the rest of the debris in the park – the 'floor of chequered marble, white on black, and a wide stone staircase with balustrades' (102), now 'littered with broken masonry and rubble' (103) – the 'Queen of the Waste Land' (101) lingers on in a different age in which she is irrelevant and disregarded. There's yet another level of irony to be discerned in Carter's representation of the Crystal Palace and its environs here, though, which is founded in the fact that any mention of the Great Exhibition in the 1960s could not help but recall the more recent Festival of Britain – indeed, the festival's inception grew out of the decision to commemorate the Great Exhibition's centenary year. In this way, argues Richard Weight, post-war Britain, desperate 'to show people at home and abroad that Britain had recovered from the war and that she was still a force to be reckoned with',[111] ostentatiously aligned itself with 'the Victorian idea of progress and...Britain's ascendance as the world's most powerful nation in the nineteenth century'[112] promoted by the original Exhibition.

The Magic Toyshop can thus be viewed as an expression of Carter's cynicism concerning patriotic ideology; a stance most clearly illustrated in an article she published in *New Society* in 1982. Entitled 'So There'll Always Be an England', this snippet of a memoir recalls Carter's experience of the phenomenon known as 'Empire Day' celebrated annually in her primary school in south London. To a great extent, it reiterates the subtext of 'My Father's House' by expressing a similar sense of the precariousness of the English identity. Empire Day is described as an overblown juvenile pageant in which, in a playground 'strung with Union Jack bunting',[113] the children parade the emblems and flags of the constituent countries that make up Great Britain – England, Scotland, Wales, England and Ulster, followed by 'symbols of England's first colonies and acquisitions'.[114] When it comes to pageantry, though, England is sadly lacking:

> Those [children] who carried the Scottish, Welsh and Ulster flags wore national costume – kilt, steeple hat, Kathleen Mavourneen headscarf; but the little girl who bore up the cross of St George wore just a regular gymslip. The lesser breeds, evidently, were picturesque; the English not. No.[115]

However, such a lack of picturesqueness does not mean that England is inferior to the others: quite the contrary. It is the dominant figure of the pageant, the Rose Queen, 'always the blondest and bluest-eyed of the 11-plus entrants',[116] who comes to symbolise a conception of England which unquestioningly assumes that 'the *idea* of Britain was an English invention...Great Britain=Greater England'.[117] Although this display of choreographed dominance and subordination is disturbingly reminiscent of fascism, it also has a ridiculous dimension: 'a cut-down version of an operetta, *Merrie England* for juveniles, in which south Londoners, several times removed from the soil, skipped round in circles whilst plaiting and unplaiting the ribbons...on a purpose-built maypole'.[118] For Carter, the whole charade is constructed around

[t]hese two images – the child in uniform and the child as rustic rose – [which] sum up the double thrust of Englishness: the hard edge, and the soft focus. There is the rigid authoritarianism that presumes a passive submission; and then there is the marshmallow sentimentality with which the English have chosen to smother their bloody, bellicose and unexemplary history in order to make it digestible.[119]

In the context of this discussion, such a statement brings us back to *The Magic Toyshop*, which reproduces the spirit of Empire Day precisely in its mingling of authoritarianism and sentimentality within the medium of theatre. Above stairs, Uncle Philip's authority is 'stifling' (73), 'heavy as Saturn' (168); but below in the puppet-theatre his kitsch displays reveal him to be 'a sentimental man, at times' (127). Thus, however ludicrous though such an assertion may at first sound, it is indeed Uncle Philip who assumes the role of the Rose Queen in this scenario. As has already been observed, he is symbolically linked with the appropriation of queenly authority; but his surname, Flower, also recalls the 'tissue-paper rose petals' and 'artificial roses' (185) that adorn this blue-eyed, fair-haired symbol of imperialism.

This alignment of Uncle Philip's toyshop with the spirit of Empire Day reveals, too, the way in which Carter foregrounds the limits of his despotism. Although the oppression experienced by the other members of the household, both male and female, is no laughing matter, the readers themselves are made aware of the inherent ridiculousness of the charade Uncle Philip perpetrates. His performances in the puppet theatre function to reveal, rather than conceal, the fact that his entire existence is a sustained enactment of authority, from 'his own, special, pint-size mug which had the word "Father" executed upon it in rose-buds' (73) – another image which links him to the Rose Queen – to his melodramatic enjoyment of food. Similarly, in 'So There'll Always Be an England', Carter portrays Empire Day as a laughable anachronism in a changing post-war world. Only the headmistress, Miss Cox (a name, note, which appears in the scatological graffiti adorning Queen Victoria in *The Magic Toyshop*), keeps it going as an annual event, in 'a state school, where one or two of the teachers were, I think, members of the Communist Party'.[120] On her retirement, Empire Day is no more, and its props 'arrive...in the playground as toys',[121] their symbolism, if it had ever been comprehended by the children at all, now forgotten. But, says Carter, she learnt 'one thing' from the 'living fossil of a pageant of Empire Day' – that 'patriotism is theatre',[122] a performance whose purpose is to perpetrate a stereotype of 'Englishness' to conceal the 'confusion'[123] of identity that lies beneath. In the same way, *The Magic Toyshop* recasts patriarchy as a performance that conceals its steady erosion from the inside, in the form of the growing disaffection of the Jowle brothers. Once Uncle Philip is brought face to face with their increasingly flagrant flouting of his authority, catching Aunt Margaret in bed with Francie, he sets fire to the toyshop, an act which is the final confirmation of his role as a cardboard cutout who goes up in flames as easily as his puppets.

The Magic Toyshop can, therefore, be read as a metaphor of the condition of England in the post-war period; a country whose position in the world has fundamentally changed, but which nevertheless remains unable to develop a new conception of itself. This is underscored by Carter's allusions to the Great Exhibition of 1851, which portray it as representative of the ruins of Victorian imperialism – yet for a sixties' readership, this reference would also recall the more recent Festival of Britain, an event that, as has already been discussed, explicitly positioned itself as the successor to the Great Exhibition. While the Festival may not be mentioned directly in *The Magic Toyshop*, Carter's references to fashions in design and interior decoration evokes a milieu shaped by Festival aesthetics, even while her narrative retreats from that environment and all it represents. In fact, Carter's disapproval of the Festival of Britain is on record: alongside her critique of Empire Day in 'So There'll Always Be an England' she dismisses it as 'the same kind of thing on a bigger scale, and perpetrated by a Labour government, too'.[124] While Carter's later work, in particular, revels in the creativity and self-indulgence of the carnivalesque, here the theatrical festival is clearly aligned with the notion of 'patriotism as theatre', bestowed on the masses from above in an attempt to maintain the status quo, rather than as something genuinely democratic, and hence potentially liberatory.

In his discussion of the Festival of Britain in *Patriots: National Identity in Britain 1940–2000*, Richard Weight says that it drew very strongly on '[t]he dominant metaphor of Britishness during this period [which] lay in the notion that the British were a family'.[125] This is a particularly apt comment in the context of my argument that *The Magic Toyshop* draws its metaphorical force from a post-war, post-Festival, post-austerity cultural context, since Carter, too, centres her narrative on the family unit. However, given Carter's sceptical opinion concerning the efficacy of public displays of nationalism intended to weld people together into a cohesive body predicated on a consensual group identity, the main family unit in *The Magic Toyshop* is distinctly dysfunctional; a disparate group of individuals in varying degrees of relationship to each other (it is, after all, composed of the remnants of other families), ruled over by a tin-pot dictator.

At this point, however, Carter is reluctant to speculate what kind of identity might evolve outside of the boundaries of the imperialist, patriarchal arena. Melanie, Aunt Margaret, Finn and Francie finally break free of Uncle Philip, but their futures are left uncertain. Aunt Margaret flees with baby Victoria in her arms, transformed into 'a goddess of fire' (197), Francie is glimpsed briefly through the smoke, and Melanie's brother Jonathon simply disappears. The novel ends with Melanie and Finn alone in the garden of the burning toyshop, 'fac[ing] each other in a wild surmise' (199). The family has rebelled, and hovers on the very edge of the possibility of change, even though its members cannot, as yet, imagine what they might do with their freedom. Indeed, the very ambiguity that surrounds Finn's role in the narrative hints at the chance that he may merely be the patriarch's successor, although it is a point on which critics of the novel differ. Jean Wyatt, for example, asserts that 'Finn makes the revolutionary gesture of forfeiting the privileges of masculinity, opening up the possibility of a different relationship between man and woman',[126] whereas the authors of *Feminist Readings/Feminists Reading* argue that Melanie finally 'accepts the role of lover, wife and mother assigned to her by society...Finn has finally "won" her from her Uncle Philip. In Carter's version of this patriarchal nightmare world, it would appear that there is no escape.'[127]

Yet the novel's refusal to commit itself to a definitive resolution in this way doesn't constitute a failure of imagination on Carter's part, but constitutes the clinching point in the argument she's been conducting throughout the narrative. What is important is not whether Melanie decides she is going to throw in her lot with Finn (whatever that might entail) but that she has reached a position where it is possible to make a decision at all. By the same token, if we interpret this text as a metaphor of English identity in the post-war period, we can see its final tableau as indicating a crucial moment in the history of a nation. In the fifties, with the phasing-out of austerity policies, Britain is faced with a choice. In spite of the fact that it has lost the dominant position it once occupied in the world, does it continue to conceptualise itself as an imperial power, carrying on increasingly anachronistic patriotic displays? Or does it work to construct a new sense of itself that embraces the confusion that the patriotric display conceals – diversity, change and relativism? As such, the conclusion of *The Magic Toyshop* pinpoints a period in which, as Richard Weight describes:

> British national identity was assailed by forces more powerful than any it had undergone before: Americanization, decolonization, black and Asian immigration, Scottish and Welsh nationalism and a drive towards European integration. Despite a desperate and often successful struggle to cling on to national traditions, the period [between 1951 and 1964] marked the end of the relatively homogeneous Britishness mapped out during the Second World War.[128]

Moreover, as an examination of her autobiographical essays demonstrates, Angela Carter does not carry out her critique from some lofty height of authorial authority. On the contrary, she clearly aligns herself, as writing subject, with this period of change. Born, almost literally, on the front line at a point in the Second World War where the maintenance of a cohesive national identity is crucial, she grows to maturity in the period where that same identity is crumbling, in spite of ever more ostentatious attempts to preserve it. Paradoxically, precisely because she is a member of a family always slightly at variance with the outside world, and the inheritor of a somewhat convoluted sense of national identity, Carter is perfectly placed to observe and record these changes with an off-centre, critical and assessing eye.

2
I'm a Sucker for the Worker Hero

In 1965, the same year in which Winston Churchill died, Angela Carter graduated from the University of Bristol with a degree in English and embarked on her writing career, publishing her first novel the following year. While there may seem to be little connection between the death of a former Prime Minister and Carter's academic achievement, it draws attention to a significant characteristic of her early work, which is written very self-consciously in and about a definitively post-Churchillian world. The spectacle of Churchill's state funeral symbolically underlines Carter's tendency to identify the sixties as a watershed decade, since those who witnessed the event viewed it as signifying, not just the death of one man, but of an era in British history. According to the *Observer*, it was 'the last time that London would be the capital of the world. This was an act of mourning for the imperial past. This marked the final act in Britain's greatness.'[1] Richard Weight, however, qualifies that statement slightly, claiming that:

> The meaning of the event for most Britons was not imperialistic in any way. What it did was to memorialize another narrative of national greatness: the Finest Hour over which Churchill had presided. His funeral richly symbolized the fact that Britishness was underpinned by the legends of the Second World War and the idea of Britain as a defiant, self-contained island rather than the motherland of an imperial diaspora.[2]

As has already been discussed in the previous chapter, Angela Carter, born in 1940 as the Allied armies poured onto the beaches of Dunkirk, was a child of Churchill's Finest Hour. More than that, she grew up in an England which drew its identity from the nationalistic myth that he had come to represent; a myth that conceptualised Britain as a country on the front line and the last line of defence against the forces of evil. Yet although she was to draw extensively on this myth in her subsequent career, she did so from a perspective that was both critical and cynical. If this tendency towards critique was evident in the novel she published in 1967, *The Magic Toyshop*, in which she revisited the cultural landscape of her childhood, it is even more overtly expressed in other novels she wrote in the 1960s. *The Magic Toyshop* may have been a deliberate exercise in nostalgia, but *Shadow Dance* (1966) and *Several Perceptions* (1968) are definitively 'sixties' novels, set in Carter's here and now – albeit with a distinctively baroque twist.

For while the crowds at Churchill's funeral may have mourned the end of empire and paid tribute to a potent symbol of British wartime heroism, a new national narrative was already moving centre stage. By 1965, Terence Conran had opened the first Habitat store on the Fulham Road, skirt hemlines were six inches above the knee, and the Beatles were about to become more popular than Jesus Christ. Britain was becoming redefined as the home 'of dynamic youth, of innovation, of popular culture and conspicuous consumption'.[3] Yet Angela Carter was not part of this London scene, having moved to Bristol in 1962, where she became, in her own words, 'a wide-eyed provincial beatnik'.[4] Her early writing, therefore, reveals her positioned between two national mythologies – the 'Finest Hour', confirmation of Britain's enduring status as a national power; and the 'Swinging Sixties', hip, chic, consumer-driven and individualistic.

Instead, Carter allies herself with the concept of the counterculture, which was not concerned with mini-skirts and pop music so much as with political and cultural revolution. Nor was it particularly preoccupied with Britishness – instead, it looked to the anti-Vietnam War demonstrations in America and the student revolutions in Paris in May 1968 in order to advocate a process of social transformation that would transcend national boundaries. The student manifesto pinned to the main entrance of the Sorbonne in Paris in May 1968 included the declaration 'Imagination is seizing power', a slogan which functions as a particularly apt summary of novels such as *Shadow Dance* and *Several Perceptions*. Both novels feature principal characters – 'heroes', as shall be demonstrated, isn't the right word at all – who enact increasingly fantastic, self-defined, lifestyles against a backdrop composed of the crumbling leftovers of Victoriana. Sheila Rowbotham has described sixties culture as 'oscillat[ing] between dramatic lunges towards modernity and nostalgic flirtations with the old which embraced the earthed simplicity of arts and crafts and the exotic coils of *fin de siècle* degeneracy',[5] and an examination of these three novels reveals that the central dynamic of *The Magic Toyshop* – a stand-off between an authoritarian, imperialistic past and a glossy, consumerist present – is typical of all the books Carter wrote during this decade.

However, *Shadow Dance* and *Several Perceptions* differ from *The Magic Toyshop* in their geographical setting, if not in their sense of cultural place. Along with the last novel Carter wrote in the sixties, *Love*, which will be discussed in detail in the following chapter, they are set in the area in which they were written, Bristol – a fact that has led Marc O'Day to classify the three together as Carter's 'Bristol Trilogy'. His essay, published in the collection *Flesh and the Mirror* edited by Lorna Sage and published in 1994, has been extremely influential in determining how these three books are regarded. Although, as he says, 'Bristol is never named as the city in which they are set, external evidence makes the autobiographical connection clear.'[6]

In *The Magic Toyshop*, as has already been discussed, Carter uses her setting – postwar Balham and the decaying remains of the Crystal Palace in Sydenham – as a means of satirising the British empire of the nineteenth century. Looking back at a period in which Britain regarded itself as an unassailable world power from the vantage point of the sixties, by which time such a belief has become unsustainable, Carter explores the mutability of national, as well as personal, identities. Yet it was Carter's move to Bristol, as much as her South London roots, which motivated this enduring interest in the changing faces of 'Englishness'; for as a symbol of decayed imperialism, Bristol could hardly be bettered. In the eighteenth century the city rivalled London as a mercantile power, since its position on the Atlantic coast enabled it to become the centre of the slave trade. It was a pivotal part of the so-called 'triangular' trade route that shipped goods to Africa to be exchanged for slaves, who were then transported to British plantations in the Caribbean and the Americas. Goods from the plantations, such as sugar, cocoa and rum, were then brought back to Bristol. In fact, the suburb of Bristol in which Carter lived in the 1960s, Clifton, was once the city's wealthiest area, developed by merchants building homes away from the docks where they plied their trade.

Post-war Bristol, however, was a very different world. The city had suffered extensively from German bombing raids targeting the Bristol Aircraft Works, the worst of which, on 24 November 1940, prompted Bristol's Lord Mayor to lament that: a 'city of churches had in one night become a city of ruins'.[7] Many historic buildings were destroyed, and

Bristol's suburbs, Clifton amongst them, badly damaged. Perhaps it was the remnants of the 'spirit of the Blitz' that these catastrophes engendered that motivated Bristol's enthusiastic participation in the 1951 Festival of Britain, which resulted in it being 'voted best festival outside of London'.[8] According to Becky E. Conekin, the official souvenir brochure written for the event was unusual in the context of the Festival as a whole, since it celebrated Bristol's colonial and commercial history and sought to reclaim it as a source of nationalistic pride. Quoting from the souvenir programme, Conekin observes:

> We are told that the first Englishman in the West Indies was from Bristol and that during the reign of Queen Elizabeth, many expeditions 'sailed from the Avon to prey upon the Spaniards, to search for gold and to develop trade'. However, it was after 1604 that 'the city's greatest period opened'. Bristol 'colonised Newfoundland...New England and Virginia...despatched Captain James to discover a northwest passage;...founded Surat; her merchants brought slaves to Africa which they exchanged for sugar in the West Indies and for tobacco in Virginia'.[9]

Conekin argues that 'the past they celebrated was quite a contrast to the one presented in the South Bank exhibitions',[10] which focused on perpetuating the post-war myth of Britain as a self-contained island nation: a view summed up in the speech given by the Archbishop of Canterbury at the Festival's opening ceremony:

> The chief and governing purpose of the Festival is to declare our belief and trust in the British way of life, not with any boastful self-confidence nor with any aggressive self-advertisement, but with sober and humble trust that by holding fast to that which is good and rejecting from our midst that which is evil we may continue to be a nation at unity in itself and of service to the world.[11]

Bristol, therefore, is a wholly appropriate setting through which to explore the two contrasting paradigms of Britishness. One, inherited from the eighteenth and nineteenth centuries, is imperialistic, regarding Britain as a country that explored and exploited the world; the other, coming to the fore following the victory of the Second World War, is insular, portraying Britain as a distinctive island nation. Carter, however, dissects both myths with equal ruthlessness. For the disaffected youth who populate *Shadow Dance* and *Several Perceptions*, the war is associated only with personal trauma, not national glory. Morris in *Shadow Dance*, for example, loses his mother in an air raid, leaving him 'on my own and the world...fallen on my head' (147). Nor has he really ever emerged from the rubble, making his precarious living from the 'dead flotsam' to be gleaned from 'the deserted, condemned old houses which the city council planned shortly to demolish' (24). The ramshackle 'business' run by Morris and his demonic partner Honey-buzzard is not in the least motivated by a desire to preserve the past, but is wholly concerned with marketing what Honeybuzzard cynically terms '*Observer* Design-for-Living Gear' (90): items that can be removed from their original context and amalgamated into fashionable design schemes. As in *The Magic Toyshop*, the past retains neither power nor meaning – instead, the bombed-out ruins of Georgian Bristol represent a period cut adrift from any consciousness of history. As Marc O'Day notes, what links *Shadow Dance* with *Several Perceptions* and *Love* is a strong sense of existing in a kind of hinterland – moral, existential, ontological and (most pertinently in the context of a study of Carter's life and times) cultural.

However, O'Day's classification of these three novels as a trilogy, is centred entirely upon his contention that they are 'a fictional media-tion of and an imaginative response to the particular place where the author lived'.[12] While this is certainly a valid summary of the trilogy, Bristol and the sixties are not all that ties the three books together. Carter might have been writing out of and about her immediate circumstances, but in the process she appears to have drawn on her adolescent experience for inspiration as well. For example, in an interview with Les Bedford in 1977, she named the formative works of her childhood as 'Webster, the Elizabethan dramatists. It wasn't anything to do with school. I just read them. I thought they were wonderful':[13] and the edgy, self-dramatising heroes of the Bristol trilogy can indeed be viewed as types of Jacobean malcontents. Another extremely pervasive referent in these novels is film, which recalls Carter's enduring fascina-tion with the medium. Charlotte Crofts makes the point that 'Carter's early fiction is saturated with allusion to cinema, not only in its direct reference to film styles, but also the experience of watching films or the fantasy of being in them.'[14] Her range of cinematic reference, however, is typically eclectic. In *Angela Carter's Curious Room* she recalls spending 'a lot of my adolescence, my lonely, brooding, gloomy adoles-cence, in the NFT...And there I watched endless film history'.[15] But the same documentary includes a poignant piece in which she recollects childhood trips with her father to the Granada cinema in Tooting, where she encountered not only 'the big-screen experience', but also the whole world of popular cinema, encapsulated in a 'dream cathedral of voluptuous wish-fulfilment architecture'. It was here she simultaneously 'fell in love with rococo' and 'fell in love with cinema'.[16]

Even if we bear in mind that Carter began to create her autobiographical persona many years after the publication of her early work, such retrospective comparisons widen the frame of reference of the Bristol trilogy beyond that proposed by O'Day. These are not *only* novels about Bristol, or even about the sixties, but also the beginning of Carter's imaginative reworking of her own history.

According to Carter, her teenage years were not particularly happy ones, marred by clashes with her mother and a flirtation with anorexia; the latter indicating, perhaps, the emergence of her enduring preoccupation with the manipulation of appearance. ('Self-consciousness had been her bane from the start' claims Lorna Sage, 'hence her anorexia'.)[17] In *Angela Carter's Curious Room*, her brother Hugh recalled Carter as a fat child – 'very fat indeed' – who lost a drastic amount of weight 'over a very short period'.[18] He refrains from using the term 'anorexia' to describe this process of dramatic reduction, but Carter herself used it quite openly, most notably in a review of *Self-Starvation* by Mara Selvini Palazzoli entitled 'Fat is Ugly'. Carter's tone in this piece is characteristically flippant:

> My qualification for reviewing her [Palazzoli's] book is that I am an ex-anorexic myself and so, in spite of her massive research, and deep and informed sympathy for women like me, still I know a trick or two that she does not (or so I fondly believe, doctor).[19]

Less characteristically, though, she justifies her approach at the very end of her discussion, asserting that her retreat into humour is a necessary coping mechanism: 'The tone of this review may be attributed to that same gallows humour with which the seventeenth century approached the subject of syphilis; some existential ills are so savage, I believe one should approach them stoically. That is, lightly.'[20] But such a qualification is in many ways unnecessary, since the comic veneer only partially obscures a depressing portrait of adolescent crisis. According to Carter, she was 'obese from infancy' (57), and although her mother strove 'to reconcile me to obesity – she would flourish Rubens and Renoir nudes before me and read aloud enticing descriptions of fat women from Victorian novels', her daughter remained convinced 'that fat was ugly, ludicrous, and disabling' (58). In her account she describes herself as descending into full-blown anorexia at around eighteen, plummeting from fifteen stone to 'between five and a half and six stone' (58) in less than a year. She attributed the trigger to 'pure sexual vanity', assuming 'that no man in his right mind could ever have been attracted to Fat Angie: therefore I reduced myself to a physical condition – that of Walking Corpse – that only a chronic necrophile could have fancied' (58). Her parents, initially horrified, finally 'concluded I was batty and left me alone' (58) – and eventually, Carter claims, she began to eat again of her own accord before ever learning that her affliction had a medical term attached to it.

Carter hints, however, at additional factors that complicated this situation. Although intelligent, passing the eleven-plus exam in order to secure a place at a direct grant school – a private school that allocated free places to those who passed an entrance examination at the age of eleven – she did not do well enough in her 'A' levels to get a place at university for the reason that 'I wasn't terribly happy, I couldn't concentrate on work, because I was far too fat, and sat dreaming of what I'd do if I were thin'.[21] Consequently, her father apprenticed her to *The Croydon Advertiser* 'on the grounds that it was a good job for a woman, and would guarantee me equal pay and career opportunities – as far up as I wanted to go, he claimed'.[22] Whenever recounting this part of her life, as the review of Palozzoli's book exemplifies, Carter tends to deploy self-deprecating, possibly self-protective, humour. She appears at this stage to have been desperate to escape from her parents, and saw marriage as the only realistic way to achieve such a goal. Thus, in 'Fat is Ugly' she quips that marriage for her was 'the only possible release from a home environment bulging with all those Renoir nudes, although my father had always told me a good job was a better bet' (58). In an interview with Lisa Appignanesi in 1987, she reiterated this statement, claiming that she only got married in order to contradict her father's opinion that journalism was a suitable profession for her: 'It was the fifties, after all. Couldn't have this man standing about talking like somebody in Shaw.'[23] In 'Fat is Ugly', though, she also picks up on Palazzoli's contention that anorexia can be traced back to tensions in the family – specifically, 'to a heightened sense of lack of personal autonomy, due to the nature of familiar relationships' (57). One of the signs that Carter was on the road to recovery, she said, was when she 'ceased to be docile at home and became obnoxious; first sign of autonomy' (58).

So, in a family where it was expected that she would enter a profession, the best form of rebellion was to rush down the aisle as soon as possible: she was only 20 when she married Paul Carter, an industrial chemist, in 1960. However, the details of this relationship, and the reasons why it ended – they were divorced in 1972, and had been separated for three years before that – were one of those aspects of her personal life that Carter kept away from public scrutiny. All that she allowed to emerge were fairly banal generalities: the most expansive public statement regarding her former husband that she ever made in an interview was in 1984, in which she told Ian McEwan that Paul Carter 'took her on Aldermaston marches, they saw Godard's *Breathless* together, he intro-duced her to the music of King Oliver and Louis Armstrong'.[24] In her own writing, it became the material for self-deprecating jokes: in 'Sugar Daddy', for example, she implied that she fell into the relationship out of pure gratitude. As a teenager, she said, 'my parents' concern to protect me from predatory boys was only equalled by the enthusiasm with which the boys I did indeed occasionally meet protected themselves against me', and therefore it was inevitable that she would fall into the arms of the first man 'who would go to Godard movies with me and on CND marches and even have sexual intercourse with me, although he insisted we should be engaged first'.[25] Privately, though, she could be far more biting. In 1974 she wrote a letter in which she observed of her ex-husband that 'I cannot imagine why – not that I ever married him – but why I hung on so long. 9 years out of my life. I have had more meaningful relationships with people I've sat next to on aeroplanes.'[26]

Nevertheless, at the time Carter's marriage enabled her to escape her parents' well-meaning attempts to control her life, particularly when Paul Carter got a job teaching chemistry at Bristol Technical College. Although it is perfectly possible to speculate that Carter would have become a writer anyway (she had already written, and thrown away, two novels), the move to Bristol was nevertheless a pivotal event in her career. It propelled her into education and, eventually, into print, because, as she told Lisa Appignanesi, 'I couldn't get a job there [Bristol] on a paper at all – nobody was interested – and so I went to university, which was quite easy because by then I was a mature student, so I was accepted on interview. So I did English at Bristol.'[27] It was an uncle, she later said, who 'realised that I was at home, wasting away, and persuaded me to go to university'.[28] Perhaps surprisingly for someone who was to become a writer to whom the label 'postmodern' was attached, she specialised in medieval, rather than modern, literature, on the grounds that it was 'a field where the Leavisites did not reach'.[29] Absorbing herself in writings of a much earlier period, therefore, represented for

Carter a way of shaking off a deferential attitude towards F.R. Leavis's still highly influential notion of the 'great tradition' – in an interview for the *Guardian*'s women's page after the publication of *The Sadeian Woman* she satirically remarked that '[s]he...[became] a medievalist because she wanted only to read Joyce and Pound, and thought it rude to have opinions about them'.[30]

Such comments indicate that Carter developed a distaste for qualitative literary classification very early on; and indeed the tendency – in her own words – 'to regard all aspects of culture as coming in on the same level'[31] was to became a hallmark of her writing style. However, this claim must be placed in context, for although Carter appears to reject the kind of intellectual elitism advocated by Leavis and his followers, in actuality the range of her literary references can be daunting. Although Carter loved the anti-naturalism of 'medieval romances and fables',[32] she read all kinds of literature from other periods, countries and modes as well – she said she was, for example, 'the only person in my year who actually read...[*Paradise Lost*] all through, including the footnotes'[33] – and in various later interviews she also cited Dostoevsky, Edgar Allen Poe, James Hogg, Robert Louis Stevenson, Isak Dinesen, Collette, Herman Melville, Charles Dickens and Racine as significant literary influences upon her early work.

Carter wrote her first published novel, *Shadow Dance*, while still an undergraduate at Bristol. She later told Ian McEwan that although she had already 'dabbled in novel writing', it was not until '[s]omeone at the university asked her why she didn't write the way she talked'[34] that *Shadow Dance* came into being. McEwan's account suggests that the novel was written in its entirety 'in the summer vacation of her second year',[35] although Carter told a slightly different story to Helen Cagney Watts a year later when she said that the writing of *Shadow Dance* was done 'during the evenings and weekends' during term-time, and the final draft 'typed up in the summer vacation'.[36] As Carter began university in 1962, this means that she wrote the novel during the 1963–4 academic year, although it was not actually published until 1966.

Reviewing the novel on its reissue in 1994, Claire Harman describes *Shadow Dance* as a novel of its period, with the action centred around 'a brilliantly evoked provincial urban landscape of the early 1960s (full of diverting period detail), complete with a moribund newsagent's shop, a filthy laundry, a cafeteria of "inescapable, undistinguishable brownness", vomiting girls and peeing dogs'.[37] This description accords closely with Carter's own assessment of *Shadow Dance*. To Olga Kenyon she summarised it as 'set in provincial bohemia during the post-beatnik, pre-hippie phase, and to that extent...about a particular area of a city where I once lived'. However, she went on to say that it was read differently by reviewers who, having no direct experience of such a seedy provincial environment in literature or in life, 'reacted with shock and disbelief to what was for them, this completely different other world, since I don't suppose they ever set foot outside of London, NW1 or NW5'. Consequently, 'because the British love to classify...I became classified as a writer of the style known as Southern Gothic'.[38] It is interesting that Carter refers to this love of classification here as a distinctively *British* trait, since the tag is actually applied to *Shadow Dance* in a review that appeared in *The New York Times* in 1967. In a piece entitled 'Grotesques', John Bowen reviews *Honeybuzzard* (the original title of the American edition of the novel) as a book with which his audience can identify, since even though it may be set in 'an unprofitable antique-shop in an English provincial city'.

> 'American readers may find Miss Carter's characters familiar... 'Southern Gothic' is a label which has been slapped on the work of Tennessee Williams, Carson McCullers and Truman Capote, among others. I'm not sure of the extent to which the 'Southern Gothic' writers actually took over the apparatus of the English Gothic novel, but I am sure enough of *their* influences on Miss Carter. She has taken the whole Southern circus – mutilation and beauty and evil, hot weather and a dark luxuriance of bizarre images – and pitched her tent in Bristol.[39]

Such an assessment of the novel raises the intriguing possibility of viewing *Shadow Dance* as the exemplification of a type of transmuted Gothic which has undergone a double transplantation, evolving into an ever more convoluted form in the process of migrating from Britain to America and back again. Carter's late work, in particular, would come to explore this process of transatlantic influence directly, but its applicability to these particular novels is somewhat tenuous, given the fact that Carter strenuously refuted the Gothic tag in connection with them.[40] Instead, she theatrically proclaimed herself irritated by this classification of her early novels: 'I knew perfectly well what a Gothic novel was. I knew it was all owls and ivy and mad passions and Byronic heroes who were probably damned, and I knew I wasn't writing them.'[41] English Gothic or Southern Gothic, it didn't matter: as far as she was concerned (so she said), she was representing the sixties as she saw and experienced it, rather than setting out to write within the confines of a particular literary mode.

If we take Carter's statement at face value, then, if *Shadow Dance* and *Several Perceptions* are Gothic, it is because the times themselves were. Indeed, Carter consistently claimed that her first novel was intended to be naturalistic. Surreal and fantastical though it is, it was 'about a perfectly real area of the city in which I lived. It didn't give exactly mimetic copies of the people I knew, but it was absolutely real as the milieu I was familiar with: it was set in provincial bohemia.'[42] She outlined her view of the sixties in an essay published in 1988 entitled 'Truly, It Felt Like Year One', in which she famously described the decade as 'living on a demolition site...living on the edge of the unimaginable'.[43] In this piece, Carter is fascinated by the extent of the social transformation effected by the children of the immediate post-war generation, who had been the principal beneficiaries of the Welfare State set up by the Attlee government in the forties. For Carter, the impetus of the sixties revolution was founded in the new educational opportunities offered to the working classes:

> I tend to blame what went on on the 1944 Education Act. Heavy irony here. Blame? Well, some people seem to see the sixties, culminating in the summer of '68 as a giant aberration in the wonderfully tranquil and cohesive history of English social class; at least, that seems to be the neo-Rightist revisionist line. So why not let a bit of soft liberal legislation carry the can. Nevertheless, the 1944 Education Act did indeed extend the benefits of further education to a select group of kids from working-class backgrounds, picked out *on account* of how they were extra-bright. Some of them were even permitted to go to Oxford and Cambridge. (Not me.) And were they grateful? Were they, hell...We'd the full force of the Attlee administration behind us, too, and all that it stood for, that lingered on after the Tories got back in.[44]

The Education Act of 1944 to which Carter refers here ensured that all children would progress into secondary education by raising the minimum school-leaving age to fifteen. In addition, their opportunities at secondary level were determined by the results of the eleven-plus examination. The minority who earned high marks in the eleven-plus were given a place at grammar school, which was the route to university and the professions, while the rest were relegated to the less prestigious environs of the secondary modern, where the curriculum was biased towards the practical rather than the intellectual. A two-tier system it might still have been, but now the recipients of higher education were decided on the grounds of intelligence, not class; and the result, according to Carter, was the establishment of 'a full-blooded, enquiring, rootless urban intelligentsia which didn't define itself as a class by what its parents had done for a living'.[45]

However, Carter is, perhaps knowingly ('Heavy irony here'), painting a somewhat utopian picture of the rise of a grammar-school-educated intelligentsia. According to Arthur Marwick, the social changes wrought by the grammar schools was limited, since

> although the potential for mobility through the education system was greater than it had been in the 1930s – rather more working-class children did now get through the eleven-plus into grammar schools – the whole system still very much replicated the division of the social structure into working, lower-middle, upper-middle, and upper classes.[46]

Nevertheless, Richard Weight, who quotes Carter in his discussion of the social consequences of the grammar school system, argues that its subsequent dismantling – a plan advanced in 1968, and carried out over the next decade – 'kicked away the only effective ladder for working-class advancement'.[47] In direct response to Carter's statement in 'Truly, It Felt Like Year One' that the Labour government 'put a stop' to grammar schools because they 'were on the point of turning into training camps for the class war' (210), Weight claims that although there was

> no evidence that the motive for abolition was quite so premeditated... there was a warped logic and a cruel irony to it. During a period in which Britain was enjoying a cultural renaissance which modernized its national identity, the institution which had done most to make that change possible was abolished'.[48]

Weight's contention here draws attention to another aspect of the sixties 'cultural renaissance' which has particular pertinence to Carter's literary output of this decade – its ephemerality. Angela Carter wrote 'Truly, It Felt Like Year One' in 1988, when Thatcherism was still at its height, and thus her depiction of the sixties is imbued with an extreme sense of nostalgia for an era which seemed to promise so much but which was in actuality so brief. 'Things were becoming accessible to me, in my early twenties, that I'd never imagined – ways of thinking, versions of the world, versions of history, of ways for society to be' (211). But, as she stresses throughout her fiction, carnival never lasts. For these children of the Education Act and the Welfare State, anything might have seemed possible, but in its radical reconfiguration of social and national identity, the revolution carried within it the seeds of its own destruction.

Shadow Dance and *Several Perceptions* may have been written while the sixties were in full swing, but they nevertheless convey a similar sense of an era heading towards an inevitable fall. Moreover, while in both their plot and their form they stress the carnivalesque mutability which Carter regards as the essence of the sixties countercultural revolution, they also focus upon the dangers inherent in living on a 'demolition site'. In fact, although 'Truly, It Felt Like Year One' remembers the sixties as one long party – it is described as both 'festal' (212) and a 'spree' (215) – remarkably little of this mood can be found in the novels set in Bristol, which focus on the nihilistic consequences of existing in a decade in which 'everyday life...took on the air of a continuous improvisation' (212). As Marc O'Day says, the Bristol Trilogy 'shows clearly how the sixties were a laboratory – or perhaps, rather, a battle-field – in the relativisation of all kinds of values: aesthetic, moral, spiritual, economic, political'.[49] To be alive in a time when anything goes may be exciting, but it is also potentially terrifying, a fact which gives these novels their dark and gothic edge.

Shadow Dance is a case in point. It is narrated from the point of view of Morris, an unsuccessful junk dealer and even more unsuccessful husband, whose neurotic and depressive perspective permeates the novel. He thinks of himself as 'a second-hand man', who 'might be totally impotent, helpless, useless as the junk in his shop'.[50] He has ambitions to be a painter, attempting to create what appear to be abstract colour-field works in 'pink and orange' (20) and 'green and white' (102). However, 'he was a bad painter and knew himself to be a bad painter and the desire to be a painter and the knowledge that he would never be a good painter burned inside him all the time' (19). What Morris is really good at is being a sidekick, or straight man, to Honeybuzzard, a figure who is Carter's embodiment of the pleasure and the dangers of the sixties. In contrast to Morris' tortuous introspection, Honeybuzzard is all appearance and no depth. Possessor of a 'flamboyant and ambiguous beauty' (55), he is superficial, artificial and contrived; his mania for dress-up and masquerade indicative of a fluid and unfixed subjectivity.

Indeed, fashion is the key to Carter's depiction of the sixties. In an essay entitled 'Notes for a Theory of Sixties Style', published in *New Society* in 1967, Carter analyses the clothing of the period, clearly revelling in the 'arbitrary and bizarre'[51] combinations of 'eclectic fragments' (106) of which sixties fashion is composed. She was not alone in this: in their book published in 1972, *Watch Out Kids*, Mick Farren and Edward Baker observe that:

> Fashions began to develop for army surplus and second hand clothes. The Cuban revolution provided a cheap and handy rebel look that could be achieved with fatigue caps and combat coats from the neighbourhood government surplus store. A church jumble sale could easily turn a teenage girl into a Victorian whore or a twenties flapper for the art school dance. The castoffs of previous generations were blended into bizarre combinations to fulfill individual and collective fantasies. Although the effect was often more Marx brothers than haute couture, it was the first time that a section of youth was working out its own fantasies without waiting for capitalist merchandising and mass media to provide them with the props.[52]

Farren and Barker focus here upon fashion as an aspect of the counter-culture's political revolution, noting that this recycling of garments and styles constitutes an anti-capitalist rejection of the commercial mass marketing of image. Carter, however, adopts a more philosophical attitude. What, she asks, do the 'fancy dress' and 'gaudy rags' (106) that constitute sixties style suggest about the changing relationship between body and identity? Because clothing has become a series of signifiers cut loose from any system of meaning, the individual can no longer hide behind a socially prescribed image: instead, everyone now has to evolve their own style, thus 'present[ing] the self as a three-dimensional art object' (106). In its resemblance to 'fancy dress' (106), sixties fashion has become disguise, opening out the possibility of 'a holiday from the persistent self' (106). But behind the dressing-up lurks serious intent:

> In the decade of Vietnam, in the century of Hiroshima and Buchenwald, we are as perpetually aware of mortality as any genera-tion ever was. It is small wonder that so many people are taking the dandy's way of asking unanswerable questions. The pursuit of magnificence starts as play and ends as nihilism or metaphysics or a new examination of the nature of goals. (108)

Honeybuzzard is the perfect example of an individual who takes 'the dandy's way of asking unanswerable questions': although the questions he poses as he passes through the many and various identities he assumes in the novel are ones to which we may not necessarily want to hear the answers. The very plasticity of his persona hints at a more nihilistic interpretation of sixties style, and one expressed by Christopher Booker in *The Neophiliacs*, a highly critical study of the period published at the very end of the decade:

> This sudden vogue among teenagers and the avant-garde middle class for colourful playthings and visual 'images' pillaged indiscriminately from a century of industrialised culture, whether *art nouveau* ties or grandfather clocks painted white or vests printed with slogans varying from 'I love The Beatles' to 'Jesus Saves', was marking the disintegration of the youthful collective fantasy into a more fragmented and inconsequential phase, in which no one 'look' or fashion would prevail, but in which titillatory images could be seized on almost at random.[53]

Angela Carter's reaction to Booker's publication – if she read it at all – is not on record, but it can, I think, be confidently assumed that she would have refuted his assessment of the sixties, which condemns the decade as a period of 'make-believe';[54] a kind of 'group fantasy' which represented 'a symptom of social disintegration, of the breaking down of the balance and harmony between individual, classes, generations, the sexes or even nations'.[55] Nevertheless, there are ways in which the direction of Booker's argument, if not his exact approach, is anticipated in this novel, written three years earlier. The reader's first view of Honeybuzzard, for example, conveys precisely the same sense of fragmentation and randomness evoked in *The Neophiliacs*:

> Honeybuzzard, lithe and slick as a stick of liquorice in his black leather jacket and corduroy trousers. Honeybuzzard, who seemed to be affecting a Groucho Marx stunt walk, his black legs scuttling in the wake of his thrust-forward torso. Honeybuzzard, crowned with an extremely large peaked cap, checked in screaming orange and shouting purple, pulled well down over his forehead ... He had on a new pair of owl-round, emphatically black sunglasses. He looked like a Hollywood starlet unsuccessfully attempting incognito. (55)

In this description, nothing matches – the sobriety of Honey's 'black leather jacket and corduroy trousers' clashing with the 'screaming orange and shouting purple' of his 'large peaked cap', all set off by sunglasses which may hide his face, but only make him more noticeable. Even his body is disjointed by his Groucho Marx walk, which grotesquely divides torso from legs. It is an elaborate performance, but its contradictoriness reveals nothing about Honey – not his occupation, his class, his politics or his character. When Morris speaks to him, '[t]he bright face under the bright cap' becomes 'a mask of nothing' (59), and all Morris can see when he attempts to look into Honeybuzzard's eyes is 'his own face blackly reflected' (60).

Honeybuzzard's dandyism, therefore, renders him opaque and oblique, whether he is resembling 'an illustration to "Goblin Market"' (130) with beads plaited through his hair, or posing as 'a song-and-dance man' (88) in a straw boater salvaged from a derelict house. Consequently, for all that he may stand as an icon of sixties fashion, Honeybuzzard is more emblematic of the loss of political and social purpose condemned by Booker, for he stands for nothing but the fulfilment of his own perverse desires: he is, as Elizabeth Wilson says of the dandy, one of those 'ambiguous rebels whose rebellion never is a revolution, but instead a reaffirmation of the Self'.[56] The fact that, to Honeybuzzard, the Self is all is confirmed by his favourite hobby. Like Uncle Philip in *The Magic Toyshop*, he is a toymaker, who makes friends and enemies together into Jumping Jacks whose actions are indissolubly tied to his whims.

Honeybuzzard is more than a sinister eccentric, for his parade of disguises conceal a sadist and, finally, a murderer. With Morris as his half-horrified, half-fascinated audience, he systematically brutalises his girlfriend Ghislaine in an escalating process of abuse, posing her for pornographic photographs, then scarring her face horrifically in an act of 'spiritual defloration' (132), and finally, in the novel's ghastly dénouement, murdering her. Even then he is not done with Ghislaine, for there are hints that he then uses her body as a prop in a blasphemous, necrophilic ceremony involving a crucifix. Nothing, it seems, is taboo as far as Honeybuzzard is concerned.

Even more horrifically – if that were possible – Ghislaine is not an unwilling victim in this process. Instead, she positively revels in an ecstasy of self-abasement. She is an active participant in Honeybuzzard's pornographic fantasies, '[a]fter each pose ... glanc[ing] questioningly up at the two men with the silent question: "Am I being wicked enough?"' (16). She seeks Honeybuzzard out the very day she is released from hospital following the knifing that has transformed her from 'a beautiful girl' (2) into 'the bride of Frankenstein' (4), 'features and all dragged away from the bone' (3). Morris, certainly, struggles to feel pity for Ghislaine, regarding her instead with a mixture of revulsion and guilt. For in his role as Honeybuzzard's 'shadow', he has been silently complicit in everything that has been meted out to Ghislaine – he was present when the pornographic photographs were taken, albeit on the opposite side of the camera, and he supports Honeybuzzard in his story that she was scarred by a gang of teenagers, even though he knows it is a lie. But viewed from the opposite side of the mirror, it is Honeybuzzard who is Morris' shadow, performing the acts he barely acknowledges he desires to commit himself. His dreams of cutting Ghislaine's face 'with a jagged shard of broken glass' (18) remain fantasy: it is Honey who translates them into reality. At the end of the novel, Morris reluctantly acknowledges the ties that bind them together, deciding 'to enter, Orpheus-like, the shadowed regions of death...and, like Orpheus, to rescue or destroy a dear companion' (181). In doing so, he leaves 'the real world' behind in order to enter 'a new dimension outside both space and time' (181). What Morris achieves there, however, is left obscure, as the novel concludes with him 'vanish[ing] into the shadows' (182).

As Lorna Sage says, *Shadow Dance* remains a remarkably shocking text, which 'crammed in ideas and themes and images that its author was to explore at leisure for years to come';[57] a comment which foregrounds the importance of the *zeitgeist* of the sixties to all of Carter's work. It is the period from which she drew her most basic inspiration, and although these 'ideas and themes and images' would go through various modulations and inflections as her career progressed, they nevertheless retain a connection to their countercultural roots. Along with its companion novel *Several Perceptions*, *Shadow Dance* draws on aspects of sixties culture in the same way as Honeybuzzard and Morris salvage artefacts from old houses, and thus they are novels that:

> uniquely crystallise the vertigo of that decade. The vertigo that had nothing to do with the ephemeral pop mythology of the Beatles or mini-skirts, but with Vietnam, with the Prague spring, culminating in the events of May in Paris, '68, when, however briefly, it seemed imagination might truly seize power. Vertigo that came from the intoxicating, terrifying notion that the old order was indeed coming to an end, vertigo of beings about to be born.[58]

Carter, though, is not referring to her own novels here, but to the work of the French new wave film-maker Jean-Luc Godard; and the applicability of this description to *Shadow Dance* and *Several Perceptions* indicates the extent to which they themselves are indebted to cinematic influences. Carter herself cited Godard as exerting particular influence upon her perception of the sixties, recalling in 'Truly, It Felt Like Year One' that:

> I saw Godard's *Breathless* when it came out in 1959, and my whole experience of the next decade can be logged in relation to Godard's movies as if he were some sort of touchstone. I suppose all I was doing was going through some kind of intellectual apprenticeship of a generalised 'European' type, and I recognised and responded to a way of interpreting the world that suited my own instincts far more than the Leavisite version I was being given at university.... The last words of *Weekend* – *fin du cinema, fin du monde* – heavens! how they struck home![59]

For Carter, Godard was the cinematographer who both defined and explained the decade to 'my generation of British adolescents that ripened, some would say like a boil, towards the end of the 1950s', to whom, she said, his films came as a 'revelation'. Through Godard, they were able to redefine themselves in a more radical mode:

> Not, as we'd been told, the children of F.R. Leavis and the Welfare State, but, in Godard's famous definition, children 'of Marx and Coca-Cola'. And more. Children of Hitchcock, Dostoevsky, Brecht – and of pulp fiction, phenomenology and the class struggle. Heady stuff, that changes you.[60]

Indeed, to align Carter's first novel with *Breathless*, Godard's first feature film, is an illuminating exercise, not because the plots echo each other in any way, but because they are so similar in terms of mood and outlook. The hero of Godard's film is a young hoodlum called Michel, who steals a car in Marseilles in order to drive to Paris, where he intends to pick up some money owing to him and effect a reunion with Patricia, a former girlfriend. On the road to Paris a policeman catches him speeding and attempts to stop him, whereupon Michel shoots and kills his pursuer with a gun he finds by chance in the glove compartment of the stolen car. Now a murderer (a fact that does not seem to disturb him overmuch), he proceeds to Paris and, in between tracking down his money and evading the police, he attempts to persuade Patricia to run away with him to Italy. In the end, however, it is Patricia who betrays Michel's whereabouts to the police, and they eventually shoot him dead.

It is a bleak story – as bleak as *Shadow Dance* – and like *Shadow Dance*, for all its meticulous indexing of place and of period (a great deal of the film was shot on location rather than on set), it is not, ultimately, realistic. Indeed, Godard himself later said of *Breathless* that 'although I felt ashamed of it at one time, I do like... [it] very much, but now I see it where it belongs – along with *Alice in Wonderland*. I thought it was *Scarface*.'[61] What makes the film particularly disturbing and surreal is its lack of contextualisation. As Wheeler Winston Dixon observes of Michel, '[h]is life, and his death, are both seen as essentially random acts, devoid of meaning and/or consequence; Michel lives only for the moment'.[62] A fan of Humphrey Bogart, whose mannerisms he continually self-consciously copies, Michel is intrinsically amoral and a compulsive fantasist who is addicted to the contemplation of his own reflection. Even his most serious crime, murder, is performed 'in character' in accordance with the dramatic demands of the part he has assumed. Patricia, a middle-class American girl, is clearly seduced by Michel's gangster persona, but although she may superficially seem to be a vulnerable innocent, in fact she is no more in touch with reality than he is. Just as there is no concrete motive underlying Michel's murder of the policeman, so the reasons for Patricia's final betrayal of him are similarly arbitrary and confused. If she had turned him in because she believed he should be punished for his crimes, both his acts and hers could be comprehended by being placed in the context of a moral framework, but in fact she accepts what he has done with perfect equanimity.

Breathless and *Shadow Dance*, therefore, inhabit the same moral (or, rather, *a*moral) universe. Honeybuzzard and Michel are both creations lacking in any sense of moral culpability, a fact that allows their creators to explore the pleasures and the dangers of absolute egotism. Moreover, their attitudes towards women are extremely similar – to Michel, any woman to whom he is not attracted is brutally dismissed as a 'dog', an attitude echoed in the casual brutality of Honeybuzzard's assertion that 'Some women you can only vivisect' (62). To complicate matters further, neither Patricia nor Ghislaine are unequivocal victims. Unsettlingly, they play the games and thus share the blame, fuelling the fantasies of the men who are both their lovers and abusers.

Both Godard's film and Carter's novel also point up their lack of moral referents through their referencing of period. The action of *Breathless* is played out in a city papered with Situationist slogans – the bedroom wall of one of Michel's former girlfriends is emblazoned with the question 'Pourquoi?', and a street flyer tendentiously proclaims

'Live dangerously until the end'. The film is made, and set, in 1960, when Situationism was at its height, and its two main characters personify the bankruptcy of the modern condition as understood by the situationists, who:

> characterised modern capitalist society as an organisation of spectacles: a frozen moment of history in which it is impossible to experience real life or actively participate in the construction of the lived world. They argued that the alienation fundamental to class society and capitalists production has permeated all areas of social life, knowledge, and culture, with the consequence that people are removed and alienated not only from the goods they produce and consume, but also from their own experiences, emotions, creativity, and desires. People are spectators of their own lives, and even the most personal gestures are experienced at one remove.[63]

Breathless thus exemplifies Guy Debord's assertion that reality in its totality is in thrall to the 'spectacle', which 'proclaims the predominance of appearances and asserts that all human life, which is to say all social life, is mere appearance'.[64]

Shadow Dance does not make overt reference to Situationism, but it echoes *Breathless* in its representation of life reduced to the commodification of appearance, an atmosphere achieved not only by Carter's self-absorbed and excruciatingly self-conscious protagonists, but also through her locating of the action in a moment when the ruins of past conflict – 'the deserted, condemned old houses which the city council planned shortly to demolish' (24) – are being swept away in favour of a gleaming world governed by the dictates of a modern consumerist style. Certainly, the encroaching presence of the brave new aesthetic environment which the Festival of Britain had claimed to prefigure in the fifties looms over *Shadow Dance*. One of Morris's acquaintances, whom he habitually bumps into at auction sales, is Oscar, 'a Design Centre obsessive, and contemporary clean lines and white paint man, who lived in a Scandinavian living box and stuffed his dustbins weekly with old, shabby, broken things for they meant nothing to him' (27–28). Although Oscar is, to a great extent, a figure of fun in the novel, Carter makes it clear that it is he, not Morris, who is most in tune with contemporary style, as illustrated by the transformation of the old café that is one of Morris' habitual haunts. Its 'grained wood' panelling and chairs and tables of 'solid and immovable oak' (29) have been exchanged for 'steel and plastic structures so light they had to be screwed into the ground to prevent them overbalancing at a touch' (29–30). Here, interior decoration takes on an overtly symbolic significance. The solidity and immovability of the old is deceptive, for it is being swept away in favour of the light, the fragile and the transient; which in turn indicates the superficiality and the vacuity of modernity.

Furthermore, although Honeybuzzard and Morris may appear to be resisting the rapidly encroaching tide of notions of modern taste influenced by 'Festival style', in fact their countercultural commitment to the recycling of the old rather than embracing the radical aesthetic changes required by the new (which demands that its adherents, such as Oscar, 'stuff...[their] dustbins weekly' with precisely the 'old, shabby, broken things' that Honey and Morris salvage) may not necessarily be as radical as they themselves would like to think. Marc O'Day argues persuasively that 'the individualism, expressiveness, private fantasy, romanticism, self-indulgence and need for change espoused by the counterculture are all valorised as values and practices of consumerism itself',[65] with the result that the boundaries between 'official and countercultural, commercial and anticommercial (if there was really any such thing)'[66] become indistinct. In Situationist terms, such a conclusion demonstrates that there is no escape from the spectacle, since in the process of resistance one only becomes more firmly embedded within it.

The resulting sense of dislocation from a world of Descartean certainty that operates according to a predictable, discernable system of cause and effect is predominant in all three books that make up the Bristol trilogy. However, it is particularly evident in the first two novels, in both of which Carter includes striking, surreal and violent moments where narrative continuity is abandoned, and events happen seemingly at random. In *Shadow Dance*, for example, an episode occurs in which the antiques shop is stormed by 'a crazy, silent, dancing crew, faltering, staggering in the ghost light, haphazardly here and there on the pavement, in the road' (114):

> The gang drew into a ragged group outside the laundry and with one accord turned and faced the shop...then one of them – Morris could not see who – pitched a brick at their window. The missile went wildly astray...but as if at a signal, they all, shouting (though the two men could hardly hear them, through the thick glass) surged across the road at the very moment when the streetlamps went out. They carried sticks and stones and broken bottles and pieces of wood with nails in them and Morris thought he caught the flicker of the blade of a knife.

Then the ponderous bicycle of a patrolling policeman rolled majes-
tically down the road and they all ran away, just like that. (115)

This bizarre incident remains unrelated to anything else that takes place
in the novel. As the passage quoted above illustrates, even Morris's
perception of the event itself remains partial, giving us no clues that
might lead us to an explanation – he cannot see who throws the first
stone at the shop window, nor can he hear, 'through the thick glass',
what the mob are shouting as they advance. Moreover, the fact that
they run away, 'just like that', at the first sign of a policeman implies a
lack of strong motivation underlying the attack, which is never explained.

A similar episode occurs in *Several Perceptions*. The chief character of
this novel, Joseph, is very reminiscent of Morris in *Shadow Dance*, with
whom he shares his melancholia, purposelessness and misogynistic
attitudes. At one point in the novel, Joseph goes to a pub for a drink
with his friend Viv and Viv's mother Mrs Boulder, and a fight breaks
out in the public bar which conveys the same impression of random
violence. Events occur which have no meaning attached to them and,
seemingly, no consequence, involving a girl with 'extraordinary
flashing black eyes and a backcombed beehive of dark hair, her 'young
man', who has 'taxidermy eyes like a dead, stuffed deer',[67] and Kay
Kyte, a character who is reminiscent of Honeybuzzard – like Honey, Kay
is a dandy who raids the ragbag of sixties style. The girl throws a glass at
Kay, and when he protests, her boyfriend makes an abortive attempt to
attack him. The whole event collapses into farce, however, when Kay
dodges, leaving the boy raving amongst the smashed glass on the floor:

'I can't control an Irish temper and she's always looked after me, I'm
three parts mental. I'm just out of a mental hospital and I'm three
parts mental, don't call me a lunatic for Christ's sake, and there you
are in your gold ear-rings and I'm looking at you, what you want to
wear golden ear-rings for if you don't want to be looked at, I'm
looking at you peacefully and you say "What's with you, friend,"
and I can't bear it, it's too much –'

The girl stood with her hands on her hips; her demonic red lips
were stretched in a flamenco dancer's artificial smile.

'It's not true,' she said. 'He's just out of the nick. God, what a liar
he is.' (52–53)

In typical Carter fashion, this scene is shot through with references to
several different literary modes. The two anonymous characters are

playing out their own 'Elizabethan tragedy' (51), while the accusation thrown at Kay by the boy – 'what you want to wear golden ear-rings for if you don't want to be looked at' – parodies a line from a scene in T.S. Eliot's modernist poem *The Waste Land* that also takes place in a pub: 'What you get married for if you don't want children?'.[68] Another way of understanding this episode, however, is to regard it, not as theatrical or poetic drama, but as film – the translation into a literary context of a cinematographic method pioneered by Godard.

Breathless introduced a technique which was to become one of Godard's trademarks; the 'jump cut', in which he would randomly excise frames of film from the reel, with the result that the action proceeds in a jerky, discontinuous fashion. Reviewing *Breathless* in *The New York Times* in 1961, Bosley Crowther regarded Godard's interruptions of continuity as underlining the film's main theme – its 'vastly complex comprehension of an element of youth that is vagrant, disjointed, animalistic and doesn't give a damn for anybody or anything, not even itself'.[69] This statement could very well be appropriated as a summary of Angela Carter's portrayal of sixties youth in the Bristol trilogy; given Carter's description of Godard's impact upon her in 'Truly, It Felt Like Year One', and the fact that such radical rejections of causality occur most blatantly in her earliest novels, a case can be made that Godard's work not only helped shape the atmosphere of these texts, but also Carter's narrative technique at this point in her career. Indeed, in the course of the bar-fight in *Several Perceptions*, Carter inserts a comment which can be seen as a narrative explication of the cinematic jump cut: 'There was a jagged atmosphere in the bar; things were happening without a sequence, there was no flow or pattern to events. Causation was still awry' (52). In other words, the setting of this text has no past and no future; only a continuous, nightmarish, present in which the spectator is presented with a chaotic jigsaw of events which do not connect, and are incapable of explanation or comprehension. Moreover, although the participants in such scenes *enact* violent emotion – to the point where injury, if not murder, appears a real possibility – Carter makes it obvious that they do not really *feel* it.

In both *Shadow Dance* and *Several Perceptions*, this sense that life is nothing more than a mechanical reiteration bereft of feeling or intent is felt particularly strongly by the novels' main characters, Morris and Joseph. Lacking a past, neither possesses any sense of continuity. While Morris has never had a father and has lost his mother – who may be dead, or may simply have abandoned him – Joseph is brought up in 'a real family', with a mother and father, '[e]verything complete' (89).

Nevertheless, he cannot connect with his personal history: when he phones his home, he experiences the sense that although

> [h]e had lived for eighteen years between the shop and the square of garden and, it seemed to him, had scarcely left a mark on the house to show he had been there, not a fingerprint on any wallpaper or a stain on the linoleum. Nothing. Only his mother crying because he was not there proved he had been there and gone. (105)

However, according to Jonathon Green, the term 'generation gap' entered the language around 1967, which suggests that Joseph's sense of being cut off from his parents' lifestyle is not nearly as unique as he might like to think. In fact, for all his endless self-dramatisation and his desire to characterise himself as some kind of brooding malcontent, he can actually be viewed as being representative of his age group, for *Several Perceptions* stresses particularly strongly that such feelings of alienation constitute an eminently appropriate response to the time. In contrast to the novel that directly preceded it, *The Magic Toyshop*, which adopts an oblique attitude towards the historical process, this novel is dated, very precisely, 'March–December 1967', and takes place against the backdrop of the Vietnam War. Joseph is a member of the immediate postwar generation who grew up with the National Health Service and the opportunities offered by free state education, but they are benefits for which he is not in the least grateful: 'Joseph had the chance of a fine education but threw it away; he had free choice on the self-service counter and voluntarily selected shit' (4). Continually oppressed by 'dreams of fires quenched with blood and bloody beaks of birds of prey and bombs blossoming like roses with bloody petals over the Mekong Delta' (4–5), Joseph simply does not see the point. Instead, he attempts suicide in his crumbling bed-sit, the walls of which are covered with pictures:

> Lee Harvey Oswald, handcuffed between policemen, about to be shot, wild as a badger. A colour photograph, from Paris Match, of a square of elegant houses and, within these pleasant boundaries, a living sunset, a Buddhist monk whose saffron robes turned red as he burned alive. Also a calendar of the previous year advertising a brand of soft drinks by means of a picture of a laughing girl in a white, sleeveless, polo-necked sweater sucking this soft drink through a straw. And a huge dewy photograph of Marilyn Monroe. (15)

Joseph's choice of pictures here represents both his private state of mind and the period in which he lives in its juxtaposition of the trivial and the horrific, the fantastic and the historical. Marc O'Day has already discussed the relevance of R.D. Laing's study of schizophrenia, *The Divided Self* (published in 1960) to *Several Perceptions*; his point that 'Joseph's sickness is...period-specific'[70] reminiscent of Carter's own statement in 'Fat is Ugly' that

> schizophrenia was the mode of the sixties. (I was a student when Laing's *The Divided Self* came out to form an instant focus for self-identification for young people away from home for the first time; they had to open a new ward in the local madhouse to deal with the resulting plague.)[71]

Joseph exemplifies the schizophrenic as defined by Laing: a person 'who may feel more unreal than real; in a literal sense, more dead than alive; precariously differentiated from the rest of the world, so that his identity and autonomy are always in question'.[72] Carter, indeed, described him as 'in a very Laingian and sixties fashion, responding to an insane world by becoming insane'.[73] But Laing also worked to break down the division between the opposing categories of 'madness' and 'sanity' asserting in his preface to the 1964 Pelican edition of *The Divided Self* that 'In the context of our present pervasive madness that we call normality, sanity, freedom, all our frames of reference are ambiguous and equivocal.'[74] Viewed from this perspective the collage of pictures on Joseph's wall can be seen as representative of the way in which society itself represents history as drama, trivialising tragic, monumental, events by reducing them to sound bites and images. The question implicitly posed by *Several Perceptions* is therefore this: how to make sense of a world in which horror is conveyed to you in such trite fragments?

Joseph's psychiatrist, Ransome, is an anti-Laingian, believing that Joseph's 'sickness is merely a failure to adjust to the twentieth century' (63):

> Let's take the Vietnam war,' Ransome went on. 'I don't think you care at all about the sufferings of the people of Vietnam, Joseph; not in any real sense of involvement with a real situation. You make no move to relieve those suffering in a real way, through voluntary service, for example. You don't even join in any organized protest. Rather, you've taken this dreadful tragedy of war as a symbolic event

and you draw a simple melodramatic conclusion from this complex tragedy – you use it as a symbol for your rejection of a world to which you cannot relate.' (63–64)

Ransome isn't necessarily wrong, since Joseph does indeed view the war as symbolic of his own inner state, but nevertheless, for many in Britain in the sixties the war became reconstructed in their personal imaginations through reference to images drawn from the media. For example, Sheila Rowbotham – who was involved in the very direct anti-war action that Ransome accuses Joseph of avoiding – describes the Vietnam War as 'my generation's Spain...the suffering of its people became imprinted on our psyches. I kept seeing the image of a strange white creature, lacerated by red wounds, the embodiment of pain.'[75] '[O]pponents of the...War', says Rowbotham, were 'haunted by the photographic images of hunted Vietnamese being lined up, the Buddhist monks' self-immolation, the TV coverage of unrelenting bombing raids'.[76] In this context, Joseph's obsessive visions of 'little children clad in flame and the Mekong Delta like one gigantic wound' (64) seem less like individual psychosis and more like a representative experience of the period.

Writing in 'Truly, It Felt Like Year One', Carter reflected on the significance of the Vietnam War for the British youth of the sixties: 'The more I think about it, the odder it seems...that so much seemed at stake in Vietnam, the very nature of our futures, perhaps.'[77] Although he would not withdraw support for the American president Lyndon Johnson, Harold Wilson nevertheless refused to lead Britain into direct involvement in the war, and therefore the country remained on the sidelines of a conflict in which it played no part. However, anti-war demonstrations, initiated in America primarily by students who were already involved in the civil rights movement, had crossed the Atlantic by 1965, when a demonstration was staged at Oxford University. Jonathon Green argues that Vietnam became such a major issue for British radicals because it gave them a focus through which to express a more general discontent with a Labour government that was reneging on the promises with which it had wooed voters in 1964: 'If the Left needed a single issue on which to focus the charge that Wilson had "betrayed" their hopes, then Vietnam was it.'[78] The results of a survey conducted after a march in October 1968 revealed that '70% of the marchers felt themselves to be demonstrating not just against the Vietnam War, but against the structure of the capitalist society in Britain'.[79] In October 1967, while Carter was mid-way through the writing of *Several Perceptions*, the Vietnam Solidarity Campaign led by Tariq Ali staged its first march, from Trafalgar Square to the US Embassy in Grosvenor Square, which attracted 10,000 participants. Sheila Rowbotham, who was there, described herself as 'exhilarated by the size of the march, a great gathering of everyone I had ever known plus thousands more besides'.[80]

Carter said that 'the positive side' of the British interest in the Vietnam War was that it fostered 'an internationalism that wasn't the least superficial. There was an extraordinary camaraderie among the rootless urban intelligensia.'[81] Although the war would not end until the mid-seventies, *Several Perceptions* reflects the sense of optimism and solidarity that was a feature of 1967, described by Carter as the year 'when things were peaking'.[82] Whereas *Shadow Dance* ends on a note of individual resolution, unresolved, *Several Perceptions* is decidedly more celebratory. Although it contains many of the same elements as Carter's first novel – most notably, the crumbling antique backdrop, the solipsistic antihero and the narcissistic dandy – they are not nearly as dark. Honeybuzzard's role is taken by Kay Kyte, who is akin to Shakespeare's Puck, whizzing through the landscape on his bicycle 'like a little Super-hero, maybe Mini Man or Mighty Moppet biking off to a meeting of the Teen Titans' (10). From his invalid mother's 'dilapidated mansion' (127), Kay presides over his 'floating world' (128) of provincial bohe-mians and hippy chicks in 'attic surroundings of faked luxury and rampant neglect' (128). The novel ends with a Christmas party, during which dreams come true. The haunted, inadequate characters that populate the narrative are all given a second chance, Joseph amongst them. Deciding to become 'friends with time again' (146), he banishes the ghost of Ransome: ' "Don't come bothering me," said Joseph. "You are only an emanation, a soothe-me. A soothe-sayer. Go away and look after the sick people" ' (147).

Yet Joseph's idea of a 'cure' is not one that Ransome would neces-sarily endorse, for the world that he re-enters remains a distinctively countercultural one. Ironically, family ties remain strong within this alternative existence, but, like Melanie's in the *The Magic Toyshop*, 'family' becomes a free-floating concept: a makeshift, reassembled version of the original. What differentiates Joseph, though, from either Morris or Melanie is that he has rejected his biological family, not lost them. Like Carter herself, he has made the journey to Bristol from the South London suburbs, which is also a shift from the respectable lower-middle classes to a kind of classless bohemia. 'His father was a newsa-gent and tobacconist who worked hard all his life. His mother was just an ordinary housewife who worked hard all her life' (6–7). But Joseph, a child of the sixties, rejects the work ethic of his parents and takes full advantage of the dole money provided by the Welfare State.

Family histories, therefore – which are also inextricably bound up in public narratives of national identity – are either abandoned or invented by the children born out of the Second World War. For them it is the war's private, not its public, consequences that have had the most impact upon their lives since it has sundered family ties rather than consolidated them. Joseph's neighbour Annie Blossom, for example, is a Barnardo's baby who has no idea who her parents might have been, but she believes 'it's possible and seems likely' (86) that her father was killed in the war. Like Morris, the war constitutes a definitive break in her personal history, which can only be filled in with conjecture.

Nevertheless, what *Several Perceptions* takes away on the one hand, it gives back on the other. Characters such as Joseph's best friend Viv, and the beautiful bohemian Kay Kyte stand in opposition to the self-sufficient solitude of Joseph and Annie, since both of them are the devoted sons of mothers. Yet these mother-figures, too, are somewhat problematic, since both seek to circumvent or negate the historical process. Terrified of growing old, the senusual and curvaceous Mrs Boulder hides 'the crumbling sandstone of her real appearance' beneath a 'painted imitation of a face' (114). Unlike Joseph, she does not achieve a recon-ciliation with time, but becomes instead completely subsumed in artifice, attending Kay's party in magnificent, drag-queen, splendour: 'her dress was tight white satin, split up one side, her spike-heeled shoes were silver and a silvery moon dust was puffed over her bouffant meringue of hair and her eyelids were silvered and her face was superb' (131). Mrs Boulder is only the first of an array of fabulously over-the-top feminine confections that parade through Carter's subsequent fiction, all of whom are as questionable as they are admirable. One the one hand, Mrs Boulder's defiant stand against time is magnificent, but on the other, it links her to the other mother in the text, Mrs Kyte. A former actress, Mrs Kyte lives in a 'slow time' (138) which refuses to move on from past to future. Like *Great Expectations'* Mrs Haversham or Norma Desmond in *Sunset Boulevard*, she gently decays along with her mansion, lost in dreams of pre-war theatrical glamour.

One of the conundrums posed by the text is whether it is possible to navigate a median line between a destructive historical process which destroys and divides, and timelessness, associated with stasis, death and illusion. It is Kay Kyte who offers the possibility of a compromise between these two extremes. The photograph of his deceased father,

'Mr Kyte the fighter pilot', who 'took part in the fire raids over Dresden' (142) may remind the reader of the novel's historical context – but Kay's attitude towards it is instructive. Rather than romanticising his father as a 'war hero' (142), he pragmatically accepts his absence as an unalterable fact, knowing that 'the dead stay dead, down in the black' (142). Nevertheless, he continues to party, fending off the inevitable with paper chains and plastic roses.

The ending of *Several Perceptions*, for all its celebratory theatrics, thus retains some of the sense of precariousness of its predecessors. Morris vanishes into the shadows in search of his demonic double and Melanie and Finn freeze in the face of an as-yet-unimagined future; while for Joseph the world remains 'full of horrible and inscrutable inhumanities' (142). The room in which the novel's concluding party takes place is dominated by a vast mirror which 'reflected the windows and the trees and darkness outside, so the crowd appeared hemmed in on all sides by dangerous night' (129): an indication, perhaps, of the inability of the counterculture to change the world. Instead, it remains a vehicle of individual, rather than collective, revelation.

3
What Were the Sixties Really Like?

Several Perceptions may conclude on a note of tentative celebration, but it is a moment of optimism which is not repeated in the final two novels Angela Carter wrote in the sixties: a foray into science fiction, *Heroes and Villains* (1969), and *Love*, which is the final novel set in Bristol. Although *Love* was published in 1971, in the Afterword written for the book's reissue in 1987, Carter emphasised that:

> *Love* was written in 1969 and the people in it, not quite the children of Marx and Coca-Cola, more the children of Nescafé and the Welfare State, are the pure, perfect products of those days of social mobility and sexual licence.[1]

If 1967 is the point at which 'things were peaking', then the novels written in the final three years of the decade reflect a rapid slide into disillusionment. Although both *Heroes and Villains* and *Love* reiterate themes and figures familiar from the earlier books, they are noticeably darker. Her characters still posture and perform as much as they have ever done, but now the façade barely conceals the desperation underlying the act. These texts also show Carter, having published three successful novels – *The Magic Toyshop* was awarded the John Llewellyn Rhys memorial prize for the best novel of 1967, and *Several Perceptions* won the Somerset Maugham Award in 1968 – beginning to reassess her own authorial intentions and techniques.

This process of artistic evolution echoes Carter's gradual shift in focus during the later years of the sixties, which moved her towards a more explicit radicalism. Although she had 'always followed politics . . . I don't think I voted until the late 1960s, and that was a partly political decision not to vote. There comes a moment when many of the things of which you have a theoretical knowledge actually apply to oneself.'[2] Some of this increased engagement with the political process was undoubtedly due to her growing feminist awareness. In 'Truly, It Felt Like Year One', Carter records a contradictory attitude towards the social roles accorded to women in the sixties. On the one hand, she celebrates the sexual revolution, contradicting the view that it 'only succeeded in putting more women on the sexual market for the pleasure of men'.[3] Instead, it allows sex to become 'a medium of pleasure', 'divorced from not only reproduction but also status, security, all the foul traps men lay for women in order to trap them into permanent relationships'.[4] But this assertion is heavily qualified, since 'there's no such thing as pure pleasure', after all.[5] In many ways, Carter claims, relationships between the sexes were actually complicated by the advent of sexual liberation, proving that 'human relations are very complex and often very painful regardless at what moment during their course sexual intercourse takes place'.[6] And it was sexual liberation's failure to iron out all the inequalities between men and women that eventually brought her to feminism, 'in the end, because still and all there remained something out of joint and it turned out that was it, rather an important thing, that all the time I thought things were going so well I was in reality a second-class citizen'.[7]

In 'Truly, It Felt Like Year One', Carter is, in some respects, reiterating a fairly standard 'how-I-came-to-feminism' narrative which can be found in many women's accounts of the sixties, bearing out the observation made by Anna Coote and Bea Campbell in *Sweet Freedom: The Struggle for Women's Liberation*, that:

> Radical politics in the 1960s provided an excellent breeding ground for feminism. Men led the marches and made the speeches and expected their female comrades to lick envelopes and listen. Women who were participating in the struggles to liberate blacks and Vietnamese began to recognize that they themselves needed liberating – and they needed it now, not 'after the revolution'.[8]

Promise of a Dream is a good example of Coote's and Campbell's point. In this memoir of the sixties Sheila Rowbotham records her own growing engagement with the women's liberation movement in terms which parallel Carter's account in essays such as 'Truly, It Felt Like Year One' and 'Notes From the Front Line'. Although deeply involved in left-wing political activism, Rowbotham said she remained unconvinced by feminism, as 'I knew it only as the suffrage movement of long ago or as a lobby of professional women for advancement at work'.[9] Instead, her younger self remains preoccupied with 'private musings about sexuality',[10] in spite of the routine sexism she experiences in the course of her political activities. For example, at a meeting of the East London Vietnam Solidarity Committee, her suggestions concerning fundraising are ignored. In a room 'dominated by unpractical but opinionated Trotskyist men', Robotham finds they 'kept cutting me out of the discussion as if I had never spoken'.[11] It is only when a visiting speaker from America alerts her to the existence of 'this thing called "male chauvinism"'[12] that Rowbotham achieves 'new insight'[13] which allows her to begin to bridge the gap between the personal and the political.

This process culminates in two very similar events that took place at the end of 1967, which Rowbotham records as absolutely crucial in shifting her consciousness towards an explicitly feminist stance:

> John Hoyland wanted to know if I would like to parade around an architectural students' ball in a mask. A friend of his, a poet and puppeteer, was making elaborate papier-mâché masks. Though mine was an unartistic white paper bag with a red nose, we were a big hit on the tube, where we were treated as minor celebrities. We waltzed around the dance floor at the ball to oohs and aahs until it was time for the next act, when the architects quickly lost interest. A strip-tease had begun on stage. I looked at the stripper through the slits in my white paper bag with a queasy sensation. Yet another of those contradictions. How was I to regard her?
>
> More masks, fairgrounds and people getting away and having fun appeared on television on 26 December in the Beatles' sly satire of 'straight' society, *The Magical Mystery Tour*. Again there was a strip-tease. As I watched the black and white television, I caught myself picking up their excitement. Suspended, I observed myself divided in two, seeing another woman's body through men's eyes. It was a moment of incongruity when the outer world and my own perceptions collided uncomfortably.
>
> At the end of 1967 I was feeling profoundly disjointed and askew. I was not, of course, the only woman sensing that personal experience was shifting in the late sixties. It was as if some hidden plate deep under the surface of appearances had moved irrevocably, sending out tiny, barely perceptible seismic shocks which were shortly to contribute to an earthquake. After this politics was never to be quite the same.[14]

There is something very Carteresque about Rowbotham's account here, with its stress upon playacting and masquerade, and the split in subjectivity engendered by a performance in which the female subject is split by being forced to confront, in the most literal of terms, the fact that – however well-educated, articulate and forceful she may be – she still lives in a world in which women's only real value resides in their sexual desirability. Furthermore, Rowbotham's dilemma recalls John Berger's memorable statement in *Ways of Seeing*, that:

> Men look at women. Women watch themselves being looked at. This determines not only most relations between men and women but also the relation of women to themselves. The surveyor of woman in herself is male: the surveyed female. Thus she turns herself into an object – and most particularly into an object of vision: a sight.[15]

Citing Berger's description of the viewer/viewed relationship in connection with Rowbotham's description of her reaction to these two strip-tease performances enables us to understand how they take on an epiphanic force in her text, not only because they mark moments of personal revelation, but also because they are representative of the experience of a great many women at this time. As Rowbotham acknowledges, 'I was not, of course, the only woman sensing that personal experience was shifting in the late sixties.' Bearing out her contention, in 'Notes From the Front Line' Angela Carter talks in very similar terms of developing

> a sense of heightened awareness of the society around me in the summer of 1968, my own questioning of the nature of my reality as a *woman*. How that social fiction of my 'femininity' was created, by means outside my control, and palmed off on me as the real thing.[16]

Like Rowbotham, Carter becomes radicalised 'primarily through my sexual and emotional life', becoming 'truly aware of the difference between how I was and how I was supposed to be, or expected to be'.[17] Part of this process involves the recognition that she

> was, as a girl, suffering from a degree of colonisation of the mind. Especially in the journalism I was writing then, I'd – quite unconsciously – posit a male point of view as a general one. So there was an element of the male impersonator about this young person as she was finding herself.[18]

In both cases, therefore, the adoption of feminism entails a shifting of viewpoints. Although both women, as speakers and writers, align themselves with a male perspective, they become uncomfortably aware that there are limits to their identification with the opposite sex – they are, to reiterate Carter's words, 'male impersonators'. And as impersonators, not the 'real' thing, they suffer from persistent double vision, since they are unable to wholly detach themselves from the object of surveillance that is also themselves. As Carter so cogently puts it – though still using the masculine pronoun – '[y]ou could walk your calf past the butcher's shop for days, but it's only when he sees the abattoir that he realises that there is a relation between himself and the butcher's shop'.[19]

But that moment of recognition, however, takes Sheila Rowbotham and Angela Carter in very different directions. Rowbotham became one of the foremost figures in a feminist movement that gathered momentum in the new decade of the seventies. Publications such as *Women's Consciousness: Man's World* and *Hidden from History*, both published in 1973, established her as an important contributor to radical feminist theory. Carter, though, retained a somewhat critical distance from the mainstream feminist movement throughout her life, in spite of her claim to be 'a rank and file socialist feminist'.[20] Alison Easton neatly describes her as 'existing in "contrapuntal relationship" with feminism's constantly evolving and internally conflicted history, never simply representing any one position and never quite in step with anyone'.[21] Carter's refusal to toe any feminist party line from the outset is evident from the last two novels she wrote in the sixties, for although this is a period in which, by her own account, she is working her way towards such an explicitly feminist position, her portrayal of the relationships between the genders is as problematic as it had ever been. In these narratives, her male and female characters engage in relationships that are nothing more than extended power plays, in which no tactics are regarded as too extreme if it means gaining dominance over the other.

This is apparent in the post-apocalyptic novel Carter wrote after *Several Perceptions*, *Heroes and Villains*. Forsaking the Georgian terraces of Bristol and the author's own immediate environment, *Heroes and Villains* takes place in a dystopian future world in which the Bomb has dropped, wiping out most of the human population. Only pockets of humanity survive, most of which are divided up into two groups – the Professors, who live in heavily protected compounds and try to salvage the knowledge and technology of the past; and the Barbarians, nomadic tribespeople, salvaging a precarious existence from the wreckage. The narrative centres upon the relationship between a Professor girl and a Barbarian boy, but it is no Romeo-and-Juliet romance. Marianne is virtually kidnapped by the Barbarian Jewel, who takes her back to his tribe, rapes her and participates with her in an enforced marriage ceremony. The novel ends with Jewel's death, and Marianne's assumption of the role of chieftain.

Carter always subsequently talked of this novel as constituting a consciously new departure for her. First of all, in an exhibition of characteristic bloody-mindedness, she decided that she was going to purposely write the kind of Gothic novel that reviewers and readers had assumed she'd been producing all along. Consequently, much of her audience probably failed to get the point, but that did not matter: it was Carter's own perverse reaction to being 'labelled very early on...as "Gothic" ', when *she* thought she was being 'naturalistic':

> I mean, people love labels. The labelling urge, this taxonomic passion, is very strong, especially in reviewers. I became, at the time, very irritated at the Gothic tag because I was, and am, a great pedant, and I knew perfectly well what a Gothic novel was. I knew it was all owls and ivy and mad passions and Byronic heroes who were probably damned, and I knew I wasn't writing them. Even though some of my heroes were quite emphatically damned, they weren't damned in the Byronic fashion, and that was why, when I set about writing my fourth novel, I very consciously chose the Gothic mode, with owls and ivy and ruins and a breathtakingly Byronic hero.[22]

In order to underline this, Carter selected as one of her prefaces to the text an extract from Leslie Fiedler's 1960 study *Love and Death in the American Novel*: 'The Gothic is essentially a form of parody, a way of assailing clichés by exaggerating them to the limit of grotesqueness.' In his analysis of Heroes and Villains, David Punter develops this notion of the Gothic as parody in relation to the novel, arguing that Carter uses the mode to 'ironically suggest...that the Gothic vision is in fact an accurate account of life, of the ways we project our fantasies onto the world and then stand back in horror when we see them come to life'.[23] This contention is backed up by Carter herself, who said, when discussing her intentions regarding *Heroes and Villains* with Les Bedford in 1977, that: 'I do think that detaching the worm from the rose and displaying it is a useful social function.'[24] However, given what Carter had already said to Bedford about the intentions behind this novel, I would suggest that the quotation from Fiedler is suggestive of her desire not merely to use the Gothic as a *means* of parody, as Punter and others have noted, but to use the Gothic *itself* parodically.

The 'tone of fake innocence'[25] that Punter observes dominating the text from the outset – bland statements suggestive of the most outrageous interpretations – in this context constitutes a kind of authorial double-dare. Keeping her face perfectly straight throughout, in *Heroes and Villains* Carter piles the Gothic clichés high enough to test the credulity of the most naïve of readers. The lush, fetid, landscapes of the apocalypse thus become suggestive of the narrative style itself: the ruined manor house in which the Barbarians camp, described as 'a gigantic memory of rotten stone, a compilation of innumerable forgotten styles now given some green unity by the devouring web of creeper, fir of moss and fungoid growth of rot',[26] illustrative of Carter's deliberate baroque extremism in which overblown modes, metaphors and motifs collide and intertwine. Her dubious hero Jewel is so 'beautifully savage' (62) that naturalism cannot contain him; instead, he is 'a fantastic dandy of the void whose true nature had been entirely subsumed to the alien and terrible beauty of a rhetorical gesture' (72). Meanwhile, his tutor Donally plays the organ in a crumbling chapel like Vincent Price in a Hammer Horror film, 'crafting a new religion' (63) with the aid of a stuffed snake and a feathered cloak.

If Carter's readers wanted Gothic, *Heroes and Villains* more than satisfied their desire. Viewed from another angle, though, this text is also a science fiction novel: a version of 'the post-apocalyptic novel which was popular in the Cold War 1950s'.[27] Whether willingly or not, Carter was already strongly identified with contemporary Gothic, but science fiction was a mode in which she had not so far participated, although she admitted to reading it 'from time to time'.[28] She was never part of the mainstream science fiction scene, but she was an admirer of some of the major British New Wave SF writers of the sixties, such as J.G. Ballard and Michael Moorcock – novelists who were using science fiction as means of trenchant social commentary and *avante garde* experimentation. Roz Kaveney, a critic who has explored Carter's links with the New Wave in her essay 'New New World Dreams: Angela Carter and Science Fiction', maintains that her expressions of esteem for such writers as Ballard, Moorcock and John Sladek were:

> an expression of a view that there were people who were doing something with narrative parallel to what she wanted to do. The New Wave were guerrillas of interior landscapes, like the Surrealists,

but not as obsessed with putting people in their proper place; they were, in brief, on her side.[29]

At this point in her writing career Carter was certainly becoming more interested in using her narratives as a way of working through ideas. Not that her work had ever been distinguished by its raw emotive outpourings, but she said that *Heroes and Villains* nevertheless demonstrated that:

> I was growing up. I was beginning to regard the work that I was doing as external as myself and in no sense fantasy wish-fulfilment or working through personal problems, personal situations in the form of a novel. I was beginning to perceive text as text, as Barthes would say, and since the work was external to me, it was a place where I could engage with ideas and with characters – well, with ideas, rather, characterised as characters and as imagery.[30]

As many critics have noted, science fiction is particularly well suited to the kind of intellectual project that Carter is describing here. Lucie Armitt, for example, argues that:

> [t]he depiction of an alternative reality is only the first step of an essential reassessment process on the part of both author and reader; making strange what we commonly perceive to be around us, primarily in order that we might focus upon existing reality afresh, and as outsiders. This is a necessary process if we are to challenge what are commonly taken for granted as 'absolutes' or 'givens'.[31]

The vantage point conferred upon the writer (and reader) of science fiction that Armitt talks of here – that of the outsider – is reiterated over and over again in definitions of the genre, summed up by Peter Nicholls as 'the great modern literature of metaphor... the literature of the outsider, in the extreme sense'.[32] This central feature of the mode chimes with Carter's own habitual assumption of the peripheral point of view; validated – as has already been noted – in her autobiographical pieces, in which she portrays herself as betwixt and between nationalities and classes, and as a much-loved daughter who is nevertheless in some respects extraneous to her parents' self-contained relationship.

Bearing this latter point particularly in mind, it is interesting to see that, in a piece published in the science fiction magazine *Vector* in 1982, Carter explicitly traces her involvement with science fiction to her childhood, when her journalist father would bring the next day's papers home from work: '*The Times* for my mother and *The Daily Sketch* for me'. At this time, *The Daily Sketch* was serialising John Wyndham's *Day of the Triffids*, which Carter says she would read 'in the small hours of those long ago sleepless nights':[33] the same nights, presumably, during which she would hear her parents through the bedroom wall 'chattering away for hours in the early morning'[34] over tea and biscuits. In this context, the separation from the self-contained parental unit is emphasised by her consumption of a form of literature that validates the perspective of outsider.

This facility of science fiction to act as the vehicle for ideas was certainly one of the main appeals the genre held for Carter. In 'Fools Are My Theme', she proceeds to draw a parallel between medieval liter-ature and science fiction; both forms of writing, she said, that demand the reader's direct participation. Her childhood reading and her university studies taught her the same lesson – '[t]hat writing is not necessarily a personal activity, not a personal experience of my feelings or person-ality, but an articulation of a whole lot of feelings and ideas that happen to be around at the time'.[35] *Heroes and Villains*, therefore, is not just a Gothic fantasy (even though it fulfils that role beautifully), but also a novel that enables Carter to reflect on the political context of the sixties; in particular, the Cold War and the growing fear of nuclear conflict it generated.

If *Heroes and Villains* is on the one hand Carter's attempt to poke fun at the 'taxonomic passion' of her reviewers, then on the other it is also taking issue with a certain kind of science fiction that failed to take the postwar political situation seriously. In 'Anger in a Black Landscape', an essay published in 1983 when the Greenham Common protests were at their height, Carter remarked that:

> One of the most curious phenomena of the postwar period has been the growth of fictions about the blissfully anarchic, tribal lives the lucky fifteen million survivors are going to lead in a Britain miracu-lously free of corpses, in which the Man with the Biggest Shot-Gun holes up in some barbed-wire enclave and picks off all comers. (Polygamous marital arrangements are often part of these fantasies.) The post-nuclear catastrophe novel has become a science fiction genre all of its own, sometimes as warning – more often as the saddest and most irresponsible kind of whistling in the dark.[36]

This essay does not mention *Heroes and Villains*, but it is nevertheless illustrative of the personal and cultural backdrop against which it was written. In it, Carter identifies herself – and, by implication, her whole generation – as 'a child of the nuclear age. I was five years old when they, or, rather, the Allies – that is, we – dropped an atomic bomb on Hiroshima.'[37] The detonation of this A-bomb, 'perpetrated – obviously – without my knowledge or consent, although they said it was for the sake of my future, changed irrevocably the circumstances in which that future life would be passed'.[38] But in this essay, as in others, Carter recalls the sixties as a decade that appeared to offer the opportunity to change that legacy, claiming that

> those long gone days of the marches from Aldermaston were some of the most moving and beautiful memories of my girlhood. It seemed, then, that in the face of those immense shows of serene public indignation – exhibitions of mass sanity, as they were – that, as had, after all, happened occasionally before, mass protest might change things.[39]

Here, Carter once again shows herself to be participating in debates to do with nationhood and British identity. The Campaign for Nuclear Disarmament (CND) was founded on 17 February 1958, in response to the exploding of the first British A-bomb the previous year. Richard Weight argues that CND was never a very effective protest body, for '[w]orthy though its aims were, the organization's membership was mostly confined to the radical middle classes and there is no evidence that it had any effect on either British opinion or on the world leaders whose fingers were on the button'.[40] However, Jonathon Green maintains that CND 'remains absolutely vital in any consideration of the Sixties. Beyond anything else it provided the first public forum for youthful rebellion.'[41] This was certainly so in Carter's case: it is evident from her essays that the marches organised by CND constituted a focus for her early radicalism.

In addition, Richard Weight points out that the organisation served a useful function as a focus for nationalist discontent: although it might have been '[p]olitically ineffective', it remains 'historically significant because it highlighted the questioning of "Pax Britannica" among middle-class Britons'.[42] According to Weight, this popular growth in cynicism concerning the Empire became a cause of great concern to the government, to the point where the name itself became untenable, replaced, increasingly, by the sobriquet 'Commonwealth'. A particularly pertinent example of this is the fate of Empire Day, the event Carter had endured in her South London primary school – in 1958, it was

renamed 'Commonwealth Day', and in 1959, in a further effort to
bolster the public's flagging enthusiasm for the concept, the short-lived
'Commonwealth Week' was launched.

> For seven days every year an exhibition would tour fifteen British
> cities. The first was opened by Princess Margaret in Liverpool in
> 1959. In the three years of its short life, Commonwealth week was a
> dismal failure. In March 1962, a report by Duncan Sandys concluded,
> with typically British understatement, that it had not 'attracted
> continuous and enthusiastic support'. Part of the reason, he said, was
> 'a lack of enthusiasm for and appreciation of the Commonwealth
> ideal amongst many teachers'.[43]

By the sixties, therefore, Britain's imperial identity had become
virtually unsustainable, eroded by a steady process of decolonisation
(India became an independent nation in 1947, and other countries
followed throughout the fifties and sixties), and by a series of crises
abroad. Consequently, says Leslie Stone, '[f]or much of the 1960s,
Britain suffered from an acute identity crisis, uncertain of its position
and status in the world, unsure of its current power and future direction.'[44] Moreover, as the Commonwealth week debacle demonstrates,
the British themselves retained little enthusiasm for the concept of
either Empire or Commonwealth.

One event in the sixties played a particularly pivotal role in changing
Britain's view of itself – the Cuban Missile Crisis of 1962. The fourteen
days during which Russia and America stood on the brink of nuclear
conflict while Britain played the role of helpless bystander hammered
home the uncomfortable realisation that America had supplanted
Britain as the dominant superpower. Like many of her generation,
Carter experienced the Cuban Missile Crisis as 'one of the great water-
sheds, certainly of my life. I think people who were born after the
Cuban Missile Crisis, who don't remember, are different because it was
touch and go for a minute there.'[45] She may have been born during the
Second World War, but this event marked the moment when she 'came
of age'.[46]

Heroes and Villains is the book in which she imaginatively explores
how life would have been had the brinkmanship practiced by Russia
and America in 1962 actually toppled the world over the edge into
nuclear catastrophe. Drawing on the kind of concerns that motivated
her participation in CND, she refuses to cast this post-apocalyptic future
in a heroic mode – unlike the kind of novels she pokes fun at in 'Anger

in a Black Landscape', in which the destruction of the world is used as a plot device to resurrect the stereotypical macho action hero. Belying any expectations that might be raised by its title, there is no hero in this novel, and no civilisation capable of being reconstructed. Even though the Professors attempt to recreate the past behind the barriers of their armed compounds it is a futile task, for however hard they work to assemble the bits and pieces of past knowledge, the framework within which it can be disseminated and understood has been destroyed beyond repair. The books they salvage are ultimately useless because they are now only collections of words that 'had ceased to describe facts and now stood only for ideas or memories' (7). For example, Marianne's father is writing 'a book on the archaeology of social theory', but only Marianne appears to realise that 'maybe nobody in the community would want to read it, except Marianne, and she might not understand it' (8). Or maybe she is not alone in this recognition, since suicide is a major cause of death amongst the members of the Professors' community.

The Barbarians, though, are no better. Painted, bejewelled and tattooed though they are their glamour is less than skin deep, as Marianne comes to realise once she has joined the tribe:

> [T]he flowing Barbarian coiffures, clogged at the roots with lice, now seemed wilfully perverse accessories and when she saw warrior garments hanging limply from nails hammered into the walls, she almost laughed to see the fragile shells of such poorly founded terror. The children suffered promiscuously from ringworm, skin diseases and weeping eye. Also rickets. (45)

Rather than representing the colourful antithesis to the drab, ultimately pointless, life of the Professors, the Barbarians are no more capable of surmounting their miserable circumstances. Scraping a hand-to-mouth existence amongst the ruins, their gaudy rags are nothing more than empty bravado.

From the beginning of the novel, Carter teases her readers with the possibility that the role of heroic saviour might be assumed by beautiful Jewel. Marianne first observes him from the balcony of her 'white tower made of steel and concrete' (1) in the course of a Barbarian raid on her compound, when he kills her brother in hand-to-hand combat. In the years that follow, she recalls his face 'with visionary clarity' (10), and their eventual reunion has about it the inevitability of romance. Nonetheless, this assumption is as illusory as Jewel himself, who may look every bit the part of romantic lead but fails dismally to fill it, with the result that he is dislodged from the dominant role he might otherwise have occupied in the text. Firstly, his treatment of Marianne leaves much to be desired, as he both rapes and beats her; but secondly (and extremely paradoxically given the physical abuse he metes out to her), he simply isn't sufficiently substantial enough. Viewed through Marianne's eyes – the dominant perspective throughout the narrative – he is nothing more than 'the furious invention of my virgin nights' (137).

Marianne levels this accusation at Jewel in a highly allegorical episode that takes place towards the end of the book, in which Carter establishes clear links between the redundancy of the heroic archetype and the collapse of imperialistic certainties. In the course of their wanderings, the Barbarian tribe reach the coast, where Marianne sees 'a time-eaten city up to its ears in the sea': a magical, evanescent sight, 'its towers, domes and roofs so mingled with their own shadows and reflections that all seemed to hang in mid-air, among clouds of night and waning stars' (137). The scene works intertextually on a number of different levels – alone together on the shore, Marianne and Jewel are reminiscent of Ferdinand and Miranda in Shakespeare's *The Tempest*, and the ruins of the city an insubstantial pageant faded which, as in Prospero's soliloquy in the original play, is intended to remind us not only that life is transient, but also to foreground the fictionality of what we are seeing. Another possible allusion is to T.S. Eliot's 'unreal city' that dominates the wasteland of contemporary culture. However, just as in Finn and Melanie's ambiguous encounter in the ruins of the Crystal Palace pleasure gardens in Sydenham, which this episode so resembles, this 'drowned town' (138) also has its roots in a real place.

It is necessarily anonymous, because the world in which 'everything had once been scrupulously named' (136) is long gone, but evidence suggests that this may be a description of Brighton – more specifically, Brighton Palace Pier, constructed in 1899. Just as the Crystal Palace was not a real palace – and rendered all the more downmarket on its relocation to South London – so the 'Palace' in Brighton Palace Pier is also a simulacrum of the real thing. It refers to the ornate pavilion constructed at the pier head, which was a kind of miniature, 'people's' version of the Brighton Pavilion, constructed for the Prince Regent in the eighteenth century. It is this oriental fantasia whose 'minarets, spires and helmets of wrought iron' can be seen 'protrud[ing] from the waters', along with 'the uppermost part of a wheel of gigantic size' (138) – the Big Wheel that was added to the pier in 1938. Nonetheless, Carter cannot resist embellishing her sources, as *The Magic Toyshop* also illustrates, and the description of the elaborately rococo clock tower, displaying a 'clock held in the arms and supported on the forward-jutting stomach of a monstrous figure... of a luxuriously endowed woman scantily clad in a one-piece bathing costume' (138) is all her own invention. What it does do is foreground the original function of the pier as a place of pure pleasure, and thus transform it into a nostalgic reminder of a past from which Marianne and Jewel are irrevocably sundered.

But while the figure on the clock tower is certainly representative of the earthy proletarian pleasures of Victorian seaside culture, from another perspective she also perpetuates Carter's on-going nationalistic metaphor. The parallels between this woman and wave-ruling Britannia are all too obvious: but this Britannia is redundant and adrift in 'the smug and serene sea' (138), not the proud representative of imperial superiority. Nor is she the only symbol of British imperialism to appear in this episode. Having seen the remnants of Brighton, Jewel and Marianne camp out on the beach; but while Jewel sleeps, Marianne sees a lion 'leap through the window hole of a chalet bungalow' and make a 'sinuous progression across the sand' (140) to stand over her sleeping husband.

Juxtaposed with the image of the ruined pier, the lion, too, takes on symbolic significance. In this context, it becomes the imperial lion, symbol of Great Britain and her empire, whose 'ancestors came over the sea in cages to delight and instruct the children of domestic times' (140) – but now it has returned to the wild, contemplating Jewel with 'infinite boredom' before 'wander[ing] off, indifferent. Back it went to the forest, such miraculous, slinking grace' (140).

In her study of the Festival of Britain, Becky Conekin notes that

[t]he Lion, denoting the 'might, dignity, power and prestige of the Empire', had been the symbol of Britain in 1924 when the British Empire Exhibition was staged at Wembley to help people focus on the glories of Empire after the disturbing events of the First World War.[47]

But in the post-nuclear war world of *Heroes and Villains* the lion, like language itself, has retained neither use nor meaning, belying George Orwell's declaration in his cultural manifesto, *The Lion and the Unicorn*, that:

[t]he Stock Exchange will be pulled down, the horse plough will give way to the tractor, the country houses will be turned into children's holiday camps, the Eton and Harrow match will be forgotten, but

England will still be England, an everlasting animal stretching into the future and the past, and, like all living things, having the power to change out of recognition and yet remain the same.[48]

In this novel, England is not so durable as Orwell imagined – or perhaps it is simply that, writing in 1941, he could not imagine anything as catastrophic as the Bomb. In 'Anger in a Black Landscape', Carter dramatises the conceptual crisis initiated by any contemplation of nuclear warfare: it is very difficult, she argues, not to think of nuclear weaponry as 'the very transcendental essence of war, and, more than that, an externalisation of all our notions of the ultimate evil. The Bomb has become a very potent, perhaps *the* most potent, symbol of Original Sin.'[49]

Therefore, this allegorical encounter between man and lion is multi-layered and complex. While, viewed from one perspective, it indicates the breaking of all ties between the individual and a sense of nationhood, it also participates in the biblical allusions which the discourse of the Bomb invites. Like Melanie and Finn before them, Marianne and Jewel are Adam and Eve facing the consequences of the Fall; and in this context, the fact that the lion does not harm Jewel constitutes a miraculous deliverance, a momentary suspension of the 'kill-or-be-killed' imperative of the post-Edenic, post-holocaust world.

However, at the same time as Carter is allegorically portraying the crisis of identity Britain was experiencing in the sixties through reference to one of the very events that emphasised the nation's loss of international status, she is also engaging in a satirical exploration of the ways in which a new sense of nationalism can be (re)constructed. In many ways, Carter's approach appears to endorse Joanne P. Sharp's argument that

[t]he nation is created not through an originary moment or culturally distinct essence but through the repetition of symbols that come to represent the nation's origin and its uniqueness. National culture and character are ritualistic so that every repetition of its symbols serves to reinforce national identity.[50]

Jewel's tutor Donally, as a former Professor, understands very well the importance of ritual and symbolism in the creation and sustenance of a coherent sense of nationhood; something he makes clear in a lengthy speech to Marianne, whom he regards as his natural ally:

'It seemed to me that the collapse of civilisation in the form that intellectuals such as ourselves understood it might be as good time as any for crafting a new religion,' he said modestly. 'If they won't take to the snake for a symbol, we'll think of something else suitable, in time. I still use most of the forms of the Church of England. I find they're infinitely adaptable. Religion is a device for instituting the sense of a privileged group, you understand; many are called but few are chosen and, coaxed from incoherence, we shall leave the indecent condition of barbarism and aspire towards that of the honest savage, maintaining some kind of commonwealth.' (63)

Jewel, whose fate is always to act as a pawn in the hands of others, is crucial to this project, having been groomed by Donally since childhood to assume the role of symbolic figurehead for this new 'commonwealth'. However, this is not a part that can be assumed or discarded at will. It is carved into his very skin, thus transforming Jewel from an individual into a piece of ritualistic paraphernalia. On their wedding night, Marianne finds that he has an elaborate portrait of the biblical Fall of Man tattooed across his back, 'a grotesque disfigurement, which fascinated her' (85). This is not just another expression of the Barbarians' love of decoration or adornment, but something far more calculated – as Jewel says of Donally: 'I think he'd like to flay me and hang me up on the wall.... He might even make me up into some ceremonial robe and wear me on special occasions' (86). As a flag or garment of state, Jewel is therefore intended to function as the kind of reiterative symbol Sharp argues is necessary for the maintenance of a national identity.

The subject Donally has chosen for the tattoo stands both alongside and against Sharp's point that a nation is *not* created through an 'originary moment', for in one sense that is precisely what Jewel's back portrays. Throughout *Heroes and Villains*, Carter plays with Edenic imagery which evokes the notion of a 'new beginning' in the persons of a second Adam and Eve. If the Bomb has cast humankind out of their secular Eden, then Donally's intention is to formulate the means by which it can be reconstituted: but he does so, as he himself admits, through the calculated recycling of Christian imagery and ceremony.

So in fact there is indeed no such thing as an originary moment in this book; only a continuation of the same mythic formulae. Sharp's observation that nations 'are not entirely invented, but constructed out of already existent elements of culture, society and mythology'[51] is a view that Carter appears to endorse. Ultimately, however, it is only undermined by the novel's ending, in which Jewel drives Donally from the tribe then changes his mind, dying in the course of a raiding party to bring him back. Jewel's motives for this abrupt *volte-face* are made clear: he has moved from being an ambivalent pawn to actively desiring the role of nationalistic symbol. Thus his decision marks, as Marianne realises, the end of innocence and 'the birth of ambition', for Jewel now wishes Donally to make him wholly figurative: the 'Tiger Man', tattooed in his entirety. As Marianne puts it, 'If I took off your shirt, I think I would see that Adam had accepted the tattooed apple at last' (146). In the event, though, it is Eve, not Adam, who is transformed, for when Jewel is killed, Marianne steps into his role. Rejecting the suggestion that she become Queen of the Barbarians she declares that instead *she* 'will be the tiger lady and rule them with a rod of iron' (150).

In many ways, this decision again tempts us with the notion that this is a genuine moment of origin, in which the imperial lion gives way to an entirely new image of nationhood represented by the tiger. And yet, although the symbols may shift and metamorphose into different forms, their actual function does not change. Because Carter employs the tactic she used before in *The Magic Toyshop*, that of freeze-framing the narrative an instant before it reaches a resolution, its validity is implicitly placed in question. While Marianne's decision to become the 'tiger lady' is capable of being envisaged as a triumphant surmounting of her circumstances, carving out a powerful position for herself within a deeply misogynistic society, the readiness with which she embraces Donally's brutal symbolism renders such a tactic distinctly dubious. Thus, if we read this novel as a satire on Britain's loss of a firmly founded sense of national identity in the postwar period, what it achieves is not a simplistic rewriting of that identity, but an interrogation of the meaning of nationhood itself. In his introduction to *Nation and Narration*, Homi K. Bhabha describes his intentions in a way that is useful for an understanding of this aspect of *Heroes and Villains*. The underlying thesis of the volume, he asserts, is a shared desire to investigate

> the nation-space in the *process* of the articulation of elements: where meanings may be partial because they are *in media res*; and history may be half-made because it is in the process of being made; and the image of cultural authority may be ambivalent because it is caught, uncertainly, in the act of 'composing' its powerful image.[52]

This is precisely what has happened by the end of Carter's novel. Writing only seven years after the Cuban Missile Crisis, she uses the science fiction plot motif of nuclear apocalypse in order to allegorically represent a very real loss of national confidence. If, at the end of the

Magic Toyshop, she portrays a Britain hesitating on the brink of the sixties, here she is representing it at the end of the decade, engaged in a desperate rear-guard action to keep competing versions of 'Britishness' from disrupting a coherent imperial façade that has actually been in the process of steadily eroding since the end of the Second World War. In this context, Marianne's lament at the loss of certainty can also be seen as a eulogy for a coherent sense of nationhood: 'When I was a little girl, we played at heroes and villains but now I don't know which is which any more, nor who is who, and what can I trust if not appearances?' (125).

Carter forsook the overtly allegorical form for her next novel, *Love*, which she called 'my farewell to the British provinces':[53] but it can also be regarded as taking up the question posed by Marianne, and stretching its implications to their furthest extreme. Lorna Sage, one of the novel's most consistent fans, describes it as 'a bitterly perfect book, a bleak celebration of the emptiness you arrive at if you rubbish the real too thoroughly';[54] an observation echoed by Linden Peach, when he argues that '[i]n *Love*, Carter suggests that "indifference", which she explored in her first novel, may be a symptom of too introverted a subjectivity'.[55] In other words, *Love* questions the ways in which we perceive the world and distinguish what is 'real' from what is not; what is external to ourselves, and what is not.

The narrative perspective of *Love* is split between the characters of Annabel and her husband Lee, but it is Annabel's view that dominates the beginning of the novel. In many ways, she is distinctly familiar, since she is another of Carter's vulnerable girl-women who inflict damage on all around them through the sheer extremity of their self-victimisation. Thus, as Sage, for example, observes, Annabel is reminiscent of Ghislaine from *Shadow Dance*; although Carter herself drew a parallel between Annabel and Joseph in *Several Perceptions*. But in spite of Carter's linking of *Love* to her other novels set in Bristol, she also made it clear that she wasn't merely reworking the same themes and ideas, but developing them in response to the changing times. *Love* was, she said, 'my farewell to the sixties. The people in it are the same people as in the earlier two novels, as I've mentioned, but they are getting older and they're losing hope and the flower-power is taking its ghastly revenge.'[56]

Accordingly, while Joseph 'is neurotic, he's just a neurotic, and if he continued to take his pills he'd have been perfectly all right, Annabel...is mad. She's not responding to an insane society, she's utterly isolated in psychosis.'[57] While Joseph represents the possibility held out by R.D. Laing – that there is more than one way of regarding the world – if Annabel stands for anything, it is the closing-down of such potential at the tail-end of the sixties. Annabel inhabits an altern-ative reality that has been 'remodelled ... entirely to her own require-ments',[58] and it is the utter horror of this retreat into psychotic isolation that makes *Love* Carter's *real* Gothic novel of the sixties. *Heroes and Villains* assembles the paraphernalia of the Gothic to create a clanking stage set, but *Love* mobilises the Gothic's tone and mode in a far subtler, sophisticated and disturbing way.

The influence of Edgar Allan Poe on the text, in particular, is indicated by the names of the main protagonists, Annabel and Lee, who, amalga-mated, form the name of the eponymous heroine of Poe's poem 'Annabel Lee'.[59] In her interview with Les Bedford, Carter admitted to an enduring 'familial attachment' to Poe, whose imagery 'I've used as a starting point for imagery of my own'. At the same time, though, she also established a certain critical distance between Poe and herself: 'I've used him a lot decoratively, but never structurally. I don't know if that makes sense. I mean, he's not an ideas man, Poe, and his obsessions – incest, necrophilia and so on – are slightly different to mine'.[60]

Nevertheless, the opening of the novel introduces the reader to the distinctly Poe-esque sense of macabre uncanniness that pervades the novel. The opening of *Love* is set within what appears to be the symbolic space that recurs throughout Carter's sixties narratives, in which the ruins of the past are indicative of the postwar dissolution of a fixed national identity. Here, it is a park on a hill above Bristol, which had once

> surround[ed] a mansion which had been pulled down long ago and now the once harmonious artificial wilderness, randomly dishev-elled by time, spread its green tangles across the high shoulder of a hill only a stone's throw from a busy road that ran through the city dockland. (1)

All that remains is 'a stable built on the lines of a miniature Parthenon' (1) and 'an ivy covered tower with leaded ogive windows' (2).

> Both these pretty whimsies were kept securely locked for fear of the despoliation of vandals but their presence still performed its original role, transforming the park into a premeditated theatre where the romantic imagination could act out any performance it chose amongst settings of classic harmony or crabbed quaintness. And the magic strangeness of the park was enhanced by its curious silence. Footfalls fell softly on the long grass and few birds sang there, but

the presence all around of the sprawling, turbulent city, however muffled its noises, lent such haunted, breathless quiet an unnatural quality. (2)

Although this scene bears some similarity to Brandon Hill, which stands above Bristol's docks, Carter's description here of the park as a 'theatre' foregrounds its primary function as a psychic, rather than historical, space, amenable to infinite transformations through the medium of the romantic imagination. Annabel, through whose eyes this scene is viewed, eschews the classicism of the stables, preferring 'the Gothic north' represented by the tower – a decision that creates the illusion of choice between rationalism and emotionalism. But an illusion is all it is, since there is in reality no way out of the monomaniacal perspective offered by Annabel; a fact indicated by Carter's description of the park entrance:

> The park maintained only a single, still impressive, entrance, a massive pair of wrought-iron gates decorated with cherubs, masks of beasts, stylized reptiles and spearheads from which the gilding flaked, but these gates were never either open or closed. They hung always a little ajar and dropped from their hinges with age; they served a function no longer for all the railings round the park were long gone and access everywhere was free and easy. (2)

This description indicates the terrifying boundlessness of Annabel's vision, since these gates are no gates at all. Not only are they themselves 'never either open or closed', the lack of fence means that they are circumvented with ease, and thus exist only as mockeries of their original function. This should be a positive metaphor, perhaps, indicating, as Carter has done in previous novels, the 'people's palaces' that replace the places and spaces of former privilege. In this passage, though, the gates serve a very different purpose, acting as markers of the universality of the uncanny in the text. In his study of the uncanny, Nicholas Royle draws attention to the characteristics of the mode in a way that is applicable to Carter's use of it in this opening scene. Through an analysis of a short story by L.G. Moberly, 'Inexplicable', he concludes that:

> First . . . it is a story about a house . . . and it begins at the threshold, with a complexity and uncertainty of crossing a threshold, with an experience of liminality (the word comes from the Latin, 'limen',

threshold). Second, it foregrounds a sense of the familiar or 'ordinary' (the house is in such an 'ordinary road lined by ordinary houses'): uncanniness is indissociably bound up with the ordinary or familiar. Finally, the opening paragraph of Moberly's story is self-reflexive in the sense that it remarks on its own participation in a certain tradition of supernatural, gothic or uncanny fiction. In signalling its own status as a story, in implicitly invoking its own fictionality, 'Inexplicable'...do not reduce but rather complicates and even deepens the singularity of its claims to a certain eerie 'reality'.[61]

The opening of *Love* corresponds to all three of the above criteria. While the park, admittedly, may not be a house in the literal sense, in her foregrounding of the otherwise useless gates, Carter nevertheless invokes the notion of the threshold (although where the boundaries of this threshold lie is anybody's guess). Moreover, the presence of this small slice of the past in the midst of 'the sprawling, turbulent city' conveys exactly that mingling of the familiar with the extraordinary pinpointed in Royle's argument; and its 'muffled noises' which gives the 'haunted, breathless quiet' of the park an 'unnatural quality' also indicates the 'auditory dimension' that Royle argues is 'crucial to a critical apprehension of the uncanny'.[62] Lastly, this passage is characteristic of the majority of Carter's fiction in refraining from concealing its status as fictional construct. The park, like the text itself, is a 'premeditated theatre', 'a pure piece of design' (1), and the deliberate placement of adjectives such as 'Gothic', 'haunted' and 'unnatural' indicative of the care with which Carter sets her scene. It is a place in which '[e]verything is subtly out of alignment. Shadows fall awry and light no longer issues from expected sources' (55).

As has already been shown, comparable scenes in *The Magic Toyshop* and *Heroes and Villains* occur as single set pieces within the text, but in *Love* the park functions as a bracketing symbol, as is perhaps appropriate in a novel which splits the narrative perspective between two characters. Lee visits it towards the end of the book, by which time husband and wife have become completely disconnected, both from each other and the world around them, caught up in a destructive triangular dynamic which includes Lee's half-brother Buzz. Annabel has already attempted suicide once, having seen Lee flirting with another girl at a party, but she herself has also engaged in a clumsy copulation with Buzz. For Lee, as for Annabel at the beginning of the novel, the park is almost entirely unreal, so completely coloured by his interior preoccupations that it is impossible to separate the subjective from the objective gaze.

This is stressed by a crucial encounter between Lee and an anonymous boy 'with wild eyes and floating hair' (100), who creeps up on Lee as he sits 'on a bench in the white shadow of the Gothic tower' (99–100). This boy has no individual identity at all, but is perceived by Lee merely as a projection of his own psyche, causing him to reflect that 'he must somehow have hired the boy to act out his ugly grief for him, like a professional mourner' (101). As 'the crazed inhabitant of the Gothic pinnacle which, appropriately enough, served as the backdrop for their balked encounter' (100), the boy also assumes the role of *spiritus loci*; a direct emanation of the place itself. Like the park, therefore, his role is purely symbolic, 'perform[ing] the function of the fool in Elizabethan drama, a reference point outside events but inside another kind of logic, the remorseless logic of unreason where all vision is deranged, all logic uncoordinated and all responses beyond prediction' (101).

The reader of the other novels in the Bristol trilogy will recognise this reference, since it relates to the disconnected logic of the jump cut that occurs in both *Shadow Dance* and *Several Perceptions*. However, while in the previous novels, such episodes were finite and self-contained, here (as the image of the park with no boundaries indicates) it spreads out to encompass the text in its entirety, for throughout Carter foregrounds the impossibility of arriving at any coherent pattern of events susceptible to rational interpretation. Her description of the consequences of Annabel's suicide attempt demonstrates this nicely:

> Afterwards, the events of the night seemed, to all who participated in them, like disparate sets of images shuffled together anyhow. A draped form on a stretcher; candles blown out by a strong wind; a knife; an operating theatre; blood; and bandages. In time, the principal actors (the wife, the brothers, the mistress) assembled a coherent narrative from these images but each interpreted them differently and drew their own conclusions which were all quite dissimilar for each told himself the story as if he were the hero except for Lee who, by common choice, found himself the villain. (43)

'What can I trust', asks Marianne towards the end of *Heroes and Villains*, 'if not appearances?' But in *Love*, appearances can never be trusted, since they are not only always *in play* (and therefore always contested), they are also always in the process of being *played out*: the sense of being an actor in a drama is an experience common to all the main protagonists. For example, the impression Lee gives of 'perfect naturalness, utter spontaneity and entire warmth of heart' (12) is, in fact, the product of his extreme self-consciousness: he has a 'wardrobe of smiles' (19) to suit every occasion. Annabel's suicide attempt may be perfectly serious, but it is portrayed as 'melodramatic' (49), a 'stale cliché' culled from scenes in ' "B" feature films' (50). Consequently, reality in this novel is 'like a flicker book' (59): a rapidly moving jumble of randomly selected images that never quite cohere into a unified whole capable of either yielding 'meaning' or drawing to a satisfactory conclusion.

The plethora of dramatic allusions in *Love* recalls the equation made by Carter in *The Magic Toyshop* between patriotism and theatre, in which the stage becomes the forum in which hackneyed metaphors of English identity are reconstituted. Here, however, Carter utilises her theatrical metaphors very differently. Her mention of Elizabethan drama (indeed, all the novels in the Bristol trilogy contain similar, if brief, references) indicates the extent to which she is making use of a central, and paradoxical, dynamic of seventeenth-century tragedy, in which, argues Jonathan Dollimore, 'contradictory accounts of experience are forced into "misalignment", the tension which this generates being a way of getting us to confront the problematic and contradictory nature of society itself'.[63] Citing this statement within the context of a discussion of *Love* is useful, not only because it summarises the collision of perspectives which both structures and fissures the text, but also because it draws attention to the social critique underlying the aesthetic exercise.

Ironically, given the extent to which *Love* is morbidly concerned with interiority, it is also the novel that arguably contains more social references than any other novel in the Bristol trilogy. In the Gothic mode, Buzz and Lee function as each other's shadow selves, suggestive, as Rosemary Jackson says of the recurring motif of the double in fantastic fiction, of 'a radical refusal of the structures, the "syntax" of cultural order ... through a radical open-endedness of being'.[64] In this novel, though, the brothers are obviously intended to be regarded as the *products* of their cultural context rather than its antitheses; something Carter makes clear by means of a detailed synopsis of their family history. As with Morris in *Shadow Dance* and Joseph in *Several Perceptions*, Carter draws on her own South London roots in her portrayal of these characters – in fact, her account closely echoes the autobiographical essays she was yet to write. (She was later to tell Lorna Sage that the street in which the brothers are raised was 'a real street', and hence untypical of her fiction, in which 'usually I describe locations with that sort of detail when they are unreal, imaginary'.)[65] Lee and Buzz are half-brothers, whose mother disappears into a psychiatric hospital after undergoing a spectacular mental breakdown. (In another swipe at her childhood *bête noire*, Empire Day, Carter has her burst in on the playground celebrations, 'naked and painted all over with cabbalistic signs' [10].) The brothers are taken in by their indomitable Trotskyist aunt – a woman distinctly reminiscent of Carter's portrayal of her own grandmother in 'The Mother Lode' – and raised amongst meticulously delineated 'scenes of urban pastorale' (11). But when their aunt dies and her house pulled down by the Greater London Council, the brothers are set adrift. Lee, who is a grammar-school boy, ends up at Bristol University, but this strengthens, rather than erodes, his bond with his secondary-modern-educated brother.

> [T]hey stayed together because they were alone in a world in which both felt themselves to be subtly at variance. . . . Their mother's madness, their orphaned state, their aunt's politics and their arbitrary identity formed in both a savage detachment for they found such detachment necessary to maintain their precarious autonomy. (11)

The vacillation of the brothers' history between stability and chaos mimics the social development of postwar Britain. They are, quite literally, products of the war, for when Lee's father is 'killed in the course of duty' (11), his mother goes 'on the game' (11), and Buzz is conceived by an anonymous American serviceman. Although they achieve some temporary measure of security with their grandmother, their identities remain fluid and unfixed, with the result that both are, to a great extent, self-made. Neither Lee nor Buzz 'carried through life the name he had been born with', and Lee has acquired a 'grammar-school accent' – which, however, tends to give way 'under stress' (47). Ironically enough, therefore, they end up as eminently fitting emanations of sixties sensibility – its (supposed) classnesses, its rebelliousness and its idealisation of unconventionality. As Marc O'Day says:

> the characters are fictional creations who in part typify various aspects of the social and sexual mobility opened up by the postwar expansion of educational opportunities, the welfare state, the widespread availability of the Pill, the 'permissive' attitudes officially marked by the reform of the laws on divorce and homosexuality, and counter-cultural hedonism. This . . . is also true of other figures in the Bristol Trilogy novels. The difference in *Love* is in the kind and amount of detail we're given, and in the intense focus on the dynamics of the triangle.[66]

In spite of the general bleakness of *Love*, Carter does have a great deal of fun with the social aspects of the novel, as is evident in her description of Lee's and Annabel's wedding day. Although Annabel's conventional middle-class parents are appalled at the match, they experience a certain second-hand *frisson* at the prospect of her marrying 'into Bohemia' (37); even though they would have perhaps preferred her to have married Buzz, whose camera suggests that he 'might be a respectable Bohemian, and would, one day, grow rich for they had read how photographers were the new aristocracy' (37).

The phrase 'new aristocracy' is deliberately placed by Carter here, for it is a term coined by *Private Eye* in 1965 to describe the elite of 'swinging London' – actors, pop stars, models, designers and photographers. Jonathon Green identifies David Bailey (the photographer whom Annabel's parents very obviously have in mind) as particularly emblematic in this respect, 'for many contemporaries the masculine embodiment of the period'.[67] It was Bailey who, in 1965, produced *The Box of Pinups*, containing thirty-six photographic portraits of the central figures in the new artistic *beau monde*:

> It really was a box...which charted the world...of the media-chic 'Stringalongs' and its aim was to capture the 'ephemeral glamour' of the era 'on the wing'. The pinups, 'the people in England who today seem glamorous' – were typified as 'isolated, invulnerable, lost' (the central adjective somewhat at odds with its bookends)'.[68]

But Green's description of *A Box of Pinups* (the quotations are from the 'Publisher's Note' to the collection, written by David Bailey and Francis Wyndham) illustrates the extent to which the 'glamorous', 'isolated' and 'lost' characters in Carter's novel typify the time's view of itself. It is an era in which image is all, and ephemeral youth cultivated for and preserved through the photographer's lens. Not surprisingly, therefore, photography is another central reference in *Love*. Buzz is, indeed, a photographer, who uses his camera as a form of mediation between him and the world, 'as if he could not trust his own eyes and had to check his vision by means of a third lens all the time so in the end he saw everything at second hand without depths' (25). But it is clear that Carter is implying a critique of photography here, not celebrating it. The photographic field is flat because it cannot replicate the third dimension, and thus Buzz's preference for using the camera as an inter-polative device between himself and the outside, 3-D, world reflects the troubling lack of feeling that characterises the text as a whole. His vision, therefore, echoes Bailey's photographic 'pinups': a series of static, essentially isolated, images of beautiful but separate selves.

It is when the photographic motif is attached to Lee, however, that its uncanny aspect is foregrounded particularly strongly. He treasures, we are told, 'two iconic photographs' (26) of scenes from his childhood, in which he attempts to anchor a stable sense of self:

> One showed a line of clean children carrying letters which together formed the exhortation: DO RIGHT BECAUSE IT IS RIGHT; the other was of a large, stern, middle-aged woman outstaring the camera with a brother on either side of her. She was their aunt. (25)

This little collection is eventually joined by a third, taken by Buzz – a photo of Lee and Annabel asleep in bed together, 'look[ing] as beautiful and peaceful as if made in heaven for one another' (26).

Lee intends these souvenirs to act as a type of historical record, but in fact they do nothing of the sort, since he can 'find no causal connection between his three photographed faces. The infant, the child and the adolescent or young man whose face was still so new, unused and incomplete seemed to represent three finite and disconnected states' (26). It is a statement that, again, takes us back to the image of the 'flicker book'. For as Annette Kuhn says, photographs are evidence only 'up to a point...Not that they are to be taken only at face value, nor that they mirror the real, nor that even a photograph offers any evident relationship between itself and what it shows.'[69] Instead, photographs are to be 'read and decoded, like clues left behind at the scene of a crime'.[70]

In her analysis, indeed, Kuhn repeatedly returns to the motif of concealed murder, her argument circling around, though never directly confronting, photography's relationship with the uncanny. For as Carter demonstrates in this novel, not only does photography have the ability to capture shadows and freeze the past, but it also occludes more than it actually reveals. While the aunt retains Carter's own grandmother's talent for being 'always and ineradicably *there*',[71] with the result that her photograph conveys no hint of ambiguity, the picture of 'a line of clean children carrying letters' is another matter. We already know that this is a photograph of Lee's school's Empire Day celebrations, but we also know what is lurking outside the frame – the spectre of the mad mother, simultaneously there and not there, a flicker out of the corner of the eye. Written out of the family history, it is her very absence from this photograph that testifies to her (late, *be*lated) presence.

While there might seem to be a world of difference between David Bailey's posed portraits, Lee's snapshots and Buzz's voyeuristic, opportunistic, photographs, all can be aligned with the notion of the sixties as itself an uncanny event. Marina Warner says of photographic technology that it 'has established former selves and the presence of people as they were when they were alive in very corner of everyday experience',[72] and this notion of the proliferation of images, both living and dead, is certainly what, for Carter, distinguishes the underlying culture of *Love*. Viewed from this perspective, the sixties is a hall of mirrors, within which reflections contemplate other reflections in a kaleidoscopic pattern that is endlessly refracted, constantly shifting – and, most importantly, never truly connecting.

Love takes up the Beatles' mantra of the sixties, 'all you need is love',[73] but then poses the question: what, exactly, *is* love? It is in Carter's conclusion that the Gothic heart of the book resides, for here sex is not a physical or emotional act, but a spectral one. For example, when Buzz and Annabel finally achieve the union each has fantasised about for so long it is inevitably (and literally) anti-climactic, as they find themselves 'embrac[ing] each others phantoms . . . connoisseurs of unreality as they were, they could not bear the crude weight, the rank smell and the ripe taste of real flesh' (94–95). And in a scene that parodies the conventions of romantic fiction, Annabel is described in terms that recall Poe's Madelaine Usher,[74] newly arisen from her coffin:

> 'I love you,' she said.
> She spoke in a sweet, fallacious music like the song of a mechanical nightingale and now she seemed to him a ghostly woman, white as a winding sheet and shrouded in hair. The darkening light seemed to pass straight through her almost dissolving edges and when she stretched out her hands towards him they looked like dried flowers, nothing but veins and transparency, and he could see the bones of her fingers through them. (62)

Love, in other words, is more like a macabre communication with the dead than a fruitful interaction between living, breathing human beings. When the characters in this novel stretch out to touch another, they only ever find spirits they themselves have conjured up from the depths of their own neediness, confusion and self-loathing. Flesh, meanwhile, decays, is discarded, cut, tattooed and generally abused. According to this twisted, disconnected logic, Annabel's eventual fate, as 'a painted doll, bluish at the extremities' with flies 'clustered around her eyes' (112) transforms her into the ultimate love object.

Just as the people in *Love* are consumed by their own nihilistic vision, so, by implication, the sixties ultimately spirals to destruction. It is a connection that has already been made by Marc O'Day, who has also argued that it is through *Love*'s photographic references that the sixties is particularly closely anatomised:

> It's generally agreed that *Love* is a farewell to the sixties and to myths of the sixties, written and set at the end of the decade. In the title of David Bailey's 1969 book of photographic portraits, which itself parodically mourns the passing of Swinging London, it's *Goodbye Baby and Amen*. I've always thought of the coffin on its cover as being, at least partly, Annabel's. Her death, too, symbolises the death of the sixties.[75]

4
A Quite Different Reality

With *Love*, Carter rounded off her literary output of the sixties, a decade in which she had married, gained a university education and become a successful and prolific novelist. In *The Magic Toyshop* and *Heroes and Villains*, she uses fantasy as means of exploring issues of nationalism and identity, while the (ostensibly) more realistic narratives of the Bristol trilogy allow her to mirror the sixties back upon itself to create a doubled reflection in which images shift and metamorphose in the endlessly refracting patterns she identifies as the essence of the period. In addition, the sixties mark the beginning of her radicalisation, a process that was to continue into the seventies.

It would be overly simplistic to argue that the death of the sixties as portrayed in *Love* also had a personal dimension as far as Carter was concerned, but she herself did admit to a certain synchronicity between her private life and public experience at the end of the decade. While she was, ironically, a married woman for most of the radical sixties, 'the sense of living on a demolition site was perfectly real, in one way, because I stopped being married in 1969'.[1] Although she was characteristically reticent about the collapse of her marriage, in 'The Quilt Maker' she has her narrator describe a pivotal event that takes place in 'the Greyhound Bus Station in Houston, Texas, with a man I was then married to' (122). In this story, the anonymous narrator is given by her – equally anonymous – husband 'an American coin of small denomination (he used to carry about all our money for us because he did not trust me with it)' (122). With it, she buys a small peach, leaving the larger one 'for somebody who wanted it more than I did' (123). Her husband, though, challenges her choice, allowing the narrator to triumphantly deliver the devastating punch line with which the story concludes:

> The point of this story is, if the man who was then my husband hadn't told me I was a fool to take the little peach, then I never would have left him because, in truth, he was, in a manner of speaking, always the little peach to me'. (123)

Whatever the truth behind this fictionalised anecdote, Carter and her husband did embark on a road trip across America by Greyhound bus in 1969, and in the words of Ian McEwan, 'after 10 years of marriage they parted company at San Francisco airport and Angela flew off to Japan'.[2] Her trip to America, land of 'hallucinatory midnight bus stations',[3] was, therefore, the precursor to a far more radical change of scene.

Carter cited several different reasons for her decision to travel to Japan in 1969. She was financially enabled to do so due to the Somerset Maugham award she had won for *Several Perceptions*, which gave her £500. Some of it was spent on the American trip, the rest on getting to Japan. In an interview for the *Guardian*'s women's page on her return to England in 1972, Carter said:

> [p]art of the condition of the Somerset Maugham award is that you should spend some of it travelling. My marriage was on the point of foundering and I think Somerset Maugham would have derived a certain pleasure from financing my running away from home, particularly since I ran away to Tokyo and Bangkok.[4]

According to her interviewer, this trip represented for Carter a way of 'actualising her fantasies, which were ones of emancipation – from marriage and from herself'. However, she was definitely not fulfilling a long-held dream of travel for its own sake, for 'living alone in a foreign land had never been a fantasy of hers'.[5] Up until 1969, she 'had, previously, never been further than Dublin, Eire':[6] and indeed, she had only hit upon Japan as an ultimate destination because 'I liked their movies'.[7] This latter point was something she enlarged upon in the course of her interview with Lisa Appignanesi, in which she said it was the result of a dare; that someone, knowing her mania for Japanese cinema, 'said to me, "Now you can go to Japan". So I had to.'[8]

All this makes her choice of country sound somewhat arbitrary, although in her introduction to a collection of essays she wrote on her experiences in Japan following her return, she rationalises her decision: 'Why Japan though? I wanted to live for a while in a culture that is not now nor has ever been a Judeo-Christian one, to see what it was like.'[9] In Susannah Clapp's 1991 interview, Carter struck a rather more flippant note on the same theme, claiming that she ended up in Japan because it was 'the only country that met her stringent criteria for a bolthole: good public transport, a non-Judeo-Christian culture and an efficient sewage system'.[10] Mocking the tone might have been, but the point itself is nevertheless serious, and has the effect of turning what at first appears to be madness into method. For all their eroticism and exoticism, Carter's writing of the sixties are written from within the very Judeo-Christian tradition Japan allowed her to escape, and it was an opportunity that Carter, a dedicated atheist, seized upon with alacrity.

As has already been discussed in the introduction, Carter's period in Japan is, to some extent, mysterious. She made a living 'one way and another':[11] Susannah Clapp says that she 'worked for a spell in the English language branch of the NHK broadcasting company',[12] and Peter Kemp that 'she subsisted by turning the English of Japanese translators into native-sounding English'.[13] She also briefly worked as a bar hostess, an experience she recorded in an essay published in *New Society* in 1972, 'Poor Butterfly'. According to Carter, she fell into this occupation purely by accident:

> The *mamma-san* explained that, as a special attraction during the festive season, she had originally intended to dress her fifteen resident hostesses in colourful national costumes from all over the world. Owing, however, to a printer's error, the postcards she commissioned to advertise her special attraction read: 'During the days before Xmas, your drinks will be served by charming and attractive hostesses ... from all over the world.' Therefore she had to go out and search for a clutch of foreigners and she was prepared to pay well over the odds for them, since the notice was so short – 30,000 yen, about £35 sterling, for five nights' work in shifts of two and a half hours.[14]

In spite of Carter's airy assertion on her return to England that she found that '[f]ending for herself on the other side of the world wasn't difficult at all',[15] 'Poor Butterfly' suggests quite otherwise. 'Caucasian girls' might be in demand as 'exotic extras' (252), but it does not mean that they are treated any more respectfully by their clients, with whom they engage 'in a kind of dextrous, cross-cultural, tightrope dance' of crude sexual allusion (a sample of which Carter purports to 'transcribe ... verbatim' [252]). Beneath the tone of arch burlesque is represented a world of enormous gender inequity and female desperation, with Carter concluding that she is spending her evenings acting as little more than 'a masturbatory device for gentlemen' (254). Little wonder that she credited Japan as the place in which 'I became radicalised, because I learnt what it is to be a woman'.[16]

Newly separated, Carter also had romantic as well as economic relationships with men during her stay in Japan. In fact, some sources assert that she went there to join someone whom she had already met, although this is a fact that comes up in the obituaries rather than in any of the interviews Carter gave in her lifetime (needless to say, it was not information that she volunteered in any of her writing of or about this period). Nicci Gerrard, for example, says that Carter 'left her husband and flew to join her Japanese lover',[17] and Paul Barker, too, claims that Carter 'joined a lover' there. Barker, though, speculates that this person might not have been Japanese: 'I think he was Korean, and Koreans are as despised in Japan as (say) Poles are in Chicago.'[18]

Whatever the truth might have been, Carter does record the story of a romance with an Oriental man, but, as is invariably the case when her material verges on the personal, she retreats behind fictional personae. The essays she wrote for *New Society* on various aspects of Japanese culture might make use of the plural (in 'Tokyo Pastoral', an essay on the suburb of the city in which she lived, she uses it continually, referring, for example, to '*our* neighbourhood')[19] but she never specifies on whose behalf she is speaking. Yet her stay in Japan inspired a number of 'hybrid' narratives, in which free use is made of the first person at the same time as the story's presentation as fiction baffles the simplistic identification of the 'autobiographical' narrative voice with that of the author herself. Not surprisingly, these stories are provocative, potentially shocking in what they appear to disclose: as Carter once said of sixties fashion, they 'mimic nakedness',[20] revealing and concealing at one and the same time.

A good example of this is the tale that opens her first collection of short stories, *Fireworks: Nine Profane Pieces*, which was published in 1974. The stories themselves, however, were written between 1970 and 1973, and, said Carter in her afterword, were 'arranged in chronological order, as they were written'.[21] This means that 'A Souvenir of Japan' can thus be assumed to have been written some time in 1970. Although Carter had published a few short stories over the years (her first, 'The Man Who Loved A Double Bass', appeared as early as 1962), she credited Japan with stimulating her interest in the form: she was inspired, she said, 'to write short pieces when I was living in a room too small to write a novel in'.[22] It is a characteristically neat turn of phrase, but when considering the relationship between life and work, it is possible to speculate that the short story mode also served a more pragmatic function for Carter, enabling her to teasingly fictionalise those experiences she did not want to record in a more unambiguous form. In fact, she comes very close to admitting as much in her afterword to *Fireworks*, when she draws a distinction between the short story and the 'tale', which:

> differs from the short story in that it makes few pretences at the imitation of life. The tale does not log everyday experience, as the short story does; it interprets everyday experience through a system of imagery derived from subterranean areas behind everyday experience, and *therefore the tale cannot betray its readers into a false knowledge of everyday experience.*[23]

'A Souvenir of Japan' should, therefore, not be viewed as a short story, or as an anecdote, but as a 'tale' in the terms outlined by Carter: a narrative that transforms 'everyday experience' into something obviously 'other'. It ostensibly relates the story of a trip taken by the Western narrator and her Oriental lover to a traditional festival, but it rapidly segues into an extended, stylised, meditation on the nature of their relationship. Against a potentially idyllic backdrop 'of shared happiness...a muted, bourgeois yet authentic magic',[24] the two principal figures are locked together in a convoluted logic of bluff and double-bluff, each trying to outdo the other in 'a silent battle of self-abnegation' (3). Even their visit to the festival is another round in their interminable battle of wills and consequently they do not stay long, for reasons the narrator explains at some length:

> the last thing in the world that I wanted was to leave the scintillating river and the gentle crowd. But I knew his real desire was to return and so return we did, although I do not know if it was worth my small victory of selflessness to bear his remorse at cutting short my pleasure, even if to engineer this remorse had, at some subterranean level, been the whole object of the outing. (3)

As a result, it is difficult to see this relationship as a romance, since it encompasses no real union of either mind or body. The differences in nationality, physiology, gender and culture between these two individuals is precisely what makes them the object of each other's desire – but it also simultaneously guarantees that such barriers can never, ever, be transcended. Witness, for example, the narrator's description of her lover:

> His hair was so heavy his neck drooped under its weight and was of a black so deep it turned purple in sunlight. His mouth also was purplish and his blunt, bee-stung lips those of Gauguin's Tahitians. The touch of his skin was as smooth as water as it flows through the fingers. His eyelids were retractable, like those of a cat, and sometimes disappeared completely. I should have liked to have had him embalmed and been able to keep him beside me in a glass coffin, so that I could watch him all the time and he would not have been able to get away from me. (6)

In a sensual passage full of intimate physical description, this man is positioned as the narrator's ultimate object of desire. Yet the discourse of exploitation and violence is a persistent undercurrent – he is pulled down by the weight of his hair; his lips are bruised and 'bee-stung'; moreover, the purple colour attributed to both lips and hair evoke shadows of old bruises. Such incipient brutality rises to the surface with the narrator's final, most outrageous, statement that her lover would be even more perfect if he were dead, 'so that I could watch him all the time and he would not have been able to get away from me'. She is not, therefore, interested in this individual as a person, only as an item to be contemplated in aesthetic terms, frozen into a changeless *objet d'arte*. Indeed, the allusion to Gauguin situates her lover within the tradition of the muse; the mute, often anonymous, receptacle for artistic inspiration.

Such an analysis suggests that Carter is deliberately inverting gender roles here, with the female protagonist taking over the role of what John Berger terms 'the "ideal" spectator', who is 'always assumed to be male'. Indeed, she could be assumed to be engaging in the very reversal of perception with which Berger challenges his readers: 'Choose from this book an image of a traditional nude. Transform the man into a woman .... Then notice the violence which that transformation does. Not to the image, but to the assumptions of a likely viewer.'[25] Perhaps this is the source of the violence that we can see inscribed upon the body of the lover. But in 'A Souvenir of Japan' the hijacking of the male gaze becomes, inevitably, entangled in issues of race as well as gender. While on the one hand the control exercised by the female gaze in this scenario challenges the customary ways in which women are fetishized when seen through men's eyes, on another, it becomes just one more example in a long tradition of the white, Western view of the alien 'Other'. In other words, the female protagonist can assume the dominant role *vis-à-vis* the gaze without any real violation of the dominant power structures, because she is adopting the customary Occidental view of the Orient.

Further examination, though, reveals the extent of Carter's game playing, for it turns out that she can claim superiority on neither count. Alone in Japan, the narrator is being forced into a continual confrontation with her own alienation; she is 'absolutely the mysterious other... a kind of phoenix, a fabulous beast'; 'an instrument... played upon an alien scale' (7). By the same token, her assumption of gender dominance is less an assertion of feminist power than a consciously defiant stand against the ingrained chauvinism of Japanese society: it is, observes the narrator, 'a man's country' (6), where women are 'valued only as the object of men's passions' (7). Yet this appears not to lead her towards critique so much as acquiescence: '[i]f the only conjunction possible to us was that of the death-defying double-somersault of love, it is, perhaps, a better thing to be valued only as an object of passion than never to be valued at all' (7). This is an unsettling assertion, since it suggests that the narrator, 'suffering from love' (8) as she is, is willing to collude in her own objectification.

However, if the narrator's assumption of dominance is not, ultimately, convincing, neither is her submissiveness. Instead, the relationship becomes a kind of sadomasochistic erotic ritual in which the roles of dominant and submissive are self-consciously enacted by both parties in order to achieve a balance of pleasure and pain. In this short story, as in her essays, Carter represents Japan as a place obsessed with mutilation of all kinds, where:

> [t]hey torture trees to make them look more like the formal notion of a tree. They paint amazing pictures on their skins with awl and gouge, sponging away the blood as they go; a tattooed man is a walking masterpiece of remembered pain. They boast the most passionate puppets in the world who mimic love suicides in a stylized fashion, for here there is no such comfortable formula as 'happy ever after'. (10–11)

The narrator draws clear parallels between the tortuous progress of her relationship and its enactment within a society in which 'monstrous passions bloom' (10) – the lover neglects and lies to the narrator precisely in order to 'savour... the most annihilating remorse' (8), while her chief value to him is 'as an instrument which would cause him pain' (11). Like the samurai or the geisha, therefore, the story's protagonists assume roles 'which transmute life itself into a series of grand gestures' (10), manipulating it to form the backdrop for their perverted passion play.

Carter's final trick, though, is the most startling of all the moves she makes in this already highly duplicitous narrative, which is to call into question the ontological status of the lover himself. Early in the story, the narrator confidently tells her readers that his name is Taro, a name she aligns with that of a character in a traditional tale: 'Momotaro, who was born from a peach' (5). She found this story, she says, '[i]n a toy store [where] I saw one of those books for children with pictures which are cunningly made of paper cut-outs so that, when you turn the page, the picture springs up in the three stylized dimensions of a backdrop in Kabuki' (5). It is easy to miss the implications of this reference – as, indeed, you are intended to, so that Carter can spring her surprise a few pages later: 'His name was not Taro. I only called him Taro so that I could use the conceit of the peach boy, because it seemed appropriate' (9). So, if Taro is not Taro, who is he? Does he actually exist at all? In spite of the detailed physical description supplied by the narrator, this figure remains shadowy for the simple reason that he does not appear in the narrative directly but only through the recollections of the narrator; recollections, indeed, which tend to focus on his absence rather than his presence. He is, ultimately, a speech effect or, to use the narrator's own words, a 'conceit', around which she can structure a story that ultimately is about nothing but her *own* desire:

> I knew him as intimately as I knew my own image in a mirror. In other words, I knew him only in relation to myself. Yet, on those terms, I knew him perfectly. At times, I thought I was inventing him as I went along, however, so you will have to take my word for it that we existed. But I do not want to paint our circumstantial portraits so that we both emerge with enough well-rounded, spuriously detailed actuality that you are forced to believe in us. I do not want to practise such sleight of hand. (8–9)

Here, the reality of the lover is simultaneously asserted and denied – he both 'exists' and is 'invented'. Moreover, the passage goes still further, proceeding to destabilise the identity of the speaker herself, who might similarly be only an invention or a speech effect. This, therefore, is Carter at her most mendacious, for 'sleight of hand' is exactly what she is practicing – she knows it, and she knows that, by now, her readers know it too. Thus, her 'word' means nothing, for it only points towards more words, more conceits, more narrative trickery. Ultimately, *both* lovers are nothing more than 'paper cut-outs' in a storybook; a storybook, moreover, situated in the context of a city that is 'a cold hall of mirrors which continually proliferated whole galleries of constantly changing appearances, all marvellous but none tangible' (9).

Mirrors become the controlling metaphor of a later story that is also published in *Fireworks*, entitled 'Flesh and the Mirror'. Again, this is a first-person narrative that invites us to suppose that Carter and the autobiographical 'I' are the same, but it also plays very similar games, deliberately destabilising the narrative voice to such an extent that it cannot be fixed to a clearly defined subject position. The plot of 'Flesh and the Mirror' concerns the experiences of an extravagantly lovelorn narrator, who has just returned to Tokyo following an extended visit to England. Her lover has not turned up to meet her as expected, and when she returns home, he is nowhere to be found. As she searches for him, 'crying bitterly...under the artificial cherry blossom' (61), she is 'delivered into the hands of a perfect stranger' with whom she goes to 'an unambiguous hotel' for a brief sexual liason. She finds her lover the next day, and together they repair to another hotel, in which they enact 'in every respect a parody of the previous night' (68). But their constant quarrelling and her persistent guilt sour the relationship, and they part a few days later.

These events may or may not be based on fact, but that tantalising possibility is precisely the point of the story, which resembles 'A Souvenir of Japan' in its artfulness. Indeed, as the story concludes, 'The most difficult performance in the world is acting naturally, isn't it? Everything else is artful' (70). Quite – there is absolutely nothing naturalistic about 'Flesh and the Mirror', caught up as it is in the disorienting perspectives of the self-dramatising subject who sees the world around her kaleidoscopically refracted through the medium of her self-absorption, 'mov[ing] through these expressionist perspectives in my black dress as though I was the creator of all and of myself, too, in a black dress, in love, crying, walking through the city in the third person singular, my own heroine' (62). The narrator's tendency to view herself 'in the third person singular' is literalised in the text, which features moments of slippage between the first and the third person, who is both 'I' and 'she'. This shifting of viewpoints becomes literally echoed in the first hotel room, which, because it has a mirror on the ceiling, reflects every nuance of the narrator's desire back to herself. As a result

she becomes both participant in and viewer of her personally orches-
trated melodrama.

> The magic mirror presented me with a hitherto unconsidered notion
> of myself as I. Without any intention of mine I had been defined by
> the action reflected in the mirror. I beset me. I was the subject of the
> sentence written on the mirror. (65)

The narrator professes herself to be horrified, for while she is used to
being 'in complicity' with her mirror 'to evade the action I/she
performs that I/she cannot watch ... *this* mirror ... reflected the embrace
beneath it without the least guile' (65). Her protestations of remorse are,
however, equally melodramatic. She claims that the mirror has betrayed
her into 'act[ing] out of character' (65), but what in fact it does is merely
motivate her to assume another persona, who enacts a 'demonstration
of perturbation [that] was perfect in every detail, just like the movies.
I applauded it' (65). Such passages make clear that there is therefore no
authentic reality to be arrived at in this narrative, only a shifting succession of identities anchored in an 'I' whose view of the world around her
fluctuates in accordance with the demands of her part. Even the long-
sought-for lover is, in the end, 'created solely in relation to myself, like
a work of romantic art' (67).

It is worth analysing 'A Souvenir of Japan' and 'Flesh and the Mirror'
in such detail because of the implications they offer for our understanding of Carter's manipulation of autobiography over this period.
The fact that such stories echo incidents and situations that are known
to have happened to Carter during her time in Tokyo encourage us to
assume that she is using her own experience as inspiration. Nevertheless, the incessant shifting (not to say shift*iness*) of the autobiographical
persona deliberately foregrounds the difficulties inherent in identifying
the teller of the story with the figure of the author herself. In the final
analysis, these are not so much travelogues as traveller's tales, which draw
on what the narrator of 'Flesh and the Mirror' describes as the 'enormous
histrionic resources' (63) of the alien landscape. Even Lorna Sage
professes herself unsure as to the provenance of this particular story,
stating that although 'I think it probably did happen', the 'whole
episode may of course have been a fantasy bred out of the city'.[26]

This growing interest in the possibilities offered by the *faux* autobiographical voice exerted an increasing influence on Carter's fiction: after
Love, which was written before her departure for Japan, she wrote no
more novels solely in the third person. *The Infernal Desire Machines of*

Doctor Hoffman, *The Passion of New Eve* and *Wise Children* are all presented as first-person confessional narratives, and all play with the vacillating perspectives of an individual subjectivity; the possibilities of performance presented by the (apparent) offer of disclosure. While *Nights at the Circus* might appear to be an exception, since it moves between third and first person points of view, it is, nevertheless, dominated throughout by the raucous voice of Carter's Cockney heroine, Fevvers, who insists on telling much of her own story directly to the reader.

Yet while the pieces published in *Fireworks* demonstrate developments in Carter's narrative technique, they do not constitute a radical departure in terms of theme. Opinion is split between those who regard Carter's time in Japan as, in the words of Marina Warner, 'mark[ing] an important transition'[27] in her work, or those who argue that it is less of a benchmark than it might appear. Linden Peach, for example, says that '[m]uch of what she wrote about Japan and produced after her stay there provides a gloss on her early fiction'.[28] He proceeds to argue that pieces in *Fireworks* and in *Nothing Sacred* evoke echoes of the earlier novels: the puppet master in the short story 'The Loves of Lady Purple' recalls the role allocated to Uncle Philip in *The Magic Toyshop*, while Carter's description of relationships in Japanese culture in 'Once More into the Mangle' and 'People as Pictures' has its exemplification in the relationship between Marianne and Jewel in *Heroes and Villains*. 'In other words', concludes Peach, 'Japan did not simply provide her with new ideas, but confirmed her in the way in which she was developing.'[29] For Marina Warner, though, Japan gave Carter 'a way of looking at her own culture which intensified her capacity to conjure strangeness out of the familiar'.[30]

However, these two points of view are not irreconcilable. Certainly, even the most casual survey of Carter's oeuvre shows that her writing did not undergo a sudden and dramatic change at the beginning of the seventies. Yet while many of the themes and scenarios that are present in the earlier novels resurface in the writing she did during and after her time in Japan, it does become more concentrated upon its own textuality, and with the problematisation of the relationship between text, author and world: an awareness that was obviously only intensified by Carter's own experience of intense alienation. The two impulses do not work against each other, though, but in tandem. For example, the relationship conducted in the break between the first and the third person in both 'A Souvenir of Japan' and 'Flesh and Mirror' indicates the possibility of an autobiographical link while at the same time making a straightforward association between author and narrator impossible.

Yet one of the ways in which attention is drawn to these stories' status as text, and not as transparent recordings of direct experience, is that they have their roots in other stories Carter had already written – the Bristol trilogy, and, most particularly, *Love*. The narcissistic self-absorption of the protagonists and their frequently vicious power plays in these short pieces are distinctly reminiscent of the tortuous interactions of Lee and Annabel. (In fact, 'Flesh and the Mirror' introduces, albeit briefly, the love triangle between a woman and two men that is the central structuring principle of *Love*.) While the Japanese pieces may contain no love suicide, they are nevertheless situated in the context of a culture in which a fate such as Annabel's is perfectly conceivable, since 'human relations either have the stark anonymity of rape or else are essentially tragic'.[31] Indeed, Carter's pronouncement with regard to Japanese culture that '[l]ove is a tragic, fated passion; yet, still, heroically, they love',[32] could perfectly well act as Lee and Annabel's epitaph. Moreover, in the essay in which this statement appears, she examines Japan's favourite art form, the comic strip, and comes to a conclusion that also evokes echoes of *Love*'s 'flicker book' sensibility:

> Since the strip, as a form, is essentially a series of stills, unfolding only in the personal time of the reader, the effect is one of continuous static convulsion. This is a condition sufficiently approximating to that of modern Japanese society.[33]

Whether through deliberate action or sheer serendipity, therefore, what Carter appears to have found in Japan was an intensified, ritualised, institutionalised version of everything that had come to most fascinate her about sixties culture: the conflation of identities and roles, the sado-masochistic potential of love, and the rejection of progression in favour of a kind of intensified stasis.

If the short stories in *Fireworks* and the pieces in *Nothing Sacred* gesture back to the fiction that Carter wrote before she arrived in Japan, then another pre-Japanese text can be proposed as not only revisiting the themes and preoccupations of her earlier work, but also illustrating her in the process of moving towards the novel she was to write next, *The Infernal Desire Machines of Doctor Hoffman*, published in 1972. An aspect of Carter's work which has been hitherto completely neglected is her writing for children, the first example of which, *Miss Z: The Dark Young Lady*, appeared the same year as *Love* – 1970. It is a short but bizarre fable, which tells the story of the eponymous Miss Z, who lives with her father 'in a Parrot Jungle': the very exotic, vaguely Latin American landscape she was to explore in her next adult novel.[34] They have moved there from 'the Human Town' because '[t]he earth is so rich… And the air is so sweet' (9), but the 'perverse' parrots make Miss Z's father 'exasperated' (5), and he kills their King with his catapult. Consequently, the parrots disappear from the jungle, leaving only bad fortune behind them: 'the well refused to give water; the cow refused to give milk; the plow refused to turn the soil; and the fire refused to light. Even the rocking chair refused to rock' (8). This rebellion against human colonisation has its intended effect: Miss Z's father, having fallen 'sick from eating poison fruit' (9), is 'overcome with remorse' (8). Threatened by starvation and the loss of her father, Miss Z embarks on a quest to negotiate the parrots' return and raise the curse.

On consulting a wise woman, she discovers that the parrots have flown 'to the place where the green lions live' (9), and she finds it with the help of a cast of fantasy characters: an ugly, outcast creature named Odd, who she bribes with cheese sandwiches; a rather lascivious dragon who demands to be paid for his aid with kisses; and an excessively narcissistic and bombastic unicorn. Following a fight between the unicorn and the ruler of the green lions, Miss Z persuades the parrots to forgive her father and to return to the Parrot Jungle. When she herself reaches home, she finds her father 'recovered from his sickness… [sitting] contentedly in his rocking chair on the porch rocking back and forth. All was in order again. Around him, treeloads of parrots sang evening songs' (30).

While this narrative may have been marketed as a children's story, it nevertheless recapitulates some familiar Carter themes. For example, Miss Z's mother's absence from the text remains unexplained – she is, simply, never mentioned – and this links Miss Z to the procession of motherless daughters who populate Carter's fiction, from Melanie to Marianne. Miss Z lives alone with her father in the Parrot Jungle but – like Marianne in *Heroes and Villains* – even while she loves him, she also possesses a keen sense of his limitations. Aided by the magic dress she has made with her own hands, Miss Z assumes the active role in the text automatically; she does not question whether questing is an appropriate role for a female protagonist, and she certainly never voices any expectation that her father will take on the mantle of hero.

Miss Z: The Dark Young Lady is also of interest in relation to Carter's critique of patriotism and the regalia of nationalism, encapsulated in the twinned figures of the lion and the unicorn. Her employment of such imagery is particularly apt when one considers her autobiographical essays which position her as suspended between a Scottish and an

English identity, as the appearance of the lion and the unicorn on the coat of arms of Great Britain dates back to the union of England and Scotland in 1603. When James VI of Scotland also became James I of England, the English lion and the Scottish unicorn were linked; a union commemorated in the nursery rhyme 'The lion and the unicorn were fighting for the crown'. *Miss Z: The Dark Young Lady* could be considered as a creative adaptation of that rhyme, in which both heraldic creatures are divested of dignity in an encounter that is more than a little ridiculous. The lion wears an ostentatious 'crown of green jade' (24), while the unicorn is vain and blustering: ' "I have destroyed more green lions than you've had hot dinners," said the unicorn. "Let me handle this" ' (20). Their duel, however, constitutes nothing more than pointless posturing: 'The lion roared and feinted with his horn, but the light was so dim, the lion was only half awake and the unicorn was almost half asleep..., and no blows were actually struck' (24). Miss Z grows 'bored with watching them trying to fight' (25), and eventually sorts them out herself: like her author, she has no particular allegiance to either lion or unicorn.

Yet there are also elements in this novel that prefigure the surreal world of *The Infernal Desire Machines of Doctor Hoffman*, the most significant of which can, once again, be extracted from the anti-climactic encounter between the lion and the unicorn. For although this incident certainly recalls the traditional nationalistic rhyme, it is also reminiscent of a central motif utilised in the 1951 Festival of Britain. The Lion and Unicorn Pavilion was an important part of the South Bank exhibition, designed to 'symbolise two of the main qualities of the national character: on the one hand, realism and strength, on the other fantasy, independence and imagination'.[35] This intention was made clear in the slogan posted above the corn dolly figures of the Lion and the Unicorn: 'We are the Lion and the Unicorn. Twin symbols of the Briton's character. As a Lion I give him solidity and strength. With the Unicorn he lets himself go...'.[36] While this dichotomy does not emerge in Carter's children's book, it is the central structuring principle in *The Infernal Desire Machines of Doctor Hoffman*, which Carter herself described as a 'dialectic between reason and passion, which it resolves in favour of reason (unlike my life)'.[37]

Perhaps because it was a text in which she contemplated the kind of tidy resolution that her life did not offer, Carter retained a marked fondness for *Hoffman* throughout her subsequent career. In 1977, she told Lorna Sage that '[t]here are passages in *Hoffman* that still give me enormous pleasure';[38] and when Olga Kenyon asked her whether she

'had a favourite among your own novels', it was *Hoffman* that she
picked. However, that did not stop her acknowledging that her readership did not, generally, share that view. At the time she was speaking to
Olga Kenyon, *Hoffman* had just been published in paperback. She gave
Kenyon a copy, while at the same time admitting that the book was
'not selling as well as I'd hoped. I'm not fashionable.'[39] Elsewhere, she
spoke of it as 'the novel that marked the beginning of my obscurity.
I went from being a very promising young writer to being completely
ignored in two novels.'[40] The other novel was *Love*, but while that 'had
been a small book, mildly commercially unviable, *Hoffman*, a big book,
was magnificently commercially unviable'.[41] Ian McEwan notes that
the novel's 'critical reception was lukewarm. It was all a little too
garishly extreme for literary tastes',[42] and many interviewers pass over it
altogether: it is simply not mentioned in the conversations Carter had
with John Haffenden or Lisa Appignanesi, nor in her commentary for
Angela Carter's Curious Room, the programme that was intended to act as
a summary of her career. As Ali Smith argues, *Hoffman* is 'Carter's lost
classic',[43] her 'far-too neglected achievement'.[44]

   True to form, *Hoffman* was written at speed; Carter told Susan Rubin
Suleiman that it took her 'three months, in a Japanese fishing village on
an island'.[45] Perhaps one of the reasons for its subsequent disappointing
reception is that it is an excessively complicated book of ideas, in which
Carter not only revisits many of her earlier preoccupations, but also
begins to amalgamate new ideas and influences: most notably, the work
of the Marquis de Sade and Jorge Luis Borges, whose works Carter
encountered in the late sixties, during or just before her stay in Japan.
In addition, Susan Rubin Suleiman says that '[i]t was in Tokyo...
around 1970, that she first came upon two books about Surrealism and
cinema that had a tremendous effect on her': Ado Kyrou's *Surréalisme et
cinema* and *Amour-érotisme et cinema*.[46] Marina Warner observes, too,
that Carter's association with Surrealism during the time she lived in
Japan was strengthened by her contact with 'French exiles from *les
evenements* of 1968 who had fetched up in Japan'.[47]

   In her essay, Suleiman goes on to cite conversations with Carter in
which she said that, at the time she was living there it was caught up in
its 'own version of 1968',[48] a statement that suggests that in the process
of running away, she actually ended up returning to a version of the
very sixties counterculture she had left behind. Following their defeat in
the Second World War, Japan had been subject to American occupation
between 1945 and 1952, during which period 'many of the central
institutions of Japanese society were reshaped. Universal suffrage was

introduced, the power of the parliament enhanced, the constitution rewritten, farmland redistributed, and the education system over-hauled.'[49] Just as Britain had done, Japan had lost its colonial empire, and was caught up in the process of redefining its own culture and its role in the wider world. Although by the sixties it was experiencing an economic boom, Japan was not immune from the student demonstra-tions of 1968, at least one of which Carter witnessed at first hand. In 'My Maugham Award', she describes seeing '[i]n the campus at Waseda University, beautiful young men with the faces of those who will die on the barricades... lobbing hand grenades at policemen'.[50]

David Punter proposes another countercultural influence on the novel, arguing that it can be read 'as a series of figures for the defeat of the political aspirations of the 1960s, and in particular of the father-figures of liberation, Reich and Marcuse';[51] certainly, *Hoffman* is, in the words of Susan Rubin Suleiman, 'a veritable collage of pre-existing genres and verbal or visual quotations',[52] many – though by no means all – of which are indebted to the ideas of the cultural revolutionaries of the sixties. Marcuse is particularly relevant: a figurehead of the revolu-tionary student movement, whose *Essay on Liberation*, published in 1969, argued for an autonomous artistic practice that would break all political and social imaginative restraints:

> Between the dictates of instrumentalist reason on the one hand and a sense experience mutilated by the realizations of this reason on the other, the power of the imagination was repressed; it was free to become practical, i.e., to transform reality only within the general framework of repression; beyond these limits, the practice of the imagination was violation of taboos of social morality, was perversion and subversion.[53]

Hoffman, it can be argued, constitutes a journey into those realms of 'perversion and subversion' that can be found through the exercise of what Marcuse termed 'the radical imagination' through which 'the rebellion and its uncompromised goals [can] be remembered'.[54] But as Punter suggests, Carter does not employ such references uncritically, stringently interrogating the potential of the radical imagination to effect any kind of real political, social or ontological change.

However, neither Punter nor Suleiman mention another writer whose work also forms an integral part of *Hoffman*'s narrative and thematic structure. The writing of Jorge Luis Borges not only gave Carter a new way of continuing her critique of imperialism, but also helped perpetuate her abiding interest in the intellectual uses of fiction, a point she made at length to Helen Cagney Watts:

> I was very impressed when I first read Borges, because of the way he grandly threw out certain traditional elements of writing fiction. I admire very much his highly schematic short stories, and also the way in which he just grandly junked things like character – which is totally in opposition to the whole idea of the short story that I was brought up with. You know, the De Maupassant short story with the hook at the end; the well-made short story in other words. So I was greatly encouraged by the way he just junked these devices, and was doing something which I found much more like the sort of things that I wanted and could do myself. What I found to be most significant for me were these highly schematic, workings-out of ideas, and that filled me with great joy because it meant that there were suddenly all these things I could do, that it was OK to do.[55]

With *Heroes and Villains*, Carter had found the freedom to engage in 'workings-out of ideas' through the science fiction medium, and this was a form that remained important to *Hoffman*, which she actually described as containing the 'most Sci Fi elements'[56] of any of her novels. But, given her assertion that, although she was 'read and reviewed by Sci Fi addicts... it's definitely not an important aspect of my writing',[57] it can be argued that Borges' work played an important part in allowing Carter to gain the confidence to 'junk character' in order to create a narrative that showcases her complex philosophical and political debate. Carter told Ian McEwan that she first read Borges in 1969 just before her Japanese interlude, an experience that caused her to feel 'she had come across a new way of writing fiction'. 'His work linked directly with the speculative and didactic medieval literature that I admired. It was very liberating, very exciting. I thought, one can do anything!.'[58]

Carter's use of Borges has been largely ignored by critics, but Lorna Sage makes a telling point when she argues that the plot of *Hoffman* recalls a passage from *The Book of Imaginary Beings* (translated in 1969):

> Borges, under the heading *Fauna of Mirrors*, is retelling an ancient Cantonese myth:

> In those days the world of mirrors and the world of men were not, as they are now, cut off from each other. They were, besides, quite different; neither beings nor colours, nor shapes were the same. Both kingdoms, the spectacular and the human, lived in harmony; you could

come and go through mirrors. One night the mirror people invaded the earth. Their power was great, but at the end of bloody warfare the magic arts of the Yellow Emperor prevailed. He repulsed the invaders, imprisoned them in their mirrors, and forced on them the task of repeating, as though in a kind of dream, all the actions of men... Nonetheless a day will come when the magic spell will be taken off.

In fact, this is more or less the plot of *Dr Hoffman* – a precarious victory for the Reality Principle.[59]

Sage's argument is very convincing but it does not go far enough, for Carter's novel does not only adopt some of its themes from Borges, but also makes use of his metafictional techniques. *Hoffman* takes the form of an autobiography composed by Desiderio, who tells the story of his quest on behalf of the Minister of Determination to discover and destroy the machines through which Doctor Hoffman institutes his reign of Nebulous Time, in which desires become manifest and warp the fabric of reality. Desiderio's journey, however, has a double and contradictory objective, for at the same time as he is seeking to annihilate desire, he is also searching for his own desire's object, Doctor Hoffman's daughter Albertina. After a journey that consists of a series of increasingly bizarre encounters, he reaches Doctor Hoffman's laboratories, where he learns that the passionate union of himself and Albertina will provide 'such a charge of energy our infinity would fill the world and, in this experiental void, the Doctor would descend on the city and his liberation would begin'.[60] Faced with the prospect of being instrumental in the final destruction of rationality, Desiderio murders both Albertina and her father, and returns to a life bereft of desire.

The narrative's status as fictionalised autobiography is heavily foregrounded from the beginning. In a separate introduction, Desiderio – now approaching the end of his life and a national hero – opens his story by contemplating the process by which he will recover and restructure his memories:

Because I am so old and famous, they have told me that I must write down all my memories of the Great War, since, after all, I remember everything. So I must gather together all that confusion of experience and arrange it in order, just as it happened, beginning at the beginning. I must unravel my life as if it were so much knitting and pick out from that tangle the single, original thread of myself, the self who was a young man who happened to become a hero and then grew old. (11)

This is very reminiscent of a narrative tactic frequently employed by Borges: that of the narrative within a narrative. 'The Library of Babel', for example, purports to be a document written by a librarian within an infinite library. The correspondence between 'real' and 'implied' author is further complicated by editorial insertions in the form of footnotes, which make reference to an 'original manuscript' by an 'unknown author'.[61] Thus, the author himself (Borges) becomes subsumed into the identity of another (the 'unknown author'); and, albeit accidentally, this relationship is rendered even more complex by the presence of the story's (actual) translator, whose initials, 'J.I.', are appended at the end of the piece.[62] Moreover, the very consciousness of textuality that this complicated structure evokes is the subject of the story, which makes the library – the home of words and books – the model of the universe itself. '[T]he Library is total'[63] and contains everything it is possible to write: one cannot step outside and assess it from a distance, but must formulate hypotheses regarding its origins and purpose from within.

The postulation of narrative as a prison-house is emphasised through the employment of ironic contradiction. Early on in the story, for example, the narrator asserts that:

> Like all men of the Library, I have travelled in my youth; I have wandered in search of a book, perhaps the catalogue of catalogues; now that my eyes can hardly decipher what I write, I am preparing to die just a few leagues from the hexagon in which I was born.[64]

Yet his description of himself as well travelled sits at odds with the circumscribed circumstances of his existence; a similar dichotomy to that evoked in *Hoffman*. Both Borges' unknown narrator and Desiderio are telling their stories in retrospect: when Desiderio ponders on the steps he must take to organise his narrative he is also drawing our attention to its status *as* narrative. The fact that his story is not being told *in media res* means that, however far-ranging his travels might be, in actuality he does not leave the room in which he is writing.

Borges uses this retrospective technique in his work time and time again – most famously in 'The Garden of Forking Paths', another narrative that provides us with insights into the themes and structure of *Hoffman*. Again, the transmission of this story is multi-layered: a fictional introduction asserts that it is a statement by a Prussian secret agent, Hans Rabener, which has been 'dictated, reread and signed by Dr. Yu Tsun, former professor of English at the *Hochschule* at Tsingtao'.[65] Moreover, because '[t]he first two pages of the document are missing',[66] the narrative begins mid-sentence. As in 'The Library of Babel' the subject of the narrative is narrative itself, described by Patricia Waugh as 'both a discussion and an example' of the contradictions that it raises, with the result that it is 'a story of a maze which is a maze of a story'.[67] The central motif is that of the labyrinth – not a physical labyrinth, but a textual one, contained in a work by Rabener's ancestor Ts'ui Pên, in which all possibilities, all reading choices, can exist in simultaneity:

> I understood, 'the garden of forking paths' was the chaotic novel; the phrase 'the various futures (not to all)' suggested to me the forking in time, not in space... In all fictional works, each time a man is confronted with several alternatives, he chooses one and eliminates the others; in the fiction of Ts'ui Pên, he chooses – simultaneously – all of them. He creates, in this way, diverse futures, diverse times which themselves also proliferate and fork.... In the work of Ts'ui Pên, all possible outcomes occur; each one is the point of departure for other forkings.[68]

The infinite variations and possibilities offered by this fictional text, however, is not echoed in the fiction in which it is embedded, as 'The Garden of Forking Paths' ends with the closing down of possibilities. For it is also a story of remorse, in which the narrator, whose 'throat yearns for the noose',[69] is consumed by guilt at the necessary – and irrevocable – murder of someone whom he had in actuality revered. He kills Stephen Albert, the only man to have reached an understanding of the true nature of Ts'ui Pên's labyrinth, as an act of necessity. The removal of the individual to which the name of Albert points transforms the designation into a floating cipher that can be used in the communication of a cryptic message. The agent's 'Secret' which he has to pass on to his employers is 'the location of the new British artillery park on the River Ancre',[70] and he therefore murders Albert in the knowledge that when the act is reported in the papers, the name of the city – Albert – will be broadcast for other Prussian agents to read.

As with 'The Library of Babel', there is a great deal in 'The Garden of Forking Paths' that is reminiscent of *Hoffman*. First of all, the centrality of Albert's name within the latter text may provide us with another gloss on the name of Desiderio's love, Albertina. Although Sage claims that she is 'named for Proust's ineffable object of desire, who's a boy in disguise',[71] it is worth considering that 'Albertina' is also the feminised form of 'Albert'. Both figures – Albert and Albertina – are central to the narrative 'in name' only, for Albertina, too, is a floating signifier, a clue, whose tangible reality remains out of Desiderio's reach for most of the novel. In addition, both murders rebound upon the perpetrator – Rabener's murder of Albert leaves him facing a future in which all is 'unreal, insignificant' in the face of 'my innumerable contrition and weariness',[72] while Desiderio feels himself to be 'condemned to disillusionment in perpetuity'; stranded in a world in which 'there were no more transformations because Albertina's eyes were extinguished' (220). Finally, and perhaps most significantly, both narratives play with temporality, for Doctor Hoffman and Ts'ui Pên substitute a linear concept of time with infinite multiplicity. Ts'ui Pên's construction of a textual 'labyrinth'[73] containing 'an infinite series of times, in a growing, dizzying net of divergent, convergent and parallel times.... [that] embraces all possibilities of time'[74] finds its echo in Doctor Hoffman's concept of 'Nebulous Time', in which 'life itself...become[s] nothing but a complex labyrinth and everything that could possibly exist, did so' (11).

This is not to suggest, however, that Borges is the only influence on *Hoffman*, nor that Carter's admiration of him is unqualified. In a review of a late work by Borges, published in 1979, she puts him in his place in no uncertain terms:

> Monstrous critical overkill of an even more upmarket kind has transformed the Argentinian *petit maître*, Borges into one of the Great Writers of our Time and his most recent collection, *The Book of Sand*...shows sign that he is content humbly to acquiesce in this opinion.[75]

Carter's equivocal opinion of Borges is written into *Hoffman*, channelled, principally, through the character of Desiderio. In his analysis of Latin American literature, *Into the Labyrinth*, Gerald Martin discusses Borges and his work in detail, portraying him a writer whose aim was nothing less but the 'impos[ition] of order on the universe by considering it a vast kaleidoscopic jigsaw puzzle'; and his work a 'compil[ation] of his own eccentric catalogue of books, writers and ideas in order to chart his *own* course through Western literature'.[76] Martin argues that although Borges conceals this egocentric drive beneath a veneer of studied, ironic, detachment:

> [i]t is, despite the mask of indifference and the pretence that all is just a game, an effort to defeat a permanent sense of loss increasingly

heightened by the passage of time, and within this, an attempt to pre-record the image of his own face for posterity.[77]

This is also an extremely apt summary of Desiderio's role in *Hoffman*, for the first page of his memoir consists of a prolonged avowal of disdain for the heroic role in terms that nevertheless instate him in a position of privilege. In spite of his claim that 'I did not want to be a hero' (11), Desiderio's self-selected status as autobiographer places him at the centre of the text – as it is intended to. His habitual pose of indifference only confirms him in this position since it is precisely this characteristic that allows him to negotiate the endlessly metamorphosing landscapes of Nebulous Time:

> I became a hero only because I survived. I survived because I could not surrender to the flux of mirages. I could not merge and blend with them; I could not abnegate my reality and lose myself for ever as others did, blasted to non-being by the ferocious artillery of unreason. I was too sardonic. I was too disaffected. (pp. 11–12)

Desiderio's modesty, like his habit of sardonic detachment, is deceptive. His claim that 'out of my discontent, I made my own definitions and these definitions happened to correspond to those that happened to be true' (13) is a masterly piece of dissimulation, since it asserts precisely what it disavows: the ability to evolve 'true' definitions and impose them on the world around him. Just as much as Borges, Desiderio has an eye on posterity throughout his narrative: as he says, 'if what I had done had turned out of the common good, I might as well reap what benefits I could from it' (pp. 220–21). The end of his introduction, indeed, revolves entirely around the notion of commemoration:

> Expect a tale of picaresque adventure or even of heroic adventure, for I was a great hero in my time though now I am an old man and no longer the 'I' of my own story and my time is past, even if you can read about me in the history books – a strange thing to happen to a man in his own lifetime. It turns one into posterity's prostitute. And when I have completed my autobiography, my whoredom will be complete. I will stand forever square in yesterday's time, like a commemorative statue of myself in a public place, serene, equestrian, upon a pediment. (13)

At the end of the novel, he returns to the conceit of the statue, picturing himself as 'an old hero, a crumbling statue in an abandoned square' (221); and bearing this in mind, the satisfied exclamation he makes on the completion of his story, 'What a thick book my memoirs make!' (221), implies that this entire exercise in autobiography is a self-conscious attempt to assure that his reputation survives his fast-approaching death.

If posterity is one of the motivating factors behind Desiderio's narrative, then grief is the other, and this, too, can be viewed as an aspect of the Borgesian performance as outlined by Martin. Desiderio's habit of disaffection is only partially successful in concealing a devastating sense of loss, because the narrative he creates not only articulates his sorrow, but also constitutes an attempt to textually recover the lost love-object. In one respect, this is Carter's literalisation of the sentiment expressed in *Love*: the construction of the beloved as a spectre, a ghostly outline conjured up out of the fevered imagination of the desperate lover who is haunted by desire. In telling the story of his series of encounters with Albertina – encounters that actually constitute a series of separations – Desiderio recuperates his lost love, a project that appears to achieve its intended aim. However, the final line of the novel, 'Unbidden, she comes' (221), is characteristically allusive, open to interpretation. Does this signal the arrival of yet another memory, or is it suggestive of a more momentous reunion?

In this narrative, therefore, that is at once so wide-ranging and yet so circumscribed, Carter draws upon Borgesian notions of the self and textuality, and also satirizes the narrative pose of the Borgesian authorial persona. Critics differ on whether Borges can be classified as a writer of Latin American magical realism – Maggie Ann Bowers, for example, argues that he

> is only considered to be a true magical realist by Angel Flores who emphasizes the influence of Borges to the extent of claiming that his 1935 collection of short fiction *Historia universal de la infamia* (*A Universal History of Infamy*) was the first example of Latin American magical realist writing.[78]

However, magical realism is a form that undoubtedly allows Carter another perspective from which to view the issue of cultural identity, for as Bowers says:

> magical realism has become associated with fictions that tell the tales of those on the margins of political power and influential society.

This has meant that much magical realism has originated in many of the postcolonial countries that are battling against the influence of their previous colonial rulers, and consider themselves to be at the margins of imperial power.[79]

If Carter's fictions up until the seventies were concerned with charting the collapse of British imperialism, then narratives such as *Hoffman* experiment with the kind of forms that arise out of the dissolution of Britain's dominance as a world power. One of the conundrums of Desiderio's story is that, all the time he is seeking to restore European Enlightenment rationalism to his country, he is aware of, and for the most part resisting, a completely different identification. He is, he confesses to his readers, 'of Indian extraction': like so many of Carter's other male characters – Morris, Joseph and Lee – his mother was a prostitute 'of the least exalted type', and consequently, says Desiderio, 'I do not know who my father was but I carried his genetic imprint on my face' (16). The contradictory subject position that results is evident in the opening of the novel's third chapter, 'The River People':

> The Portuguese did us the honour of discovering us towards the middle of the sixteenth century but they had left it a little late in the day, for they were already past their imperialist prime and so our nation began as an afterthought, or footnote to other, more magnificent conquests. (67)

In this passage, Desiderio's assertion aligns him with both the original inhabitants of the country, who are discovered by the Portuguese, and with the nation that results from that act of conquest. He never quite loses a faint nostalgia for an alternative history that is only partially his (and unrecoverable anyway), in the same way as he mourns for Albertina while also justifying his murder of her. As Aidan Day says of that act, 'doing the right thing does not, can not, exorcise desire, and it presents the desire that has been limited as continuing to haunt and frustrate the mind because though it has been banned, it cannot be exorcised'.[80] The same can be said of histories that counteract the official record: while they may be banned, they nonetheless survive on the periphery of the dominant culture. *Hoffman*, in fact, marks the beginning of Carter's more overt use of her interest in unofficial forms of storytelling: an interest that was to lead her, later in the decade, to the rewritten fairy tales of *The Bloody Chamber*.

Another major intertextual reference in *Hoffman* – again, one that is also important to *The Bloody Chamber* – is to the work of the eighteenth-century pornographer, the Marquis de Sade. As with Borges, Carter does not put the Marquis to use in *Hoffman* uncritically, for it is a text that not only contains allusions to Sadeian plots and situations, but also satirises the behaviours and attitudes of de Sade himself. As was to become clear in *The Sadeian Woman*, a study of de Sade that Carter published in 1979, her use of such references constitute a way in which she can voice her evolving feminist concerns. It constitutes, though, a controversial enterprise, for while second wave feminism was raising many women's consciousness, it seems to have sent Carter's in the opposite direction: to the gutter rather than the stars. But there Carter found a striking and disturbing way of showcasing female victimisation, for instead of turning away from de Sade's vicious treatment of his sexual partners, she confronts him head-on. In this way, she denies him what he most desires – the disgusted opposition that would confirm him in his sacrilege – and instead allows the extremity of his perversion to render him ridiculous.[81]

This technique, which foreshadows the argument that Carter would later deploy in *The Sadeian Woman*, is first evident in *Hoffman*, which features a monstrous caricature known only as the Count. However, the association between Carter's Count and the historical Marquis is quite obvious (with, as both Linden Peach and Aiden Day have noted, a dash of Dracula thrown in for good measure).[82] Sally Robinson has persuasively argued that it is in *Hoffman* that Carter begins to evolve her own brand of gender politics, which separate 'woman' as biological entity from 'woman' as cultural category. It is with the latter, says Robinson, that she is most concerned, regarding 'gender as a relation of power, whereby the weak become "feminine" and the strong become "masculine". And because relations of power can change, this construction is always open to deconstruction.'[83] Thus the Count's monstrous perversity, which the novel disturbingly realises, is inherently unstable, for it will always go 'too far' and collapse in an anti-climactic event. As Robinson argues:

> Carter makes explicit the 'underside' of narrative and history through the use and abuse of pornographic narrative conventions. This 'underside' – the mechanics of desire and pleasure as they function beneath the violent and de-humanising fictions of masculinist pornographic narrative – is brought to the surface and, thus, problematised the identification that is necessary in order for pornography to do its 'work'.[84]

A good example of Carter's use and abuse of pornographic conventions is an episode in which Desiderio and the Count visit the 'House of

Anonymity' (129), a brothel in which every perverse desire can be satisfied. But in Carter's hands it becomes an allegorical space in which relations are rendered down to their fundamental and most brutal constituents. On their arrival, Desiderio and the Count don 'black tights made in such a way that, once we put them on, our genitals remained exposed in their entirety, testicles and all', and 'hood-like masks' (129). In this way, the punters are reduced to their basic male function: as Desiderio unenthusiastically notes, these costumes are 'unaesthetic, priapic and totally obliterated our faces and our self respect; the garb grossly emphasized our manhoods while utterly denying our humanity' (130). So phallic authority is rendered ridiculous in the very extremity of its authority, for everything in this house is subordinated to it – monkeys are 'living candelabra' (130), lions serve as sofas and brown bears as armchairs, while the prostitutes themselves are caged pieces of 'venereal statuary' (131). Desiderio is shocked by these women, whom he considers to have 'passed beyond, or did not enter, simply humanity. They were sinister, abominable, inverted mutations' (132), but he is unable to see what Carter's vicious caricature makes so obvious to her readers: that their monstrosity reflects their role as emanations of male desire itself at its most monstrous. As Sally Robinson says of this passage, 'Desiderio's confusion here marks the contradictions Carter sees in the construction of Woman through pornographic narrative... [he] is forced to confront his complicity in the dehumanisation of the objects of his desire.'[85]

The Count (and by extension Desiderio, at this point in the text) thus becomes another manifestation of one of Carter's favourite figures: the puppet master. The Count is a 'bad actor', whose poses are both 'lurid' and 'ludicrous' (123), and the women he encounters, tied to him by market forces or simple physical force, have no choice but to move according to the dictates of his starkly self-reflexive desires. The Count, therefore, lives in a solipsistic universe in which his own excesses are merely reflected back upon their originator, and as with Carter's other puppeteers, such as Uncle Philip and Honeybuzzard, it is this that is his undoing. In the House of Anonymity, he reduces his chosen prostitute to 'a bleeding moan' (137), but when he, his valet Lafleur and Desiderio are shipwrecked upon the coast of Africa after having been kidnapped by pirates, he is cast out of his monomaniacal universe into the midst of a scenario over which he appears to have no control:

> Oh, what a bedraggled demiurge he was! His black tights were all tattered and torn, so a fringe of toe peeped out at the foot of each, and his prick hung out of the aperture as limp and woebegone as a deflated balloon. He limped like an eagle with a broken wing. (157)

Here, the very costume that put the Count's priapism on display now showcases his inadequacy, and appears to make him pathetic parody of his former self. Yet he is not as entirely powerless as he seems, for Desiderio notes that the Count's desire nevertheless remains the controlling element in this scenario. Presented with a black chieftain presiding over a tribe of cannibalistic amazons, the Count identifies him as 'my hypocritical shadow, my double, my brother': a role he assumes, says Desiderio, because 'such was the Count's desire that he should be and do so' (159). The Count's insatiable desire is therefore seen as consuming itself in the most literal of terms, since he is 'boil[ed] up for soup' even while he 'laugh[s] with joy – pure joy' (163) at experiencing his own pain.

The Count's sadism, though directed so horrifically at others, is ultimately revealed to be auto-sadism, for when all other variations on suffering have been satiated, there is inevitably nowhere – and *no one* – else left to exploit. As for Desiderio, in a relationship reminiscent of that between Honeybuzzard and Morris in *Shadow Dance*, he trails along behind the Count, a fascinated voyeur despite himself. But he occupies the position of sadist in his own right only intermittently, since as many critics have already observed, his assumption of masculine authority is undercut in other episodes in which he is forced to assume a 'feminine' passivity. For example, while accompanying a travelling carnival, he is raped by an entire troupe of Arab acrobats. In the course of 'the most comprehensive anatomy lesson a man ever suffered', he is 'intimately ravaged' and reduced to a 'blubbered wreck' (117). This experience is recalled to him when he is later forced to witness Albertina's rape by a herd of centaurs: he 'suffer[s] with her for I knew from my own experience the pain and indignity of a rape' (179).

But if Desiderio's consciousness has been raised it is not by much, for Carter has not forsaken one of the most unpalatable concepts of her early work – that victimisation entails a certain amount of complicity. The rape Albertina suffers is extremely brutal, but after the event she implies that the source of the event originates from her own fantasies, 'convinced that even though every male in the village had obtained carnal knowledge of her, the beasts were still only emanations of her own desires, dredged up from the dark abysses of the unconscious' (186). This is a controversial conclusion to draw, since it implies that the sexual sadism and extreme misogyny that characterises the Sadeian libertine may in fact be an accurate depiction of sexual politics – moreover, even women gain perverse pleasure from participation in such fantasies.

Again, this foreshadows Carter's argument in *The Sadeian Woman*, in which she draws on the two female stereotypes offered by de Sade – the passive victim, Juliette, or Justine, the female sadist. In Albertina, though, the two positions combine, making her the passive victim of her own sadistic impulses.

This, then, is the central question behind *Hoffman*: where do our fantasies come from? Do they depict reality, or form it? In an environment in which 'our desires . . . had achieved their day of independence' (186), all the protagonists can come up with are hackneyed stereotypes gleaned from myth and pornography, in which everyone is entrapped within a system that offers them a stark choice – between dominance or submission; victimiser or victimised; rapist or raped. Doctor Hoffman claims that 'mine is not an either/or world' but 'an and + and world' (206), yet Desiderio's experiences up to this point have confirmed that an 'either/or world' is precisely what Nebulous Time has become. This is not, in other words, a letting loose of imagination, but merely a more extreme version of the power relationships that sustain mundane reality. Like Desiderio, we have only been fooled into thinking that we are in the realm of radical fantasy: when he finally meets Doctor Hoffman, he is disappointed to find him a dried-up and emotionless little man, 'cold, grey, still and fathomless' (204), 'a man without desires' (211). Meanwhile, the 'true acrobats of desire' (215) are revealed to be little more than lab rats, mechanically rutting in cages in order to produce the 'eroto-energy' (214) that powers Nebulous Time.

In this novel at least, therefore, fantasy manifestly fails to work as an effective subversive force. As Susan Rubin Suleiman says, this speculation that desire might power a revolution is what makes the novel Surrealist, since the Doctor 'scientifically literalis[es] the Surrealist dictum that desire makes the world go round'.[86] However, it is a revolution that ultimately fails to take place, and not because of Desiderio's murder of Hoffman. It was simply never going to happen, for in fact the choice between realism and fantasy was always illusory. In Marcuse's terms, the radical imagination is not overthrown but defeated by being shown to never have been all that radical in the first place. Far from being revolutionary, the imagination never breaks free from the prevailing status quo but merely shores up the symbols and images that sustain it. Such a conclusion does not necessarily mean that fantasy does not have the power to change reality, but it does hint at the complexity of the question

Carter poses – how can we truly liberate our fantasies without recourse to ready-made symbolism which merely perpetuates the existing imbalances of power within society? It was a question she was to work out in the fiction she wrote following her return to England in 1972.

5
My Now Stranger's Eye

Angela Carter ended her sojourn in Japan the way she had begun it – in flight. Just as she had run away from England in order to get away from her husband, so she ran away from Tokyo to get away from her lover; or at least that was what she said to Catherine Stott in an interview she gave for publication in the *Guardian*. Finding her refusal 'to wash his socks or the dishes...incomprehensible', she hints that he decided to transform her into a wife: 'After a while he decided the time had come to really lobotomise me. So here I am – back in Islington, having sort of fled.... You would really have to do yourself over to marry a Japanese.'[1]

At this stage, she told Stott, she was contemplating further travels, 'fully expecting to be drawn further and further East until, who knows, the only thing she is certain of is that her next novel is to be called "The Great Hermaphrodite" and is all about the pan-sexual revolution'.[2] This is a fair summary of what was to become *The Passion of New Eve*, but the novel took five more years to come to fruition, during which time Carter did not settle anywhere for long. She had no permanent home in England in the year following her return: Susannah Clapp records her as spending most of it 'living in the poet Fleur Adcock's East Finchley Flat, then [she] left for Bath, which was "writhing in the last gasp of flower power"'.[3] Things may not have been quite so simple as Clapp (or, more probably, Carter) makes it sound, for during her time in London Carter had become embroiled in another ill-advised relationship. Carmen Callil, recalling her first meeting with Carter in London in 1972, said that Carter's 'first words' to her were 'that the man she was living with had thrown a typewriter at her the night before: did I recommend she leave him?',[4] and in her letter to Neil Forsyth Carter – somewhat melodramatically – describes her move to Bath as

133

yet another escape. 'I nearly got murdered & if he ever comes within 20 miles of me again I shall call the police':[5]

> I am in Bath due to a serious* [*written up in margin: an authentic Freudian slip – I intended 'series'; it wasn't serious, because not much ever is, perhaps] of serio-comic mishaps involving a psychopath; the police; and my father's sudden desire to know where I was. So he gave me enough money to buy a (very) small house in a place where he thought I wouldn't get into trouble.[6]

Carter must have appreciated the irony, for having married to escape her father's benign dictatorship, at the age of thirty-four a series of flights from men had caused her to end up back where she started. On the other hand, as she says in 'Sugar Daddy' and 'My Father's House', the power-balance of the relationship had by now altered. At around the same time as she moved to Bath her father moved back to his original hometown of Banff in Aberdeenshire, thus 'complet[ing] the immigrant's journey... from A to B and back again',[7] which meant that Carter's independence was not, in fact, seriously threatened. In many ways, it improved their relationship, as her later tribute to him in 'Sugar Daddy' testifies.

And she did still travel. She went to Turkey, and to Russia, and even spent three months back in Tokyo gathering material for *New Society* essays. However, her return to Japan did not arouse any nostalgic memories: in her letter to Neil Forsyth, written after her return, she told him that 'I have more or less finished with Japan, now: it is too sad for me.... After six weeks in Tokyo, that fine, clear Japanese depression settles in one's head like the jewel in the head of the wise toad.'[8] From this letter it is clear that this was not a particularly happy period as far as Carter was concerned, particularly since she was earning only a precarious living from her writing. She got a grant from the Arts Council, and wrote 'for the tit-mags until the friend who commissioned the porn insulted his bosses [sic] popsy, so *that* source of income dried up'.[9] She facetiously said she was 'toy[ing] with the idea of marrying money',[10] but in fact she extended her interest in pornography and began writing a book on the Marquis de Sade. It was a project that arose out of her association with Carmen Callil, who in 1972 asked her if she would write a book for her yet-to-be established feminist press, Virago.

So by 1974 Carter had begun work on both *The Passion of New Eve* and *The Sadeian Woman*, although they did not appear in print until 1977 and 1979 respectively – a dramatic change from the sixties, in which she produced four novels in as many years. Certainly, the pressure to earn a living inhibited her production of fiction, since it was the non-fiction that provided her with a much-needed source of income. Interviewed by Alex Hamilton in 1979, she initially blamed *Hoffman* for this state of affairs. Because it had turned out to be 'commercially unviable' she said, 'she had to scrape around to make a living which is contraproductive'. However, to her interviewer's evident confusion, she immediately began to offer a series of alternative excuses for her period of novelistic non-productivity:

> Then she says she was having a nice time and adds that no, she wasn't having a nice time. Then she says she couldn't think of anything to write about. Then she says that she is forced to confess that the psychic compulsion evaporated when she left her husband.[11]

This latter statement is particularly intriguing, implying that Carter's earlier fictional output might have been some kind of therapy; an artistic escape from an unhappy situation. Yet it could also be another instance of the old family talent for magical realism resurfacing, since it suggests an emotional engagement with the process of writing that sits at odds with Carter's consistently repeated assertion that what interested her most was using her fiction as the forum for working out intellectual ideas. In 'Fools Are My Theme', indeed, she takes precisely the opposite tack, arguing that it was her love of the kind of experimental intellectualism that characterised *Hoffman* that led to what she regarded as her decline: 'Autobiographically, what happened next, when I realised that there were no limitations to what one could do in fiction, was just what happened when people tried to get out of genre into mainstream... I stopped being able to make a living.'[12]

According to Lorna Sage, Carter did herself few favours during this fallow period. She had 'no secure relationship with a publisher – between 1971 and 1977 she moved from Hart-Davis to Quartet to Gollancz',[13] and she also changed agents in 1973; a decision that, she told Forsyth, further financially disadvantaged her because 'my cast-off agent withholds my checks'.[14] Perhaps as a consequence, the seventies also saw her becoming, says Lorna Sage,

> painfully prickly about reputations. When she filled in an author's publicity form for Gollancz, who published *The Passion of New Eve* in 1977, there was a section asking her to list her previous publications. Angela wrote simply '7 novels', without giving even the titles.[15]

In spite of the fact that she was struggling to get another book-length project underway, Carter was still writing her 'tales'. *Fireworks* was published in 1974, and although it consisted largely of stories she had composed in Japan, the last in the collection in particular reflects the disillusionment of return. Because the stories were published in the order in which they were written, we can presume 'Elegy for a Freelance' to have been composed around 1973, the period in which Carter was at her lowest ebb. The title itself, which does not bear an immediately obvious relationship to the story, could thus be considered an ironic reflection on the author's own rootless, unattached and nomadic circumstances, although this is not one of Carter's teasing 'Is-it-autobiography-is-it-not?' narratives. Instead, it is an elegy for a failed revolution – or rather, for the idealism that believed that revolution would change the world – and, as such, is also Carter's last farewell to the utopian aspirations of the counterculture.

The story is told in the first person by a female narrator, who recalls her past existence as the member of a radical revolutionary cell. Along with her lover, known only as 'X', she lives in an attic on the fourth floor of a 'tall and narrow'[16] house in a decaying London square, from which she witnesses the disintegration of a decadent and corrupted society. The 'innocent slave of bourgeois aesthetics' (106), the narrator finds the crumbling city a compelling spectacle: 'voluptuous, oppressive, corrupt, self-regarding London, marinating in the syrup of her own decay like *baba au rhum*, while the property speculators burrow away at her guts with the vile diligence of gonococci' (106).

The narrator's perceptions render this urban landscape exotic and perilous: like other middle-class Carter heroines before her, she luxuriates in the *frisson* caused by being in the midst of the utterly different. And the most obvious manifestation of this difference is X himself, who is the latest and the last incarnation of Carter's most disturbing male characters such as Honeybuzzard, Buzz and Jewel. From the window of their attic, he scans people in the square below through the telescopic sights of his rifle, 'practicising indifference' (105); to the narrator, he makes 'assassination sound as enticing as pornography' (108). He recalls his predecessors' utter egocentricity, too, 'engag[ing] in conspiracies because you believed the humblest objects were engaged in a conspiracy against you' (108). The narrator's reaction to X is also familiar, for if he is Honeybuzzard or Buzz, she reflexively falls into the role of a Ghislaine or an Annabel: a woman who has such an unstable sense of self that she willingly submits to playing a bit part in the violent fantasies of another. The voices of her fictional forerunners, as well the recollection of their fates, echo through her protestations of love, which reveal her pathetic, unthinking, naivety: 'I went into his world when I fell in love with him and felt only a sense of privilege in its isolation. We had purposely exiled ourselves from the course of everyday events and were proud to live in parentheses' (105). There's another echo discernable too, of course, that of the Carteresque persona in the Tokyo narratives, who is as spellbound by the spectacle of the alien Other as her lover is with her, with the result that they become mutually complicit participants in an ultimately destructive relationship. 'Your kisses along my arms were like tracer bullets. I am lost. I flow. Your flesh defines me. I become your creation. I am your fleshly reflection' (108).

There is, however, a crucial difference here. This narrative is being related in retrospect by an older, perhaps wiser, certainly more cynical voice that is fully cognisant of the limitations of its vision. Neither Ghislaine nor Annabel survive to see through the object of their masochistic obsession, but this figure not only does that, but disposes of him herself. When X goes too far, murdering their landlord and stealing his money, she and the other members of the cell mount a coup, in recognition of 'our common responsibility as his cause in the random nature of his effect' (116). Following a trial, they hang X from a tree on Hampstead Heath; an event the narrator approaches with chilling detachment:

> When X realised there was no hope for him, he relapsed into silence but, when I slipped the noose around his neck, he asked me if I loved him. I was surprised at that – it seemed to me so far from the point; but I replied, yes, I *had* loved him and I tested the running knot. (118)

The moment when X 'dance[s] exuberantly' at the end of the rope (118) is highly significant, for it marks the moment when the tables are definitively turned on the puppet master, who now is dancing to someone else's tune. Nevertheless, Carter leaves in doubt the issue of whether the narrator has achieved any real measure of freedom by escaping from his clutches, for in many ways, rather like Marianne in *Heroes and Villains*, she ends up only confirmed in her monstrosity. The story's ending is worthy of Dostoevsky or Poe, with the surviving members of the cell squabbling about how to dispose of the body of the landlord, whose blood is leaking through the floorboards, while outside 'the coup had taken place... All the time we had been plotting, the generals had been plotting and we had known nothing. Nothing!' (120).

It is perfectly possible to interpret 'Elegy for a Freelance' as a satire upon the politics of the counterculture, which in this story consists of bourgeois youngsters playing at radicalism while hopelessly out of touch with the real revolutionary forces in society. But in reality it is more about the seventies than it is about the sixties – a point underlined by that the fact that passages in the story echo, virtually word-for-word, extracts from an essay Carter wrote for *New Society* in 1972, *'Fin de Siècle'*. In this piece, Carter casts 'my now stranger's eye'[17] over London, seeing the city as 'an infinitely accommodating whore... over-ripe, voluptuous, oppressive, corrupt, self-regarding, inward-turning who costs twice as much to love as any *grande horizontale* in the entire history of the world'. Although '[a]ge, alas, cannot wither her' (154), London is corrupt and fetid, 'wear[ing] the self-conscious quaintness of parochialism like a singularly unbecoming national dress' (154). So much for the optimism of the sixties in which, '[f]or a brief season, it seemed the old barriers of class and privilege were, if not actually down, at least crumbling' (154). The seventies are not a fair exchange, obscuring the hopeful slogans of the previous decade with words that 'bear... not peace, but a sword: "Support the Stoke Newington Eight", "Armed love", "To hell with the Stoke Newington Eight", "Support the dockers", "Smash the dockers", "Support the IRA", "Smash the IRA"' (155). And while the infrastructure of the city slowly grinds to a halt – '[t]he telephones very often do not work' and '[s]ometimes buses come; sometimes they do not' (154) – popular culture takes refuge in a nostalgic recreation of the past that is 'itself a sickness of the sensibility. Nostalgia, accompanied by the impotent rage that shrieks and gibbers from the hoardings, adds up to a manic-depressive sickness' (156).

While Carter had been away, a Conservative government had come to power. Under the leadership of Edward Heath, it optimistically embarked upon a policy of expansion that, according to Christopher Booker, 'unleashed on Britain's cities the greatest concentration of redevelopment they had ever known'.[18] It is the result of this 'spurious boom in share-dealing and property'[19] that Carter memorably characterises as London's 'ill-favoured offspring, all concrete, glass, steel, chrome and dead' (154). As Carter suggests, the subsequent depression also left its pathological inscription upon the London landscape. Peter Ackroyd, too, observes that in the seventies London's dockside became deserted, 'with echoing warehouses and waste ground the only visible remnant of what had once been one of the city's glories',[20] and proceeds to describe the state of the city in this period in terms very similar to Carter's:

> London lost its vivacity, and much of its energy. The sudden decay
> of trade and commerce, in a city devoted to them, provoked

considerable dismay and anxiety. For a while it seemed that its life
was being stopped. This in turn led to concern among those who
administered the city. London was sick, and needed a fresh access of
life and trade.[21]

The year in which Carter wrote '*Fin de Siècle*', 1972, marked the beginning of this phase of decline, described by Richard Weight as

the most dreadful of the postwar era, a litany of racial conflict in
England, nationalist discontent in England and Wales, war in Ireland
and perpetual strikes everywhere. According to Francis Wheen, 'If
the Sixties were a wild weekend and the eighties were a hectic day at
the office, the Seventies were one long Sunday evening, heavy with
gloom and torpor'.[22]

Carter herself may have been raised in an environment of 'a perpetual
Sunday afternoon',[23] but the 'long Sunday evening' of the seventies
carried with it no such comforting connotations. Just at the point
where the country appeared to be opening itself up to influences and
ideas from outside, and thus to the chance of real cultural change,
Britain turned in upon itself. In this respect, Arthur Marwick, like
Richard Weight, identifies 1972 as a benchmark moment: '[i]t was the
year of the IRA bomb outrage at Aldershot in which five civilians died;
and it was also the first year since before the First World War in which a
union picket lost his life (albeit in an unfortunate accident)'.[24]

In one sense, this insularity was not surprising, as society really did
appear to be in danger of crumbling from within. The period of Edward
Heath's government was plagued by widespread industrial action: in
the winters of both 1972 and 1973 the miners went on strike, bringing
blackouts across the country, and in December 1973 the Prime Minister
instituted a three-day working week in a desperate attempt to save valuable fuel. It was estimated that in 1972 the number of working days lost
because of strikes amounted to 23,909,000.[25]

Britain may have been preoccupied with its own internal crises, but it
was also, paradoxically, poised on the brink of a momentous political,
social and cultural revolution that would see it turning away from its
traditional identification with the Commonwealth in order to become
part of the European Union. 1972 was, again, a significant year for
Britain in this regard, since this was when Britain signed the treaty that
would enable the country to take, in the words of the Prime Minister,
'our rightful place in a truly united Europe'.[26] However, Richard Weight

argues that 'the isolationism which two world wars had bred had not dissipated',[27] and that '[t]he folk memory of the Second World War continued to grip the British imagination'.[28] While the 'island nation' myth may still have retained its potency, the narrative of Empire that it had superseded, though dead, was – perhaps – not buried. Christopher Booker for one argues that the most devastating aspect of the political unrest of the seventies, the IRA bombing campaign on the British mainland, was caused by the long-term consequences of Britain's imperialistic past coming home to roost:

> By the 1970s...the dismantling of the British Empire...was, with the exception of the 'problem' of Rhodesia, virtually complete. Indeed there were those who saw the most intractable crisis which continued to confront the United Kingdom through the Seventies, that in Northern Ireland, as a ghostly epilogue to the whole Imperial story, appropriately centred on the unhappy island where Britain's 'overseas expansion' had first begun eight hundred years before.[29]

In the early seventies in particular, therefore, British identity was in crisis. Society, beleaguered from within and without, seemed to be on the verge of disintegration – according to Arthur Marwick, by 'the end of 1973 and the beginning of 1974 press, television and political platforms were dominated by the question "Is Britain ungovernable?"'.[30] All of this underlies Carter's response to the Britain in which she found herself upon her return from Tokyo, and it provides a particular context for the series of essays she wrote for *New Society* on British cities and cultural life between 1970 and 1976. Four of these essays were republished in *Nothing Sacred* in 1982, grouped together under the title 'England, Whose England?', with additional commentary provided by the author. Interestingly, her introduction makes no mention of the condition of England at the time the essays were originally written, but is instead a potted version of the essay 'So There'll Always Be an England', Carter's reminiscences of her primary school's Empire Day celebrations in the 1940s.[31] Carter records the demise of Empire Day with obvious pleasure: its 'strange innocence...is *happily* irrecoverable' (my italics).[32] In its place, she offers her own 'explorations of the concept of Englishness, and of certain myths of Englishness as they manifest themselves in various English places', replacing a homogenous and stereotyped portrayal of English identity with one that is far more diverse, contradictory – and, most importantly, open to question.

Three of the four essays are about the north of England – displaying what Carter, partially the product of South Yorkshire mining stock, claims to be 'a certain regional bias'[33] – but in 'Bath, Heritage City' Carter confronts the myth of Englishness that she personally finds most inimical. In her preface, Carter underlines the equivocal nature of her response: while 'Bath was a lovely place in which to live ... it is England at its most foreign to me; as self-conscious a performance as Miss Cox's "Empire Day"' (70). Yet she hardly needs to state this so obviously, since her self-conscious desire to puncture Bath's bourgeois complacency is evident from the very beginning of the essay:

> Getting a buzz off the stones of Bath, occupying a conspicuous site not fifty yards from the mysterious, chthonic aperture from which the hot springs bubble out of the inner earth, there is usually a local alcoholic or two on the wooden benches outside the Abbey. On warm summer afternoons they come out in great numbers, as if to inform the tourists this city is a trove of other national treasures besides architectural ones. Some of them are quite young, one or two very young, maybe not booze but acid burned their brain cells away, you can't tell the difference now.[34]

Although the first sentence begins by evoking the very traditional, anachronistic, view of Bath that sustains the heritage industry, Carter is apparently making a move to undermine it by introducing a human, and contemporary, dimension to the scene. However, as her conceit becomes more elaborate, this sense of human interest becomes harder to sustain, for in an ironic reversal that recalls the central conflict of *The Infernal Desire Machines of Doctor Hoffman*, the fantasy of Bath is portrayed as in many ways more 'real' than the down-and-outs and eccentrics that populate its streets. Bath's prosperous Palladian façades may indeed be beautiful, but, says Carter, '[o]ur perceptions of the city are modified by those of everybody else who has ever been here and thought that it was beautiful. It is more than the sum of its parts' (165). To a great extent, Bath is an unreal city. At its 'most beautiful when remembered' (163), it is an 'icon of sensibility' – a nostalgic symbol of an 'England' that has never really existed apart from within art: 'the pictures of John Piper and Michael Ayreton and the Nashes. Mervyn Peake showed its demonic aspect. In fiction, the novels and anthologies of Walter de la Mare; in music, Brittain's setting of "The splendour falls on castle walls"' (165).

   Bath's inhabitants therefore become emanations of the city's sensibility, its distinctive 'charm' – which for Carter is a loaded word, for what, she asks, does charm conceal? 'Charm, the English disease; charm, mask of dementia? The fine-boned, blue-eyed characteristically English madness' (161–62). In the course of the essay, which is, naturally, as much about the author as it is about Bath, Carter is brought face to face with an uneasy confrontation with an unwillingly inherited cultural legacy: 'an Englishness I attempt to deny by claiming Scottish extraction' (164). It is precisely this sense of simultaneous belonging-and-not-belonging that she emphasises in her autobiographical essays; and it is also worth considering her tendency in interviews to both claim and decry the attribute of charm in connection with her own work. Her early novels, she was to say, were distinguished by her attempt to 'charm': 'to try and seduce, and perhaps to rape, my readers'.[35] In 'Notes From the Front Line', for example, she confessed that 'when I was younger and perhaps bruised more easily . . . I used the strategy of charm a good deal – I attempted to disarm with charm'.[36] But charm is 'a great handicap':[37] it is, she writes in 'The Mother Lode', 'our curse'.[38] Owning up to it, though, forces her into an uneasy complicity with her English roots; and, hence, English madness.

That Carter was becoming more preoccupied with issues of personal identity is indicated by that fact that this was the period in which she began writing more overtly about herself, moving away from 'hybrid' narratives into an apparently more straightforwardly autobiographical mode: both 'The Mother Lode' and 'My Father's House' were published in 1976. However, as has already been argued in previous chapters, such pieces should not be taken at face value. Post-Japan, Carter was experimenting with the first-person voice in her novels and short stories as well as in her journalism, and the ease with which these pieces can be aligned with her fiction indicates that they may well be more artful than a strictly documentary interpretation would allow. Japan was certainly a motivating force in this desire to construct for herself a mongrel identity, split between the conflicting imperatives of her English and Scottish roots. Lorna Sage has a point when she says that the time Carter spent away 'confirmed her in her sense of strangeness'.[39] But perhaps these interventions in the autobiographical mode were also a writerly experiment: a defiant assertion of self, of the importance of *her* self, *her* voice, in a period she clearly felt marked a crisis point in her career.

In this respect, the fact that Carter began writing for radio in the seventies is significant, since it can be regarded as a move that was the logical extension of her increasing fascination with personal and subjective points of view. In her preface to a collected edition of four of her scripts for radio, Carter claims that she began 'writing for radio, myself, because of a sound effect. I made it quite by accident.'[40] Contradicting the apparent artlessness of this initial impulse, in her preface she rationalises in detail the multiple attractions that radio held for her; among them its 'capacity to render the inner voice, the subjective interpretation of the world ... It is, *par excellence*, the medium for the depiction of madness; for the exploration of the private worlds of the old, the alienated, the lonely.'[41] It could therefore be said that radio drama strips away the veneer of charm to reveal the 'English disease' that charm conceals, for here there is no appearance to deceive: only words.

As Charlotte Crofts has said in her study of Carter's writing for radio, film and television, Carter's radio scripts suggest 'that radio might offer a unique space for the articulation of (female) subjectivity because of its reliance on the voice'.[42] Crofts proceeds, though, to argue that the liberatory possibilities suggested by such a statement are in fact not wholeheartedly endorsed in the plays, which also 'give ... material voice to mouthpieces of patriarchal culture'.[43] To complicate matters further, not all these 'mouthpieces of patriarchal culture' are men: as Crofts points out, female figures, such as Granny in *The Company of Wolves*, are also suggestive of 'female collusion in the patriarchal suppression of female sexuality'.[44] But one voice remains dominant throughout: that of Carter herself, whose role as storyteller is foregrounded in the verbal performance.

In addition, Crofts also observes that Carter's work for radio can be linked to her short stories on both the literal and the formal level. Not only do both 'Lady of the House of Love' and 'The Company of Wolves', stories that appear in *The Bloody Chamber* collection she published in 1979, begin life as plays for radio, but they resemble each other in that both short story and radio play:

> paradoxically contain more imaginative space precisely because of their 'lack'. The 'blindness' of radio, the absence of visual stimuli, necessitates the stimulation of the listener's imagination ... creating space for their active involvement in the process of meaning production ... The lack of narrative space in short fiction contributes to its open-endedness as a medium, demanding a similarly active readership.[45]

The same point is made by Carter, who constructs 'the presence of the margin of the listener's imagination'[46] as crucial to the radio play; but it is worth observing that the sparseness of both media also creates an audience more reliant on the author, whose words are spun out of air and the dark. As Carter says in her preface to *Come Unto These Yellow Sands*, 'the writer who gives the words to these voices retains some of the authority of the most antique tellers of tales'.[47]

For all that Carter liked to portray this period as the nadir of her career, it was hardly prolonged, for by 1976 both her personal and professional life was beginning to improve. While living in Bath, she met the man who was to become her second husband, Mark Pearce, 'who was mending the roof of the house opposite, came in to paint her ceiling, "and never left"'.[48] In spite of the eighteen years difference in their ages (Carter was the older), the relationship was the most successful and stable of her life, and marked the end of her 'flights' from one man to another. By 1977, the couple had settled in a house in The Chase, Clapham, a move that took Carter very nearly back to her family roots in Balham. Additionally, in 1976 she gained the post of Arts Council for Great Britain Fellow in Creative Writing at Sheffield University, which allowed her to finally enjoy the benefits of a stable income.

But in her seventh novel, *The Passion of New Eve*, Carter returned once again to past history. The novel's American setting draws on the road trip Carter made with her first husband at the end of the sixties that culminated in her journey to Japan. Recollecting the novel in an interview given ten years after its publication, Carter made the connection clear:

> *The Passion of New Eve* was written, oh, ten, twelve years ago, and the vision of America was based on a Greyhound bus trip I took through the States – forgive me, the vision of the United States: one has to be very specific – was based on a Greyhound bus trip I took with my then husband in the summer of 1969, when one really did feel that it couldn't hang on much longer, when the war had been brought home. The feeling of New York there is only very slightly exaggerated. A picture not of how it *was* in New York, but of how it *felt* in that summer of 1969.[49]

Carter's portrayal of New York in this, the most mannered of her novels, transforms it into a city of nightmare, 'a lurid, Gothic darkness'[50] that 'shimmered and stank' (11), in which feminists, blacks and anarchists run out of control. Her narrator, Evelyn, 'a tender little milk-fed English lamb, land[s] plop! heels first in the midst of the slaughter' (9). Having expected 'a clean hard bright city where towers reared to the sky in a paradigm of technological aspiration' (10), he is completely unable to comprehend the chaos in which he finds himself, and embarks on a series of bizarre adventures in the course of which both his identity and his body become transformed.

In *Angela Carter's Curious Room*, Carter suggested that she had attached great hopes to *The Passion of New Eve*, which was intended as:

> my great bid for the European serious novel, it was my great bid for...I'm not going to say it was my great bid for fame, because it wasn't a bid for fame, it was a kind of bet with myself, that I wanted to write what seemed to me a deeply, serious piece of fiction about gender identity, about our relation to the dream factory, our relation to Hollywood, our relation to imagery.[51]

This is indeed a 'serious' book, which is perhaps why Sage dismisses it as 'raw and savage'.[52] Carter forsook much of her humour (and certainly her 'charm') in order to mount an openly polemical attack on socially sanctioned fictions of all kinds, from mythic matriarchs to cinematic *femmes fatales*. As she wrote in *The Sadeian Woman* – published two years later, but researched in tandem with the writing of this novel – 'All the mythic versions of women, from the myth of the redeeming purity of the virgin to that of the healing, reconciling mother, are consolatory nonsenses; and consolatory nonsense seems to me a fair definition of myth anyway.'[53] The time she had spent in a non-Judeo-Christian culture had only intensified her distain for myth, and for any feminist system that appealed to it.

The novel opens with a meditation on the manufactured nature of symbols, through the male narrator Evelyn's nostalgic recollections of the iconic movie star Tristessa, a member of 'the queenly pantheon of women who expose their scars with pride, pointing to their emblematic despair as a medieval saint points to the wounds of his martyrdom' (6). She is a modern archetype of feminine suffering, whose greatest roles are images of doomed Gothic romanticism: Madelaine in *The Fall of the House of Usher* and Catherine Earnshaw in *Wuthering Heights*. In Evelyn's knowing introduction, Tristessa emerges as pure symbol, a manifestation of the collective cultural fascination with the sadomasochistic spectacle of female tragedy. However, Evelyn teasingly hints that knows more than he is letting on here, for he clearly possesses information that he is not yet prepared to share with the reader: 'Tristessa. Illusion. Enigma. Woman? Ah!' (6).

Just as in *The Infernal Desire Machines of Doctor Hoffman*, therefore, what we are reading is a fictional autobiography, related not only with all the benefit of hindsight, but also all the possibility for deception that hindsight allows. In this respect Evelyn's opening contemplation of both Tristessa and the quality of the film on which her image is preserved becomes a meditation on the ability of art to triumph over time. But it is a precarious and partial victory, since although Tristessa 'would always be beautiful so long as celluloid remained in complicity with the phenomenon of persistence of vision...that triumph would die of duration in the end' (5). Desiderio's enduring fear that he will not be remembered after his death is replaced with an acceptance that all images must eventually fade, even one so resonant as Trisessa's.

What Evelyn's arch asides only partially reveal, though, is that this image was never authentic in the first place. In the course of the narrative, Tristessa is revealed to be a fake: a transvestite who 'had made himself the shrine of his own ideas, had made of himself the only woman he could have loved!' (128–29). However, given that Evelyn himself has undergone an enforced sex change by this time, becoming Eve, 'a perfect specimen of womanhood' (68), his/her entire first-person narrative is revealed as an extended exercise in gender masquerade. The masculine point-of-view reproduced in the first chapters is itself an act of narrative transvestism, told by a woman who is recollecting a gender perspective that s/he no longer shares. Alison Lee's point is pertinent here; that although at this point in the text '[l]ogically the speaker is Evelyn . . . it could also be argued that the speaker is an Evelyn who has been temporarily remembered by Eve'.[54]

Gender identity, reproduced and enacted through the medium of the autobiographical text, becomes an extended performance – the narrative equivalent of cross-dressing – and Carter uses this 'cross-narrative' form to viciously critique the kind of essentialist thinking that was an influential aspect of second wave feminism in the seventies. In 1976, the American feminist Adrienne Rich published *Of Woman Born: Motherhood as Experience and Institution*, in which she argues that the earliest religions were matriarchal, and that 'periods of human culture' have existed 'which have shared certain kinds of woman-centered beliefs and woman-centered organization'.[55] Images produced by such cultures 'express an attitude toward the female charged with her intrinsic importance, her depth of meaning, her existence at the very center of what is necessary and sacred'.[56] As the 'Mother Goddess is gradually devalued and rejected; the human woman finds her scope and dignity increasingly reduced'.[57] While Rich does not advocate a return to some kind of pre-patriarchal religious system, such extracts demonstrate that she nevertheless endows the image of the Mother Goddess with positive, potentially liberatory, properties.

Rich's approach was echoed in an even more extreme form by another American radical feminist, Mary Daly. Her book *Gyn/Ecology* was published a year after *The Passion of New Eve*, but its argument exemplifies the views Carter held in such distain. For Daly, patriarchy has appropriated all meanings, myths and symbols to itself in an act of 'Goddess Murder',[58] with the result that women, denied a sense of autonomous selfhood, 'become carriers and perpetrators of patriarchal myth'.[59] The solution posited by Daly lies in 'recognizing that the attempt to murder her [the Goddess] – mythically and existentially – is radically wrong, and demonstrating through our own being that this deed is not final/irrevocable. The deed can be revoked by re-invoking the Goddess within.'[60]

In *The Passion of New Eve*, Carter takes such ideas and stretches them to a ludicrous extent. The Goddess is indeed re-invoked in this novel in the form of Mother, the ultimate radical essentialist feminist, 'the hand-carved figurehead of her own, self-constructed theology' (58). The state of abject awe to which Evelyn is reduced at the sight of her is illustrative of Daly's point that the masculine principle is motivated to brutally suppress the female principle by fear, since 'Female Selves are so terrifying to the patriarchal male that he must reverse/reduce them'.[61]

> Before this overwhelming woman, the instrument that dangled from my belly was useless. It was nothing but a decorative appendage attached there in a spirit of frivolity by the nature whose terrestrial representative she had, of her own free will, become. Since I had no notion how to approach her with it, she rendered it insignificant; I must deal with her on her own terms. (60)

Yet in the realm of Mother, 'myth is a made thing, not a found thing' (56). Far from being some mystical priestess, Mother is a talented scientist who has deliberately carved her own body into the statuesque, many-breasted form that deprives Evelyn of his manhood, both metaphorically and literally. At the core of Mother's motivation lies an extremely calculated political agenda, and all the mystical hocus-pocus surrounding her is nothing more than a rather obvious contrivance. For instance, Evelyn's comment that sitting in Mother's lap was 'like being seated at the console of a gigantic cinema organ' (65) is reinforced when, like a cinema organ, she descends through 'a trap-door in the floor . . . smiling cheerfully' (67). The accompanying music, meanwhile, blares out of hidden hi-fi equipment rather than issuing from heavenly choirs.

Mother, then, is unencumbered by taste or restraint, relying on the sheer potency of her manufactured symbolism to maintain her power: a power she underlines in her castration of the male subject. This is, again, in line with the discourses of the kind of radical feminism typified by Rich and Daly. Neither proposes that the Goddess has some kind of spiritual pre-existence; instead, they utilise her as a symbol of female energy and suppressed female histories. Mother's creation of Eve from Evelyn is a similarly calculated manipulation of the symbolic. Believing that 'Woman has been the antithesis in the dialectic of creation quite long enough', she decides to 'make a start on the feminisation of Father Time' (67) by creating a second Eve from a male body, then fertilizing the body of the new woman with its own male sperm. In so doing, she recalls the kind of agenda put forward in the notorious 'SCUM (Society for Cutting Up Men) Manifesto' issued by Valerie Solanis in 1967: 'It is now technically possible to reproduce without the aid of males (or, for that matter, females) and to produce only females. We must begin immediately to do so.'[62]

Nor do the analogies with radical feminism end there. Evelyn's castration, in which Mother 'cut off all my genital appendages in a single blow, caught them in her other hand and tossed them to Sophia, who slipped them into the pocket of her shorts' (70–71), is the ultimate in stereotypical feminist revenge fantasy. And not only is Evelyn forcibly created woman, s/he is then educated in 'every kitsch excess of the mode of femininity' (71) by being subjected to Tristessa's entire cinematic oeuvre. This is not to say that Mother is oblivious to the distinction between 'essential' femaleness and constructed 'femininity', for even Eve herself, in a rhetorical expostulation addressed to Tristessa, expresses doubts as to whether 'Mother wanted me to model my new womanhood upon your tenebrous delinquescence and so relegate me always to the shadowed half being of reflected light'. Instead hindsight, again, comes into play here. The older Eve who is telling the story has come to 'suspect some other, subtler reason' behind Mother's use of Tristessa's image, because 'now I know that Mother knew your extraordinary secret' (71–72).

Such statements raise the possibility that what Mother intends to do is to put Eve through a process analogous to that endured by every woman who becomes, in Daly's memorable terms, a 'Painted Bird', who is 'given an artificial self ... cosmeticized by her tormentor to such an extent that she is unrecognizable to her own kind'.[63] Eve is, in other words, being compelled to recognise how femininity, like myth, is 'a made thing, not a found thing' – a statement that acquires added force when applied to Tristessa (for whom Daly's notion of the 'Painted Bird' is particularly apt). For what Eve's narrative has steadily been moving towards from its inception is the moment when Tristessa's real identity is unveiled; the point at which 'the parted strands of silver' (127) of her g-string reveal 'the rude, red-purple insignia of maleness, the secret core of Tristessa's sorrow, the source of her enigma, her shame' (128).

Carter's attitude towards Tristessa, one of her great performers, is distinctly mixed. In one respect, Tristessa is absolutely admirable, holding her magnificent fiction together 'only by means of a massive effort of will and a massive suppression of fact' (129). She is an expression of Carter's enduring fascination with the cinematic *femme fatale*, 'somebody who has been completely constructed by the rules of the cinema, really on terms quite strictly of what *men* want from goddesses'.[64] These are Carter's own words, though, and they are suggestive. While on one level, Eve and Tristessa appear to share an ambiguous gender identity, what they also have in common is the retention, to a certain degree at least, of a masculine viewpoint. Eve has been forced to assume a gender s/he never identified with him/herself; with the result that s/he becomes 'my own masturbatory fantasy' (75), while Tristessa, for all her feminine glamour, cannot relinquish 'the awfully ineradicable quality of his maleness' (173). He is 'too much of a woman...for the good of the sex' (173), for he incarnates the male fantasy of woman to perfection.

Heather L. Johnson argues that *The Passion of New Eve* appears to be drawing on narratives of transsexuality that were beginning to appear in the late sixties and early seventies, a period which

> saw the establishment of gender identity clinics and research programmes devoted to the study of gender dysphoria syndrome. The First International Symposium on Gender Identity was held in London in July 1969 and was widely reported in the media. Yet...it was not just professional psychologists and social science researchers who recorded accounts of gender transgression; the men (and less commonly the women) who cross-dressed or underwent sex-reassignment surgery began to write about their experience.[65]

The novel is indeed amenable to such comparisons, although there is no record of how many of these accounts, if any, Carter read. Certainly, however, Tristessa illustrates the 'transvestite influence'[66] that Carter perceived within seventies fashion. In a *New Society* essay, 'The Wound in the Face', published in 1975, Carter observed that make-up had returned to the female fashion scene, 'recapitulat[ing] the glazed, self-contained look typical of times of austerity'.[67] Whereas the face of the sixties either barely wore cosmetics, or were 'cosmetics used as a satire on cosmetics' to create an 'utterly monstrous'[68] look, the seventies created a generation of women who looked like female impersonators.

> Is it that the physical image of women took such a battering in the 1960s that when femininity did, for want of anything better, return, the only people we could go to find out what it had looked like were the dedicated male impersonators who had kept the concept alive in the sequinned gowns, their spike-heeled shoes and their peony lipsticks? Probably. 'The feminine character, and the ideal of femininity upon which it is modelled, are products of masculine society,' says Theodor Adorno. Clearly a male impersonator knows more about his idea of the character he is mimicking than I do, because it is his very own invention, and has nothing to do with me.[69]

The ambivalent attitude Carter displays here towards such figures can be detected in her creation of Tristessa, a being who incarnates and disseminates an image of woman as victim whose greatest virtue lies in her capacity to endure suffering. In 1984, Carter told John Haffenden that although '[q]uite a number of people read *The Passion of New Eve* as a feminist tract...in fact there is quite a careful and elaborate discussion of femininity as a commodity'.[70] There is nothing wrong, therefore, with female impersonators so long as nobody mistakes their performance of the male fantasy of femininity as representative of real women and their situation – but the danger posed by Tristessa's public face is that that is exactly what has happened. Through the mechanism of the Hollywood Dream Factory, Tristessa has become a universal symbol, a marketable icon, whose image has transcended its creator. However, Carter then proceeds to undermine this conclusion by making the relationship between (feminine) image and (male) flesh completely notional later on in the novel. When Eve and Tristessa make love in the desert, 'his flesh...that seemed made of light' (147) is at odds with his physically masculine role in the sexual act as Eve describes it, during which 'the glass woman I saw beneath me smashed under my passion and the splinters shattered and composed themselves into a man who overwhelmed me' (149).

This is event is a meaningful coupling in a novel within which most sexual encounters are enforced – Eve's last sexual experience as a man and his first as a woman are both rapes. In her poetic description of the union of Tristessa and Eve Carter turns to her medievalist roots in order to evoke the allegory of the virgin and the unicorn. The unicorn, symbol of innocence and purity, can only be trapped by using a virgin as bait, since both are uncorrupted beings. The analogy is quite explicit: Tristessa approaches Eve 'as warily as the unicorn in the tapestry at the Musée de Cluny edges towards the virgin' (146), and 'like the unicorn, he knelt beside me in his sacral innocence and laid his hallucinated head in my lap' (147).

Under the circumstances, of course, this cannot be anything other than an ironic invocation. Eve, a man who has become a woman and been sexually active in both incarnations, hardly qualifies for the role of virgin, and the 'sacral innocence' that she attributes to Tristessa emanates not from a divine source so much as the 'celestial limelight' (147) that surrounds the stars in the Hollywood firmament ('"More stars than there are in heaven," had been MGM's motto' [147]). Carter's utilisation of this allegory, though, can be better understood in self-referential terms, since her primary source here is a little-known early work of her own: *Unicorn*, a poem published in 1966. As the title indicates, this similarly constitutes an ironic exploration of the unicorn myth, in which a group of 'strip-club agents cramped in cabinet de voyeur'[71] recruit 'the only virgin to be had' – a girl who is 'raw and huge' with 'breasts like carrier bags'. The unicorn's phallic function is evident throughout the poem: his 'full splendour...manifests itself most potently / at twilight. Then the horn sprouts, swells, blooms / in all its glory'. However, the presence of the male voyeurs deprives him of phallic authority, as they are ultimately manipulating the unicorn as well as the virgin. As Charlotte Crofts, the only critic to have subjected this poem to scrutiny, points out:

> Carter's poem is radical in suggesting that the unicorn (representing phallic masculinity) is a fabulous beast (cultural construction), which can be caught (sustained) only by the virgin (the equally constructed myth of femininity). Rather than simply describing or, worse, reinscribing the patriarchal status quo, the network of looks in *Unicorn* functions to foreground the mechanisms by which these gendered identities are culturally constructed. In other words, the poem works to radically challenge notions of gendered identity by drawing attention to the constructedness of both masculinity and femininity.[72]

The focus of Crofts' analysis is not Carter's novels, but the fact that her summary of *Unicorn* is also an exact description of the result of Eve and Tristessa's union in *The Passion of New Eve* demonstrates how close the two pieces are thematically. *Unicorn*, through its use of 'off-stage' directions, points to the constructedness of both myth and gender, and in the blatant artificiality of Tristessa's and Eve's bodies *The Passion of New Eve* does the same; Tristessa's 'apprehensive' attitude towards 'the masculine apparatus of which he now found himself the master' (146) reminiscent of the way in which the unicorn's horn is registered as an appendage that is acquired (or attached) rather than innate: 'SEE THE HORN / (bend the tab, slit in slot / marked 'x')'.

Establishing a comparison between *Unicorn* and *The Passion of New Eve* in this way encourages us to think of the novel as an elaborate allegory of gender identity, which is indeed how it is most often read. However, while it is certainly open to such theoretical interpretations, the book is no different from any of Carter's other texts in also situating itself within a defined social context. 'The Wound in the Face' proposes a link between extreme versions of femininity and a climate of social austerity, which suggests that Tristessa, in particular, is a figure anchored in, and expressive of, a particular place and time: in this case, America in the summer of 1969. In an echo of her comments to Lisa Appignanesi, Carter told Olga Kenyon that:

> [t]he novel was sparked off by a visit to the USA in 1969. It was the height of the Vietnam war, with violent public demos and piles of garbage in New York streets. If you remember, it was the year of gay riots in Greenwich Village, when they even chucked rocks; so my scenario of uprisings isn't all that far-fetched. [73]

What Carter is referring to here are the famous Stonewall Riots, an event that was pivotal to the establishment of the Gay Liberation Movement in America. When police raided the Stonewall Inn in Greenwich Village on 27 June 1969 – arresting, amongst others, three drag queens – they sparked off violent resistance amongst the gay community. Riots broke out over a period of two days involving more than 4000 participants, and although they included gays and lesbians as well as drag queens, Jerry Lisker in *The New York Daily News* reported it as almost exclusively a piece of transvestite street theatre:

> Last weekend the queens had turned commandos and stood bra strap to bra strap against an invasion of the helmeted Tactical Patrol

Force...Queen Power reared its bleached blonde head in revolt...
'We may have lost the battle, sweets, but the war is far from over,'
lisped an unofficial lady-in-waiting from the court of the Queens.[74]

There is little obvious resemblance between Tristessa and these militant
drag queens, since Tristessa wishes to conceal, not flaunt, his/her 'trans'
identity, thus suppressing the dissident potential it offers. Nevertheless,
once 'outed' as a transvestite, the very assiduousness with which s/he
has preserved the illusion of femininity foregrounds its status as
performance, and thus renders it capable of being read from a radical
perspective.

On a more general level, though, the Stonewall Riots were just one
facet of widespread social disaffection in America at the end of the
sixties. Protests against the Vietnam War were ongoing and vociferous,
while radical feminist groups such as SCUM were advocating guerrilla
action against the oppressive patriarchy. In its Manifesto, SCUM argued
for 'selective and discriminate' acts of 'destruction and killing', and
stated that, while 'SCUM will never instigate, encourage or participate
in riots of any kind or any other form of indiscriminate destruction', it
'will coolly, furtively, stalk its prey and move in for the kill'.[75] As Carter
says in her conversation with Appignanesi, when considered within its
social context, her portrayal of New York in *The Passion of New Eve* – in
which 'female sharpshooters took to sniping from concealed windows
at men who lingered too long in front of posters outside blue movie
theatres' (17) – no longer seems quite so fantastic.

Moreover, this novel also explores the balance of power between
Britain and America in the late sixties and early seventies. National
identity and gender identity collapse into each other at this point:
'Englishness' is gendered 'feminine', while 'American-ness' is 'masculine'.
Evelyn is the most obvious example of this, dislodged from the privileged position conferred upon him by his masculinity the moment he
touches down in New York, whose streets he wonders in 'dazed innocence' (13). His behaviour towards Leilah, the prostitute whom he picks
up and subjects to 'beatings...and degradations' (28) can be viewed as
a desperate attempt to redress the balance – although ironically, of
course, it does nothing of the sort, for Leilah is actually Mother's agent,
who (as in the case of the virgin with the unicorn), is using her body as
bait. While she may notionally be American, Tristessa in her feminine
incarnation is also identified as 'foreign' within a New World context –
after all, her two most iconic roles are as Cathy in *Wuthering Heights* and
as Madeleine in The *Fall of the House of Usher*. While the former is,

obviously, English, the latter establishes a link with a Europeanised Southern Gothic tradition exemplified by Poe. Moreover, her house of 'heaped glass hoops' (110) in the middle of the desert can be viewed as a debased version of the Crystal Palace, and thus as another of Carter's symbolic spaces in which the notion of Empire is both evoked and critiqued. While the original was full of the marvellous products of the British imperialist project, Tristessa's houses kitsch film memorabilia, to much the same ludicrous effect. The Great Exhibition exhibited 'a comic mixture of objects:...railway locomotives, pins, taxidermy, nude statues and Gothic stoves':[76] Tristessa's contains exquisitely-crafted wax models of the most tragic products of the Hollywood dream factory: Jean Harlow, James Dean, and Marilyn Monroe amongst them. But Tristessa's version of the Crystal Palace, too, is destroyed – by Zero, the militant misogynist who positions himself as Tristessa's antagonistic antithesis.

Zero, who kidnaps and rapes Eve following her escape from Mother, is the most blatant representative of American-ness, which in this book is gendered aggressively masculine. He is as much a blatant parody of masculinity as Tristessa is of femininity, for he takes the American myth of pioneering individualism to its extreme. A poet who has 'abandoned verbalisation as a means of communication' (85), he lavishes more care and attention on his extensive gun collection than he does on his seven wives, whom he keeps in conditions of utmost degradation. Yet he also exemplifies America's growing vulnerability at the end of the sixties, for his excessive macho posturing conceals a deep-seated insecurity concerning his virility. Zero is, indeed, an empty signifier, for he is sterile. Only the murder of Tristessa, he believes, will restore his potency, since he is convinced that 'the movie actress had performed a spiritual vasectomy on him' (92).

Locked up in his desert compound with his harem and his guns, Zero can therefore be regarded as emblematic of the kind of extreme nationalism that has spawned such phenomena as the American militia movement, described by Stuart Sim as:

> an intriguing, and worrying, blend of nationalism and religion... [that] pictures itself as an embattled minority within the United States, striving to defend the constitution from those who would seek to amend or overturn any of its basic principles, such as, crucially, the right to bear arms.[77]

Sim proceeds to point out that women are regarded as a particular threat as far as such movements are concerned, since they traditionally have a very masculine, control-orientated ethos, with deeply traditional ideas about gender roles and sexual politics... That anxiety, stemming from the emergence of the 'modern woman' (a phenomenon more marked in American than European society), led to a reassertion of masculine values within Protestant fundamentalism in the late 19th and early 20th centuries in America, that still marks out the movement today.[78]

Bearing Sim's comments in mind, it might seem somewhat inappropriate to argue that Mother, too, could be considered 'American' on the same terms as Zero. But this is a novel, after all, in which gender has been cut away from the biological body, and both Mother and Zero are militant grotesques, potent and dangerous combinations of religious fundamentalism and dogmatic, dogged, individualism. Hatred and fear of the 'Other' lies at the core of both their philosophies, which in turn become emblematic of American anxieties in the sixties and seventies. While Britain officially entered the Common Market on 1 January 1973, thus – however unenthusiastically – aligning itself with a European identity, America under the Nixon administration was in the midst of crisis. The president was the first in history to be forced to resign his office, while massive popular protests brought the Vietnam War to an ignominious close in 1975, when American helicopters airlifted the remaining troops out of Saigon.

As far as Carter was concerned, though, it was this event that at least partially redeemed America, and she regarded it as 'their finest hour... in human terms... the single most glorious event since the abolition of slavery'.[79] In *The Passion of New Eve*, however, the balance of power between Old and New worlds remains unresolved. Mother, realising that her manipulation of myth is meaningless, and that thus 'she never really existed',[80] deteriorates into a mad vodka-swigging derelict, while Eve leaves the coast of America for – where? That question hangs in the air unanswered, for Carter does not anchor Eve's autobiographical voice in any kind of context. Instead, it issues from somewhere on the ocean, bound to an inexorable replaying of the past and the ever-present image of Tristessa, who 'often comes to me in the night, serene in his marvellous plumage of white hair' (191).[81] Perhaps the best way to comprehend this (non)conclusion is through reference to a passage from *The Sadeian Woman*:

The goddess is dead.
And, with the imaginary construct of the goddess, dies the notion of eternity, whose place on this earth was her womb. If the goddess is

dead, there is nowhere for eternity to hide. The last resort of homecoming is denied us. We are confronted with mortality, as if for the first time. (110)

The Passion of New Eve, like its predecessor, was not a great critical success for Carter; indeed, she told Olga Kenyon that 'only *Gay News* gave me a really sympathetic review'.[82] Things were shortly to change, however, for under the prompting of her editor at Gollancz, Liz Calder, Carter began writing different kinds of stories, which, collected, were to become one of her most successful books – *The Bloody Chamber*, published in 1979. She had been interested in fairy tale for a long time, and in 1977 had published a translation of Charles Perrault's fairy tales, also for Gollancz. Carter's views regarding fairy tale has been well documented, but is summed up in the opening lines of her introduction to *The Virago Book of Fairy Tales*, published in 1991:

> Although this book is called 'The Virago Book of Fairy Tales', you will find very few actual fairies within the following pages ... for the term 'fairy tale' is a figure of speech and we use it loosely, to describe the great mass of infinitely various narrative that was, once upon a time and still is, sometimes, passed on and disseminated through the world by word of mother – stories with no known originators that can be remade again and again by every person who tells them, the perennially refreshed entertainment of the poor.[83]

For Carter, the virtue of the fairy tale lies in its status as an inherently democratic narrative form, always open to appropriation and interpretation. Admittedly, though, there is a certain inconsistency in this opinion as far as she is concerned, since – as has already been discussed with regard to her radio plays – the mode as she defines it places the figure of the storyteller centre stage. She (and it almost always is 'she', says Carter) is the figure who 'has tailored the story personally, to suit an audience of, say, children, or drunks at a wedding, or bawdy old ladies, or mourners at a wake – or, simply, to suit herself'.[84] And Carter certainly did 'suit herself' with regard to the stories in *The Bloody Chamber*, as the amount of controversy they have continued to generate indicates that pleasing her audience by providing them with a comfortably reassuring read did not feature on her list of priorities. A major source of that controversy lies in the fact that, all the time that she was working on *The Bloody Chamber* stories, she was still trying to complete *The Sadeian Woman*.

Remarks Carter made to Les Bedford around this time indicate that *The Sadeian Woman* was becoming a rather tiresome burden as far as she was concerned. As she said, she had already been working on it for three years, and was by now desperate 'to finish the book for my own peace of mind'.[85] Indeed, three years may have been a slight underestimate of the period of time she had been researching de Sade, since she had claimed to Neil Forsyth that 'most of the notes for the Sade book are completed' in August 1974. She had, apparently, looked into using the material for a PhD thesis, 'but plans thwarted by a) bureaucracy of London University, b) a feeling...that I could use the material better, ultimately, in a novel'.[86] This is, however, slightly at odds with Carmen Callil's assertion that *The Sadeian Woman* had always been intended as a book for Virago Press. Carter never did submit it as a PhD. thesis, though, and *The Sadeian Woman* was indeed eventually published as one of Virago Press' inaugural titles.

But Carter's ongoing research on pornography certainly had an obvious impact upon her creative writing. The stories in *The Bloody Chamber* may draw on the basic narratives of some of our culture's most well-known fairy tales, such as 'Beauty and the Beast' and 'Little Red Riding Hood', but every one of them is shot through with a Sadeian sensibility. Again, her interview with Les Bedford makes this association perfectly clear, in which she says of the title story in the collection, a rewrite of 'Bluebeard', that she 'did actually manage to get in most of de Sade, which pleased me'.[87]

The Sadeian Woman is therefore a key text for the understanding of Carter's fiction of the seventies, lurking in the background of everything else she wrote in this period (an observation that adds another twist to a remark she made to Les Bedford, that de Sade was 'like Rasputin...he won't die').[88] *The Sadeian Woman* appears, initially at least, to set itself up as a kind of *apologia* for de Sade, conferring upon him the status of 'moral pornographer', a figure defined by Carter as:

> an artist who uses pornographic material as part of the acceptance of the logic of a world of absolute sexual licence for all the genders, and projects a model of the way such a world might work. A moral pornographer might use pornography as a critique of current relations between the sexes. His business would be the total demystification of the flesh and the subsequent revelation, though the infinite modulations of the sexual act, of the real relations of man and his kind. Such a pornographer would not be the enemy of women, perhaps because he might begin to penetrate to the heart of the

contempt for women that distorts our culture even as he entered the realms of true obscenity as he describes it. (19–20)

Whereas pornography conventionally portrays infinite modulations of the sexual act which excludes any awareness of 'the social context in which sexual activity takes place, that modifies the very nature of that activity' (16), de Sade's work threatens to demystify the flesh by rendering apparent the radical asymmetries of power that dictate the nature of sexual relationships. More than that, argues Carter, he is radical because he is capable of imagining women as sexually active beings, rather than the mute recipients of male desire:

> He was unusual in his period for claiming rights of free sexuality for women, and in installing women as beings of power in his imaginary worlds. This sets him apart from all other pornographers at all times and most other writers of his period. (36)

However, much as Carter might admire de Sade – for his atheism, his defiant obscenity, for 'the ferocity of his imagination' (32) – she is also highly critical. By the end of the book, she has concluded that he is, after all, a 'simple pornographer' (132), since he dare not explode all the taboos upon which his art depends: '[h]is perversion . . . is almost like a magic circle which he has constructed around himself to preserve himself from the terrible freedom to which his ideas might lay him open' (132). This means that the liberatory possibilities offered by the Sadeian woman are curtailed, for in the final analysis she 'subverts only her own socially conditioned role . . . not . . . her society, except incidentally, as a storm trooper of individual consciousness' (133).

The Bloody Chamber thus becomes another means by which Carter can contend with de Sade – it is Margaret Atwood who has adroitly summed it up as 'a "writing against" de Sade, a talking-back to him'.[89] The villains in these stories, both male and female, are capable of being viewed as prototypes of the Sadeian libertine, while the heroines tread an ambiguous, risky path towards the satisfaction of their own desires. This is well illustrated in the story that begins the collection and gives it its title, 'The Bloody Chamber'. It is narrated from the point of view of the libertine's naïve victim – his fourth wife, who like her predecessors is doomed to satisfy his nihilistic appetite, 'that reality of his that came to life only in the presence of its own atrocities'.[90] The 'atrocious loneliness' the narrator perceives in 'his blind, shuttered eyes' (35) is a direct echo of Carter's description in *The Sadeian Woman* of 'the lonely freedom of the libertine, which is the freedom of the outlaw, a tautological condition that exists only for itself and is without any meaning in the general context of human life' (99).

However, in its original context this passage refers to a woman, not a man. It appears in a chapter on de Sade's Juliette, a woman who frees herself from the strictures of socially sanctioned femininity by becoming a monster in the mould of the Marquis himself. The narrator of 'The Bloody Chamber' goes some – though not all – the way towards this identification, a process obvious from the outset of the narrative. From the beginning, Carter makes the economic imperatives underlying the narrator's decision to marry the Bluebeard figure clear: raised by her mother in genteel poverty, she cannot help but be attracted to a man who is 'rich as Croesus' (10). Thus, even as the story opens, she is already positioned as to a certain extent an active participant in her fate, a complicity that becomes even more obvious when the Marquis' coded allusions to his desires stir an answering response in her. When he gives her as a wedding present a 'choker of rubies, two inches wide, like an extraordinarily precious slit throat', and she spies the 'sheer carnal avarice' the sight of his bride wearing it arouses in him, she 'sense[s] in myself a potentiality for corruption that took my breath away' (11). Carter makes it apparent that this is the libertine's ultimate trick: he does not force the narrator to do anything, but instead lures her on through the careful cultivation of her own libidinous instincts.

> Your thin white face, chérie; he said... Your thin white face, with its promise of debauchery only a connoisseur could detect.
> A log fell in the fire... I felt as giddy as if I were on the edge of a precipice; I was afraid... not so much of him... I was not afraid of him; but of myself. I seemed reborn in his unreflective eyes, reborn in unfamiliar shapes. (20)

'The Bloody Chamber' therefore exemplifies Carter's enduring refusal to allow women the consolatory role of victim. These heroines do not fatalistically lie back and think of England, but instead join in, often enthusiastically, the process of their own defloration. So in Carter's version of the tale, Red Riding Hood not only sleeps with the wolf, she strips both him and herself, and burns their clothes in the fire to signify the irrevocableness of the act. The tiger's bride willingly joins him amongst the 'gnawed and bloody bones' (66) that stand as evidence of his carnivorous appetites, while the female vampire in 'The Lady of the House of Love' preys on young men, as much dedicated to the satisfaction of her own destructive desires as any of de Sade's regiment of monstrous women.

Sally Keenan has argued of *The Sadeian Woman* that it displays 'almost heretical disagreement with certain aspects of feminist thinking current in the 1970s'.[91] In its equally strong rejection of idealistic notions of maternity and its refutation of the high moral ground to which only innocent victims can lay claim, the same could be said of *The Bloody Chamber*. Such implications were passed over by many of the reviews and early critical analyses, which approached the collection as typical of the kind of feminist revisionism of traditional tales that was becoming a fashionable endeavour during the 70s and 80s, exemplified in the work of such writers such as Anne Sexton, Robin McKinley, Jane Yolen and Tanith Lee. But slightly later critics such as Robert Clark and Patricia Duncker reacted strongly against Carter's conflation of fairy tale and pornography. Duncker, for example, argues that both forms encode a misogyny that cannot simply be excised. Carter may think she is subverting these modes from within, but in actuality she cannot help but 'rewrite...the tales within the strait-jacket of their original structures', and thus she 'merely explains, amplifies and re-produces rather than alters the original, deeply, rigidly sexist psychology of the erotic'.[92] Such controversies though, have ensured the enduring visibility of *The Bloody Chamber*, which continues to be one of Carter's most widely discussed texts.

The Bloody Chamber was a benchmark text for Carter in another way, too. In *The Sadeian Woman* she asserts that the point at which de Sade's radical project founders is when the figure of the mother is on the verge of becoming a fully eroticised being. In the end, though, de Sade cannot bring himself to take that final step, ensuring that the mother remains 'the primal "good" object' (134) against which the excesses of the libertine are directed. But in 'The Bloody Chamber', Carter restores the mother to the narrative as an autonomous figure, for in a neat turning of the tables it is she who rides in to save her daughter. She may have been 'an ex-colonial', said Carter in 1987, but she is, nevertheless 'a nice mother...the right kind of person'.[93] Her 'adventurous girlhood in Indo-China', has stood her in good stead: she has already 'shot a man-eating tiger with her own hand' (7), and she faces the Marquis as if he were merely another rogue predator, shooting him in the head with her late husband's service revolver.

Carter was consistent in her claim – which her autobiographical essays suggest springs from her own experience – that 'a woman's relationship with her mother is very, very difficult...much more difficult, much more complicated, much more obscure than a boy's relationship with a father',[94] which is perhaps why she chose to write such a relationship out of most of her fiction. But while *The Passion of New Eve* replaces simple absence with 'Mother', a monstrous archetype of maternity, in 'The Bloody Chamber' she is simply 'a mother', whose attachment to her daughter is so strong that a simple conversation about gold bath taps arouses a '*maternal telepathy* that sent my mother running headlong from the telephone to the station' (40) [italics Carter's]. The figure of the grandmother fares less well in this text – in 'The Company of Wolves' she is reduced to an unmourned heap of bones beneath the bed, and in 'The Werewolf' she *is* the wolf, killed off by her granddaughter. In the books to come, though, Carter begins to conflate the two figures of mother and grandmother, which results in the creation of fiercely maternal characters whose age places them in an ambivalent relationship with the girls who could equally as well be their granddaughters as their daughters – and may in biological fact be neither. It would, once again, be simplistic to say that we can see Carter using her fiction to make peace with her mother, but from *The Bloody Chamber* onwards it does begin to display markedly more tolerance of the maternal figure.

So although Carter may have returned to England in 1972, *The Bloody Chamber* marked her real homecoming, in both personal and professional terms. Settling in South London with Mark Pearce, she had returned, quite literally, to the scenes of her childhood; something she did in her writing, too, for her rewritten fairy tales, with their scenes of metamorphosis from man to wolf, woman to tiger, recall a comment Carter made to Lisa Appignanesi, that the first stories she ever wrote as a child were all 'about animals'.[95] And, more generally speaking, they demonstrated her forsaking the Oriental and North and South American landscapes that had characterised her writing of the seventies for something, if not yet quite English, certainly Northern European. In fact, they were mostly written during her time at Sheffield, which was why, she said, 'they are all such cold, wintry stories'.[96]

Lorna Sage also credits *The Bloody Chamber* with confirming Carter in the role of public storyteller, maintaining that '[t]he fairytale idea enabled her to *read* in public with a new appropriateness and panache, as though she was *telling* these stories'.[97] Carter took on, in other words, the role of Mother Goose as understood in the terms outlined by Marina Warner: subversive, ribald, emblematic of 'female sexual knowledge and power'.[98] And this analogy also holds true in another context. Warner comments that 'in popular narratives, their shuttles flashing back and forth between oral warp and literary woof, the character of the teller encloses the tenor of the tale; . . . the teller enters and takes part in the story, becomes a protagonist':[99] Carter, at this point in her career, did indeed begin to become a protagonist in her own story, an autobiographical narrative that, over the years, became ever more self-contained and self-referential. The first major interviews with her, conducted by Les Bedford for Sheffield University Television and by Lorna Sage for *New Review*, both appeared in 1977.[100] In Sage's interview, in particular, it is possible to see Carter playing up the authorial persona she had already established the year before in 'The Mother Lode' and 'My Father's House', delivering what amounts to a virtual *précis* of these pieces: her birth 'as Dunkirk fell', the evacuation of the family to Wath-upon-Dearne, the tough-as-old-boots 'Yorkshire granny', the mixed national identity.[101] She ended the decade, therefore, having not only re-established her career, but also having created a public identity for herself: that of the teller of tales.

6
You Write From Your Own History

The final year of the seventies began with another Winter of Discontent: on 27 January 1979, 1.5 million public service sector workers staged a day of action, followed by a series of selective strikes across the country. In May, the Conservatives won the general election, bringing Britain's first female Prime Minister to power. Angela Carter's view of Margaret Thatcher – one shared with many of Britain's intelligentsia – was characterised by horror tinged with unwilling fascination. In an essay written for the *New Statesman* in 1983, when Mrs Thatcher was running for re-election, she presents her as a wholly artificial monster, nothing more than a 'complex of signs labelled Margaret Thatcher'.[1] Under the influence of her 'media advisors', she has been turned 'into a comicbook superheroine', an effect achieved 'not by toning down her patent absurdity but by playing it up'.[2] So the Thatcher image does not attempt to pass itself off as naturalistic: instead, '[w]e are told exactly how she does it and then invited to applaud', for 'the image is more important by far than the meaning behind it'.[3] In this piece, Margaret Thatcher emerges as a grotesque, a pantomime dame, an imperialistic wet dream run riot. What she is, in other words, is the living embodiment of 'patriotism as theatre' and thus the natural inheritor of the crown of the Rose Queen that was discarded in the aftermath of Empire Day. As Carter says:

> Perhaps it was inevitable that in our post imperial anomie, and hangover after the two-hundred-year spree, Britain should throw up the apparatus to create a twopenny halfpenny demagogue of the kind known and feared throughout the Third World. Should release the madwoman who'd always been gibbering in the Tory attic, with its lugubrious lumber of Union Jack draped gallows...And should give this symbolic entity the keys to the whole asylum.[4]

One of the defining characteristics of Margaret Thatcher's government was her attempt to redefine Britishness on her own terms. Richard Weight, indeed, calls her 'the most nationalistic Prime Minister of the postwar era'.[5] Her avowed intent was not just to revive Britain's economic fortunes, but 'to renew the spirit and solidarity of a nation'.[6] Notoriously, Margaret Thatcher promoted a return to 'Victorian values', which she defined as 'the values when our country became great ... As our people prospered, so they used their independence and initiative to prosper others.'[7] Thus, she presided over what Weight describes as the 'reviv[al] of nineteenth-century British nationalism, presenting the self-reliant individual as the microcosm of a proud, self-reliant nation'.[8]

This nationalistic revival attained its apotheosis in the Falklands War of 1982, in which the British armed forces repelled an Argentinian attempt to reclaim the British-occupied Falkland Islands in the South Atlantic. According to Eric J. Evans, public opinion polls suggested that 80 per cent of the population supported the Government's decision to send a military task force to the Falklands, and in the aftermath of victory Margaret Thatcher's speeches utilised the discourse of nationalism to ever more Churchillian effect:

> We have ceased to be a nation in retreat. We have instead a new-found confidence – born in the economic battles at home and tested and found true 8,000 miles away. We rejoice that Britain has rekindled that spirit which has fired her for generations past and which today has begun to burn as brightly as before. Britain has found herself in the South Atlantic and will not look back from the victory she has won. When we started out there were the waverers and the faint-hearts, the people who thought we could no longer do the great things we once did, those who believed our decline was irreversible, that we could never again be what we were, that Britain was no longer the nation that had built an empire and ruled a quarter of the world. Well they were wrong.[9]

In fact, the war led many commentators to make direct comparisons between Margaret Thatcher and Churchill, as evidenced by Max Hastings's and Simon Jenkins's assertion that '[i]t is doubtful if any other British Prime Minister since Churchill ... would have sent the task force and supported it right through to victory'.[10]

The Falklands War also marked an increase in overt control of the press by the state. Coverage of the war was rigidly supervised and censored by the government, whose relations with the BBC, in particular, was hostile throughout the 1980s. Alistair Davies and Alan Sinfield claim that the BBC 'came under sustained pressure from the government' during this period, because of attempts to present even-handed coverage of Northern Ireland and the Falklands War.

> Through its power to set the level of the licence fee, the government (by reducing its resources) forced the BBC to make fundamental changes to the way it operates, with the result that many programmes are no longer made by the BBC's permanent staff but are commissioned from independent production companies. For the Thatcher government's supporters, the government's approach brought a new efficiency to the BBC; to its detractors, it represented a conscious attempt to dismantle the Corporation, in part to free government from an immensely powerful restraint, in part to make possible the sale of the BBC to commercial organisations sympathetic to the Conservative party.[11]

The Conservative government of the eighties sought to exert control over all aspects of the arts by using the same tactic; reducing and controlling state funding in order to force the arts to make up the short-fall by functioning as businesses seeking corporate sponsorship. As Davies and Sinfield argue, not only did this compromise their ability to produce experimental, less 'popular' work (since corporations were unlikely to fund anything that would not be profitable), but it also changed public perception of the cultural function of the arts:

> The election in 1979 of Margaret Thatcher as Prime Minister brought a fundamental change ... to the notion that the arts had anything to contribute to national morale or self-consciousness. In particular, the idea (current since 1945) that the arts provided an indispensable national forum – in which current views of the world could be questioned or contested, and through which new views could be disseminated – was rejected as the self-serving justification of a subsidised left-wing elite.[12]

No wonder that Salman Rushdie, Angela Carter's great friend and artistic contemporary, regarded Thatcherist Britain in despair: 'nanny-Britain, strait-laced Victorian Britain, thin-lipped jingoistic Britain, is in charge. Dark goddesses rule; brightness falls from the air.'[13] Carter and Rushdie both actively campaigned against the Falklands War: Veronica Horwell, for example, recalls meeting both of them at 'a public meeting at the ICA of dissenters from the victory flypasts'.[14] Carter was convinced that the advent of Thatcherism necessitated a return to the kind of political activism that had characterised the sixties, but pessimistic about the possibility of this happening in actuality in the context of the eighties. In 'Anger in a Black Landscape', published in 1983, she argues vehemently against both the Falklands War and the siting of Cruise missiles in Britain, events that meant, she said, 'my forties began, as my twenties had done, in a fury of rage'.[15] However, she is not very optimistic regarding the chances that her call to 'rage, rage against the dying of the light'[16] will gain much response, for not only have '[w]e ... learned to live with the unthinkable and think it',[17] but we are also handicapped by the fact that the British are 'an exceedingly law-abiding race', who don't 'want to make a fuss – another British characteristic'. Although Carter 'include[s] myself in this',[18] towards the end of the essay she juxtaposes her 'English' passivity with 'Scottish' intransigence, which has given her 'a hereditary facility for vituperation'.[19]

So, while public protests might have been muted in a dominant atmosphere of passivity, Carter exercised her Scottish 'facility for vituperation' through her fiction. In the process, she finally became an established literary figure, producing work that exhibited precisely what Davies and Sinfield argue what the government found most inimical about the arts: the stringent interrogation of current world views, and the dissemination of new and radical ideas. (Carmen Callil sums her up as 'the prime representative of a British personality that had not been privatised away'.)[20] Her novels in particular can be viewed as positioning themselves in ironic relationship to the Thatcherist return to 'Victorian values'. *Nights at the Circus* (1985), and *Wise Children* (1991) both revisit the *fin de siècle*, the moment when the Victorian period was drawing to a close, in order to mount a critique of notions of the very notions of nationalism and empire Thatcherism was attempting to revive. Moreover, both texts make liberal and overt use of Carter's enduring metaphor of 'patriotism as theatre' taken to ever more grotesque extremes. *Nights at the Circus* is set in the music hall and the circus, while *Wise Children* juxtaposes downmarket 'popular' theatre, such as musical revues and pantomime, against 'legitimate' theatrical productions, and the novels' major characters (Fevvers in *Nights at the Circus* and the Chance twins in *Wise Children*) work to undermine culturally-determined categories of class, taste and nationalism. These texts can be viewed as Carter's riposte to Thatcherist policies and politics; its attack upon the independence of the arts, and its promotion of an aggressive patriotism which overtly drew upon the jingoistic rhetoric of war and empire.

Both *Nights at the Circus* and *Wise Children* are also distinguished by their renewed interest in 'Englishness'; but one that stands in direct contradiction to Thatcherist versions of national identity. Although she fails in her attempt to get to Japan, Fevvers mirrors her author's own travels through Russia: but her voice remains stridently, defiantly, Cockney, as does the narrative of Dora Chance, whose sojourn in Hollywood does nothing to impinge upon her identity as Balham born and bred. Bearing this in mind, it is ironic that Carter began this decade of her life once again abroad, this time in America. It was, however, for very different reasons from her previous visit to the States at the end of the sixties, which culminated in her running away from her husband to Japan and another man, for at the beginning of the eighties she was travelling in a professional capacity, as Visiting Professor on the writing programme at Brown University in Providence, Rhode Island.

It was an experience Carter recorded in an essay written, as ever, for *New Society*, 'Snow-Belt America', in which she offers a generally favourable impression of Providence, which she depicts as a kind of transatlantic version of Balham. A small city, with a shrinking, melting-pot population, in suspension between decline and upswing, it was, notes Carter approvingly, founded by a man who:

> was expelled from the commonwealth of Massachusetts in 1636 for saying he didn't think the king had any right to cede land that belonged to the Indians. He had a good civil rights all round, and let in Jews and Quakers once he had a place of his own'.[21]

So although on first glance Providence 'appears to present an apt and homogenous face. That bony, uncomfortable, New England face, with the blue, fantatic's gaze', '[o]n closer examination, this New England face...dissolves'.[22] It is replaced by a variety of colours, ethnicities and accents – Portuguese, Italian, Lusitanian, Afro-American – living in suburbs that are on the verge of being appropriated by the more prosperous middle classes.

'Snow-Belt America' also shows Carter laying claim to her old, familiar position of outsider. Having described the different ethnic communities of Providence and provided a thumbnail sketch of the city's history, she then withdraws, claming to 'understand none of all this...I can't get a grip on it'.[23] Presented with 'a plurality of worlds',[24] she 'can't put all these separate conditions together and make sense of them, and nobody seems to try, anyway'.[25] But it is not plurality that is the problem: instead, it is the encroaching spectre of homogeneity that she finds threatening, the point at which 'houses retreat behind prim hems of grass...No laughter of children. No graffiti in Portuguese, no hearts or names of footballers.'[26] Although Carter herself may have become increasingly respectable, 'Snow-Belt America' shows her allegiance still lying with the 'peculiar, rootless, upward, downward, sideways socially mobile...twilight zones'[27] that characterise her own personal history.

The eighties therefore saw Carter settling down only in the broadest sense of the term – in what Lorna Sage describes as 'a most vagrant fashion. She had travelled all over the place for jobs, residencies, and tours, and the Clapham house was always being changed around.'[28] She spent a fair amount of the decade abroad: as well as the stint in Providence, Rhode Island, she spent three months as writer in residence at the University of Adelaide in 1984, and short periods of successive years back in America: 1985 in Austin, Texas; 1986 in Iowa City; and 1988 in Albany, New York State. She also taught part-time on the writing MA at the University of East Anglia between 1984 and 1987, and occasional workshops elsewhere. By all accounts, she enjoyed teaching and was good at it, becoming a generous mentor to many talented aspiring writers in both Britain and America. The novelist Pat Barker, who was tutored by Carter at a residential creative writing workshop held at Lumb Bank in West Yorkshire in the early eighties, described her as 'a born teacher as well as a born writer', who was 'very good at recognizing people with very dissimilar talents from her own'.[29]

Carter also continued to work in other media. Her interest in radio lasted until the early years of the eighties – her last radio play was broadcast in 1984, by which time she was beginning to write cinematic adaptions of her own fiction. She began work on a film script of 'The Company of Wolves', already a radio play and a short story, in 1982. Produced by Neil Jordan, it was released in 1984. According to Jordan, Carter gained a great deal of satisfaction from her involvement with the production: '[s]he was thrilled with the process, because she loved films, and had never really been involved in one'.[30] In 1988, her adaptation of her second novel, *The Magic Toyshop*, was released as a feature film in 1987 and broadcast on ITV the following year.[31] It may be that this transition from radio to film indicates in a shift in Carter's own conception of her artistic status. While, as has already been discussed in the previous chapter, radio became her way of asserting her voice at a time when she felt it was not being heard, her writing for cinema and TV showcases her status as a successful writer. She made sure that she kept control of her ideas, too: Charlotte Crofts notes in relation to *The Magic*

Toyshop that Carter's inclusion in the process of the adaptation of her own text was 'unusual' in television, in which the script is usually written by a commissioned 'third party'.[32]

Carter's growing prominence as a writer – marked out by her move from the 'invisibility' of radio to the 'visibility' of the screen – was also supported by her non-fiction. By the early years of the eighties, she was not only firmly established as a creative writer, but also as the author of cultural criticism, a status marked in 1982 by the publication of *Nothing Sacred*, the first collection of her journalism, by Virago Press. In the context of a study of the relationship between her life and her writing, this is a significant event, since it anthologised her autobiographical essays – 'The Mother Lode' and 'My Father's House' as well as the *New Society* articles written in Japan – and thus made her life (or at least her version of it) available for wider public scrutiny. Carter's growing identity as a deliberately apostrophised version of herself was perpetuated in a series of 'interviews with the author' that took place throughout the eighties that are quite as interested in her as in whatever piece of work the interview was intended to promote. However, with both interviewer and interviewee drawing on the same source material, they demonstrate a tendency to become locked into a self-reaffirming loop of autobiographical reminiscence. In John Haffenden's interview published in *The Literary Review* in 1984, for example, he opens by referring directly to 'The Mother Lode', while the interview Carter gave to Ian McEwan in the same year for *The Sunday Times Magazine* goes over the ground covered by both 'The Mother Lode' and 'My Father's House', with any remaining gaps filled by Carter herself. For example:

> Her mythomania is evident in her playful account of the early life. She was born in Eastbourne in 1940 at the time of Dunkirk – 'not the best possible moment', with 'bombs falling all around'. Her granny, who had come down to supervise the birth, decided the family would be safer in the South Yorkshire coalfields. And why safer there? 'Because lots of little old ladies like my granny would be standing on slag heaps waving their fists at the sky and shouting 'Bugger off, Hitler!'. And so it was that granny 'put us all into a great big box and took us up to Yorkshire'.[33]

While MacEwan wryly acknowledges Carter's inveterate tendency towards 'mythomania' Carter's interjections nevertheless keep the familiar 'cabaret turn' on track, so close to her written account that they could almost be direct quotations.

In both the interviews cited above, Carter was promoting the first novel she had written since *The Passion of New Eve*, seven years previously. Yet *Nights at the Circus* had been longer than that in the making. To Ian MacEwan, she claimed that she had first had the idea almost ten years previously, but 'I had to wait till I was big enough, strong enough, to write about a winged woman'.[34] If this is the case, then she began to think about what would become *Nights at the Circus* around the mid-seventies; a speculation that takes on particular interest in the light of a comment made by Carmen Callil in her obituary on Carter, in which she said that in her last two novels, Carter 'wrote about the people she loved most, her husband Mark (*Nights at the Circus*) and her son Alexander, born eight years ago (*Wise Children*)'.[35] Callil's statement raises the intriguing possibility that not only do the last novels have a marked autobiographical basis, but also that they provided Carter with a way of going beyond the story of her life presented in the essays in a way that was not too overtly confessional.

Nights at the Circus can therefore be viewed as a combination of critique and celebration – critique of Britain under Thatcherism, but also a personal celebration of a relationship that, unlike previous ones, was not based on disappointment or exploitation. Friends commented on the harmoniousness of the Clapham household: Marina Warner, for example, recalled after Carter's death how 'she found happiness with her second husband',[36] while Lorna Sage describes Carter and Pearce as very much a couple, 'wearing identical surplus navy greatcoats outdoors, announcing their unanimity, and accentuating their height'.[37] It is difficult not to assume – as Carter's critics indeed tend to – that this contentment affected her portrayal of the central romance of *Nights at the Circus* between the winged Cockney *arieliste* Fevvers and the American journalist Jack Walser. Although it is impossible to ascertain exact dates, it is worth speculating that Carter's comment to MacEwan that she began thinking about a winged woman nearly ten years before the novel's publication indicates a chronological synchronicity between Fevvers's inception and the early period of Carter's relationship with Mark Pearce.

Most of the novel is concerned with tracing the two protagonists' progress through a series of picaresque adventures, and although this was hardly a new plot structure as far as Carter is concerned, the spirit in which these travels are conducted and their conclusion is very different. Marianne, Desiderio and Eve all end their journeys with the loss of the beloved, the protagonist's desire for whom is at least half-imaginary anyway, but *Nights at the Circus* ends with a true lovers' reunion. Although this is not to say that the characters don't have to endure a considerable amount of adversity beforehand, for both Fevvers and Walser undergo a period of strenuous reconstruction before they become capable of embarking upon the kind of satisfactory relationship Carter clearly wishes them to achieve. For example, Walser's initial view of Fevvers is sceptical, since he is trying to unmask her as a fake, but his trials and tribulations with the circus bring him to the point where he can accept both Fevvers and her wings. At the beginning of the novel, the matter of Fevvers's authenticity as a winged woman looms large, even when 'those notorious and much-debated wings' are

> stowed away for the night under the soiled quilting of her baby-blue satin dressing-gown, where they made an uncomfortable-looking pair of bulges, shuddering the surface of the taut fabric from time to time as if desirous of breaking loose ('How does she do that? pondered the reporter').[38]

In the end, though, the wings cease to matter to Walser, to whom Fevvers becomes simply the beloved. His real revelation at the text's conclusion is not the realisation that Fevvers really is a winged woman, but his willingness to acknowledge the perils of love, 'for now he knew the meaning of fear as it defines itself in its most violent form, that is, fear of the death of the beloved, of the loss of the beloved, of the loss of love. It was the beginning of an anxiety that would never end, except with the deaths of either or both' (292–93).

Fevvers, though, is put through the same process, for love is something she also must learn to take at face value. If Carter's previous romantic history had been characterised by a series of flights from one relationship to the next, then Fevvers becomes the literal personification of her author's own progress towards a stable, mutually beneficial partnership. Throughout the novel, Fevvers lurches from one exploitative association to another – Madame Schreck exhibits her as a freak in her Sadeian brothel; Mr Rosencreutz attempts to sacrifice her in order to gain eternal youth; the Russian Grand Duke lures her to his mansion in order to make her, quite literally, into his toy. Fevvers escapes from all these situations, through not only the use of her wings, but also her innate intelligence and – *in extremis* – direct authorial intervention.

Indeed, her 'much-debated' wings are something of a mixed blessing to Fevvers, simultaneously making her a both a freak and a fortune. As Walser observes early in the novel, 'on the street, at the soirée, at lunch in expensive restaurants with dukes, princes, captains of industry and punters of like kidney, she was always the cripple, even if she always drew the eye and people stood on chairs to see' (19). Fevvers may market this difference and profit from it, but she is eventually led to recognise that this is a perilous path. Lured into the clutches of the Russian Grand Duke by presents of diamonds and the promise of more, Fevvers is fatally mistaken in her assessment of him as nothing more than 'a punter good for a touch' (172). So desperate does her situation become that she can only be saved through the use of an egregiously implausible twist in the narrative. But this is the experience through which Fevvers, as she herself admits, has ' "learned my lesson" ' (192), realising that material transactions are no substitute for love. She ends the novel, no longer 'Winged Victory' nor the 'Cockney Venus', nor under any of the other sobriquets that have been freely attached to her throughout the narrative, but as simply a 'happy young woman' (295) whose laughter rings out across the dawn of a new century.

That is not to say, though, that the conclusion of *Nights at the Circus* is wholly unproblematic. As it turns out, Fevvers has indeed been fooling Walser all along, for in the course of their reunion he discovers that she is not 'the "only fully-feathered intacta in the history of the world" ' (294). As we know by now that Fevvers is indeed 'fully-feathered', this means that her real confidence trick has entailed the concealment of her loss of virginity. The issue of her wings has functioned as a red herring (so to speak), diverting both Walser's and the readers' attention away from the real secrets in a narrative in which the sexual defloration Fevvers must have experienced somewhere along the way has simply been edited out.

This has implications for our understanding of the autobiographical elements within the novel, which are rendered questionable from the start. Indeed, Walser's initial interview with Fevvers, in which she tells the story of her upbringing and early career, demonstrates that it is in her narrative that much of its most fantastical elements reside. In asking Walser to believe that she possesses the power of flight – a belief he strenuously denies, and which she refrains from proving beyond doubt – Fevvers is continually, and deliberately, undermining the authenticity of her own autobiographical narrative. Moreover, it is further destabilised by Lizzie's presence at the interview, for the adding of her voice to Fevvers' story does not authenticate it by anchoring it in a verifiable truth. Instead, Lizzie's frequent interjections only renders it, in quite literal fashion, more duplicitous, as 'the convolutions of their joint stories' makes Walser feel like 'a sultan faced with not one but two Scheherezades, both intent on impacting a thousand stories into the single night' (40). Fevvers' reliance on Lizzie as her partner in the performance of a kind of autobiographical double act is indicated by her tendency to fall 'silent' (51) and become 'ill-at-ease' (42) whenever Lizzie leaves the room.

However, Walser's complete preoccupation with Fevvers' claim to be a winged woman causes him, 'connoisseur of the tall tale' (11) though he might be, to miss quite another story lurking in the subtext of their outrageous account. It is at the points where this alternative narrative threatens to come to the surface that Fevvers' and Lizzie's partnership is most obviously discernable, since they keep one another in check. This tendency is shown, for example, when Fevvers describes the marriage of one of the former whores in Ma Nelson's brothel to an unnamed member of the aristocracy:

> Well, married they were and a very refined affair it was, in St John's, Smith Square, she in off-white because he'd given out she is a provincial widow. And, afterwards, at the reception, which was held in the Savoy Hotel, nothing but the best –
> ' – he chokes to death on the *bombe surprise*,' said Lizzie, and emitted a sudden, fierce cackle, for which Fevvers reproved her with a look. (46)

The potentially explosive subject of the *bombe surprise* is one to which Lizzie returns when telling Walser about her sister Isotta's ice-cream parlour in Battersea, and again his attention is diverted by Fevvers:

> 'Best ice-cream in London, sir. Best cassata outside Sicily. Old family recipe. *Il mio papa* brought it with him. As for our *bombe surprise* – '
> 'Ooops!' interpolated Fevvers, who, at that moment, by some accident, had contrived to overturn her powerbox. What a mess! It took a moment or two to dust the spilled powder off the things on the dressing-table and then it was she herself who continued. (47)

So misdirected is Walser that he is even inveigled by Lizzie into sending mysterious encoded communications from Russia via the diplomatic bag through which he files his news reports, thus unwittingly aiding the revolutionary Bolshevik cause. But his distraction is excusable, since he is handicapped by his obsession, 'the sudden sting of jealousy that struck him when he thought of Fevvers "alone", "unaccompanied", in her gaudy dress in the Grand Duke's arms'. Had he not been, speculates the third-person narrative voice, he might 'have spotted the code; the secret writing. Have found a story, there, that would have turned him back into a journalist, again' (181).

The blunting of Walser's journalistic acumen – itself an amusing tactic from an ex-journalist who admitted to 'a demonic inaccuracy as regards fact'[39] – allows the narrative's most subversive undercurrents to proceed without hindrance or interrogation. Even when, in a confessional mood at the end of the novel, Fevvers tells Walser that '[t]hose letters we sent home by you in the diplomatic bag were news of the struggle in Russia to comrades in exile, written in invisible ink' (292), the full implications of this is left to the reader to work out for themselves. But it is this admission that achieves a final, definitive, undercutting of Fevvers' triumphant laughter with which the text closes, the laughter that 'began to twist and shudder across the entire globe, as if a spontaneous response to the giant comedy that endlessly unfolded beneath it' (295).

Although her eighth novel was primarily reviewed as a comedy – Carolyn See in *The New York Times* described it as 'a mad mixture of Mary Poppins, Djuna Barnes's "Nightwood", Greek mythology and reruns of "The Bionic Woman" '[40] – Carter herself said that 'the idea behind *Nights at the Circus* was very much to entertain and instruct'.[41] A burlesque fantasia on one level it may be, but on another it is a deadly serious satire on nationalism and identity that positions itself in ironic counterpoint to the public rhetoric of Thatcherism. Malcolm Bradbury describes Thatcherist Britain as 'a patriotic place, ostensibly secure in interests and historical identity. A war in the Falklands and an aggressive policy on cooperation with Europe asserted as much: Britain was Britain, a long-term democracy with a sovereign identity, and not Europe',[42] which is an apt description of the target of some of Carter's most vicious satire in *Nights at the Circus*. When Walser, still in search of a story, follows Fevvers to Colonel Kearney's circus, he joins the troupe of 'Buffo the Great, the Master Clown' (116), where he becomes 'the Human Chicken' (152). But clowning, in this novel, is serious business: 'the terrible Buffo' (116) specialises in 'violent slapstick' (117) in an act centred upon disintegration and death. And it is Buffo who inherits the Rose Queen's crown – nationalism is now, not theatre, but circus show.

The nationalistic aspects of Buffo's act are rendered obvious from the start. Buffo, like Fevvers, is 'Cockney bred and born; his *real* name was George Buffins, but he had long ago forgotten it, although he was a great patriot, British to the bone, even if as widely travelled as the British Empire in the service of fun' (118). When Buffo 'dies' at the culmination of his act, his comedy coffin is 'draped with the Union Jack' (117), but he refuses to acknowledge his own demise. Instead, he 'bursts through the coffin lid! Right through. With a great, rending crash, leaving behind a huge silhouette of himself, in the flimsy wood'

(118). In his malign version of the resurrection, Buffo is reminiscent of Christ, and Christian imagery is, indeed, repeatedly attached to him. Given Carter's dedicated atheism, though, this does nothing to counteract Buffo's role as a grotesque incarnation of an imperialistic spirit that strenuously resists all attempts to lay it decently to rest. Instead, Buffo persists in grimly grinding through his act to the point where all restraint is lost.

In the clowns' final show, the horror that has always lain at the heart of their performance threatens to dramatically rupture the carnivalesque surface of the spectacle in the same way as Buffo bursts through the lid of his coffin. Adopting a patriarchal role reminiscent of *The Magic Toyshop*'s Uncle Philip, one of Carter's earlier representatives of 'patriotism as theatre', Buffo presides over the 'the Feast of Fools' (175) in a horrible parody of 'the loving father about to divide meat between his children' (176). But there is every risk that the 'bloody streamers' (176) attached to his carving knives may metamorphose into authentic blood when his 'reason snap[s]' (177) and he becomes genuinely homicidal. Even then, because 'the show must go on', the other clowns collude to disguise the fact that attempted murder is taking place right before the eyes of the audience. Thus:

> even if Buffo at last *had* contrived to plunge his carving knife into the viscera of the Human Chicken, nobody in that vast gathering of merry folk would ever have been permitted to believe it was real manslaughter; it would have seemed, instead, the cream of the jest. (177)

In 'Masochism for the Masses' written only a year before the publication of *Nights at the Circus*, Angela Carter portrays Margaret Thatcher herself as a low-brow performance artist: she is 'Bennie Hill *en travestie*',[43] and 'the "bad guy" in wrestling...like Mick MacManus'.[44] So parodically stylised has she become, says Carter, that 'it's a wonder her perorations aren't drowned by peals of mirth each time she opens her mouth, and unpleasantly significant that they are not'.[45] In this context, Buffo can be regarded as a savagely ironic reflection of Thatcher, in the sense that he functions as her mirror image. While she becomes ever more absurd but still no-one laughs, his descent into genuine insanity is greeted with ecstatic mirth. His performance is curtailed within the 'O' of the circus ring – when he leaves it, he is carted away to a lunatic asylum – while hers threatens to become ever more universal and inescapable, representative of 'a transcendent Britishness rising above mere sectarian strife such as the class struggle'.[46] The dawn of the twentieth century should – as Lizzie and her fellow Bolsheviks so devoutly hoped – have heralded the death of empire, but Buffo represents its refusal to lie down and die. On the contrary, its efforts to incarnate itself become ever more desperate and unrestrained. Whereas in her earlier novels such as *Love* Carter depicts love as spectral, manifested in the figure of the revenant, here the role of spectre becomes associated with blind nationalism, motivated by neither intellect nor purpose.

Thatcherism well understood the value of invoking the spirit of nationalism, for as Eric J. Evans argues, while radicalism in the late eighteenth and early nineteenth centuries might have been inspired by 'a vigorous patriotic tradition', that was lost when the rhetoric of patriotism 'became appropriated by the right wing of the political spectrum during the imperialist expansion of the late nineteenth century...In the 1980s a populist of genius drew upon it to devastating effect.'[47] Carter's late novels respond to this by invoking the 'spirit' of patriotism in its literal sense as 'phantom', haunting a society that should long since have witnessed its passing. She makes use of such metaphors in 'Masochism for the Masses', in which she argues that the Conservative election campaign of 1983 attempted to conflate the distinction between government and nation to the point that:

> a vote for Thatcher is a vote, not for the Tories, but for Britain. If you believe in Britain, clap your hands, and Britain, like Tinkerbell in Peter Pan will rise from her deathbed. And. And then, do what? But what Britain will do after this, to change the metaphor, Lazarus-like resurrection is also left vague, except, like any revenant, she will be less corporeally substantial and, presumably, no longer need nourishment, health care, education or employment.[48]

John Bayley is correct, I think, in his argument that 'Mrs. Thatcher as the national anti-heroine...looms in the background of Carter's work'. In his argument – which quite fortuitously draws on iconography that recurs in all her writing – Thatcher and Carter together 'could be seen as making a new heraldic opposition on the royal crest: the lion and the unicorn still fighting for the crown'.[49] While Thatcher is the patriarchal, phallic woman, Carter is 'the supreme subversive', who offers images of a 'new woman [who] combines correctness with being a sort of jolly feminine Tom Jones'.[50] Extending the analogy beyond that proposed by Bayley, it could be argued that what Carter also intends is an undercutting of Thatcherist imperialistic rhetoric in a way that is not 'jolly' in the least.

So, while *Nights at the Circus* creates a personal happy ending for its main characters, it loads their optimism concerning the coming century with heavy irony. This dichotomy between personal fulfilment and public disillusionment that had come to characterise Carter's own life was thrown into further relief by the birth of her son, Alexander, in November 1983. Motherhood had not intentionally featured on Carter's agenda: at the age of 43 she 'simply found herself pregnant and decided to go ahead with it'.[51] On the one hand it was an undoubtedly happy event; but on the other her experience of childbirth only strengthened her firmly held belief that Britain was 'going to hell in a handbasket'.[52]

Towards the end of Carter's pregnancy her blood pressure went up to unacceptable levels and, 'the day after judging the Booker'[53] she was confined to hospital, from which she wrote to Lorna Sage venting her fury at her dictatorial consultant obstetrician, 'a Thatcher-clone'[54] who advised Carter to consider giving up the baby after the birth.

'How is your husband feeling?' she asked.
I paused to think of the right way of putting it and she said quickly: 'I know he's only your common law husband.'
While I was digesting this, she pressed down on my belly so I couldn't move and said:
'Of course you've done absolutely the right thing by *not* having an abortion but now is the time to contemplate adoption and I urge you to think about it very seriously.'
That is *exactly* what she said! Each time I think about it, the adrenalin surges through my veins. I want to kill this woman. I want the BMA to crucify her. I want to rip out her insides.[55]

It is evident that this letter served as the raw material for an essay entitled 'Notes from a Maternity Ward' published in the *New Statesman* a month later. The tone of the published piece is – probably fortunately – rather more temperate. Although the consultant is still described as 'an unreconstructed 'Thatcher clone – that is, she looks like Thatcher minus the peroxide and the schlap', she is given due credit for being 'a good doctor',[56] and while the anecdote concerning her recommendation of adoption is left in, it is off-set by Carter's description of the consultant's change in attitude after the birth. When Alexander is 'chuckling in a glass box like a very expensive orchid', she becomes 'nice as pie. Well done, she says.'[57]

This essay, a rare venture outside the territory marked out in Carter's usual autobiographical repertoire, presents the reader with an intriguing mixture of the personal and the political, as Carter begins by making characteristic use of her own experience as a launching point for wider social critique. She gave birth in the South London Hospital for Women by Clapham Common, an 'elegant, red-brick building', 'very well equipped' and 'convenient for Clapham South tube station'.[58] Although manifestly providing (appallingly insensitive consultants apart) a valuable service to women, particularly to those 'whose religion specifies they be treated by doctors of the same sex', the hospital was scheduled for closure as part of the Conservative party's endeavour to cut costs in the NHS, which gives Carter the opportunity to take the government to task for putting the market economy before compassion and simple common sense. The only way of saving it, Carter sarcastically opines, is 'if the Minister of Health turns into a woman tomorrow . . . especially if (s)he then converted to Islam'.[59] Not that being female guarantees any degree of instinctive sympathy for other women. The figure of the consultant demonstrates this, and she, of course, stands in a synecdochal relationship to that other woman bestriding British politics, society and culture, who has rejected all identification with other members of her sex.

Carter's political invective in this essay, however, proceeds to modulate into a meditation on motherhood itself, a preoccupation that initially appears to stand somewhat at odds with its beginning:

> The midwife shows me how to put the baby to the nipple. 'Look deep into his eyes,' she says. 'It helps with the bonding.' Good grief! Aren't we allowed any choice in the matter, he and I? Can't I learn to love him for himself, and vice versa, rather than trust to Mother Nature's psychological double bind? And what of his relationship with his father, who has no breasts?[60]

For Carter, therefore, 'bond' does not signify emotional attachment so much as restraint: she is innately suspicious of a love that arises from biological imperative rather than autonomous decision. 'Constrained affection; what resentment it will breed, in time . . . he is doomed to love us, at least for a significant initial period, because we are his parents. The same goes for us. That is life. That's the hell of it.'[61] However, there is one 'mercy': the 'specific urgencies of the neonate' divert his parents' attention away from '[t]he TV news' that 'gobs out fresh horrors into the living room every evening'. Public imperatives become subordinate to domestic ones, with the result that 'that appalling dichotomy – the one between our lives as we live them and the way that forces outside ourselves shape them for us – seem less desperate than usual'.[62] Although Britain remains a society run by lunatics and megalomaniacs, motherhood at least provides a buffer from the horrors going on outside the enclosed world centred upon the demands of the infant.

From odd comments dropped here and there it is obvious that Carter never regretted the consequences of her unplanned pregnancy. It appears, for example, to have allayed anxieties about her body that had endured following her anorexic period as a teenager. To Peter Kemp she said that she had become 'nicer as a middle-aged person than I was as a girl. When I was 18 or 19, I became self-inducedly very thin and morbid. But after I had my little boy . . . I was just fatter in the way one so often is, and I felt so much better for it.'[63] And she was more than capable of dropping the occasional rather mumsy aside into her writing, describing herself in a contribution to a feminist recipe book published in 1987 as 'a middle-aged non-vegetarian yet nevertheless of the whole-food tendency, whose small son has never tasted Coca-Cola'.[64]

However, 'Notes from a Maternity Ward' aside, Carter resisted invitations to talk about her relationship with her son at length. Although happy to be photographed with Alexander (a particularly touching one of the family group is attached to Ian MacEwan's 1984 article), and to conduct interviews with him around,[65] she did not give away a great deal aside from the fact that 'I like the man and the boy I live with very much'.[66] When, in her 1987 interview, Lisa Appignanesi asked Carter directly about how she had been affected by the birth of her son, she launches into a long response, but one from which it is very difficult to extract much personal information:

> Well, it's cut [time to write] . . . right down, actually, because they do take up a lot of time. They demand it, and you don't mind giving it to them. Also, for a student of human nature, which I suppose I am by profession, they're very interesting things to have around. God knows, you learn a lot about human beings from looking at a child . . . Obviously intellectual activity and small children are incompatible, unless you really are furiously interested in their development, unless you've got philosophical concern with how this person grows out of this little fleshy seed. But also I tend to think Wordsworth was right about children – I do think that they have something from . . . some glory about them.[67]

It seems obvious from this that she was finding motherhood fascinating, and rewarding, in its way, even though she was inevitably having to restructure her habits of working: 'I sit at home in my quiet room and think a lot. I *used* to think a lot. Now I do a lot of finger painting, actually.'[68] But her retreat into the third person – something she does not do when asked about earlier parts of her life already covered by her autobiographical essays – introduces a certain sense of distance indicative of a reluctance to reveal intimate details. Indeed, when subsequently asked by Appignanesi whether 'she might write something about this', Carter's answer, though hesitant in the extreme, is an unequivocal negative: 'Well, I think, I think…well, it's very difficult because I have a great resistance to writing about it, because of…Oh, because of lots of reasons.'[69]

Yet, in her next novel she returned to the issue that had preoccupied her in 'Notes from a Maternity Ward' – the nature of the biological bond. It was a question over which she had actually been pondering since at least 1976, where in 'The Mother Lode' she comments that one of the things she most admired about Japanese society was

> their tolerant acceptance of the involuntary nature of family life. Love in the sense of passionate attachment has nothing to do with it; the Japanese even have a different verb to define the arbitrary affection that grows among these chance juxtapositions of intimate strangers.[70]

In 'Sugar Daddy', published in the same year as 'Notes from a Maternity Ward', Carter returns to the same topic; that of

> the curious abyss that divides the closes kin…the tender curiosity appropriate to lovers is inappropriate, here, where the bond is involuntary…He is my father and I love him as Cordelia did, 'according to my natural bond'. What the nature of that 'natural bond' might be, I do not know, and besides, I have a theoretical objection to the notion of a 'natural bond'.[71]

Carter's use of Shakespearean references here is appropriate, since it anticipates what was to become her last, and arguably most popular, novel: *Wise Children*. In some senses, *Wise Children* accommodated 'a very definite shift in her work' she attributed to her changed domestic situation; 'I find myself', she said to Anna Katsavos in 1988, 'thinking much more simply because I'm spending so much time with a small child'.[72] As a consequence, she claimed, she now played less complex games with her reader than she used to. *Wise Children* bears this out to some extent, being somewhat less obscurely eclectic in its sources than many of Carter's previous novels. However, it is still an intertextual riot: as Kate Webb says in her essay 'Seriously Funny: *Wise Children*', the novel 'not only steals freely from other literary texts but also takes from the texts of other people's lives and uses these too'.[73] At its base, though, it is a sustained allusion: Carter told Susannah Clapp that her 'original plan had been to write a novel in which all the Shakespeare plots were to be replayed by her Cockney song-and-dance-heroines and their family. In the end she couldn't get them all in: there's no *Two Noble Kinsman*, and ... no *Titus Andronicus*.'[74] To Lorna Sage, she described it as an expression of her desire to write a book that was distinctively different from *Nights at the Circus*, which was 'a big thick heavy nineteenth-century novel'. In contrast, she wanted *Wise Children* to have 'more holes in the text, it should be airy, with spaces on the page ... I wanted a transparent prose that just ran, and I wanted it to be very funny'.[75]

Carter had very decided views on Shakespeare, whom she desired to rescue from the 'shadow of Leavis' and the clutches of 'high' culture, which she considered to be an inappropriate place for him anyway. Instead, she always argued that he should be approached as a popular writer: 'the intellectual equivalent of bubble-gum', but one who 'can make twelve-year-old girls cry, can foment revolutions in Africa, can be translated into Japanese and leave not a dry eye in the house'.[76] In her final interview for the BBC, Carter traced her interest in Shakespeare back to her childhood, when her mother would tell her daughter all about the 'Lilian Bayliss popular productions' she had seen at the Old Vic in her own girlhood, with the result that Carter grew up 'completely steeped in the lore, language and culture of Shakespeare, miserable, rotten, reactionary old bourgeois old fuddy-duddy that he is'.[77]

Wise Children, for all its differences from the novel that preceded it, thus reproduces the duality of 'public' and 'private' preoccupations that also distinguishes *Nights at the Circus*, for in it Shakespeare is explored both as repository of national identity and in the context of his significance within Carter's own family history. Carter herself claimed that she made free use of biographical material in her writing of this book. In her interview with Carter in 1991 Susannah Clapp makes the observation that 'the London that it rejoices in is in part the South London of Carter's childhood',[78] which Carter remembered at a time when it 'was still the place where retired music-hall artistes lived. I had a friend whose lodger was a retired one-legged adagio dancer – honestly.'[79]

Entwined as he is with her personal narrative, the figure of Shakespeare thus becomes the means whereby Carter can recover a personal history that is distinctively, specifically, maternal. Because Carter's love of the Bard is inherited directly from her mother, he functions as a link between two women who are otherwise so separated in time, experience and character. While Carmen Callil suggests that Carter is celebrating her *own* experience of motherhood in this novel, some of Olive's story – her love of fashion, of the theatre, of 'Society' (though not her 'passion for respectability')[80] – is also recorded in *Wise Children*. The parallels are noted by Susannah Clapp:

> As a cashier in Selfridges in the Twenties, she [Olive] eyed with some envy the Dolly Sisters, the Hungarian mistresses of Gordon Selfridge, who spent lavishly in the store, and who appear on the cover of *Wise Children* with sequins like windmill sails on their heads and breasts, and ostrich feather skirts.[81]

Shakespeare therefore stands in a complex relationship to this text in terms of both its public and private dimensions. As a symbol that connects Carter to her mother, he can be regarded as performing a function analogous to that of the rose tree – a gift to Carter from her mother – with which 'The Mother Lode' concludes. Although at the time, Carter says, she was 'a little disappointed by it', it assumes a new significant to her older (and *wiser*) self. 'Of all the presents of all the birthdays of a petted childhood, the rose tree is the one I remember best and it is mixed up, now with my memory of her.'[82]

But remembering her mother through the medium of the rose tree also takes us back to Carter's on-going manipulation of nationalistic myth and symbol which is incarnated in the figure of the Rose Queen, versions of whom so often recur in her work. Here Shakespeare again plays a pivotal role: as England's national playwright, whose official birthday of April 23rd is also St George's Day, he could be considered the ultimate representative of 'patriotism as theatre'. Moreover, the motif of the rose in its patriotic aspect can be attached to Shakespeare quite readily – one of the theatres with which he was associated was the Rose, situated on Bankside in South London, and it was there that *Henry VI*, a play which depicted the origins of the War of the Roses, was performed for the first time.

Paul N. Siegel has noted how readily Shakespeare is appropriated to serve nationalistic interests, in the context of which he:

> represents 'Englishness', and unchanging and deeply conservative national tradition yearning for empire...The bourgeoisie reaches

back beyond its own historical advent and claims continuity from a heritage lost in the past, but representing the proud fusion of bourgeoisie and aristocracy, parliament and monarchy, which is 'English culture' with the Bard of Avon at its heart.[83]

Carter writes such acts of appropriation into *Wise Children*, in which the founder of the Hazard dynasty, Ranulph, one of 'the great, roaring, actor-managers'[84] of the Victorian era, assumes the mission of 'tak[ing] Shakespeare where Shakespeare had never been before' (17). It is a project that takes him '[o]ff to the ends of the Empire' (17); a clear indication that England's cultural touchstone is being used to reinforce a hegemonic imperialist ideology. As Aiden Day says, '[t]he description of the tour draws a parallel between Ranulph's proselytising on behalf of Shakespeare and England's imperial occupation of – and renaming of – territories across the globe'.[85] However, this is an Angela Carter novel: such a state of affairs cannot remain unchallenged for long. Ranulph's triumphant progress across all the 'pink on the map of the world' (17) duly descends into multiple murder and suicide, for upon discovering that his wife, Estella, is having an affair with a fellow-actor, he kills the lovers and himself in accordance with the most time-honoured tradition of Elizabethan revenge tragedy. In this, he becomes distinctly reminiscent of Buffo: both characters take on a quasi-religious role within their texts, and both suffer a spectacular fall from grace.

One of *Wise Children*'s preoccupations is with charting the fluctuations in Shakespeare's value as a cultural icon from the turn of the century onwards, and with Ranulph's demise there is nowhere to go but down. In the process, Shakespeare's role as the lynchpin of English national identity becomes steadily eroded. By the eighties, the period of the novel's present, Ranulph's grandson Tristram is trading on his position as a member of one of Britain's great theatrical dynasties in order to present a game show which, perhaps in homage to Thatcherist enterprise culture, glories in the title of 'Lashings of Lolly' (11).[86] Paradoxically, while the Shakespeare industry – what Terence Hawkes has so disparagingly termed 'Bardbiz'[87] – flourishes, what Tristram's so downmarket, yet so successful, show illustrates is the loss of any sense of a distinctively 'British' national culture and of Shakespeare's capacity to act as its guarantor. While Ranulph attempted to take Shakespeare to America and died in the attempt, by the eighties the power balance between Britain and America has been turned on its head. Now it is America that dictates the content of British culture, appropriating the role as guardian of the 'meaning' of Shakespeare along the way. In *Wise Children*, this process begins in the thirties, with a Hollywood adaptation of *A Midsummer Night's Dream* which takes flagrant liberties with the original (Shakespeare is credited with contributing 'additional dialogue' [108]).[88] Ranulph's (supposed) son, Melchior Hazard, enters into this grandiose project under the illusion that he will be perpetuating his father's imperialistic ambitions, and by 'acquiring control over the major public dreaming facility in the whole world' will enact 'Shakespeare's revenge for the War of Independence' (148). That he is sadly mistaken in this assumption is underlined by a comic incident involving a casket of earth from Stratford upon Avon he has brought with him to Hollywood. On the first day of shooting, Melchior ceremoniously displays the casket 'as if it were the Holy Grail' (134), and scatters the earth it contains upon the ground of the facsimile Forest of Arden. But this casket of what Melchior so sententiously proclaims to be 'English earth, perhaps some of the most English earth of all...For it is earth from William Shakespeare's own home town' (134) is in fact nothing of the sort. Nora and Dora, upon discovering that the original contents have been used as kitty-litter by the cat belonging to the film's leading lady, have actually secretly replaced it with soil from the set. Thus, Melchior's aim of bringing part of England to Hollywood by sprinkling authentic Shakespearean earth 'all over the wood near Athens, as a consecration of the grounds' (129), becomes nothing more than a returning to Hollywood of what it already owns.

Britain's cultural and political decline is further underscored in *Wise Children* through the character of Gorgeous George, an end-of-pier entertainer who specialises in crude seaside-postcard humour. The fact that he shares a first name with George Buffo and, what's more, with England's patron saint, indicates his dubious status as the last, most down-at-heel, incarnation of the Rose Queen. Public displays of patriotism are George's stock-in-trade: the finale of his act begins with him singing, 'in a voice heavy with emotion' (66), patriotic songs such as 'Rose of England' and 'Land of Hope and Glory'. But he is more than just a conduit for English sentiment and coarse humour, for when he strips off his clothes George is revealed as a most literal embodiment of the imperialistic spirit – 'an enormous statement' upon whose body is tattooed 'a complete map of the entire world' (66). It is a patriotic portrait, too, since most of it is 'filled in brilliant pink, although the limelight turned it into a morbid, raspberry colour that looked bad for his health' (67). Mercifully, George's 'privates' are concealed by a g-string 'made out of the Union Jack'; but that does not hide the position of the Falkland Islands, which – indicating Carter's own bent for scatological humour – can be seen 'disappear[ing] down the crack of his bum' (67).

In spite of the rapturous enthusiasm of George's audience, however, this is no more than empty show. In the words of Kate Webb:

> Unlike St George of old, Gorgeous George no longer wins battles and rules the waves; he merely represents the idea of conquest. He is a walking metaphor, and effete mirror-image. George shows us an empire falling: having once dominated the world, this Englishman can now be master of only one space: his own body.[89]

Indeed, allusions to the Falkland Islands aside, this whole scene harks back to one of Carter's earlier novels. Nora and Dora see George's performance on Brighton Pier, the ruins of which were evoked in *Heroes and Villains*. There, the statue of the woman on the clock tower evoked memories of Britannia, but a Britannia disinherited and adrift, and the pier itself emblematic of the collapse of imperialistic pride in the wake of nuclear conflict. Gorgeous George fulfils much the same function, emphasised by the novel's insistence on charting his continuing decline. He plays the part of Bottom in the disastrous production of *A Midsummer Night's Dream*, and is last encountered by Nora and Dora as a down-and-out on a street corner, 'the outlines of Europe and Africa' forlornly exposed 'between the edges of his unspeakable shirt, off which the buttons had all fallen' (196).

Wise Children is therefore merciless in its anatomisation of the disintegration of Empire, which is seen as being completely unable to withstand the American incursion into the British cultural arena. This theme, of course, has particular resonance within the context of the eighties, a period in which Anglo-American relations were conducted under the aegis of the 'close, even suffocating personal warmth'[90] between Margaret Thatcher and Ronald Reagan. From 1983 to 1988, US Cruise missiles were stationed in British military bases; an event which became a predictable target for Carter's wrath. 'How *did* it happen that this island has become a moored aircraft carrier for instruments of destruction?', she asks in 'Anger for a Black Landscape'. The answer, she argues, lies in a British character honed in

> an exceedingly long history of militarism and of compliance with authority and are reluctant to lose the residual conviction that to be British involves some kind of guarantee against destruction. ('Britons never shall be slaves.') After all, we haven't been invaded by a foreign

army for a thousand years! No. Nowadays, we invite the buggers in
and call it NATO.[91]

What Gorgeous George exemplifies is a Britain only capable of trading
on sentimental images of an idealised glorious past, and it is that very
inability to let go of the past that has led Britain into becoming a pawn
in a militaristic game whose rules are dictated by America. While
Margaret Thatcher had been forced out of office in 1990, a year before
the publication of *Wise Children*, it is her policies that clearly dictate
Carter's portrayal of national identity in this novel.

There are other forms of invasion besides the purely militaristic, of
course, and Shakespeare, again, plays a pivotal role in this, for the
eighties was also the decade in which the campaign to rebuild an identical
simulacrum of the Globe Theatre on the site of the original gained
momentum. Although Carter does not refer to this phenomenon in any
of her writings, it is something of which she could not have been
unaware, and it is perfectly possible to see this as forming part of the
backdrop to *Wise Children*. Work had begun on clearing the Bankside
site for construction at the time Carter was writing the novel, although
it was not officially opened until 1997, five years after her death. The
movement to create an exact working replica of the Globe gathered
pace at a time in which the arts were becoming rebranded as an
'industry', and Shakespeare himself an ever more marketable product of
'English Heritage'. However, Terence Hawkes, adopting a different slant
on the issue, observes that the campaign to construct a reproduction of
the Globe was spearheaded by an American, Sam Wanamaker, causing
him to question whether 'Bardbiz... [is] merely the continuation of
American foreign policy by another means'.[92]

It is therefore somewhat ironic that the modern construct now
known as Shakespeare's Globe Theatre is also reminiscent of previous
attempts to showcase a national identity: namely, the Great Exhibition
and its successor the Festival of Britain. Shakespeare featured prominently
in the Festival of Britain, in particular, where the gallery in the Lion and
Unicorn pavilion included:

five sets for Shakespeare plays which were shown in miniature theatres
grouped in front of a screen in the form of an open book. Opposite
this was a showcase filled with volumes of translations of the poet's
work in forty foreign languages, together with a number of English
editions.[93]

In the Festival guide, Shakespeare, who 'enshrined his mother-tongue in monumental plays', becomes a pivotal figure in the development of English as the dominant world language, 'a mother tongue' through which 'today, two hundred and fifty million people can converse together'.[94] Although 'warlike achievements were strictly excluded'[95] from the pavilion, assumptions concerning the fundamental beneficence of British cultural imperialism clearly were not.

There are no direct allusions to the Festival of Britain in *Wise Children*, although Nora and Dora Chance, Ranulph Hazard's illegitimate grand-daughters, do own 'a unique example of an authentic Highland-style grandfather clock... [that] was exhibited at the Great Exhibition of 1851' (4). It is, says Dora, who narrates the novel in her own inimical fashion, 'the only castrato grandfather clock in London' (4). In this image, Victorian imperialism is cut down to size yet again, deprived of its masculine authority by the figure of Grandma. 'Great, tall, butch, horny mahogany thing' it might be, but as a clock, it is absolutely useless, 'giv[ing] out the hours in a funny little falsetto ping and always the wrong hour... It was all right until Grandma fixed it. All she did was tap it and the weights dropped off. She always had that effect on gentleman' (4).

The clock is passed down to Nora and Dora through the paternal line, but in its grandiose and rather absurd Highland embellishments – which 'consists of a full set of antlers, eight points, on top of it' (4) – it evokes echoes of Carter's own Scottish antecedents; while Grandma comes more or less straight from the pages of 'The Mother Lode'. She is a slightly diluted version, true, with a talent for motherhood that seems to have passed Carter's real grandmother by. While the grandmother in 'The Mother Lode' is a 'domineering old harridan, with... [a] rough tongue and a primitive sense of justice',[96] who nags her daughter endlessly, Nora and Dora's Grandma '[takes] to children like a duck to water' (28). They also have significantly different speech patterns: Carter's gran 'talked broad Yorkshire till the day she died',[97] but Grandma does not 'so much talk as elocute. She rhymed "sky" with "bay", and made "mountaynes" out of "molehills", except sometimes she forgot herself, the air turned blue' (27). The aura of gentility is no more than skin deep, then – at base Grandma possesses the same 'architectonic quality',[98] as Carter's grandmother, 'solid-built like an armoured car' (27) and with the same disregard for societal niceties. Grandma is, I think, another indication that in this novel Carter is forging links with a maternal, rather than paternal, past by filling in the gap usually left by the absent mother in her work with an enduring matriarchal presence that is even capable of dispensing advice from beyond the grave.

This allows Grandma to function as a relatively stable point in an otherwise continuously fluctuating text in which reality is continually being reconfigured; a narrative movement encapsulated in Carter's dual attitude towards Shakespeare. As Kate Webb puts it, 'Shakespeare may have become the very symbol of legitimate culture, but his work is characterised by bastardy, multiplicity and incest; the Hazard dynasty may represent propriety and tradition, but they, too, are an endlessly orphaned, errant, and promiscuous bunch.'[99] It is this very duality, this inability to be fixed to any singular meaning or origin, that casts questions over this novel's status as fictional autobiography. Although Carter may have openly admitted to drawing on her own family history in its construction, *Wise Children* is no less concerned with problematising the process of life writing than its predecessors. Because there are always at least two possible versions of every event, the facts required to create an authoritative account of a life are simply not available; and *Wise Children* ostentatiously displays its lack of veracity. It is, for a start, verbal reminiscence rather than published autobiography, for it is told by 'Dora Chance in her ratty old fur and poster paint, her orange (Persian Melon) toenails sticking out of her snakeskin peep-toes, reeking of liquor...in the Coach and Horses' (227). In a narrative in which both paternity and maternity are perpetually in question, official records such as birth, marriage and death certificates – evidence upon which a biographer depends – are replaced by the jumbled 'archeology' of Dora's desk containing 'fraying envelope[s]' (12) of theatrical memorabilia.

This is autobiography as scrap-book, the gaps between the pictures filled in with tall stories and outrageous conjecture. Children – and as Kate Webb says, this is 'a novel composed entirely of twins'[100] – appear more or less out of thin air, quite adrift from their parents; whoever they might be. Nora and Dora never know their mother, who they have been told died just after their birth, but they have a superabundance of fathers: Melchior, 'who did the biological necessary', while his brother Peregrine '*passed* as our father – that is, he was the one who publicly acknowledged us when Melchior would not' (16–17). However, as far as the brothers are concerned there is also 'a gigantic question mark over the question of their paternity' (21), for neither Melchior nor Peregrine may be the true sons of Ranulph Hazard, nor may they be the 'true' fathers of their own children. In this novel, as Dora observes, a father really is 'a moveable feast' (216). The narrative achieves its most outrageous

sleight of hand with regard to parenthood in the final pages, when
Peregrine magically reveals a final set of twins:

> Brown as a quail, round as an egg, sleepy as a pear. I'll never know
> how he got it in his pocket.
> 'Look in the other one, Dora.'
> One each. They were twins, of course, three months old, by the
> look of them. (226)

Although the babies have an origin story attached to them – their father
is supposedly Tristram's twin brother Gareth, a priest who disappeared
into the jungles of South America years before – it is not one to which
Dora attaches much credence. They are, simply, 'our babies' (227), for it's
finders' keepers as far as children in this novel are concerned. Nora and
Dora themselves know this better than any, having been brought up by

> Grandma Chance, the grandma who fixed the grandfather clock, the
> grandma whose name we carry, she was no blood relation at all, to
> make confusion worse confounded. Grandma raised us, not out of
> duty, or due to history, but because of pure love, it was a genuine
> family romance. (12)

Throughout the novel, Dora staunchly maintains that, while ' "Father" is
an hypothesis…"mother" is a fact' (223), yet, as Peregrine points out, her
own family history stands in direct contradiction to that axiom. Instead,
'[m]other is as mother does' (223), and 'family' is something created out
of love and choice, not biology nor duty. As in *Nights at the Circus*, public
satire is juxtaposed with a ringing endorsement of the value of human
affection. 'It is a characteristic of human beings, one I've often noticed,
that if they don't have a family of their own, they will invent one' (165),
says Dora, voicing a theme that appears in most of Carter's fiction, which
has persistently upheld the benefits of the makeshift family.

One of the things that characterises Dora's narrative is her outrageous
optimism. While she has lived long enough to experience tragedy, she
keeps it at arms length, thus transforming what could have been a
sob-story into a comedic triumph. That is quite a feat, given that
Nora and Dora are faded, aging showgirls, living in a shabby house
in a run-down part of London. The high point of their career was their
involvement in a massive Hollywood flop, and now they have nothing
to look forward to but death. Even their acquisition of the twins does
not entirely negate this, for although they know that they now 'can't

afford to die for at least another twenty years' (230), they are also aware that their survival is not guaranteed. All one can do accept that 'What you see is what you get. Only the here and now' (144). But *Wise Children* takes as its axiom a quotation from *Mansfield Park*: 'Let other pens dwell on guilt and misery' (163), and while tragedy is acknowledged, it is deliberately written out of the narrative. 'I refuse point-blank to play in tragedy' (154), proclaims Dora: and it is a point of principle to which she doggedly adheres throughout the story of a life that encompasses two world wars, several deaths, and a career that, apart from a brief moment in their marketable youth, has been on an almost continual downward slide.

In this respect, *Wise Children* may possess not one, but two, presiding spirits. While Shakespeare – the Shakespeare of the South Bank, the writer of low comedy and high romance – is dominant, perhaps another influence can be discerned behind Dora's voice. In 1990, a year before the publication of *Wise Children*, Carter wrote a review of a biography of the actress Louise Brooks for the *London Review of Books*. Carter was a long-time fan of Brooks, particularly of *Pandora's Box*, an adaptation of Wedekind's *Lulu* directed by George Pabst in 1929. As far as Carter was concerned, '[t]he role of Lulu ... is one of the key representations of female sexuality in twentieth-century literature':[101] and she declared in *Nothing Sacred* that 'should I ever have a daughter, I would call her ... Lulu'.[102] The Chance twins are certainly visually reminiscent of Brooks, adopting at the age of fifteen her iconic bob, '[h]alf a yard of black satin that turned into our cheeks like commas' (80); and they also share her self-awareness – her capacity to 'always enjoy ... the spectacle of herself'.[103] Indeed, the association between the Chance twins and Lulu comes very close to being overt when Dora's Hollywood lover, a writer known as Irish, takes it into his head to educate her alphabetically: the affair lasts long enough for her to reach 'W. for Wedekind' (144).

More than that, though, the Chance twins' misadventures mimic Brooks' picaresque career, which Carter described as 'one of varied sexual encounters, booze, violent reversals of fortune, a good deal of laughter, and fairly continuous intellectual activity'.[104] For Brooks, who began her stage career, too, as a hoofer in musical revues, only achieved enduring iconic status in old age, when *Pandora's Box* – as great a cinematic flop on its release as *Wise Children*'s *A Midsummer Night's Dream* – was rediscovered. In the interim, she had become a recluse in New York, living on gin and the charity of a former boyfriend, but she ended her days in relative respectability being interviewed by film studies students and writing her memoirs. Nora and Dora may not be on quite the same level, but they too represent the ability to hang on against all the odds until the next upturn in their fortunes, regaining a certain notoriety as bit-players in a film now shown at art-house cinemas in Notting Hill, and on which Ph.D's are written. Like Louise Brooks, their younger selves are captured on celluloid, 'stored away, like jam, for winter' (125); and although this makes their awareness of the ravages of time sometimes painfully acute, they can still revel in their own small share of belated fame.

Nora and Dora face their inescapable mortality, therefore, with relative equanimity. While death cannot be circumvented, they nevertheless to make the best of such life as is left to them, vowing to 'go on singing and dancing until we drop in our tracks' (232). Yet the air of breezy fatalism with which *Wise Children* ends is, in retrospect, sadly apposite. Not long after Carter had finished writing the novel, she was diagnosed with lung cancer, and the disease progressed quickly. Although she had been troubled by persistent coughs for some time previously, and had been to see her GP on a number of occasions, she was not referred to a consultant until the disease was in its advanced stages. Lorna Sage attributes the cause of Carter's illness to the fact that she had been a life-long smoker, even though she 'had given up smoking years before, when she was pregnant with Alex'.[105] Veronica Horwell's obituary for *The Guardian*, though, gives an indication of what a slippery subject for biography Carter can be, for she recalls finding Carter 'smoking cigarettes in a bad-prefect-behind-the-bike-shed way on the seat by the Underground' in the period when 'she must have known about her cancer'.[106]

Whatever the facts, Carter resembled her characters in accepting her fate with stoicism (Salman Rushdie recalls a telephone conversation with her in which she described herself as possessing a 'strong streak of Oriental fatalism'),[107] while also refusing to give in gracefully. She was working on a final TV script, *The Holy Family Album*, when she fell ill: an expression of both her fierce atheism and her love of surrealist art, it consisted of a sequence of religious paintings presented as if they were a collection of photographs, taken by God the Father, depicting a pictorial narrative of Christ's life. After taking the viewer through the different stages of the Christian story, '[t]he dreadful secret of the Holy Family Album'[108] is finally revealed – in a reversal of the Oedipal dynamic, God has planned the death of his son all along. The final horror is that this act of familial murder is not treated with the revulsion it merits; instead, the sadomasochistic image of Christ's bleeding and brutalised body becomes the defining icon of Western culture, to be displayed and venerated. Although Carter initially conceived the script as a series of images with no voiceover, it was at the suggestion of the producer that she provided an off-screen narration. Her illness posed some difficulties in that respect, since the lung cancer meant that her voice changed between retakes, 'and it was actually quite difficult to match because ... her voice had changed quite a lot'.[109]

But on the most literal of levels, Carter was not going quietly. The programme, which Sage describes as 'attack[ing] God the Father for the tortures inflicted on His son in the name of Love',[110] was predictably controversial. When it was broadcast in December 1991, *The Daily Telegraph* (again, predictably), saw it as 'undeniably offensive, not to say blasphemous',[111] while *The Times* described it as 'so offensive to Christians that, hardly surprisingly, some have called for it to be banned'.[112] According to the programme's producer, John Ellis, Carter was furious that she was not given the opportunity to publicly defend the programme, a task that was taken on Channel 4's commissioning editor for Arts and Music, Waldemar Januszczak.

The lack of analysis surrounding *The Holy Family Album* has meant that the views Carter expressed within this work still have not been widely considered. As Charlotte Crofts, the only critic to have analysed this production in any detail, says, it 'has, in effect, been edited from the Carter canon':[113] the script has not been published in the Chatto & Windus editions of either Carter's dramatic work or her journalism. This has the effect of allowing critics' dismissal of the programme, which Crofts describes as 'the most outspoken manifestation of an atheism and materialism which underpins Carter's oeuvre as a whole',[114] to stand more or less unchallenged.

Crofts proposes that 'Carter's choice of *The Holy Family Album* as a title is possibly a direct reference to Marx and Engels', *The Holy Family*, a polemic diatribe against the followers of Hegelian idealism'.[115] However, it is also possible to approach this work as also an attack upon, not just Christianity, but also upon its function as underpinning a sense of British national identity. *The Holy Family Album* opens with a contemplation of the album itself, and '[a]s Carter's narration begins, the camera zooms in on a gold lock and key on the right-hand side of the album. We see the key turn as if by magic and the album cover swings open.'[116] This is not a unique conceit – Crofts regards it as 'a deliberate reference to the opening film credits of *Jamaica Inn* and *Rebecca*'[117] – but it is also employed in the opening frames of a film commissioned by the Festival of Britain in 1951, entitled *Family Portrait*. It begins with 'a picture of a hand opening a photograph album', while a 'male voice-over explained that: 'Perhaps because we in Britain live on a group of small islands – we like to think of ourselves as a family, and, of course, with the unspoken affection and outspoken words that families have ... And so the Festival of Britain is a kind of family reunion.'[118]

Whether or not the comparison is intentional[119] it is nevertheless enlightening, since it enables the possibility of drawing a parallel between the 'holy family' and the nationalistic family, which Carter portrays in identical terms: patriarchal, authoritarian and riven by destructive oedipal power-plays. In 'The Lion and the Unicorn', George Orwell has famously described England as 'a rather stuffy Victorian family... [with] its private language and its common memories... at the approach of an enemy it closes its ranks',[120] and it is precisely this claustrophobic image of family that Carter unequivocally rejects throughout her fiction, where the closed ranks of the biological family is replaced with a much more flexible and inclusive unit held together by affection, not blood. *The Holy Family Album* can, therefore, be viewed as the final, most radical, word on an issue that is explored and debated throughout her work.

The central importance that the figure of the mother came to assume within this version of family Carter came so strongly to endorse is indicated by a charming little children's story she wrote some time late in her career, but which was not published until eight years after her death. *Sea-Cat and Dragon King* stands in direct comparison to the children's book published in the seventies, *Miss Z: The Dark Young Lady*, for whereas mother is ignored and forgotten in the earlier text, here she assumes the central role. While Miss Z's mother is absent, and her father more of a hindrance than a help, here it is the infinite resource-fulness of Sea-Cat's mother that saves the day. And she does so, not by questing or adventuring, but through the exercise of her maternal and domestic skills. Sea-Cat and his mother 'live at the bottom of the sea'[121] in 'an elegant house... [whose] walls were made of pieces of driftwood of the most fantastic shapes all woven together' (12). However, explains the narrator, sea-cats, like land cats, suffer from being in water, and Sea-Cat's mother worries that her son 'look[s] like a wet hearthrug and was always catching chills' (21). Consequently, she makes him a coat that is both decorative and useful: 'a closely fitting, elegantly tailored, wonderfully complicated, waterproof, decorative, scintillating catsuit' (24).

This catches the attention of the Dragon King, who is 'ugly as he was old' (35), but who yearns to be beautiful. When he kidnaps Sea-Cat in order to steal his suit, Sea-Cat talks himself out of the situation, demon-strating a confidence that, again, is directly attributed to his mother's talents. In response to Dragon-King's demands to hand over the suit because 'I am Dragon King, Lord of the Ocean, and I am much more important than a humble little Sea-Cat' (61), Sea-Cat can draw on the sense of self-worth that is his mother's devotion has given him. 'Sea-Cat knew he was important because his mother loved him, and he said,

"I can never give away my catsuit because my mother knitted it for me and I could never give away my mother's present, because she knitted it for me with love" ' (62). Instead, Sea-Cat takes Dragon King home, where his mother designs, knits and decorates a beautiful suit for Dragon King, which transforms him into 'a complete festival in himself alone' (89). In the process, he comes to appreciate that solitary power is no substitute for friendship and family, and the story ends in a carnival mood, with Sea-Cat and Dragon King showing off Sea-Cat's mother's ingenious and spectacular suits to '[a]ll the creatures of the ocean bottom' (92).

In *Sea-Cat and Dragon King*, therefore, patriarchal authority comes to acknowledge the strength and value, not only of the maternal bond, but also of the family based around the figure of the mother. In place of God the Father, Emperor or King, we have a mother, any mother, who will exercise considerable cleverness and ingenuity in sustaining a healthy, happy and inclusive family.

Such declarations of devotion from mother to son are all the more touching in when considered in the context of Carter's illness, a fact that not even maternal resourcefulness could change. Professionally, she continued writing for as long as she was able, editing a second book of fairy tales for Virago Press from her hospital bed[122] – although she was too ill to write an introduction, a task eventually done on her behalf by Marina Warner – and she left various ideas for further projects among her papers. With an eye, now, to posterity, Carter also continued to maintain tight control over her public persona, as evidenced by her final interview for the BBC's *Omnibus* programme. It is quite remarkable that a woman who was as near death as Carter – she died a month after filming – should choose to participate in such a project, particularly one which involved speaking at such length. At this stage in her illness, as the programme clearly shows, this was difficult for her. Friends and colleagues such as John Ellis, however, argue that it was motivated by the fact that Carter still felt 'unrecognised'.[123] The *Omnibus* programme was, therefore, her final assertion of her importance: it was her own obituary, in which she presented a conclusive verdict upon her own work and recapitulated the public story of her life for the last time. And even if she had not been confronting mortality on a personal level while she was writing *Wise Children*, she was now able to use it as a vehicle through which to express, albeit in a roundabout way, her attitude towards her own death:

Basically, *Wise Children* is a comedy, and in cultural terms, comedy stands for fertility, continuance, a sense of the protean nature of the world, of the inextinguishable, unappeasable nature of the world, the unappeasable nature of appetite and desire, which isn't necessarily a tragic thing, it's the motor that keeps us going, it's the desire to go on, that everything is going on. That the fact that you're not there to see the cherry tree next year – to introduce a Japanese motif here – the fact that you're not here to see the cherry tree next year doesn't mean the cherry tree's disappeared. It means that the cherry tree's doing its own thing in its own space and time, and that's how it should be.[124]

Parts of the *Omnibus* documentary which contain footage of Carter at home with her family, are extremely poignant; but nevertheless, this part of her life remains unexpressed and unexplored in both Carter's own commentary and that provided by friends and colleagues such as Lorna Sage and Neil Jordan. Such obliqueness prompted Daniel Johnson, reviewing the programme in *The Times*, to complain that it only presented the viewer with an 'idealised portrait' of the author, since '[w]e learned nothing about their family except the private world which Angela invented for herself'.[125] The author, however, had retained control of the script of her life to the last.

Angela Carter died at home on 16 February 1992. Her funeral was a private, family affair, but was followed by a more public commemoration of her life on 29 March. Carter herself had wanted her friends to gather and watch her favourite films at the Granada cinema in Tooting: the place where, as a child, she had been initiated by her father into the delights of popular cinema. In the event, this proved impossible since the Granada had been turned into a Gala bingo hall, so the Ritzy at Brixton stood in as a substitute. The invitation to this 'celebration of her life' was in true Carter style: 'bright pink, opening up like a stage set with curtains, and showing animals, flowers and birds, including a parrot with an RSVP in its beak'.[126] Deliberately secular, the party at the Ritzy featured readings from Carter's work, the playing of her *Desert Island Discs* selection, and a speech from Tariq Ali about her politics. The tone was determinedly up-beat: according to Carter's agent Deborah Rogers, the aim was to: ' "Celebrate: honour, observe, hallow, ritualise, exalt, glorify, revere, venerate, acclaim, applaud, cheer, laud carouse, rejoice, revel . . . It sums up our theme." '[127]

Conclusion: Posthumous Fame is no Comfort at All

In 1981, BBC Radio 3 broadcast Angela Carter's drama on the turn-of-the-century novelist Ronald Firbank, a project that Charlotte Crofts has argued shows her 'formally challeng[ing] biography as a genre'.[1] It was intended, Carter said, as an 'artificial biography',[2] but it is also possible to claim that in this play she exposes the underlying artificiality of *all* biography. The play's title, 'A Self-Made Man' is itself indicative of Carter's interest in Firbank as a writer who creates his own authorial persona:

> As with a medieval saint or any other legendary being, fabulous narratives proliferated around his dandified, powdered, occasionally rouged, inimitable figure as he flitted about the cities of the world...
>
> As with all such narratives, they may be only loosely based on real events and capable of many different interpretations.[3]

The play purports to make use of the archival materials conventionally used by the biographer, such as Firbank's 'own fiction and letters',[4] and eyewitness accounts supplied by his contemporaries. However, as Charlotte Crofts says, Carter does this 'not to build unified character, but to deconstruct it; not to create a whole picture, but to fragment the image'.[5] The result is a 'polyvalent, polysemic approach [that] offers a multi-perspectival, rather than limited, view of the lives of her biographees'.[6] As Carter's last two novels, in particular, demonstrate, autobiography is similarly contingent. The accounts of their own lives offered by both Fevvers and Dora Chance are destabilised, not because they do not tell us enough, but because they tell us too much. Fevvers and Lizzie collaborate in the construction of an increasingly incredible account, acting as guarantors only of one another's tall stories. Similarly, Dora Chance tells, not a tale, but 'a tale and a half' (227) for, 'drunk in charge of a narrative', she can't 'keep a story going in a straight line' (172).

In these narratives – indeed, in much of what she wrote from the seventies onwards – Carter is mimicking in fiction what she was also doing with her own life story. Her autobiographical essays are, similarly, not a means of revelation, but rather of disguise, creating a crafted persona for public display. That is not to say that they don't tell us 'facts' about her life, but, as I have argued from the outset, the essays present us with a selective set of details which Carter reiterates, but upon which she does not elaborate, in the interviews she gave as her career gathered pace through the seventies and eighties. As she self-mockingly lamented to Lorna Sage following their first interview in 1977, 'I only have the one script, alas'.[7] This may be a comment that marks a point of departure from her loquacious, ever-inventive fictional autobiographers, who have *too many* scripts, if anything, but the end result is much the same: autobiography becomes, not a window upon the 'real' subject, but a screen of words behind which the subject is concealed from public view. Lorna Sage argues that Carter 'went in for the proliferation, rather than the death, of the author';[8] yet it is that very multiplicity, the creation of a narrative that functions as a hall of mirrors reflecting multiple images, that is the author's most effective disguise.

Therefore, Carter's literary life is the story of a life that merges with the fiction, which means that, as Lorna Sage has similarly observed, 'you cannot, in the end, separate the woman and the writer'.[9] In other words, it is possible to put the story of the life alongside the work and see them operating on the same level, for while the life informs the work, the work also informs the recording of the life. In fact, as Carter's 'tales' of the seventies show particularly well, the 'life story' is not accorded the privileged, separate, status of autobiography, but becomes, in the final analysis, just another story.

The narrative of Carter's life is, in many ways, a contradictory one, but Carter plays on these contradictions rather than suppressing them, since it is these very inconsistencies and paradoxes that lie at the heart of her conception of herself as a writer. The most fundamental of these comes to the fore once her attachment to place is considered, and her career mapped geographically. It should be noted that, for all her reputation as a traveller, a self-described 'connoisseur of cities, of American, Asiatic and even European cities',[10] it is to London that Carter always returned. Indeed, the journey she makes eventually virtually doubles back upon itself, for her upbringing in Balham and her death in Clapham comes close to forming a circle, with Clapham Common at its centre. It was within this circle that Olive and Hugh first met, and to which, after all her flights from men, her evasions and adventures, that Carter finally returned and formed her own, chosen, family.

Almost a circle, though, but not quite, for its symmetry – and along with it the neatness of the metaphor – is irremediably skewed and complicated by issues of origin. Carter's mother and father may have met 'on the tennis courts of respectable Clapham',[11] but neither of them quite belonged there. Carter's father was Scottish, and her mother was from Battersea, the product of a South Yorkshire mother and an East Anglian father. Both, therefore, were themselves immigrants or the products of immigration – furthermore, although Carter might staunchly, repeatedly, describe herself as a 'born-and-bred south Londoner',[12] she was actually born in Eastbourne. And it is for these reasons that in 'So There'll Always Be an England', she can say of 'a black girl' that 'she is no more English than I am. Like me she was only born here.'[13]

Carter's writerly identity, therefore, originates from the paradox created out of the contradiction between 'born-and-bred' and 'only born'; she is simultaneously deeply English, yet also deeply not. It is from this self-constructed position that her concern with issues of national identity arise, since she is consistently concerned with disrupting the comforting, homogenous conceptions of 'Englishness' she claims to have found so offensive from childhood onwards. As the comments cited above indicate, Carter is both drawn to and refutes an English identity, and much of her writing vacillates around this very issue. She deplored many facets of the English character as she saw it: the tendency towards a specious kind of charm; passivity in the face of authority ('If the British weren't so bloody nice, there'd be a bloody revolution', she opines in *'Fin de Siècle'*);[14] a preference for patriotic nostalgia rather than political activism. Yet, typically, she also sees the cracks and inconsistencies that point to another version of Englishness, which for her is brought to the fore in the divide between north and south London, 'a city divided in two by water'.[15]

As is clear in all her writing, in all genres, Carter staked her claim very firmly in the south of the city, what she described in *Wise Children* as 'the left-hand side, the side the tourist rarely sees, the *bastard* side of Old Father Thames' (1). In 'D'You Mean South?', an essay written in 1977 shortly after her move to Clapham, she defines the dominant characteristics of the South Londoner as if they were her own: 'We are always on the defensive. We rarely look you straight in the eye...And we are always complaining...We exhibit many of the more unattractive personality traits of the colonised.'[16] Yet the sense of identification indicated by the use of the communal 'we' is never anything less than uneasy, for South London itself has a dual personality, split between its working-class roots and the bourgeois impulse to 'better' oneself. Thus the area encompasses what Carter describes as:

> [t]he entire Rive Gauchy bit, in fact, from seedy bohemia to radical chic, to kids called Gareth and Emma playing with their Galt toys on the floor of the bank while – *at the same time* – down the road, an old lady in the pub removes her teeth in order to sing 'Some of these days' with passion and vibrancy, to tumultuous applause.[17]

Carter herself is situated on both sides of the divide: brought up to view South London as 'home' she might have been, yet her return is indistinguishable from the incursion of other middle-class migrants from across the river. It is an incongruity of which Carter is fully, resignedly, aware: 'So here they come, and I come back, don't I? And try to pretend I've never been away.'[18]

It is this doubleness, this simultaneous co-existence of contrary states and divisions within divides, which exemplifies both Carter's writing practice and her constructed autobiographical self. In her interrogation of what being 'English' really means, a concern she traces back to her own hybridity, she keeps returning to the tension created by the opposition between north and south; proletariat and petit bourgeois; charm, and the madness that charm conceals. Her allusions to such national events and institutions as the Great Exhibition and Shakespeare embody this: the Great Exhibition is of no interest to her until *after* its relocation from Hyde Park to Sydenham: her Shakespeare is not the canonical dramatist of the Leavisites, but a crowd-pleaser whose plays were performed in Bankside theatres. The Festival of Britain, too, an event that I would argue does much to inform Carter's critique of nationalism, particularly in her earlier novels, may have been conceived on and controlled from the North bank of the Thames, but its main exhibition was sited on the South side. What all of these sites have in common is that their location away from the centre of national power undermines them from within. While their overt intent is to endorse the status quo, the paradox conferred upon them by their geographical position challenges the stringent categorisations – between north and south, rich and poor, powerful and powerless, 'high' culture and 'low' culture – upon which the assumption of hegemonic control is predicated. Thus, albeit involuntarily, they foreground the theatricality underlying constructions of identity, both personal and national, and reveal them to be instead willed, provisional and thus open to question. If the aim of Empire Day was to perpetuate 'the sense of a special destiny',[19] built upon a unified conception of Englishness, then Carter's is to shatter that image in order to reveal the competing histories and identities it seeks to gloss over.

Throughout this study, I have argued that one site is worthy of particular consideration in relation to Carter's writing: the Lion and Unicorn pavilion included in the South Bank exhibition of the 1951 Festival of Britain, which claimed to showcase the distinctively 'British' character. Carter was, not surprisingly, no supporter of the Festival, but a peculiar synchronicity can be discerned between Carter's rejection of homogenous concepts of nation and selfhood, and the pavilion's depiction of Britishness as inherently dualistic. It is a contradictory impulse represented in the figures of the Lion and the Unicorn: while the Lion represented 'solidity and strength', the Unicorn exemplified the carnivalesque impulse to 'let himself go'.[20] The extent to which this event in general and this exhibition in particular influenced Carter's representation of national identity is impossible to prove; but, serendipitously or not, it assumes a peculiar pertinence in relation to her work. As I have already explained in the introduction to this study, it has frequently been observed that Carter's writing is characterised by disjunction and contradiction, split as it is between fabulation and political purpose. Carter's flights of fantasy are always wedded to an astute awareness of place, time and social context. In *The Sadeian Woman*, for example, she argues that:

> Fine art, that exists for itself alone, is art in a final state of impotence. If nobody, including the artist acknowledged art as a means of knowing the world, then art is relegated to a kind of rumpus room of the mind, and the irresponsibility of the artist and the irrelevance of art to actual living becomes part and parcel of the practice of art.[21]

This is very definitely not what Carter was about: 'a lot of my conscious energy', she once said, 'is devoted to demythologising things'.[22] It mattered very much to her, too, that her readers realised this, a fact she emphasised to Kate Webb in 1985: 'All art is political and so is mine. I want readers to understand what it is that I *mean* by my stories . . .'.[23]

It is quite evident that what Carter means her readers to understand is the materialistic practice underlying her baroque and mannered narratives, and did not see fantasy as necessarily inimical to realism, yet is it also obvious that she found readers' tendency to see the two as incompatible extremely irritating – a point she made particularly forcefully in her final interview:

> I've got absolutely nothing against realism, but there is realism and realism. I mean, the questions that I ask myself, I think they're very much to do with reality. I would like, I would really like, to have had the guts and the energy, and so on, to write about people having battles with the DHSS, but I haven't, I've done other things. I mean, I'm an arty person. OK, I write overblown, purple, self-indulgent prose. So fucking what?[24]

Carter's, therefore, is a literary persona founded on the conflation of opposites that exist side by side, unreconciled into a seamless whole. One of the best analogies of this identity and the narrative approach that results is provided by 'The Granada, Tooting', an extract from *Angela Carter's Curious Room* that was reprinted in *Shaking A Leg*. In this piece, Carter works up her anecdote regarding her childhood trips to the cinema with her father into a metaphor that becomes a final summary of her authorial technique. What appealed to her, she said, was not only the treat of her father's undivided attention, nor the films they saw there, but the building itself, 'with its mix of the real and false – real marble hugger-mugger with plaster, so you have to tap everything to see if it sounds hollow or solid'. It is to this experience that she attributes 'a tension within me that was never resolved, the tension between inside and outside, between the unappeasable appetite for the unexpected, the gorgeous, the gim-crack, the fantastic, the free play of the imagination… and harmony, order. Abstraction. Classicism.'[25] The Lion and the Unicorn, Englishness and Scottishness, rationalism and fantasy – in Carter's life story, as in her work, nothing is ever unified, or exists on one level alone.

This latter point is relevant to another glaring incongruity in relation to Carter's life – her habit of self-concealment versus her personal ambition. The desire for privacy on the part of any author is perfectly understandable; but Carter certainly did not crave anonymity. As her attitude towards literary prizes clearly indicates, she wanted both artistic success and public recognition. Lorna Sage, for example, describes her as 'a caustic and far-from-disinterested commentator on the British literary scene. She minded about prizes and reputations because she minded about reaching readers:'[26] similarly, Carmen Callil commented that 'Angie knew what she was worth...No lack of Booker or Whitbread prizes could draw from her more than a cantankerous affirmation of "what-do-you-expect?" Like Fevvers...she flew over prizes spitting deprecations on those below.'[27] Callil implies that it rankled with Carter that, while she had been a Booker judge (in 1983) none of her own books had ever been shortlisted for either the Booker or the Whitbread.

But, as Callil also says, Carter's '[r]age and a razor-sharp mind made her a difficult person to give prizes to: she was no compromiser'.[28] By the eighties, the Booker prize had become what Malcolm Bradbury describes as 'a key cultural institution[29] – in the words of Nicci Gerrard, writing in 1989: 'Publishers plan around it, Christmas shopping is simplified by it, list editors' careers can be made by it.'[30] As the furore over *The Holy Family Album* illustrates, Carter was never averse to giving offence, and thus was perhaps not the most comfortable candidate for such a mainstream award. The closest she came to it was in 1984, when many people expressed shock that *Nights at the Circus* did not reach the short list – Sara Maitland called it 'a demonstration of philistinism', Nicci Gerrard 'a baffling act of cowardice'.[31] The prize was eventually won by Anita Brookner's *Hotel du Lac*, the kind of book Carter deplored:

> I must say that I'm not really all that much in favour of the bourgeois novel that opens a door to show a world that only the very few belong to, but to which many readers may well be 'aspiring'. For example, the recently published *Hotel du Lac* seems to me a complete fantasy world.[32]

Her acid comments on Brookner – 'I've got absolutely nothing against Brookner, of course, one writes as one does'[33] – seem particularly loaded when one considers that she had just taken the prize that Carter herself so coveted.[34] Daniel Johnson claims that Carter 'had become very grand by the end of her life, a sublimation of the narcissism which was evidently part of her invented personality from the beginning',[35] which is a less diplomatic version of Callil's classification of Carter as someone who 'knew what she was worth'.

It is therefore is distinctly ironic that in Carter's case her posthumous career has far outstripped the success she enjoyed while she was alive. The explosion of interest in her work following her death is summarised by Paul Barker:

> She dies untimely, and everyone suddenly bursts out weeping. The obituaries give her better notices than anything she ever wrote

received in her lifetime. Her books sell out within three days of her death. She becomes the most read contemporary author on English university campuses. Her last story, finished during her final illness, sells 80,000 copies in paperback. She has arrived. But she is dead.[36]

Many of Carter's critics and friends have voiced an opinion that this would not have happened if Carter had lived – Nicci Gerrard, for example, observes that on her death, Carter's novels 'became her oeuvre, ready for academic discussion and instant reappraisal',[37] while Paul Barker quotes Marina Warner describing the phenomenon as 'a popular necrophilia'.[38] It certainly allowed for her work to be tidily categorised and pigeonholed; a process that she had stringently resisted during her lifetime, but which began almost immediately she had gone:

> Margaret Atwood's memorial in the *Observer* opens with Carter's 'intelligence and kindness' and goes on to construct her as a myth-ical fairy-tale figure: 'The amazing thing about her, for me, was that someone who looked so much like the Fairy Godmother . . . should actually *be* so much like the Fairy Godmother. She seemed always on the verge of bestowing something – some talisman, some magic token . . .'. Lorna Sage's obituary in the *Guardian* talked of her 'powers of enchantment and hilarity, her generous inventiveness' while the *Late Show*'s memorial on BBC2 had the presenter calling her the 'white witch of English literature', J.G. Ballard a 'friendly witch', and Salman Rushdie claimed 'English literature has lost its high sorceress, its benevolent witch queen . . . deprived of the fairy queen we cannot find the magic that will heal us' and finished by describing her as 'a very good wizard, perhaps the first wizard de-luxe'.[39]

However, as Merja Makinen's summary of these highly similar descrip-tions of Carter following her death demonstrates, a great many of these idealistic labels were applied to Carter by those very critics and friends who saw the critical rush to assess her work as reductive. Nevertheless, their idealistic testimonials arise out of an understandable desire to eulogise a great friend who had died in the most tragic of circum-stances, and they were not, in fact, permitted to stand unchallenged for long. Makinen's essay, published in the autumn of 1992, was the first example of this wish to redress the balance, cautioning that 'this concurrence of white witch/fairy godmother mythologizing needs watching',[40] and in 1995 Nicci Gerrard warned against attempts 'to

reduce ... [Carter's] mocking iconoclasm into something more comfortable and less dangerous'.[41]

I do not think, though, that the 'fairy godmother' stereotype dominates contemporary views of Carter. If any stereotype defines how we
regard her now it is, probably inevitably, that shared by other authors
whose lives were cut short in the midst of their careers, such as Sylvia Plath
and Virginia Woolf: the tragic image of the writer who died too young.
Yet this goes hand-in-hand with a suspicion of the impulse to idealise
the figure of the dead writer, illustrated by a recently-published collection
of essays edited by Andrew Motion, to which the writer Ali Smith
contributes a piece on Carter. Allying Carter with figures such as Katherine
Mansfield, Sylvia Plath and Christopher Marlow could, again, be conducive
to romanticised reduction; fruitless speculation as to how her career
might have developed, had she lived. The essays contained in Motion's
collection do go some way down this road: in his introduction, Motion
admitts that the writers had been encouraged

> to talk about certain key themes: what did we lose by the early death
> of the people they were talking about; what might have happened to
> them, and what might they have written, had they lived for longer;
> how does their early death affect our reading of their work.[42]

Allied to this endeavour, however, is a scepticism regarding the nature
of the biographical process: looming large in Ali Smith's essay is a
consideration of the constructed nature of the Carter image, the 'work-
aday transformation into the performance of herself'[43] exemplified by
the creation of a staged photograph taken in her study in 1989. Here,
Carter's knowing construction of an authorial persona is foregrounded,
and the indeterminate status of the product, suspended as it is between
'fact' and 'fiction', acknowledged.

It has become a convention among Carter critics to express reluctance
at the point of closure, in deference to Carter's own disinclination to
commit herself to definitive conclusions. Linden Peach asserts in his
'Postscript' that 'I have deliberately avoided writing a "conclusion" to
this critical study ... because I do not believe that Carter herself
approved of conclusions',[44] and Charlotte Crofts, referring back to
Peach's statement, ends with an 'Envoi', a reference to 'the end of
Nights at the Circus, as a suitable subtitle with which to qualify the
conclusiveness of a conclusion'.[45] There is no need of such qualification
in the case of this study, however. Complete closure is impossible in the
case of a literary life, for such a life continues for as long as an audience

for that author still exists. Most of Carter's writing remains in print: it is read by general readers and studied at universities, and has lost none of its capacity to shock, startle and delight.[46] Whether Carter would appreciate this is another matter: as she wrote somewhat prophetically in 'Notes from the Front Line' in 1983, 'posthumous fame is no comfort at all'.[47]

Notes

Introduction: Is she fact, or is she fiction?

1. Daniel Johnson, 'Books Barely Furnish a Room', *The Times* (16 September 1992), p. 3.
2. Ali Smith, 'Get Carter', in Andrew Motion, ed., *Interrupted Lives* (London: National Portrait Gallery Publications, 2004), pp. 80–95 (p. 92).
3. Angela Carter, 'Trouser Protest', in Joan Smith, ed., *Shaking A Leg: Collected Journalism and Writings* (London: Chatto & Windus, 1997), pp. 113–17 (p. 113). Originally published in *New Society*, 20 November, 1975.
4. Angela Carter, 'The New Vegetarians', in *Shaking A Leg*, pp. 79–83 (p. 79). Originally published in *New Society*, 4 March 1976.
5. Joan Smith, 'Introduction', *Shaking A Leg*.
6. Angela Carter, 'The Quilt Maker', in *Sex and Sensibility: Stories by Contemporary Women Writers from Nine Countries* (London: Sidgwick & Jackson, 1981), pp. 120–40 (p. 121). All subsequent references in the text are to this edition.
7. Rita Felski, *Beyond Feminist Aesthetics: Feminist Literature and Social Change* (Cambridge, MA: Harvard University Press, 1989), p. 86.
8. John Haffenden, 'Magical Mannerist', *The Literary Review* (November, 1984), pp. 34–38 (p. 34). Reprinted in Haffenden, *Novelists in Interview* (London: Methuen, 1985).
9. In Carter's preface to 'Sugar Daddy', she is at pains to point out that ' "Carter" is the name of my first husband, not that of my father'. Angela Carter, 'Sugar Daddy', in Ursula Owen, ed., *Fathers: Reflections By Daughters* (London: Virago Press, 1983), pp. 20–30 (p. 20). The text of the essay, though not the introduction, is reprinted in *Shaking A Leg*, pp. 19–29.
10. Haffenden, p. 34
11. Paul Barker, 'The Return of the Magic Story-Teller', *The Independent on Sunday* (8 January 1995), pp. 14 and 16 (p. 14).
12. Olga Kenyon, 'Angela Carter', *The Writer's Imagination* (Bradford: University of Bradford Print Unit, 1992), pp. 23–33 (p. 23).
13. Angela Carter, 'The Mother Lode', in *Shaking A Leg: Collected Journalism and Writings* (London: Chatto & Windus, 1997), pp. 2–15 (p. 3). Originally published in *New Review*, 1976. Reprinted in Angela Carter, *Nothing Sacred: Selected Writings* (London: Virago Press, 1982), pp. 3–19.
14. Ibid., p. 23
15. Lorna Sage, *Angela Carter* (Plymouth: Northcote House, 1994), p. 22. An earlier version of this book, entitled *Death of the Author*, was published in *Granta*, 41 (1992).
16. Sage, *Angela Carter*, p. 4.
17. Lisa Appignanesi, *Angela Carter In Conversation* (London: ICA Video, 1987).
18. Felski, p. 100.
19. Kim Evans (dir.), *Angela Carter's Curious Room*, Omnibus (BBC2, 15.9.92).

20. Felski, p. 112.
21. Laura Marcus, *Auto/biographical Discourses* (Manchester: Manchester University Press, 1994), p. 280.
22. Judith Butler, *Gender Trouble* (London and NY: Routledge, 1990), p. 147.
23. Ibid., p. 136.
24. Marcus, p. 280.
25. Angela Carter, 'Preface', *Come Unto These Yellow Sands* (Newcastle upon Tyne: Bloodaxe Books, 1985), p. 7.
26. Haffenden, p. 36.
27. Angela Carter, 'Notes from the Front Line', in *Shaking A Leg*, pp. 36–43 (p. 38) (italics Carter's). Originally published in Michelene Wandor, ed., *Gender and Writing* (London: Pandora Press, 1983).
28. Joseph Bristow and Trev Lynn Broughton, 'Introduction', in Bristow and Broughton, eds., *The Infernal Desires of Angela Carter: Fiction, Femininity, Feminism* (Harlow: Addison Wesley Longman, 1997), p. 6.
29. Appignanesi, *Angela Carter in Conversation*.
30. Carter, 'The Mother Lode', p. 12.

1 Alienated is the only way to be

1. Angela Carter, 'The Mother Lode', in *Shaking A Leg: Collected Journalism and Writings* (London: Chatto & Windus, 1997), pp. 2–15 (p. 3).
2. Ibid.
3. Ibid.
4. Ibid.
5. Ibid., p. 2.
6. Ibid., p. 3.
7. Lorna Sage, *Angela Carter* (Plymouth: Northcote House, 1994), p. 5.
8. Carter, 'The Mother Lode', p. 3.
9. Ibid., pp. 3–4.
10. Ibid., p. 9.
11. Ibid., p. 7.
12. Ibid.
13. Ibid.
14. Ibid., p. 8.
15. Ibid.
16. Ibid., p. 9.
17. Ibid., p. 8.
18. Ibid., p. 9.
19. Ibid., p. 11.
20. Ibid., p. 12.
21. Ibid., p. 11.
22. Ibid., p. 14.
23. Ibid., p. 5.
24. Ibid., p. 6.
25. Ibid., p. 14.
26. Lorna Sage, 'A Savage Sideshow', *New Review*, 4:39/40, pp. 51–57 (p. 53).
27. Carter, 'The Mother Lode', p. 3.

28. Richard Weight, *Patriots: National Identity in Britain 1940–2000* (London: Pan Books, 2002), p. 30.
29. A.J.P. Taylor, *English History 1914–1945* [rev. edn] (Oxford: Oxford University Press, 1975), p. 486.
30. Weight, p. 65.
31. Lisa Appinanesi, *Angela Carter in Conversation* (London: ICA Video, 1987).
32. Carter, 'My Father's House', in *Shaking A Leg*, pp. 15–19 (p. 18). Originally published in *New Society*, 1976. Reprinted in Angela Carter, *Nothing Sacred: Selected Writings* (London: Virago Press, 1982), pp. 20–25.
33. Ibid., p. 18.
34. Ibid.
35. Ibid., p. 16.
36. Ibid., p. 18.
37. Ibid., p. 16.
38. Ibid., p. 18.
39. Ibid., pp. 18–19.
40. Ibid., p. 19.
41. Ibid.
42. Sage, *Angela Carter*, p. 7 [italics Sage's].
43. Carter, 'Sugar Daddy', in *Shaking A Leg*, pp. 19–29 (p. 19). First published in Ursula Owen, ed., *Fathers: Reflections By Daughters* (London: Virago Press, 1983), pp. 20–30.
44. Ibid., p. 26.
45. Sage *Angela Carter*, p. 7.
46. Carter, 'Sugar Daddy', p. 25.
47. Ibid.
48. Ibid., p. 24.
49. Carter, 'The Mother Lode', p. 2.
50. Carter, 'Sugar Daddy', p. 24.
51. Ibid., p. 19.
52. Ibid., p. 25.
53. Ibid., p. 24.
54. Ibid., p. 28.
55. Carter, 'The Mother Lode', p. 9.
56. Ibid., p. 13.
57. Ibid., p. 10.
58. Ibid.
59. Carter, 'Sugar Daddy', p. 22.
60. Ibid., p. 25.
61. Ibid., p. 27.
62. Ibid., p. 26.
63. Carter, 'The Mother Lode', p. 9.
64. Carter, 'Sugar Daddy', p. 20.
65. Ibid., p. 21.
66. Ibid., p. 26.
67. Joan Smith, 'Introduction', *Shaking A Leg*.
68. Kim Evans (dir.), *Angela Carter's Curious Room*, *Omnibus*, BBC2, 15 September 1992.
69. Carter, 'The Mother Lode', p. 14.

70. Evans, *Angela Carter's Curious Room*.
71. Carter, 'The Mother Lode', p. 10.
72. Appignanesi, *Angela Carter in Conversation*.
73. Sage, 'A Savage Sideshow', p. 54.
74. Ibid.
75. 'Angela Carter's Curious Room'.
76. Sage, *Angela Carter*, p. 6.
77. Carter, 'The Mother Lode', p. 14.
78. Ibid., p. 15.
79. Ibid.
80. Angela Carter, 'Edward Shorter: *A History of Women's Bodies*', in *Shaking A Leg*, pp. 70–73 (p. 71). Originally published in *New Society*, 24 February 1983.
81. Sage, *Angela Carter*, p. 15.
82. Sara Mills, *et al.*, *Feminist Readings/Feminists Reading* (Brighton: Harvester Wheatsheaf, 1989), p. 134.
83. Lucie Armitt, *Contemporary Women's Fiction and the Fantastic* (Basingstoke: Macmillan, 2000), p. 203.
84. John Haffenden, 'Magical Mannerist', *The Literary Review* (November 1984), pp. 34–38 (p. 35).
85. Moira Waterson, 'Flights of Fancy in Balham', *Observer Magazine* (11 November 1986), pp. 42–45 (pp. 42, 45).
86. Ibid., p. 45.
87. David Marquand, 'Sir Stafford Cripps', in Michael Sissons and Philip French, eds., *Age of Austerity* (Harmondsworth: Penguin, 1964), pp. 173–95 (pp. 173–74).
88. Susan Cooper, 'Snoek Piquante', in Sissons and French, eds., pp. 35–57 (pp. 35–36).
89. Juliet Gardiner, *From the Bomb to the Beatles: The Changing Face of Post-War Britain 1945–1965* (London: Collins & Brown, 1999), p. 31.
90. Cooper, in Sissons and French, eds., p. 37.
91. Angela Carter, 'Truly, It Felt Like Year One', in Sara Maitland, ed., *Very Heaven: Looking Back at the 1960s* (London: Virago, 1988), pp. 209–16 (p. 210).
92. Angela Carter, *The Magic Toyshop* [1967] (London: Virago, 1981), p. 55. All subsequent references in the text are to this edition.
93. This is anachronistic reference within a novel supposedly set in the fifties, since the first colour supplements did not appear in Britain until 1964. If we take Carter's word that *The Magic Toyship* is set in the era of her childhood, then this is an example of the kind of 'demonic inaccuracy as regards fact' (Peter Kemp, 'Magical History Tour' [*Sunday Times*, 9 June 1991]) that compromised her early career in journalism.
94. Ian Cox, *The South Bank Exhibition: A Guide to the Story it Tells* (H.M. Stationary Office, 1951), p. 6.
95. Ibid., p. 8.
96. Gardiner, p. 59.
97. Appignanesi, *Angela Carter in Conversation*.
98. Roy Strong, 'Prologue: Utopia Limited', in Mary Banham and Bevis Hiller, eds., *A Tonic to the Nation: The Festival of Britain 1951* (London: Thames and Hudson, 1976), p. 8.
99. Cox, p. xxxii.

100. Ibid., p. 7.
101. Michael Frayn, 'Festival', in Sissons and French, pp. 330–52 (p. 331).
102. Lorna Sage, 'Angela Carter', in Malcolm Bradbury and Judy Cooke, eds., *New Writing* (London: Minerva, 1992), pp. 185–93 (p. 190).
103. Haffenden, p. 35.
104. Paterson, p. 45.
105. Cox, p. 23
106. R.D. Russell and Robert Goodden, 'The Lion and Unicorn Pavilion', in Banham and Hillier, eds., p. 99.
107. Emma Parker, 'The Consumption of Angela Carter: Women, Food and Power', *Ariel: A Review of International English Literature*, 31, 3 (July 2000), pp. 141–69 (pp. 144–45).
108. Aidan Day, *Angela Carter: The Rational Glass* (Manchester: Manchester University Press, 1998), p. 24.
109. John R. Davis, *The Great Exhibition* (Stroud: Sutton Publishing, 1999), p. 34.
110. Ibid., p. 36.
111. Weight, p. 191.
112. Ibid., p. 192.
113. Angela Carter, 'So There'll Always Be an England', in *Shaking A Leg*, pp. 185–89 (p. 185). Originally published in *New Society*, 7 October 1982.
114. Ibid., p. 186.
115. Ibid., p. 185.
116. Ibid.
117. Ibid., p. 186.
118. Ibid.
119. Ibid., p. 187.
120. Ibid., p. 185.
121. Ibid., p. 187.
122. Ibid.
123. Ibid., p. 188.
124. Ibid., p. 186.
125. Weight, p. 201.
126. Jean Wyatt, 'The Violence of Gendering: Castration Images in Angela Carter's *The Magic Toyshop, The Passion of New Eve*, and "Peter and the Wolf"', in Alison Easton, ed., *Angela Carter: Contemporary Critical Essays* (Basingstoke: Macmillan, 2000), pp. 58–83 (p. 72).
127. Sara Mills *et al.*, p. 138.
128. Weight, p. 211.

2 I'm a sucker for the worker hero

1. *Observer*, 31 January 1965, quoted in Richard Weight, *Patriots: National Identity in Britain 1940–2000* (London: Pan Books, 2002), p. 454.
2. Weight, pp. 454–55.
3. Juliet Gardiner, *From the Bomb to the Beatles: The Changing Face of Post-War Britain 1945–1965* (London: Collins & Brown, 1999), p. 150.
4. Lorna Sage, 'A Savage Sideshow', *New Review*, 4:39/40, pp. 51–57 (p. 54).

5. Sheila Rowbotham, *Promise of A Dream: Remembering the Sixties* (London: Penguin Books, 2000), p. xiv.
6. Marc O'Day, '"Mutability is Having a Field Day": The Sixties Aura of Angela Carter's Bristol Trilogy', in Lorna Sage, *Flesh and the Mirror: Essays on the Art of Angela Carter* (London: Virago Press, 1994), pp. 24–58 (p. 25).
7. http://www.members.lycos.co.uk/brisray/bristol/blitz1.htm, accessed 11 August 2004.
8. Becky E. Conekin, *'The Autobiography of a Nation': The 1951 Festival of Britain* (Manchester: Manchester University Press, 2003), p. 164.
9. Ibid.
10. Ibid.
11. Archbishop of Canterbury, Speech, 17 July 1950, quoted in Conekin, p. 17.
12. Ibid., p. 26.
13. Les Bedford, 'Angela Carter: An Interview' (Sheffield: Sheffield University Television, 1977).
14. Charlotte Crofts, *'Anagrams of Desire': Angela Carter's Writing for Radio, Film and Television* (Manchester: Manchester University Press, 2003).
15. Kim Evans (dir.), *Angela Carter's Curious Room*, Omnibus, BBC2, 15 September 1992.
16. Angela Carter, 'The Granada, Tooting', published in *Shaking A Leg: Collected Journalism and Writing* (London: Chatto & Windus, 1997), p. 400. This is an extract from the script of the *Omnibus* documentary *Angela Carter's Curious Room*.
17. Sage, *Angela Carter* (Plymouth: Northcote House, 1994), p. 28.
18. *Angela Carter's Curious Room*.
19. 'Fat is Ugly', in *Shaking A Leg*, pp. 56–60 (p. 56). All subsequent references are from this edition. First published in *New Society*, 28 November 1974.
20. Ibid., p. 60.
21. Olga Kenyon, 'Angela Carter', *The Writer's Imagination* (Bradford: University of Bradford Print Unit, 1992), pp. 23–33 (p. 23).
22. Appignanesi, 'Angela Carter in Conversation'.
23. Ibid.
24. Ian McEwan, 'Sweet Smell of Excess', *Sunday Times Magazine* (9 September 1984), pp. 42–44 (p. 43). The fact that this is just about all Carter ever said publicly about her first marriage is evident in the obituaries and articles written following her death, which mention it in passing if at all. Only the anonymous writer of an obituary published in *The Times* says (presumably drawing on McEwan's interview) that her first husband 'took her on peace marches and introduced her to jazz' ('Angela Carter', *The Times* [17 February 1992], p. 15).
25. Angela Carter, 'Sugar Daddy', in *Shaking A Leg*, pp. 19–29 (p. 22).
26. 'A Letter From Angela Carter', in *The European English Messenger*, 4,1 (Spring, 1996), pp. 11–13 (p. 12).
27. Appignanesi, *Angela Carter in Conversation*.
28. Kenyon, p. 24.
29. McEwan, p. 43.
30. Alex Hamilton, 'Sade and Prejudice', *The Guardian* (30 March 1979), p. 15.
31. John Haffenden, 'Magical Mannerist', *The Literary Review* (November 1984), pp. 34–38 (p. 36).
32. Kenyon, p. 24.

33. Bedford, 'Angela Carter: An Interview'.
34. McEwan, p. 43.
35. Ibid.
36. Helen Cagney Watts, 'An Interview with Angela Carter', *Bête Noir*, Vol. 8 (1985), pp. 161–76 (p. 166).
37. Claire Harman, 'Demon-lovers and Sticking-plaster', *Independent on Sunday* (30 October 1994), p. 37.
38. Kenyon, p. 165.
39. John Bowen, 'Grotesques', *The New York Times Book Review* (19 February 1967), p. 44.
40. A contrary argument is provided by Linden Peach, in *Angela Carter* (Basingstoke: Macmillan, 1998), who argues of the Bristol trilogy that '[e]ach novel, at various levels, including parody, is indebted to Euro-American Gothic.... Carter pursues themes and motifs from nineteenth-century American writers.... [Her] view of American Gothic writing was undoubtedly mediated through Leslie Fiedler's *Love and Death in the American Novel* (1960) which quickly became required reading for students of literature' (27).
41. Bedford, 'Angela Carter: An Interview'.
42. Haffenden, p. 35.
43. Angela Carter, 'Truly, It Felt Like Year One', in Sara Maitland, ed., *Very Heaven: Looking Back at the 1960s* (London: Virago, 1988), pp. 209–16 (p. 211).
44. Ibid., p. 210.
45. Ibid.
46. Arthur Marwick, *British Society since 1945* [rev. edn] (London: Penguin, 1996), p. 56.
47. Weight, p. 379.
48. Ibid.
49. O'Day, p. 57.
50. Angela Carter, *Shadow Dance* [1966] (London: Virago Press, 1994), p. 19. All subsequent references are to this edition.
51. Angela Carter, 'Notes for the Theory of Sixties Style', in *Shaking A Leg*, pp. 105–09 (p. 105). First published in *New Society*, 14 December 1967. Reprinted in Angela Carter, *Nothing Sacred: Selected Writings* (London: Virago Press, 1982), pp. 85–90.
52. Mick Farren and Edward Barker, *Watch Out Kids* (London: Open Books, 1972).
53. Christopher Booker, *The Neophiliacs: A Study of the Revolution in English Life in the Fifties and Sixties* (London: Pimlico, 1992), p. 239.
54. Ibid., p. 12.
55. Ibid., p. 59.
56. Elizabeth Wilson, *Adorned in Dreams: Fashion and Modernity* (London: Virago Press, 1985), p. 183.
57. Sage, *Angela Carter*, p. 9.
58. Angela Carter, 'Jean-Luc Godard', in *Shaking A Leg*, pp. 380–81 (p. 381). From *Visions*, Channel 4, 11 May 1983.
59. Carter, 'Truly, It Felt Like Year One', p. 211.
60. Angela Carter, 'Jean-Luc Godard', p. 380.
61. Jean-Luc Godard, quoted in Wheeler Winston Dixon, *The Films of Jean-Luc Godard* (Albany: State University of New York Press, 1997), p. 18.
62. Ibid., p. 17.

63. Sadie Plant, *The Most Radical Gesture: The Situationist International in a Postmodern Age* (London: Routledge, 1992), p. 1.
64. Guy Debord, *The Society of the Spectacle*, quoted in Plant, p. 169.
65. O'Day, p. 31.
66. Ibid., p. 35.
67. Angela Carter, *Several Perceptions* [1968] (London: Virago Press, 1995), p. 51. All further references are from this edition.
68. T.S. Eliot, *The Waste Land*, in The Waste Land *and Other Poems* (London: Faber & Faber, 1972), p. 29.
69. Bosley Crowther, review of *Breathless* in *The New York Times* (8 February 1961), p. 26.
70. O'Day, p. 43.
71. Carter, 'Fat is Ugly', p. 56.
72. R.D. Laing, *The Divided Self* (London: Penguin, 1965), p. 42.
73. Bedford, 'Angela Carter: An Interview'.
74. R.D. Laing, Preface to Pelican edition of *The Divided Self*, September 1964.
75. Rowbotham, p. 171.
76. Ibid., p. 155.
77. Carter, 'Truly, It Felt Like Year One', p. 212.
78. Jonathon Green, *All Dressed Up: The Sixties and the Counterculture* (London: Pimlico, 1999), p. 260.
79. Ibid., p. 271.
80. Rowbotham, p. 155.
81. Carter, 'Truly, It Felt Like Year One', p. 212.
82. Angela Carter, *Nothing Sacred: Selected Writings* (London: Virago Press, 1982), p. 84.

3   What were the sixties really like?

1. Angela Carter, *Love* [1971] (London: Pan Books Ltd, 1988 [rev. edn]), p. 113. All subsequent references are from this edition.
2. John Haffenden, 'Magical Mannerist', *The Literary Review* (November 1984), pp. 34–38 (p. 34).
3. 'Truly, It Felt Like Year One', in Sara Maitland, ed., *Very Heaven: Looking Back at the 1960s* (London: Virago, 1988), pp. 209–16 (p. 214).
4. Ibid.
5. Ibid.
6. Ibid.
7. Ibid., p. 215.
8. Anna Coote and Bea Campbell, *Sweet Freedom: The Struggle for Women's Liberation* [2nd edn] (Oxford: Blackwell, 1987), p. 5.
9. Sheila Rowbotham, *Promise of A Dream: Remembering the Sixties* (London: Penguin Books, 2000), p. 159.
10. Ibid., p. 160.
11. Ibid.
12. Ibid., p. 161.
13. Ibid., p. 162.
14. Ibid., pp. 162–63.

15. John Berger, *Ways of Seeing* (London: Penguin Books, 1972), p. 47.
16. Angela Carter, 'Notes from the Front Line', in *Shaking A Leg: Collected Journalism and Writings* (London: Chatto & Windus, 1997), pp. 36–43 (pp. 37–38).
17. Ibid., p. 39.
18. Ibid., p. 38.
19. Haffenden, p. 34.
20. Helen Cagney Watts, 'An Interview with Angela Carter', *Bête Noir*, 8 (1985), pp. 161–76 (p. 163).
21. Alison Easton, 'Introduction', *Angela Carter: Contemporary Critical Essays* (Basingstoke: Macmillan, 2000), pp. 1–19 (p. 3).
22. Les Bedford, 'Angela Carter: An Interview' (Sheffield: Sheffield University Television, 1977).
23. David Punter, *The Literature of Terror: A History of Gothic Fictions from 1765 to the Present Day* (London: Longman, 1980), p. 398.
24. Bedford, 'Angela Carter: An Interview'.
25. Punter, p. 396.
26. Angela Carter, *Heroes and Villains* [1969] (London: Penguin, 1981), p. 31. All subsequent references are from this edition.
27. Linden Peach, *Angela Carter* (Basingstoke: Macmillan, 1998), p. 86.
28. Angela Carter, 'Fools Are My Theme', in *Shaking A Leg*, pp. 31–36 (p. 32). First published as 'Fools Are My Theme: Let Satire Be My Song', in *Vector*, 109 (Easter 1982).
29. Roz Kaveney, 'New New World Dreams: Angela Carter and Science Fiction', in Lorna Sage, ed., *Flesh and the Mirror*, pp. 171–88 (p. 174).
30. Bedford, 'Angela Carter: An Interview'.
31. Lucie Armitt, ed., *Where No Man Has Gone Before: Women and Science Fiction* (London: Routledge, 1991), pp. 1–12 (pp. 9–10).
32. Peter Nicholls, 'The Monsters and the Critics', in Peter Nicholls, ed., *Explorations of the Marvellous* (London: Fontana, 1978), p. 180.
33. Carter, 'Fools Are My Theme', p. 32.
34. Angela Carter, 'The Mother Lode', in *Shaking A Leg*, pp. 2–15 (p. 10).
35. Carter, 'Fools Are My Theme', p. 33.
36. Angela Carter, 'Anger in A Black Landscape', in *Shaking A Leg*, pp. 36–52 (p. 44). First published in Dorothy Thompson, ed., *Over Our Dead Bodies: Women Against the Bomb* (London: Virago Press, 1983).
37. Carter, 'Anger in a Black Landscape', p. 43.
38. Ibid., pp. 43–44.
39. Ibid., p. 48.
40. Richard Weight, *Patriots: National Identity in Britain 1940–2000* (London: Pan Books, 2002) p. 287.
41. Jonathon Green, *All Dressed Up: The Sixties and the Counterculture* (London: Pimlico, 1999), p. 23.
42. Ibid.
43. Ibid., p. 289.
44. Leslie Stone, 'Britain and the World', in David McKie and Chris Cook, eds., *The Decade of Disillusion: British Politics in the Sixties* (London and Basingstoke: Macmillan, 1972), p. 122.
45. Carter, 'Fools Are My Theme', p. 32.
46. Ibid.

47. Becky E. Conekin, *'The Autobiography of a Nation': The 1951 Festival of Britain* (Manchester: Manchester University Press, 2003), p. 94.
48. George Orwell, 'The Lion and the Unicorn: Socialism and the English Genius', in *The Collected Essays, Journalism and Letters: Volume 2* (London: Penguin, 1970), p. 99.
49. Carter, 'Anger in a Black Landscape', p. 45.
50. Joanne P. Sharp, 'Gendering Nationhood: A Feminist Engagement with National Identity', in Nancy Duncan, ed., *Body Space: Geographies of Gender and Sexuality* (London: Routledge, 1996), pp. 97–108 (p. 98).
51. Ibid.
52. Homi K. Bhabha, ed., 'Introduction' to *Nation and Narration* (London: Routledge, 1990), p. 3.
53. Bedford, 'Angela Carter: An Interview'.
54. Sage, *Angela Carter*, p. 20.
55. Peach, p. 65.
56. Bedford, 'Angela Carter: An Interview'.
57. Ibid.
58. Ibid.
59. Linden Peach, who also makes this observation, assumes that this was intentional on Carter's part, arguing that the name 'Annabel Lee in Poe's poem is...divided to provide the names of two of the leading protagonists' (*Angela Carter*, p. 62). He did not, though, have access to Carter's interview with Les Bedford, in which she claimed to have been unaware, consciously at least, of the connection:

> The girl in *Love* was called Madelaine for a long time, after Madelaine Usher, but then I thought, well, that's cheap, that's giving the game away, and I changed her name to Annabel which has no...of course, it has even more literary connotations. I was completely...I hadn't realised that until this moment. It's Annabel Lee!

60. Bedford, 'Angela Carter: An Interview'.
61. Nicholas Royle, *The Uncanny* (Manchester: Manchester University Press, 2003), p. 136.
62. Ibid.
63. Jonathan Dollimore, *Radical Tragedy* [rev. edn] (Brighton: Harvester Wheatsheaf, 1989), p. 39.
64. Jackson, p. 87.
65. Lorna Sage, 'A Savage Sideshow', *New Review*, 4, 39/40, pp. 51–57 (p. 55).
66. Marc O'Day, ' "Mutability is Having a Field Day": The Sixties Aura of Angela Carter's Bristol Trilogy', in Lorna Sage, *Flesh and the Mirror: Essays on the Art of Angela Carter* (London: Virago Press, 1994), pp. 24–58 (p. 48).
67. Green, p. 74.
68. Ibid., pp.74–75.
69. Annette Kuhn, *Family Secrets* (London: Verso, 1995), p. 11.
70. Ibid., p. 12.
71. Carter, 'The Mother Lode', p. 9.
72. Marina Warner, *Fantastic Metamorphoses, Other Worlds* (Oxford: Oxford University Press, 2002), p. 163.

73. Patricia Juliana Smith has also used this pun, as the title for an essay on *Love*, 'All You Need is *Love*: Angela Carter's Novel of Sixties Sex and Sensibility', *The Review of Contemporary Fiction* (Fall, 1994), pp. 24–29.
74. In fact, Carter originally intended Annabel's name to be Madelaine, after Poe's heroine. For details, see n. 58.
75. O'Day, p. 47.

4   A quite different reality

1. Angela Carter, 'Truly, It Felt Like Year One', in Sara Maitland, ed., *Very Heaven: Looking Back at the 1960s* (London: Virago, 1988), pp. 209–16 (p. 213).
2. Ian McEwan, 'Sweet Smell of Excess', *Sunday Times Magazine* (9 September 1984), pp. 42–44 (p. 43).
3. Angela Carter, 'My Maugham Award', in *Shaking A Leg: Collected Journalism and Writing* (London: Chatto & Windus, 1997), pp. 203–04 (p. 203). First published in *The Author*, Autumn 1970.
4. Catherine Stott, 'Runaway to the Land of Promise', *Guardian* (10 August 1972), p. 9.
5. Ibid.
6. Carter, 'My Maugham Award', p. 204.
7. Ibid.
8. Lisa Appignanesi, *Angela Carter in Conversation* (London: ICA Video, 1987).
9. Angela Carter, introduction to 'Oriental Romances – Japan', in *Nothing Sacred: Selected Writings* (London: Virago Press, 1982), p. 28.
10. Susannah Clapp, 'On Madness, Men and Fairy-Tales', *The Independent on Sunday* (9 June 1991), pp. 26–27 (p. 26). That she went to Japan to escape a 'Judeo-Christian culture' became Carter's stock answer whenever asked about this period of her life.
11. Ibid.
12. Clapp, p. 26.
13. Peter Kemp, 'Magical History Tour', *Sunday Times* (9 June 1991). Page number unavailable.
14. Angela Carter, 'Poor Butterfly', in *Shaking A Leg*, pp. 249–54 (p. 249). First published in *New Society*, 16 March 1972. Reprinted in *Nothing Sacred: Selected Writings* (London: Virago Press, 1982), pp. 44–50.
15. Ibid. Carter reiterated this in her interview with Les Bedford, in which she portrayed her time in Japan as a chance to grow up and make the discovery that 'organising my life' was actually 'a piece of cake, it's very easy to do this'.
16. Olga Kenyon, 'Angela Carter', *The Writer's Imagination* (Bradford: University of Bradford Print Unit, 1992), pp. 23–33 (p. 25). However, perhaps this statement should be reconsidered in the light of Carter's later claim to Lisa Appignanesi that 'I was being a bit facetious there'.
17. Nicci Gerrard, 'Angela Carter is Now More Popular than Virginia Woolf...', *Observer Life* (9 July 1995), pp. 20, 22–23 (p. 22).
18. Paul, 'The Return of the Magic Story-Teller', *Independent on Sunday* (8 January 1995), pp. 14, 16 (p. 14).
19. Angela Carter', 'Tokyo Pastoral', in *Shaking A Leg*, pp. 231–34 (p. 232). First published in *New Society* (11 June 1970). Reprinted in *Nothing Sacred*, pp. 29–33

(my italics). This is an excellent example of Carter's sophisticated evasion technique, since she may either be speaking about herself and another person (or persons), or on behalf of the neighbourhood in general.

20. Carter, 'Notes for a Theory of Sixties Style', in *Shaking A Leg*, pp. 105–09 (p. 105). First published in *New Society* (14 December 1967). Reprinted in *Nothing Sacred*, pp. 85–90.

21. Angela Carter, 'Afterword to *Fireworks*', in *Burning Your Boats: Collected Short Stories*, pp. 459–60 (p. 460).

22. Ibid., p. 459.

23. Ibid. (my italics).

24. Angela Carter, *Fireworks* [1974] (London: Virago Press, 1987 [rev. edn]), p. 2. All subsequent references are to this edition.

25. Berger, *Ways of Seeing* (London: Penguin Books, 1972), p. 64.

26. Lorna Sage, *Angela Carter* (Plymouth: Northcote House, 1994), p. 27.

27. Marina Warner, 'Obituary: Angela Carter', *The Independent* (18 February, 1992). Page numbers unavailable.

28. Linden Peach, Angela Carter (Basingstoke: Macmillan, 1998), p. 20.

29. Ibid., pp. 20–21.

30. Marina Warner, 'Obituary: Angela Carter', *Independent* (18 February 1992).

31. Angela Carter, 'Once More Into the Mangle', in *Shaking A Leg*, pp. 244–48 (p. 248). First published in *New Society* (29 April 1971). Reprinted in *Nothing Sacred*, pp. 38–44.

32. Ibid., p. 247.

33. Ibid., p. 245.

34. Angela Carter, *Miss Z: The Dark Young Lady* (London: Heinemann, 1970), p. 5. All subsequent references are to this edition.

35. Laurie Lee, 'The Lion and the Unicorn', in Ian Cox, *The South Bank Exhibition: A Guide to the Story It Tells* (H.M. Stationary Office, 1951), p. 67.

36. R.D. Russell and R. Goodden, 'The Lion and Unicorn Pavilion', in Mary Banham and Bevis Hiller, eds., *A Tonic to the Nation: The Festival of Britain 1951* (London: Thames and Hudson, 1976), p. 100.

37. Quoted in Sage, *Angela Carter*, p. 34.

38. Lorna Sage, 'A Savage Sideshow', *New Review*, 4, 39/40, pp. 51–57 (p. 56).

39. Kenyon, p. 25.

40. Clapp, p. 26.

41. Stott, p. 9.

42. McEwan, 'Sweet Smell of Excess', p. 44.

43. Ali Smith, 'Angela Carter', in Andrew Motion, ed., *Interrupted Lives* (London: National Portrait Gallery Publications, 2004), pp. 80–95 (p. 87).

44. Ibid., p. 88.

45. Susan Rubin Suleiman, 'The Fate of the Surrealist Imagination in the Society of the Spectacle', in Sage, ed., *Flesh and the Mirror*, pp. 98–116 (p. 100).

46. Ibid., p. 99.

47. Warner, 'Obituary: Angela Carter'.

48. Suleiman, p. 99.

49. Tessa Morris-Suzuki, *Re-Inventing Japan: Time, Space, Nation* (NY and London: M.E. Sharpe, 1998), pp. 171–72.

50. Angela Carter, 'My Maugham Award', p. 204.

51. David Punter, *The Hidden Script: Writing and the Unconscious* (London: Routledge, 1985), p. 31.
52. Suleiman, p. 103.
53. Herbert Marcuse, *An Essay on Liberation* (Boston: Beacon Press, 1969), p. 29.
54. Ibid., pp. 44–45.
55. Helen Cagney Watts, 'An Interview with Angela Carter', *Bête Noir*, 8 (1985), pp. 161–76 (p. 172).
56. Kenyon, p. 25.
57. Ibid., p. 26.
58. McEwan, p. 43.
59. Sage, *Angela Carter*, p. 34.
60. Angela Carter, *The Infernal Desire Machines of Doctor Hoffman* [1972] (Harmondsworth: Penguin, 1982), p. 215. All subsequent references are to this edition.
61. Jorge Luis Borges, 'The Library of Babel', in *Labyrinths: Selected Stories and Other Writings* (London: Penguin, 1970), pp. 78–86 (p. 80).
62. The initials 'J.E.I.' stand for James E. Irby, Emeritus Professor of Modern Latin American Literature at Princeton University.
63. Borges, 'The Library of Babel', p. 81.
64. Ibid., pp. 78–90.
65. Borges, 'The Garden of Forking Paths', *Labyrinths*, pp. 44–54 (p. 44).
66. Ibid.
67. Patricia Waugh, *Metafiction* (London: Methuen, 1984), p. 137.
68. Borges, 'The Garden of Forking Paths', p. 51.
69. Ibid., p. 45.
70. Ibid., p. 45.
71. Sage, *Angela Carter*, p. 34.
72. Borges, 'The Garden of Forking Paths', p. 54.
73. Ibid., p. 50.
74. Ibid., p. 53.
75. Angela Carter, 'Latin Rhythms', in *Shaking A Leg*, pp. 459–61 (p. 460). First published in *New Society* (28 June 1979).
76. Gerald Martin, *Journeys Through the Labyrinth: Latin American Fiction in the Twentieth Century* (London: Verso, 1989), p. 157. (Italics mine).
77. Ibid., p. 158.
78. Maggie Ann Bowers, *Magic(al) Realism* (London: Routledge, 2004), p. 17. Her reference is to Angel Flores, 'Magical Realism in Spanish American Fiction', in Lois Parkinson Zamora and Wendy Faris, eds., *Magical Realism: Theory, History, Community* (Durham, NC and London: Duke University Press), pp. 285–303.
79. Ibid., p. 33.
80. Aidan Day, *Angela Carter: The Rational Glass* (Manchester: Manchester University Press, 1998), p. 90.
81. One of the characteristics of the Count as Carter portrays him is that he needs an audience in order to fully savour his perversions, as in the incident in which he buggers his valet in front of Desiderio: ' "Watch me! Watch me!" he cried, as though, in order to appreciate the effect of his own actions, he had to know that he was seen' (125).
82. Margaret Benedikz makes the excellent point that while 'Carter appropriates and parodies characteristics of the Sadeian libertine in ... the Count', he is

also 'a conglomerate and critique of other figures'. He is, in other words, a 'collage [which] draws attention to the fragmentation of identity and the construction of representation'. *Storming the Sadeian Citadel: Disturbing Gender in Angela Carter's Fiction of Transition*, unpublished PhD thesis (Stockholm University, 2002), p. 70.

83. Sally Robinson, 'The Anti-Hero as Oedipus: Gender and the Postmodern Narrative in *The Infernal Desire Machines of Doctor Hoffman*', in Sally Keenan, ed., *Angela Carter: Contemporary Critical Essays* (Basingstoke: Macmillan, 2000), pp. 107–26 (p. 107).
84. Robinson, pp. 115–15.
85. Ibid., pp. 116–17.
86. Suleiman, p. 108.

5   My now stranger's eye

1. Catherine Stott, 'Runaway to the Land of Promise', *Guardian* (10 August 1972), p. 9.
2. Ibid.
3. Susannah Clapp, 'On Madness, Men and Fairy-Tales', *The Independent on Sunday* (9 June 1991), pp. 26–27 (p. 26).
4. Carmen Callil, 'Flying Jewellery', *Sunday Times* (23 February 1992), p. 6.
5. Neil Forsyth, 'A Letter From Angela Carter', *The European English Messenger* V/1 (Spring 1996), pp. 11–13 (p. 13).
6. Ibid., p. 11. Italics inserted by Forsyth.
7. Angela Carter, 'Sugar Daddy', in *Shaking A Leg: Collected Journalism and Writings* (London: Chatto & Windus, 1997), pp. 19–29 (p. 20).
8. 'A Letter From Angela Carter', p. 11.
9. Ibid., p. 12.
10. Ibid.
11. Alex Hamilton, 'Sade and Prejudice', *The Guardian* (30 March 1979), p. 15.
12. Angela Carter, 'Fools Are My Theme', in *Shaking A Leg*, pp. 31–36 (p. 35).
13. Lorna Sage, *Angela Carter* (Plymouth: Northcote House, 1994), p. 31.
14. 'A Letter From Angela Carter', p. 12.
15. Sage, *Angela Carter*, p. 31.
16. Angela Carter, 'Elegy for a Freelance', in *Fireworks* [rev. edn] (London: Virago Press, 1987), pp. 103–20 (p. 109). All subsequent references are to this edition.
17. Angela Carter, '*Fin de Siècle*', in *Shaking A Leg*, pp. 153–57 (p. 154). First published in *New Society* (17 August 1972).
18. Christopher Booker, *The Seventies: Portrait of a Decade* (London: Allen Lane, 1980), pp. 12–13.
19. Arthur Marwick, *British Society since 1945* [rev. edn] (London: Penguin, 1996), p. 184.
20. Peter Ackroyd, *London: The Biography* (London: Vintage, 2000), p. 762.
21. Ibid., p. 763.
22. Richard Weight, *Patriots: National Identity in Britain 1940–2000* (London: Pan Books, 2002), p. 475.
23. Angela Carter, 'The Mother Lode', in *Shaking A Leg*, pp. 2–15 (p. 3), p. 14.
24. Marwick, p. 184.

25. Ibid., p. 261.
26. Edward Heath, speaking the House of Commons debate on entry into the EU, 28 October 1971, quoted in Weight, p. 484.
27. Weight, p. 491.
28. Ibid., p. 492.
29. Booker, p. 104.
30. Marwick, p. 222.
31. This is yet another example of Carter's penchant for recycling her own work. In the same year in which *Nothing Sacred* appeared, 1982, *New Society* published 'So There'll Always Be an England', which is a longer, more elaborate version of the introduction to 'England, Whose England?'. Because they have the same date of publication it is unclear whether Carter was inspired to write the longer piece having written the commentary for *Nothing Sacred*, or if she was plagiarising her own essay for the introduction. She is certainly plagiarising the Empire Day episode in *Love*.
32. Angela Carter, *Nothing Sacred: Selected Writings* (London: Virago Press, 1982), p. 60.
33. Ibid.
34. Angela Carter, 'Bath, Heritage City', in *Shaking A Leg*, pp. 161–65 (p. 161). First published as '"Bathed in Englishness", Bath' in *New Society* (18 September 1975). First reprinted in *Nothing Sacred*, pp. 71–76.
35. Les Bedford, 'Angela Carter: An Interview' (Sheffield: Sheffield University Television, 1977).
36. Angela Carter, 'Notes from the Front Line', in *Shaking a Leg*, pp. 36–43 (p. 37).
37. Bedford, 'Angela Carter: An Interview'.
38. 'The Mother Lode', p. 13.
39. Sage, *Angela Carter*, p. 29.
40. Angela Carter, 'Preface' to *Come Unto These Yellow Sands* (Newcastle upon Tyne: Bloodaxe Books, 1985), p. 9. Also published in Angela Carter, *The Curious Room: Collected Dramatic Works* (London: Chatto & Windus, 1996), pp. 497–502.
41. Ibid.
42. Charlotte Crofts, *'Anagrams of Desire': Angela Carter's Writing for Radio, Film and Television* (Manchester: Manchester University Press, 2003), p. 48.
43. Ibid., p. 52.
44. Ibid., p. 55.
45. Ibid., p. 23.
46. Carter, *Yellow Sands*, p. 11.
47. Ibid., p. 13.
48. Susannah Clapp, 'On Madness, Men and Fairy Tales', p. 26.
49. Lisa Appignanesi, *Angela Carter in Conversation* (London: ICA Video, 1987).
50. Angela Carter, *The Passion of New Eve* (London: Virago, 1977), p. 10. All subsequent references are to this edition.
51. Kim Evans (dir.), *Angela Carter's Curious Room*, (BBC2, 15.9.92).
52. Sage, *Angela Carter*, p. 36.
53. Angela Carter, *The Sadeian Woman* (London: Virago, 1979), p. 5. All subsequent references are to this edition.
54. Alison Lee, 'Angela Carter's New Eve(lyn): De/Engendering Narrative', in Kathy Mezei, ed., *Ambiguous Discourse: Feminist Narratology and British Women*

Writers (Chapel Hill: University of North Carolina Press, 1996), pp. 238–49 (p. 239).

55. Adrienne Rich, *Of Woman Born: Motherhood as Experience and Institution* (London: Virago Press, 1977), p. 93.
56. Ibid.
57. Ibid., p. 120.
58. Mary Daly, *Gyn/Ecology* (London: The Women's Press, 1979), p. 107.
59. Ibid., p. 109.
60. Ibid., p. 111.
61. Ibid., p. 357.
62. Valerie Solanis, 'SCUM (Society for Cutting Up Men) Manifesto', http://www.indiana.edn/~rterrill/Text-SCUM.html, accessed 07 December 2004.
63. Daly, p. 334.
64. *Angela Carter's Curious Room.*
65. Heather L. Johnson, 'Transgressive Symbolism and the Transsexual Subject in Angela Carter's *The Passion of New Eve*', in Joseph Bristow and Trev Lynn Broughton, eds., *The Infernal Desires of Angela Carter: Fiction, Femininity, Feminism* (London: Longman, 1997), pp. 166–83 (p. 172).
66. Angela Carter, 'The Wound in the Face', in *Shaking A Leg*, pp. 109–13 (p. 110). First published in *New Society* (24 April 1975). Reprinted in *Nothing Sacred*, pp. 90–95.
67. Ibid.
68. Ibid., p. 111.
69. Ibid., p. 110.
70. John Haffenden, 'Magical Mannerist', *The Literary Review* (November 1984), pp. 34–38 (p. 36).
71. Angela Carter, *Unicorn* (Leeds: Location Press, 1966). No page numbers available.
72. Crofts, p. 94.
73. Olga Kenyon, 'Angela Carter', *The Writer's Imagination* (Bradford: University of Bradford Print Unit, 1992), pp. 23–33 (p. 31).
74. Jerry Lisker, 'Homo Nest Raided, Queen Bees are Stinging Mad', *The New York Daily News* (6 July 1969). www.trikkx.com/history2.html, accessed 11 December 2004.
75. SCUM Manifesto.
76. J.R. Piggott, *Palace of the People: The Crystal Palace at Sydenham 1854–1936* (London: Hurst & Company, 2004), p. 21.
77. Stuart Sim, *Fundamentalist World: The New Dark Age of Dogma* (Cambridge: Icon Books, 2004), pp. 10–11.
78. Ibid., p. 83.
79. Appignanesi, *Angela Carter in Conversation.*
80. Ibid.
81. In interview with Lisa Appignanesi, Carter tantalisingly hinted that there was more to Eve's eventual fate than she disclosed in the novel saying 'there's a story to the ending of *The Passion of New Eve*, but I won't tell it now'.
82. Kenyon, p. 31.
83. Angela Carter, 'Introduction', *The Virago Book of Fairy Tales* (London: Virago Press, 1991), p. ix.
84. Ibid.

85. Bedford, 'Angela Carter: An Interview'.
86. 'A Letter From Angela Carter', p. 13.
87. Bedford, 'Angela Carter: An Interview'.
88. Ibid.
89. Margaret Atwood, 'Running with the Tigers', in Lorna Sage, ed., *Flesh and the Mirror*, pp. 117–35 (p. 120).
90. Angela Carter, *The Bloody Chamber And Other Stories* [1979] (London: Vintage, 1995), p. 34. All subsequent references are to this edition.
91. Sally Keenan, 'Angela Carter's *The Sadeian Woman*: Feminism as Treason', in Joseph Bristow and Trev Lynn Broughton, eds., *The Infernal Desires of Angela Carter: Fiction, Femininity, Feminism* (Harlow: Addison Wesley Longman, 1997), pp. 132–48 (p. 134).
92. Patricia Duncker, 'Re-Imagining the Fairy Tales: Angela Carter's Bloody Chambers', *Literature and History* (Spring 1984), X:I, pp. 3–14 (p. 6).
93. Appignanesi, *Angela Carter in Conversation*.
94. Ibid.
95. Ibid.
96. Haffenden, p. 36.
97. Sage, *Angela Carter*, p. 40.
98. Marina Warner, *From the Beast to the Blonde: On Fairytales and their Tellers* (London: Chatto & Windus, 1994), p. 65.
99. Ibid., p. 131.
100. Although Les Bedford's interview with Carter was not widely disseminated, and is still not referred to in the majority of critical analyses, it is 'major' in the sense that it is Carter's first filmed interview, and a very early attempt to assess her work to date.
101. Lorna Sage, 'A Savage Sideshow', *New Review*, 4, 39/40, pp. 51–57 (p. 53).

6 You write from your own history

1. Angela Carter, 'Masochism for the Masses', in *Shaking A Leg: Collected Journalism and Writings* (London: Chatto & Windus, 1997), pp. 189–95 (p. 189). First published as 'Masochism for the Masses: Election '83', *New Statesman* (3 June 1983).
2. Ibid., p. 191.
3. Ibid., p. 192.
4. Ibid., p. 194.
5. Richard Weight, *Patriots: National Identity in Britain 1940–2000* (London: Pan Books, 2002), p. 569.
6. Margaret Thatcher, Conservative Political Centre Summer School, Cambridge, 6 July 1979, quoted in Peter Riddell, *The Thatcher Government* [rev. edn] (Oxford: Basil Blackwell, 1985), p. 1.
7. Margaret Thatcher, *Weekend World* (January 1983), quoted in Riddell, p. 8.
8. Weight, p. 570.
9. Quoted in Eric J. Evans, *Thatcher and Thatcherism* (London: Routledge, 1997), p. 96.
10. Max Hastings and Simon Jenkins, *The Battle for the Falklands* (London: Michael Joseph, 1983), quoted in Riddell, p. 219.

11. Alistair Davies and Alan Sinfield, 'Class, Consumption and Cultural Institutions', Davies and Sinfield, eds., *British Culture of the Postwar: An Introduction to Literature and Society 1945–1999* (London: Routledge, 2000), pp. 139–45 (p. 143).
12. Ibid., p. 141.
13. Salman Rushdie, *New Statesman*, 10 April 1983.
14. Veronica Horwell, 'Wicked with Words', Guardian (18 February 1992), p. 33.
15. Angela Carter, 'Anger in A Black Landscape', in *Shaking A Leg*, pp. 36–52 (p. 50).
16. Ibid., p. 52.
17. Ibid., p. 51.
18. Ibid., p. 46.
19. Ibid., p. 51.
20. Carmen Callil, 'Flying Jewellery', *Sunday Times* (23 February 1992).
21. Angela Carter, 'Snow-Belt America', in *Shaking A Leg*, pp. 279–83 (p. 281). First published in *New Society* (5 March 1981).
22. Ibid. This description of the 'New England face' can also be found Carter's two stories about the axe murderess Lizzie Borden. In 'The Fall River Axe Murders', first published in the same year as 'Snow-Belt America' – 1981 – and anthologised in *Black Venus* (London: Chatto & Windus, 1985), Lizzie is described as possessing a 'jutting rectangular jaw and those mad eyes of the New England saints' (119). In 1991, Carter published a second short story – included in the posthumously-published collection *American Ghosts and Old World Wonders* (London: Chatto & Windus, 1993) – entitled 'Lizzie and the Tiger', in which stress is again laid on Lizzie's 'new England jaw' and 'ice-blue eyes' (7). The melting-pot identity of Providence thus seems infinitely preferable to the inheritance of murderously repressive and repressed Puritanism that is the legacy of the country's founding fathers.
23. Carter, 'Snow-Belt America', p. 282.
24. Ibid.
25. Ibid., p. 283.
26. Ibid.
27. Lorna Sage, 'A Savage Sideshow', *New Review*, 4, 39/40, pp. 51–57 (p. 53).
28. Lorna Sage, *Angela Carter* (Plymouth: Northcote House, 1994), p. 50.
29. 'Pat Barker', in Donna Perry, ed., *Backtalk: Women Writers Speak Out* (New Brunswick: Rutgers University Press, 1993), pp. 43–61 (p. 48).
30. Neil Jordan, quoted in *Angela Carter's Curious Room*, p. 507.
31. For further discussion of the history of the production, dissemination and reception of the film of *The Magic Toyshop*, see Charlotte Crofts, *'Anagrams of Desire': Angela Carter's Writing for Radio, Film and Television* (Manchester: Manchester University Press, 2003), p. 128.
32. Crofts, p. 128.
33. MacEwan, p. 42.
34. Ibid., p. 44.
35. Carmen Callil, 'Flying Jewellry'.
36. Marina Warner, 'Obituary: Angela Carter', *The Independent* (18 February 1992), p. 25.
37. Sage, *Angela Carter*, pp. 50–51.
38. Angela Carter, *Nights at the Circus* [1984] (London: Vintage, 1994), pp. 7–8. All subsequent references are to this edition.

39. Peter Kemp, 'Magical History Tour', *Sunday Times* (9 June 1991).
40. Carolyn See, 'Come On and See the Winged Lady', *The New York Times*, 24 February 1985.
41. John Haffenden, 'Magical Mannerist', *The Literary Review* (November 1984), pp. 34–38 (p. 36).
42. Malcolm Bradbury, *The Modern British Novel 1878–2001* [rev. edn] (London: Penguin, 2001), p. 445.
43. Angela Carter, 'Masochism for the Masses', p. 190.
44. Ibid., p. 192.
45. Ibid., p. 190.
46. Ibid., p. 193.
47. Evans, p. 121.
48. Carter, 'Masochism for the Masses', p. 193.
49. John Bayley, 'Fighting for the Crown', *The New York Review of Books* (April 23 1992), pp. 9–11 (p. 11).
50. Ibid.
51. Sage, *Angela Carter*, p. 51.
52. Callil, 'Flying Jewellery'.
53. Sage, *Angela Carter*, p. 51.
54. Ibid., p. 52.
55. Ibid., p. 51.
56. Angela Carter, 'Notes from a Maternity Ward', in *Shaking A Leg*, pp. 29–31 (p. 29). First published in *New Statesman* (16–23 December 1983).
57. Ibid., p. 30.
58. Ibid.
59. Ibid. In spite of Carter's suspicion that the hospital would eventually be sold 'to bloody BUPA' (30), it was not. Following its closure in July 1984, it was occupied by protestors until March 1985. Given that one of the themes in this essay is the fact that female solidarity is not an automatic given, it is exquisitely ironic that the occupation was eventually ended when forty women police officers stormed the building to evacuate the female squatters.
60. Ibid.
61. Ibid., pp. 30–31.
62. Ibid., p. 31.
63. Peter Kemp, 'Magical History Tour'.
64. 'Angela Carter's Potato Soup', in Sue O'Sullivan, ed., *Turning the Tables: Recipes and Reflections from Women* (London: Sheba Feminist Publishers, 1987), pp. 111–13 (p. 112). Carter said her choice of recipe was typical of the kind of 'hearty fare' she knew 'best how to cook, due to a life spent on a relatively limited income in mostly northern climates' (p. 111).
65. John Haffenden, for example, describes interviewing Carter while 'her baby Alexander consumes the room and threatens the interview with healthy hubbub' (p. 34), while Mary Harron's conversation with the author is:

> interrupted by the cries of her ten-month-old son, Alexander. Playing back the tape of the interview you hear Alexander in the foreground, sometimes gurgling merrily and sometimes creaming, and in the background his mother conducting a deadly analysis of the literary world, the class system and current feminism while attempting to feed him a rusk.

(' "I'm A Socialist, Damn It! How Can You Expect Me to be Interested in Fairies?" ', *Guardian*, 25 September 1984, p. 10).

66. Peter Kemp, 'Magical History Tour'.
67. Appignanesi, *Angela Carter in Conversation*.
68. Ibid.
69. Ibid.
70. Angela Carter, 'The Mother Lode', in *Shaking A Leg*, pp. 2–15 (p. 9).
71. Angela Carter, 'Sugar Daddy', in *Shaking A Leg*, pp. 19–29 (p. 28).
72. Anna Katsavos, 'An Interview with Angela Carter', *The Review of Contemporary Fiction* (Fall 1994), pp. 11–17 (p. 15).
73. Kate Webb, 'Seriously Funny: *Wise Children*', in Lorna Sage, ed., *Flesh and the Mirror: Essays on the Art of Angela Carter* (London: Virago Press, 1994), pp. 279–307 (p. 295).
74. Susannah Clapp, 'On Madness, Men and Fairy-Tales', *Independent on Sunday* (9 June 1991), pp. 26–27 (p. 27).
75. Lorna Sage, 'Angela Carter', in Malcolm Bradbury and Judy Cooke, eds., *New Writing* (London: Minverva, 1992), pp. 185–93 (p. 185).
76. Ibid., p. 186.
77. 'Angela Carter's Curious Room'.
78. Clapp, p. 26.
79. Lisa Appignanesi, *Angela Carter in Conversation*. Such statements recall the claims Carter made regarding her early novels set in Bristol, that they were reflections of bizarre reality rather than the products of her own fertile imagination.
80. Carter, 'The Mother Lode', p. 12.
81. Clapp, 'On Madness, Men and Fairy-Tales', p. 26. In this interview, Carter made the additional claim that another pivotal source for *Wise Children* was her memory of her Aunt Kit, whose ambition to ' "go on the Halls" ' was baffled by 'a prim headmistress' who forced her to take an office job instead. 'Kit was dippy – in the war she took to roaming the streets during the blackout, "she adored seeing those flying bombs" – and was "rabidly frigid". She had a miserable life and a bleak death.' In *Wise Children*, Carter rewrites Aunt Kit's history in order to give her the show-business career she wanted, and a happy ending.
82. Carter, 'The Mother Lode', pp. 14–15.
83. Paul N. Siegel, *The Gathering Storm* (London: Redwords, 1992), p. viii.
84. Angela Carter, *Wise Children* (London: Vintage, 1992), p. 14. All subsequent references are to this edition.
85. Aidan Day, *Angela Carter: The Rational Glass* (Manchester: Manchester University Press, 1998), p. 197.
86. This is a connection also made by Kate Webb when she says that Carter 'picks up on the more recent Thatcherite humour of Harry Enfield's "Loads a'money", turning it into Tristram's ghastly catchphrase "Lashings of Lolly" ' (297). Eric J. Evans's description of Enfield's comic creation as a 'dominant symbol...of materialist Britain in the late 1980s and early 1990s...offer[ing] a course stereotype of "wad-wielding" vulgarity, judging everything in terms of immediate material gain' (121) functions as a very apposite summary of the target of Carter's satire here.

87. Terence Hawkes, 'Bardbiz', in *Meaning by Shakespeare* (London: Routledge, 1992), pp. 141–53.
88. Not only was this Carter's favourite play in the Shakespearean canon – 'because it's beautiful and funny and camp' (Clapp, 'On Madness, Men and Fairy-Tales', p. 27) – but she is also gesturing towards the 1935 film of *A Midsummer Night's Dream* directed by Erich von Stroheim. Her enduring affection for this film is underlined by the fact that she chose to be filmed watching it with Mark and Alexander in the documentary *Angela Carter's Curious Room*, screened after her death in 1992.
89. Webb, p. 286.
90. Evans, p. 92.
91. Carter, 'Anger in a Black Landscape', p. 47.
92. Hawkes, p. 153.
93. D. Russell and Roberd Goodden, 'The Lion and Unicorn Pavilion', in Mary Banham and Bevis Hiller, eds., *A Tonic to the Nation: The Festival of Britain 1951* (London: Thames and Hudson, 1976), pp. 96–101 (p. 98).
94. Laurie Lee, 'The Lion and the Unicorn', in Ian Cox, *The South Bank Exhibition: A Guide to the Story It Tells* (H.M. Stationary Office, 1951), p. 67.
95. Russell and Goodden, p. 96.
96. Carter, 'The Mother Lode', p. 9.
97. Ibid., p. 8.
98. Ibid.
99. Webb, p. 282.
100. Clapp, 'On Madness, Men and Fairy-Tales', p. 27.
101. Angela Carter, 'Barry Paris: *Louise Brooks*', in *Shaking A Leg*, pp. 387–92 (p. 388). First published as 'Brooksie and Faust' in *London Review of Books* (9 March 1990).
102. Angela Carter, *Nothing Sacred: Selected Journalism and Writings* (London: Virago Press, 1982), p. 118.
103. Carter, 'Barry Paris: *Louise Brooks*', p. 388.
104. Ibid.
105. Sage, *Angela Carter*, p. 58.
106. Veronica Horwell, 'Wicked with Words', *The Guardian* (18 February 1992), p. 33.
107. Salman Rushdie, 'Angela Carter 1940–92: A Very Good Wizard, A Very Dear Friend', *New York Times Book Review* (8 March 1992), p. 5.
108. Carter's voice-over for *The Holy Family Album*, quoted in Crofts, p. 184.
109. John Ellis, quoted in Crofts, p. 185.
110. Sage, p. 59.
111. Crofts, p. 170.
112. Ibid., p. 185.
113. Ibid., p. 168.
114. Ibid., p. 169.
115. Ibid., p. 170.
116. Ibid., p. 176.
117. Ibid.
118. H. Jennings, *Family Portrait 1951: A Film on the Theme of the Festival of Britain, 1951*, quoted in Conekin, p. 91.
119. John Ellis says the impetus behind the programme was Carter's love of surrealist painting and a desire to upset religious imagery, and *Family*

Portrait was never mentioned at any point in its conception and production (interview 22 February 2005).

120. George Orwell, 'The Lion and the Unicorn: Socialism and the English Genius', in *The Collected Essays, Journalism and Letter: Volume 2* (London: Penguin, 1970), p. 88.

121. Angela Carter, *Sea-Cat and Dragon King* (London: Bloomsbury, 2000), p. 9. All references are to this edition.

122. Carmen Callil says that she was still 'fiddling' with the manuscript in Brompton Hospital a month before her death, ' "just finishing this off for the girls" ' ('Flying Jewellery', p. 7).

123. Interview 22 February 2005.

124. *Angela Carter's Curious Room*.

125. Daniel Johnson, 'Books Barely Furnish a Room', *The Times* (16 September 1992), p. 3.

126. Valerie Grove, 'If I Should Die, Think Only This of Me', *The Times* (27 March 1992), p. 1.

127. Ibid.

Conclusion: Posthumous fame is no comfort at all

1. Charlotte Crofts, *'Anagrams of Desire': Angela Carter's Writing for Radio, Film and Television* (Manchester: Manchester University Press, 2003), p. 86.

2. Angela Carter, letter to Glyn Dearman, quoted in *Come Unto These Yellow Sands: Four Radio Plays by Angela Carter* (Newcastle upon Tyne: Bloodaxe Books, 1985), p. 504.

3. Angela Carter, 'A Self-Made Man', in *The Curious Room: Collected Dramatic Works* (London: Chatto & Windus), p. 136.

4. Ibid., p. 122.

5. Crofts, p. 72.

6. Ibid., p. 73.

7. Quoted in Lorna Sage, *Angela Carter* (Plymouth: Northcote House, 1994), p. 22.

8. Sage, *Angela Carter*, p. 58.

9. Ibid., p. 1.

10. Angela Carter, 'My Maugham Award', in *Shaking A Leg: Collected Journalism and Writing* (London: Chatto & Windus, 1997), pp. 203–04 (p. 203).

11. Alex Hamilton, 'Sade and Prejudice', *Guardian* (30 March 1979), p. 15.

12. Angela Carter, 'D'You Mean South?', in *Shaking A Leg*, pp. 177–81 (p. 179). First published in *New Society* (28 July 1977).

13. Angela Carter, So There'll Always Be an England', in *Shaking A Leg*, pp. 185–89 (p. 189).

14. Carter, *'Fin de Siècle'*, in *Shaking A Leg*, pp. 153–57 (p. 154).

15. Carter, 'D'You Mean South?' p. 177.

16. Ibid., p. 179.

17. Ibid., p. 181.

18. Ibid.

19. Carter, 'So There'll Always be an England', p. 187.
20. R.D. Russell and Goodden, 'The Lion and Unicorn Pavilion', in Mary Banham and Bevis Hiller, eds., *A Tonic to the Nation: The Festival of Britain 1951* (London: Thames and Hudson, 1976), pp. 96–101 (p. 100).
21. Angela Carter, *The Sadeian Woman: An Exercise in Cultural History* (London: Virago Press, 1979), p. 13.
22. Mary Harron, ' "I'm A Socialist, Damn It! How Can You Expect Me to be Interested in Fairies?" ', *Guardian* (25 September 1984), p. 10.
23. Unpublished interview with Kate Webb, 18 December 1985. Cited in 'Seriously Funny: *Wise Children*', in Lorna Sage, ed., *Flesh and the Mirror: Essays on the Art of Angela Carter* (London: Virago Press, 1994), p. 338.
24. *Angela Carter's Curious Room.*
25. Angela Carter, 'The Granada, Tooting', in *Shaking A Leg*, p. 400.
26. Sage, *Angela Carter*, p. 41.
27. Callil, p. 7.
28. Ibid.
29. Malcolm Bradbury, *The Modern British Novel 1878–2001* [rev. edn] (London: Penguin Books, 2001), p. 420.
30. Nicci Gerrard, *Into the Mainstream: How Feminism Has Changed Women's Writing* (London: Pandora Press, 1989), pp. 52–53.
31. Ibid., p. 57.
32. Cagney Watts, Helen, 'An Interview with Angela Carter', *Bête Noir*, 8 (1985), pp. 161–76 (p. 171).
33. Ibid.
34. The Booker Prize is usually awarded in October. Carter was interviewed by Cagney Watts in November.
35. Johnson, Daniel, 'Books Barely Furnish a Room', *The Times* (16 September 1992), p. 3.
36. Barker, Paul, 'The Return of the Magic Story-Teller', *The Independent on Sunday* (8 January 1995), pp. 14, 16 (p. 14).
37. Nicci Gerrard, 'Angela Carter is now more popular than Virginia Woolf...', *Observer Life* (9 July 1995), p. 20.
38. Barker, p. 14.
39. Merja Makinen, 'Angela Carter's *The Bloody Chamber* and the Decolonisation of Female Sexuality', in Easton, ed., *Angela Carter: Contemporary Critical Essays* (Basingstoke: Macmillan, 2000), pp. 20–36 (pp. 20–21).
40. Ibid., p. 21.
41. Gerrard, 'Angela Carter is now more popular than Virginia Woolf...', p. 22.
42. Andrew Motion, 'Introduction', Andrew Motion, ed., *Interrupted Lives* (London: National Portrait Gallery Publications, 2004), p. 9.
43. Ali Smith, 'Get Carter', in Motion, ed., pp. 80–95 (p. 81).
44. Linden Peach, *Angela Carter* (Basingstoke: Macmillan, 1998), p. 159.
45. Crofts, p. 194.
46. Unfortunately, the same is not true of Carter's work in other media. *The Magic Toyshop* is deleted and unavailable, while the DVD of *The Company of Wolves* is only available in North American format – although the scripts of both films, along with the scripts of the radio plays, have been published in *Angela Carter's Curious Room: Collected*

Dramatic Writings. As has already been discussed in Chapter 6, the script of *The Holy Family Album* has never been published, nor has the programme been rebroadcast.

47. Angela Carter, 'Notes from the Front Line', in *Shaking A Leg*, pp. 36–43 (p. 41).

Bibliography

Primary

Angela Carter, *Shadow Dance* [1966] (London: Virago Press, 1994).
——, *Unicorn* (Leeds: Location Press, 1966).
——, *The Magic Toyshop* [1967] (London: Virago, 1981).
——, *Several Perceptions* [1968] (London: Virago Press, 1995).
——, *Heroes and Villains* [1969] (London: Penguin, 1981).
——, *Miss Z: The Dark Young Lady* (London: Heinemann, 1970).
——, *Love* [1971] (London: Pan Books Ltd, 1988) [rev. edn].
——, *The Infernal Desire Machines of Doctor Hoffman* [1972] (Harmondsworth: Penguin, 1982).
——, *Fireworks* [1974] (London: Virago Press, 1987) [rev. edn].
——, *The Passion of New Eve* (London: Virago, 1977).
——, *The Sadeian Woman: An Exercise in Cultural History* (London: Virago Press, 1979).
——*The Bloody Chamber And Other Stories* [1979] (London: Vintage, 1995).
——, 'The Quilt Maker', in *Sex and Sensibility: Stories by Contemporary Women Writers from Nine Countries* (London: Sidgwick & Jackson, 1981), pp. 120–40 (p. 121).
——, *Nothing Sacred: Selected Writings* (London: Virago Press, 1982).
——, 'Sugar Daddy', in Ursula Owen, ed., *Fathers: Reflections By Daughters* (London: Virago Press, 1983), pp. 20–30.
——, *Nights at the Circus* [1984] (London: Vintage, 1994).
——, *Black Venus* (London: Chatto & Windus, 1985).
——, *Come Unto These Yellow Sands: Four Radio Plays by Angela Carter* (Newcastle upon Tyne: Bloodaxe Books, 1985).
——, 'Truly, It Felt Like Year One', in Sara Maitland, ed., *Very Heaven: Looking Back at the 1960s* (London: Virago, 1988), pp. 209–16.
——, ed., *The Virago Book of Fairy Tales* (London: Virago Press, 1991).
——, ed., *The Second Virago Book of Fairy Tales* (London: Virago Press, 1992).
——, *Wise Children* (London: Vintage, 1992).
——, *American Ghosts and Old World Wonders* (London: Chatto & Windus, 1993).
——, *Burning Your Boats: Collected Short Stories* (London: Chatto & Windus, 1995).
——, *The Curious Room: Collected Dramatic Works* (London: Chatto & Windus, 1996).
——, *Shaking A Leg: Collected Journalism and Writings* (London: Chatto & Windus, 1997).
——, *Sea-Cat and Dragon King* (London: Bloomsbury, 2000).

Secondary

Ackroyd, Peter, *London: The Biography* (London: Vintage, 2000).
Appignanesi, Lisa, *Angela Carter In Conversation* (London: ICA Video, 1987).
Armitt, Lucie, ed., 'Introduction', *Where No Man Has Gone Before: Women and Science Fiction* (London: Routledge, 1991), pp. 1–12.

Armitt, Lucie, *Contemporary Women's Fiction and the Fantastic* (Basingstoke: Macmillan, 2000).

Atwood, Margaret, 'Running with the Tigers', in Lorna Sage, ed., *Flesh and the Mirror: Essays on the Art of Angela Carter* (London: Virago Press, 1994), pp. 117–35.

Barker, Paul, 'The Return of the Magic Story-Teller', *The Independent on Sunday* (8 January 1995), pp. 14, 16.

Bayley, John, 'Fighting for the Crown', *The New York Review of Books* (23 April 1992), pp. 9–11.

Bedford, Les, 'Angela Carter: An Interview' (Sheffield: Sheffield University Television, 1977).

Benedikz, Margaret, *Storming the Sadeian Citadel: Disturbing Gender in Angela Carter's Fiction of Transition*, unpublished PhD thesis (Stockholm University, 2002).

Berger, John, *Ways of Seeing* (London: Penguin Books, 1972).

Bhabha, Homi, K., ed., 'Introduction' to *Nation and Narration* (London: Routledge, 1990).

Booker, Christopher, *The Seventies: Portrait of a Decade* (London: Allen Lane, 1980).

Booker, Christopher, *The Neophiliacs: A Study of the Revolution in English Life in the Fifties and Sixties* (London: Pimlico, 1992).

Borges, Jorge Luis, 'The Garden of Forking Paths', in *Labyrinths: Selected Stories and Other Writings* (London: Penguin, 1970), pp. 44–54.

Borges, Jorge Luis, 'The Library of Babel', in *Labyrinths: Selected Stories and Other Writings* (London: Penguin, 1970), pp. 78–86.

Bowen, John, 'Grotesques', *The New York Times Book Review* (19 February 1967), p. 44.

Bowers, Maggie Ann, *Magic(al) Realism* (London: Routledge, 2004).

Bradbury, Malcolm, *The Modern British Novel 1878–2001* [rev. edn] (London: Penguin, 2001).

Bristow, Joseph and Trev Lynn Broughton, eds., *The Infernal Desires of Angela Carter: Fiction, Femininity, Feminism* (Harlow: Addison Wesley Longman, 1997).

Butler, Judith, *Gender Trouble* (London & NY: Routledge, 1990).

Cagney Watts, Helen, 'An Interview with Angela Carter', *Bête Noir*, 8 (1985), pp. 161–76.

Callil, Carmen, 'Flying Jewellery', *Sunday Times* (23 February 1992), p. 6.

Clapp, Susannah, 'On Madness, Men and Fairy-Tales', *The Independent on Sunday* (9 June 1991), pp. 26–27.

Conekin, Becky, E., '*The Autobiography of a Nation': The 1951 Festival of Britain* (Manchester: Manchester University Press, 2003), p. 164.

Cooper, Susan, 'Snoek Piquante', in Michael Sissons and Philip French, eds., *Age of Austerity* (Harmondsworth: Penguin, 1964), pp. 35–57.

Coote, Anna and Bea Campbell, *Sweet Freedom: The Struggle for Women's Liberation* [2nd ed.] (Oxford: Blackwell, 1987).

Cox, Ian, *The South Bank Exhibition: A Guide to the Story It Tells* (H.M. Stationary Office, 1951).

Crofts, Charlotte, '*Anagrams of Desire': Angela Carter's Writing for Radio, Film and Television* (Manchester: Manchester University Press, 2003).

Crowther, Bosley, review of *Breathless*, *The New York Times* (8 February 1961).

Daly, Mary, *Gyn/Ecology* (London: The Women's Press, 1979).

Davies, Alistair, and Alan Sinfield, 'Class, Consumption and Cultural Institutions', in Davies and Sinfield, eds., *British Culture of the Postwar: An Introduction to Literature and Society 1945–1999* (London: Routledge, 2000), pp. 139–45.

Davis, John R., *The Great Exhibition* (Stroud: Sutton Publishing, 1999).

Day, Aidan, *Angela Carter: The Rational Glass* (Manchester: Manchester University Press, 1998).

Dollimore, Jonathan, *Radical Tragedy* [rev. edn] (Brighton: Harvester Wheatsheaf, 1989).

Duncker, Patricia, 'Re-imagining the Fairy Tales: Angela Carter's Bloody Chambers', *Literature and History* (Spring 1984), X:I, pp. 3–14 (p. 6).

Easton, Alison, 'Introduction', in Alison Easton, ed., *Angela Carter: Contemporary Critical Essays* (Basingstoke: Macmillan, 2000), pp. 1–19.

Eliot, T.S., The Waste Land *and Other Poems* (London: Faber & Faber, 1972).

Evans, Eric J., *Thatcher and Thatcherism* (London: Routledge, 1997).

Evans, Kim (dir.), *Angela Carter's Curious Room, Omnibus* (BBC2, 15.9.92).

Farren, Mick and Edward Barker, *Watch Out Kids* (London: Open Books, 1972).

Felski, Rita, *Beyond Feminist Aesthetics: Feminist Literature and Social Change* (Cambridge, MA: Harvard University Press, 1989).

Forsyth, Neil, 'A Letter From Angela Carter', in *The European English Messenger*, 4, 1 (Spring 1996), pp. 11–13.

Gardiner, Juliet, *From the Bomb to the Beatles: The Changing Face of Post-War Britain 1945–1965* (London: Collins & Brown, 1999).

Gerrard, Nicci, *Into the Mainstream: How Feminism Has Changed Women's Writing* (London: Pandora Press, 1989).

Gerrard, Nicci, 'Angela Carter is now more popular than Virginia Woolf...', *Observer Life* (9 July 1995), pp. 20, 22–23.

Green, Jonathon, *All Dressed Up: The Sixties and the Counterculture* (London: Pimlico, 1999).

Grove, Valerie, 'If I Should Die, Think Only This of Me', *The Times* (27 March 1992).

Haffenden, John, 'Magical Mannerist', *The Literary Review* (November 1984), pp. 34–38.

Hamilton, Alex, 'Sade and Prejudice', *Guardian* (30 March 1979), p. 15.

Harman, Claire, 'Demon-lovers and Sticking-plaster', *Independent on Sunday* (30 October 1994), p. 37.

Haron, Mary, ' "I'm A Socialist, Damn It! How Can You Expect Me to be Interested in Fairies?" ', *Guardian* (25 September 1984), p. 10.

Hawkes, Terence, 'Bardbiz', in *Meaning by Shakespeare* (London: Routledge, 1992), pp. 141–53.

Horwell, Veronica, 'Wicked with Words', *The Guardian* (18 February 1992), p. 33. http://www.members.lycos.co.uk/brisray/bristol/blitz1.htm, accessed 11 August 2004.

Johnson, Daniel, 'Books Barely Furnish a Room', *The Times* (16 September 1992).

Johnson, Heather L., 'Transgressive Symbolism and the Transsexual Subject in Angela Carter's *The Passion of New Eve*', in Joseph Bristow and Trev Lynn Broughton, eds., *The Infernal Desires of Angela Carter: Fiction, Femininity, Feminism* (London: Longman, 1997), pp. 166–83.

Kaveney, Roz, 'New New World Dreams: Angela Carter and Science Fiction', in Lorna Sage, ed., *Flesh and the Mirror: Essays on the Art of Angela Carter*, pp. 171–88.

Keenan, Sally, 'Angela Carter's *The Sadeian Woman*: Feminism as Treason', in Joseph Bristow and Trev Lynn Broughton, eds., *The Infernal Desires of Angela Carter* (Harlow: Addison Wesley Longman, 1997), pp. 132–48.

Kemp, Peter, 'Magical History Tour', *Sunday Times* (9 June 1991).

Kenyon, Olga, 'Angela Carter', in *The Writer's Imagination* (Bradford: University of Bradford Print Unit, 1992), pp. 23–33.

Kuhn, Annette, *Family Secrets* (London: Verso, 1995).

Laing, R.D., *The Divided Self* (London: Penguin, 1965).

Lee, Alison, 'Angela Carter's New Eve(lyn): De/Engendering Narrative', in Kathy Mezei, ed., *Ambiguous Discourse: Feminist Narratology and British Women Writers* (Chapel Hill: University of North Carolina Press, 1996), pp. 238–49.

Lee, Laurie, 'The Lion and the Unicorn', in Ian Cox, ed., *The South Bank Exhibition: A Guide to the Story It Tells* (H.M. Stationary Office, 1951), p. 67.

Lisker, Jerry, 'Homo Nest Raided, Queen Bees are Stinging Mad', *The New York Daily News* (6 July 1969). www.trikkx.com/history2.html, accessed 11 December 2004.

Makinen, Merja, 'Angela Carter's *The Bloody Chamber* and the Decolonisation of Female Sexuality', in Alison Easton, ed., *Angela Carter: Contemporary Critical Essays* (Basingstoke: Macmillan, 2000), pp. 20–36 (pp. 20–21).

Marcus, Laura, *Auto/biographical Discourses* (Manchester: Manchester University Press, 1994).

Marcuse, Herbert, *An Essay on Liberation* (Boston: Beacon Press, 1969).

Marquand, David, 'Sir Stafford Cripps', in Michael Sissons and Philip French, eds., *Age of Austerity* (Harmondsworth: Penguin, 1964), pp. 173–95.

Martin, Gerald, *Journeys Through the Labyrinth: Latin American Fiction in the Twentieth Century* (London: Verso, 1989).

Marwick, Arthur, *British Society since 1945* [rev. edn] (London: Penguin, 1996).

McEwan, Ian, 'Sweet Smell of Excess', *Sunday Times Magazine* (9 September 1984), pp. 42–44 (p. 43).

Michael Frayn, 'Festival', in Michael Sissons and Philip French, eds., *Age of Austerity* (Harmondsworth: Penguin, 1964), pp. 330–52.

Mills, Sara, *et al.*, *Feminist Readings/Feminists Reading* (Brighton: Harvester Wheatsheaf, 1989).

Morris-Suzuki, Tessa, *Re-Inventing Japan: Time, Space, Nation* (New York and London: M.E. Sharpe, 1998).

Nicholls, Peter, 'The Monsters and the Critics', in Peter Nicholls, ed., *Explorations of the Marvellous* (London: Fontana, 1978).

O'Day, Marc, ' "Mutability is Having a Field Day": The Sixties Aura of Angela Carter's Bristol Trilogy', in Lorna Sage, ed., *Flesh and the Mirror: Essays on the Art of Angela Carter* (London: Virago Press, 1994), pp. 24–58.

Orwell, George, 'The Lion and the Unicorn: Socialism and the English Genius', in *The Collected Essays, Journalism and Letters: Volume 2* (London: Penguin, 1970), pp. 74–134.

O'Sullivan, Sue, ed., *Turning the Tables: Recipes and Reflections from Women* (London: Sheba Feminist Publishers, 1987).

Parker, Emma, 'The Consumption of Angela Carter: Women, Food and Power', *Ariel: A Review of International English Literature*, 31, 3 (July 2000), pp. 141–69.

Peach, Linden, *Angela Carter* (Basingstoke: Macmillan, 1998).

Perry, Donna, 'Pat Barker', in Donna Perry, ed., *Backtalk: Women Writers Speak Out* (New Brunswick: Rutgers University Press, 1993), pp. 43–61.

Piggott, J.R., *Palace of the People: The Crystal Palace at Sydenham 1854–1936* (London: Hurst & Company, 2004).

Plant, Sadie, *The Most Radical Gesture: The Situationist International in a Postmodern Age* (London: Routledge, 1992).

Punter, David, *The Literature of Terror: A History of Gothic Fictions from 1765 to the Present Day* (London: Longman, 1980).

Punter, David, *The Hidden Script: Writing and the Unconscious* (London: Routledge, 1985).

Rich, Adrienne, *Of Woman Born: Motherhood as Experience and Institution* (London: Virago Press, 1977).

Riddell, Peter, *The Thatcher Government* [rev. edn] (Oxford: Basil Blackwell, 1985).

Robinson, Sally, 'The Anti-Hero as Oedipus: Gender and the Postmodern Narrative in *The Infernal Desire Machines of Doctor Hoffman*', in Sally Keenan, ed., *Angela Carter: Contemporary Critical Essays* (Basingstoke: Macmillan, 2000).

Rowbotham, Sheila, *Promise of A Dream: Remembering the Sixties* (London: Penguin Books, 2000).

Royle, Nicholas, *The Uncanny* (Manchester: Manchester University Press, 2003).

Rushdie, Salman, *New Statesman*, 10 April 1983.

Rushdie, Salman, 'Angela Carter 1940–92: A Very Good Wizard, A Very Dear Friend', *New York Times Book Review* (8 March 1992), p. 5.

Russell, R.D. and R. Goodden, 'The Lion and Unicorn Pavilion', in Mary Banham and Bevis Hiller, eds., *A Tonic to the Nation: The Festival of Britain 1951* (London: Thames and Hudson, 1976), pp. 96–101.

Sage, Lorna, 'A Savage Sideshow', *New Review*, 4, 39/40 (July 1977), pp. 51–57.

Sage, Lorna, 'Angela Carter', in Malcolm Bradbury and Judy Cooke, eds., *New Writing* (London: Minverva, 1992), pp. 185–93.

Sage, Lorna, *Angela Carter* (Plymouth: Northcote House, 1994).

Sage, Lorna, ed., *Flesh and the Mirror: Essays on the Art of Angela Carter* (London: Virago Press, 1994).

See, Carolyn, 'Come On and See the Winged Lady', *The New York Times*, 24 February 1985.

Sharp, Joanne P., 'Gendering Nationhood: A Feminist Engagement with National Identity', in Nancy Duncan, ed., *Body Space: Geographies of Gender and Sexuality* (London: Routledge, 1996), pp. 97–108.

Siegel, Paul N., *The Gathering Storm* (London: Redwords, 1992), p. viii.

Sim, Stuart, *Fundamentalist World: The New Dark Age of Dogma* (Cambridge: Icon Books, 2004).

Smith, Ali, 'Get Carter', in Andrew Motion, ed., *Interrupted Lives* (London: National Portrait Gallery Publications, 2004), pp. 80–95.

Smith, Patricia Juliana, 'All You Need is *Love*: Angela Carter's Novel of Sixties Sex and Sensibility', *The Review of Contemporary Fiction* (Fall, 1994), pp. 24–29.

Solanis, Valerie, 'SCUM (Society for Cutting Up Men) Manifesto', http://www.indiana.edn/~rterrill/Text-SCUM.html, accessed 07 December 2004.

Stone, Leslie, 'Britain and the World', in David McKie and Chris Cook, eds., *The Decade of Disillusion: British Politics in the Sixties* (London and Basingstoke: Macmillan, 1972).

Stott, Catherine, 'Runaway to the Land of Promise', *Guardian* (10 August 1972), p. 9.

Strong, Roy, 'Prologue: Utopia Limited', in Mary Banham and Bevis Hiller, eds., *A Tonic to the Nation: The Festival of Britain 1951* (London: Thames and Hudson, 1976), p. 8.

Suleiman, Susan Rubin, 'The Fate of the Surrealist Imagination in the Society of the Spectacle', in Lorna Sage, ed., *Flesh and the Mirror: Essays on the Art of Angela Carter*, pp. 98–116.

Taylor, A.J.P., *English History 1914–1945* [rev. edn] (Oxford: Oxford University Press, 1975).

Warner, Marina, 'Obituary: Angela Carter', *The Independent* (18 Febuary 1992), p. 25l.

Warner, Marina, *From the Beast to the Blonde: On Fairytales and their Tellers* (London: Chatto & Windus, 1994).

Warner, Marina, *Fantastic Metamorphoses, Other Worlds* (Oxford: Oxford University Press, 2002).

Waterson, Moira, 'Flights of Fancy in Balham', *Observer Magazine* (11 November 1986), pp. 42–45.

Waugh, Patricia, *Metafiction* (London: Methuen, 1984).

Webb, Kate, 'Seriously Funny: *Wise Children*', in Lorna Sage, ed., *Flesh and the Mirror: Essays on the Art of Angela Carter* (London: Virago Press, 1994), pp. 279–307.

Weight, Richard, *Patriots: National Identity in Britain 1940–2000* (London: Pan Books, 2002).

Wilson, Elizabeth, *Adorned in Dreams: Fashion and Modernity* (London: Virago Press, 1985).

Winston Dixon, Wheeler, *The Films of Jean-Luc Godard* (Albany: State University of New York Press, 1997).

Wyatt, Jean, 'The Violence of Gendering: Castration Images in Angela Carter's *The Magic Toyshop, The Passion of New Eve*, and "Peter and the Wolf"', in Alison Easton, ed., *Angela Carter: Contemporary Critical Essays* (Basingstoke: Macmillan, 2000), pp. 58–83.

Index